ALSO BY RACHEL LYON

Self-Portrait with Boy

Fruit of the Dead

A NOVEL

Rachel Lyon

SCRIBNER

New York London Toronto Sydney New Delhi

Scribner

An Imprint of Simon & Schuster, LLC

1230 Avenue of the Americas

New York, NY 10020

First Scribner hardcover edition March 2024

SCRIBNER and design are trademarks of Simon & Schuster, LLC

Simon & Schuster: Celebrating 100 Years of Publishing in 2024

For information about special discounts for bulk purchases, please contact Simon & Schuster Special Sales at 1-866-506-1949 or business@simonandschuster.com.

The Simon & Schuster Speakers Bureau can bring authors to your live event. For more information or to book an event, contact the Simon & Schuster Speakers Bureau at 1-866-248-3049 or visit our website at www.simonspeakers.com.

Interior design by Kyle Kabel

Manufactured in the United States of America

3   5   7   9   10   8   6   4   2

Library of Congress Cataloging-in-Publication Data is available.

ISBN 978-1-6680-2085-2
ISBN 978-1-6680-2087-6 (ebook)

For my mother
and my daughter

There are places like this everywhere,
places you enter as a young girl,
from which you never return.

—Louise Glück, *Averno*

Contents

CONTENTS

Fruit ^{of}_{the} Dead

Fruit of the Dead

A Snare for the Bloom-Like Girl

On the last day of camp the barn is hot and crowded. River Rock's final production, weeks in the prepping, is happening at last, and the casualties so far are minor. At the eleventh hour the old dog stuffy was misplaced, so the role of Toto is played by somebody's plush Pikachu. During the first scene change the butcher paper backdrop ripped clear through the tempera gray farmhouse. But the audience, made up of parents who haven't seen their kids in weeks, is generous. They crouch at the front, filming on their phones. They applaud spontaneously. They laugh. They aww.

Now, Soul Patch Adam strums a guitar accompaniment from the hayloft as eleven-year-old Glinda almost hits her high notes. *Come out, come out, wherever you are*: Cory's cue. Through the barn's side door she ushers a dozen seven- and eight-year-olds. They enter shyly, they enter hammily, some cowering, some twirling, each dressed in their own interpretation of Munchkin couture: stripes on stripes and polka dots on plaid, dandelions wilting behind dirty ears. Towels tied under chins for capes; underwear on heads, leg holes framing eyes like aviator goggles. A charmed murmuring percolates among the audience. First-Act Dorothy, a cushion-faced redhead with a lateral lisp who does a spot-on Judy Garland, gargles her vowels, and the Munchkins join in, and though a couple of children do leave the stage altogether, opting to sing their parts from their parents' sweaty arms, everything is going fine, until—

A lull. Soul Patch Adam vamps. It is Spenser Picazo's turn to deliver his one line.

We thank you very sweetly, Cory whispers from the first row.

The audience behind her shifts and coughs.

For doing it so neatly, she says with an encouraging smile, but it is no use. River Rock's youngest camper has gone uncharacteristically mute. Below his painted-on mustache his mouth is small and quivering. Behind his silicone strap-on glasses, his eyes are very wide. He stares into the crowd with increasing panic, scanning the strangers' faces. Cory reaches for him, but it's too late, his small mouth crumples and a high-pitched whine escapes. Cory, crouching, guides him offstage. As she leads him out the barn door she hears Glinda's aristocratic trill: *Let the joyous news be spread: the wicked old witch at last is dead!* and Soul Patch Adam launches into "Ding Dong," and the audience claps along.

It is cooler outside than in the thermos of a barn. Ferns clustered by the clapboard buzz with cicadas or whatever, shivering in the blessed breeze. Beyond the trampled hill, punctuated here and there by abandoned sports equipment, clouds rest upon the farthest and bluest of the White Mountains. Cory kneels beside poor Spenser on the grass and rubs his back. He shudders violently.

It's okay, she says. Stage fright is the worst. But sometimes it's good to do what scares you.

He tugs the emergency-orange band of his glasses from his curly head and lets them fall down around his neck. Without them his wet little eyes are naked and unmagnified. He looks less cartoonish and even more pathetic.

It's *not—stage fright*, he snuffles.

What, then?

I want my— His voice cracks, and with renewed despair, he says: I want my *mo-om*.

She's not here?

No. He wipes his nose, smudging his mustache halfway across his face.

Who's picking you up?

My *dad*, he grumbles. My little *sister.*

That's fun, isn't it?

He frowns at her and puts his glasses back on with a sound of disgust.

Won't you see your mom soon?

No.

After a moment, Cory recalls a minor drama. Late one evening, weeks ago—eons ago in camp time—she was in the Red House, half reading a months-old magazine, half listening to the other counselors play poker on the musty carpet, when a phone call jangled the landline. Soul Patch Adam was sent to fetch the boy from bed. A hush fell over the room when Spenser was brought in, bleary-eyed and puny, holding a stuffed animal rendered character-less by years of sweaty nights and laundering. The older counselors made halfhearted attempts to hide their beers as he was led into the kitchen, where the old communal laptop sat beside the Mr. Coffee and the dial-up modem, and they all listened to the blee-blee-bleep of a FaceTime call, holding their breath, afraid that something terrible had happened. And then, the voice of Spenser's mother, loving, exhausted, divine: *Hi, Spense! Hi, big boy! Do you want to meet your baby brother?* The poker game continued.

3

Oh, Cory says. Your mom's probably with the new baby, huh.

Spenser shoves his face into her chest, bereft. It is too much for him.

Okay, she says, gently relocating him from breast to shoulder. Yeah, that's hard, isn't it.

He climbs into her lap to weep. From the barn a new song rises into the afternoon. *Follow the yellow brick road*, the children chant, and chant again. She rocks him in time to the beat—*Follow, follow, follow, follow*—humming along, the sad little seven-year-old perspiring in her arms, but no longer crying. Spenser, young as he is, has a reputation as a high-strung weirdo, given to nightmares, benign groping, and high-decibel freak-outs about minor slights and changes in plan, but she can't bring herself to roll her eyes about him as the other counselors do. They are callous in a way she has never known how to be. She feels for the boy, even or especially when he loses his shit. It's not his fault. He is too young for sleep-away camp. Too young to be away from his mom. And, honestly, Cory can sympathize. She, too, both wants and does not want to go home. To the hot city that smells of bus exhaust and baking trash. To the too-small uptown apartment she shares with her own mother, a verified bitch. Worst of all, to her unknowable future.

Working at River Rock was hardly Cory's ideal way to spend the summer after her senior year of high school. Had she gotten into her first- or second- or even third-choice college—had she gotten into even one of her so-called safety schools—she might soon be leaving the city for a college-sponsored bonding trip, five nights of camping in canyons under the Utah stars, say; community service in Flint, Michigan. Her mother might have rewarded her by letting her tag along with the coven of classmates currently gallivanting

4

around Europe on what looks on social like a wild and glamorous backpacking tour. They have eaten pot pastries in Amsterdam, they have clubbed in Berlin, they have sunned on a beach in Crete. They have taken selfies with waxed-chested European men signing *peace* with their feminine fingers, cigarettes hanging limply from unsmiling lips. Such trips would be a reach for her, socially and financially, at the best of times, but given that she lost her scholarship and landed herself on academic probation, given that she got into, count them, zero colleges, these times are literally the worst. Her mother, always unlikely to shell out for frivolous expenses, has limited ability and no interest in sponsoring *fun*.

I will find a way to pay for classes, she told Cory in May. *I will find a way to pay for summer school. I will shell out for another round of SATs and APs. I will support you while you do an internship. I will even help you get an internship. You know I know people. You could fetch coffee, learn the ropes, at, I don't know, Condé Nast—or, hey, Google. What about Google? I could call Radha.*

Oh my god, *Mom.*

Don't Oh-my-god-Mom me. Plenty of kids your age would die for an internship at Google.

You don't know shit about what kids my age would die for.

Fine, Cory. What would you die for. Tell me. I'm all ears.

For money. For a driver's license and a car. For a future like an open road; for freedom. For a life that tastes like that feeling she used to have nowhere but at summer camp, lying on the big flat rock at the top of the hill with her hand in the damp hand of a friend as the Perseids came unraveled from the sky, silver threads pulled quick from the infinite embroidery above them.

But a sustained feeling of awe at the glory of infinity is not among the benefits of the dull and unimaginative summer occupations her mother suggested. There was some discussion of taking intro-level classes at NYU or CUNY, but one look at a course catalog brought on a paralysis of indecision. *What interests you?* her mother asked. *What do you want to do?* These were questions she could not answer. As far as she can tell she has no interests, no desires except to spend time outdoors, far away from home, to lose herself in the intricacies of a landscape, to bliss out under the ever-changing sun. So in the heady humid days of early June she watched the rest of her graduating class leave town to run their victory laps around the globe, and descended into a fog of sleep and phone and fighting with and avoiding fighting with her mother. For a month they lived together like anxious strangers, extending some semblance of détente as long as they both could, only to erupt with sudden rage into vigorous, nonsensical arguments.

It was after one of these that Cory called up her old summer camp director and begged for a job. Because she was a minor and had no experience, and because it was mere weeks before Junior Camp was to commence, they stuck her with the little ones, the sevens, eights, and nines. Here she has spent the bulk of the summer in a kind of apprenticeship to Vermont Jen, tight of lip and plentiful of body hair, who's been a counselor at River Rock since at least the nineties, playing diplomat, comforting the bullied, tending to cuts, bruises, and bites, laundering pee-soaked sheets, cleaning vomit from the crevices between floorboards, and getting increasingly sunburned, lonely, and discouraged.

Applause from the barn. The sounds of conversation and metal folding chairs creaking and scraping on the wood floor: intermission. She is still singing quietly to the child in her lap. He is totally relaxed, as if hypnotized by the minor key, the cyclical tune that has somehow segued out of her sing-along. It is a slow and simple song her mother used to sing, Medieval in melody, Gothic in content. She has not heard it in at least a decade, but it is coming back to her now, phrase by mysterious phrase, through the years and miles. She is not sure of every word—some information has been damaged in recovery—but for the most part it seems to have been securely encoded:

> Good my mother, whence are you
> of folk born long ago?
> Why are you gone away from all
> you ever seemed to know?

> For while you linger here among
> the olive trees, old maid,
> the women here would welcome you
> in halls of stone and shade.

As the campers' parents make their way outside to stretch their legs, Cory lowers her voice, self-conscious, and lets the words of the song become a hum. At the top of the hill, a figure stands apart. He is tall and broad, big-bellied but elegant, dressed in white and beige, and rippling subtly in the heat, as if appearing to her through liquid. He is watching her. How long has he been watching her? Her humming fades.

After a moment her view of him is blocked and she feels a hand on her shoulder.

Want me to take him to his dad? Soul Patch Adam juts his decorated chin at the boy in her lap, glancing not unnoticeably at her tits.

Oh, she says, pulling up her shirt. Sure, yeah.

I've been looking for an opportunity to talk to him, Adam says.

To Spenser? she asks, confused, and the child's eyes blink open.

Spenser's *dad*. Adam gives her a look as if she should know. Rolo Picazo? He's, like, major.

Major what? she says. The name seems familiar and yet divorced from meaning, the way some household names do, absorbed half consciously via radio or television, glanced at in headlines of articles she'd never take the trouble to read.

Major macher, Adam says.

Major what? she says again, altering her emphasis.

Dude's a world mover. Southgate Pharma? Ever heard of it? I'm going to see if I can finagle an internship.

Something inside her wilts a little. Cool, she says.

Adam extends a hand to poor Spenser and addresses the boy with false cheer: Let's go find your daddy, 'kay, champ?

The boy gets up, limp, forlorn, and follows Adam up the hill. In the absence of the child's body, her skin feels cooler. She stands and stretches, breathes the air, brushes the grass from her shorts, looks off into the mountains. She is running her hands through her too-short hair—an amateur cut-and-dye job, cotton candy pink, the handiwork of another counselor, big mistake—when she glances up to see that the rippling man is still watching her.

A tiny girl in a yellow dress is tugging on his belt. He pays the child no attention. Cory raises a hand to wave, to show him that she sees him. He does not wave back. He just looks and looks. His gaze is hard and hungry. It could consume her, she thinks, if she let it.

After the play and the curtain calls and the 4 p.m. dinner of hot dogs and Boca burgers in the meadow, after the last of the campers have hugged and been torn from their friends, forever changed, after the staff's final huddle and posthuddle vent sesh, commences the long and dreaded process of all-camp cleanup. Cory and Iris, Dora, Melissa, and New Jen spend three or four hours cleaning the girls' cabins and tossing into trash bags all that the eighty-odd female-identifying campers have left behind: the mud-caked beach towels and experiments in tie-dye; the crumpled letters, torn postcards, and rain-damaged paperbacks; the mostly empty bags of chips and candy wrappers; the tampons wrapped in toilet paper, the blood-stiffened underwear shoved under mattresses; the half-empty bottles of body wash, nauseatingly sweet; the acne ointments and hair removal creams; the razor blades and eyelash curlers; the henna, hair dye, makeup, and dozens of bottles of nail polish with glam and wacky names: Bet on Rouge and Mello Yello, Dancing Queen and Tender Is the Night. They pocket the ones they like and toss the rest.

At sundown they pause to paint their toenails on the porch of the Red House and pass around Iris's last remaining joint. In the lull when the sun has sunk, leaving behind a pastel mess of yellow, blue, and pink, among the lingering smells of ash and marijuana, nitrocellulose, soil, and woods, somebody asks:

So what's everyone doing after this?

New Jen and Melissa are going back to college next month. Iris and Dora are leaving for a rented ramshackle house everyone calls Château Relaxeau, which they share with four other painfully cool River Rockers Cory knows. Jealous, Cory says, and, after a moment, she gives in to the urge to complain that she's dreading going back to live with her mom.

Come with us! they clamor. It will be so fun! You can crash on the couch till you find a job. You can sleep in my bed. Or mine! We can cuddle puddle!

How would it be. She tries to imagine. She has been to the Château once before, for a big postcamp party last August, at the end of her final summer as a camper. She recalls the cigarette-burnt living room carpet, the mildewed bath towels, a vinyl cushion on a toilet seat, grandmotherly pink. One of the roommates is a bassist named Garrett whom Cory's had a crush on since she was ten. He's three or four years older and so thin he's concave, with bird-bone shoulder blades, sad brown eyes, and a girlfriend named after a mermaid.

Sounds amazing, she says, then lowers her eyes to her dirty toes, nestled in the soles of her pastel purple, ethylene vinyl acetate sandals. On the toenails pool ten puddles of Emerald City green.

I don't know if I could be in the same house as Garrett Pollack, she admits.

Oh my god, says Iris, laughing, you'd get over that so fast.

Dora agrees: Garrett is such a dork.

Wait, says New Jen, you have a thing for Pollack?

You could totally fuck him, Melissa says with the authority of an older girl. You're so much prettier than Ariel.

Oh my god, says Cory, I am *not*.

Yes you are, Melissa says—

Iris says, You're definitely the prettiest girl at camp.

Stop, Cory pleads.

—and cooler, too, Melissa says. Ariel may seem chill, but she's so insecure.

Hot mess, New Jen says.

Well, says Cory, her face warming, if hot mess is his type, maybe I do have a chance.

The girls laugh, then go quiet, finishing their manicures. The insectoid symphony of nightfall mingles shrilly with a bass beat drifting up the hill. Through the trees they can just make out the glow of the Rec Hall windows, where the other counselors are cleaning the kitchen and laying out a final feast of leftovers.

Whatever you do, says New Jen, who's a psych major, don't feel you have to go back to a shitty situation. You're eighteen now. You can make your own decisions. If things with your mom are toxic, you can make a new family, a family of choice.

The others nod, waving their hands in the summer air and blowing on their fingernails. After a moment, Iris has the bright idea to make of the barn one last joyful jumble. A flower fight! The plan is met with enthusiasm. Dora brings an ancient boom box, New Jen a dollar-store disco ball they found wedged behind a toilet, who knows why.

The paper poppies were Cory's invention. Assembled by herself, half a dozen other counselors, and a few brownnosing campers over the past few weeks, they are shaped like shuttlecocks, coins of cork coated in glue and dipped in glitter, a red crepe-paper ruffle attached to each. For weeks they have been accumulating in the Art Shack in preparation for their appearance at the outset of act 2. This afternoon, after hours of mind-numbing manufacture and weeks of picking glitter and Elmer's glue from her fingerprints, after Spenser's meltdown, after intermission, it was at last their time to shine. The green-faced kid who played the Witch delivered her line with relish—*Poppies!* she snarled, flicking her cape. *Poppies shall put them to sleep!*—and, from behind the butcher paper backdrop, atop a stepladder, Cory dropped the sparkling confections. They twirled as they fell—as intended!—gorgeously aerodynamic, shedding glitter as they went, splitting the sunshine that flooded sideways through the barn's wide windows. Second-Act Dorothy stretched and yawned; the Tin Man cried for help; the Scarecrow kvetched; the Lion dropped backward, feet to the sky, eliciting laughter. The young actors played drowsy, and the audience awakened.

Now, in the rotating colored lights, to '90s R & B, the paper twirls and the glitter falls again, stray flakes alight and glinting, the girls all loose and laughing. Shoes are kicked off. Melissa puts on the Witch's hat and does a great impression. Someone tosses Cory the Lion's rubber mask; she puts it on and promptly stumbles. Iris, falling on top of her in a fit of giddy laughter, wails, I have to pee! and staggers up again, followed by the others, leaving Cory all alone on the broad barn floor, laughing in a heap of paper poppies. The others are just outside, watering the ferns, ha-ha. Mid-hilarity her laughter fades into a kind of charged euphoria. All the long, exhausting day she's craved this. Solitude at last.

Soon, this moment will be nothing more than memory. The paper flowers all around her. The centuries-smoothed wooden floor below. How running her bare toes over its dry surface sends shivers through her spine. The sounds of her friends outside, the CD skipping on an unresolved chord. The smells of hot dogs, dirty hair, and perspiration; the taste of salt on her upper lip. The tingling of the marijuana in her jaw and cozy feel of her head inside a shell, protected. Imagine it: her brain inside her head inside the lion mask, an oyster inside an oyster shell inside an oyster shell. Deep within the doubled chassis nestles everything, for better and for worse, that makes Cory Cory, yet no more than a corrugated ball of tender muck, synapses snapping like microscopic firecrackers. The weed has left her in a state of benign wonder. It is a miracle, a miracle! to be eighteen, alive, and high.

She holds a crepe petal between her thumb and finger and squeezes, enjoying the give of its minute ridges and grooves. She tosses a poppy in the air, watches it twirl and land on her belly. Pulls her phone from her pocket and repeats the gesture, leaving her finger on the screen to make a mesmerizing little video. She opens social and experiments, altering colors, filters, contrast, settling eventually on a prismatic filter that multiplies and exaggerates the glitter-cast rainbows. Posting the video, she location-tags it the way she has everything she's posted from camp: *Never-Never Land*. She is watching it, pleased with her artistry, and rewatching it, when a notification buzzes. A text from her mother. Another video, this one in China. An aerial view of rice paddies. The sound of the plane is loud and startling. She turns off her phone before it ends. The subtext is too annoying. Look at me, and my glamorous life. Look where I can go, what I can see, with my decades of education and experience. Cory slides the phone back into her pocket. The temptation overcomes her to doze off, overwhelmed and hidden behind her mask, amid the pretty mess.

And perhaps she has dozed off for a moment, because now her friends' voices are lost in the shrill pulse of the crickets, and she is awakening to the fact that she is no longer alone.

The rippling man stands above her. His bulk blocks the wavering rainbow lights. His face is cast in shadow, but she can tell he's looking down at her, head cocked, teeth gleaming. Even if he were not holding the hands of two small kids—fairy child on the left, in a yellow summer dress; on the right, nearsighted Spenser—she'd know immediately that he is the giant who watched her from the hill.

There she is, says Spenser.

The man is massive, easily six and a half feet tall and more than a couple of hundred pounds, but his voice is low and tender when he replies, Well done, bud.

The boy glows in the light of his dad's approval.

Cory, I presume.

She pushes up onto an elbow, but the lion mask slips down, partially concealing him. In a brief, out-of-body moment she wonders what it's like to see herself through his eyes. I'm not Cory, she says in a deep voice. I'm king of the jungle. *Rawr!*

Spenser laughs and gets into her lap.

What are you still doing here? she says.

We came back for you, Spenser says.

You what? She tugs the mask off. The air is cool on her damp brow.

Last day of camp, sire? the man observes, ignoring his son.

She wipes the perspiration from her lip and forehead with the back of her hand and fusses with her hair, which has gotten matted down inside the mask. She worries for a moment he might know she's stoned, then lets the worry go. He's a dad, but not *her* dad. She has no dad. Still, it catches her by surprise sometimes, this spontaneous yearning for a man's approval, like knocking into a forgotten bruise. Under his gaze she goes suddenly shy, and addresses his son instead:

Yeah, what a summer, huh? How'd you like your first year at River Rock?

Spenser has busied himself pulling on the frayed denim of her shorts. His eyes have disappeared behind a fog on his glasses lenses.

That's my sister, he says, pointing at the girl.

What's her name?

Fern.

Hi, Fern, Cory says, smiling at the child, but she retreats behind the girthy leg of her father, who points at Spenser and says,

Thing One over here tells me you're his favorite counselor.

That's sweet, says Cory.

He's having a hard time letting you go.

The man's focus on her is so intense she feels it like a tickle at the back of her neck, in her belly, in her you-know-what, which pulses and dampens involuntarily: a pleasurable feeling that is not a sign of pleasure, not exactly, not necessarily. It happens, has been happening, for years, anytime she thinks of sex or sex-adjacent things—or even

14

things that have nothing to do with sex but nevertheless evoke it, that fall in the uncanny valley where appetizing and nauseating meet. Sticky fingers. Beanbag chairs. The way boys pile upon each other on the football field, bodies upon bodies upon bodies upon mud. Iris scratching a bug bite on her inner thigh, the way her eyes dim with pleasure, the ugly pink welt of it, dark blood breaking the surface of the swollen skin in the tracks of her fingernails. Certain insinuating words—hump, mount, slit, muck—which the simple act of repeating to herself, under her breath, can transport her to a state of near hypnosis. The feeling, despite herself, of being watched.

Spenser, the man says. Did you have something you wanted to say?

Spenser mumbles into her shirt.

What did you want to say to Cory? the man asks again. Look her in the eye when you talk to her.

Spenser fixes his eyes on her and the fog on his lenses evaporates a little. Come with us to Pluto, he says like a little alien.

Um. She laughs and glances at his father, not understanding.

Phrase it as a question, says the dad.

Come with us to Pluto? he repeats, raising his eyebrows and two upturned hands.

It's a diner, the man says. Up Route 37. We had lunch there a couple weeks ago, before I dropped Spenser off. These two can't get enough.

Waffles! says Spenser, and shoves a fist into the air, narrowly missing Cory's chin.

That's right. And what are you going to get, Fern?

In an impossibly sweet, high voice, the girl replies: Chocka-chip pancakes.

Ooh, yum, says Cory indulgently.

Does that sound good?

It does sound good. It sounds more than good. The very thought of food ignites in Cory a voracious hunger. But she has responsibilities here. Any moment, presumably, Iris and the rest will be back with brooms and mops and Murphy's oil.

I shouldn't.

He sighs and addresses the children: She *shouldn't*.

Prompted, the kids emit whines of protest.

He shrugs at her, renouncing responsibility. He stoops to casually pick up a paper poppy. What will you eat here? he asks, as if addressing the flower.

She thinks herself into the walk-in, where she and Iris sometimes go to attend to their munchies. What's in there now? Leftover potato salad, days-old wilted greens, the cookie dough that last time left her doubled over in stomach pain, all of it soon to be thrown out.

And surely your dining companions can't be half as charming as these little fools. Not every night you get to eat out with Milhouse and Tinker Bell.

The little fools in question grin, and their father smiles as if he has already won. His thick fingers squeeze a paper petal, dropping glitter onto the floor, and again she pulses. *Dude's a world mover*, Adam said. Could that be true, and if it is, what could a man like that want with an eighteen-year-old loser like her, shitty pink hair and no future to speak of, barely a camp counselor, for god's sake. Somewhere deep within her, the answer to these questions lurks, hungry, in the dark.

From her lap, Spenser recites: Sometimes it's good to do what scares you.

Well said, son! The boy's dad holds the flower out to her, an invitation, and his lips are soft, his eyes large, deep set, and mournful, the irises as dark and opaque as the pupils within, and she

16

feels tugged toward him, a corporeal acquiescence, as natural and strangely physical as if he had her on a leash. Inadvertently she smiles.

When he speaks again his voice is low and growling: Let's go for a drive.

Whatever he might want with her, wherever he might take her, chances are it is better than what awaits her at home. Fear is better than boredom, she reasons, danger trumps familiarity, the unknown is always more interesting than the known. So it is with some reluctance, but not much, that she rises. Glitter comes unstuck from her bare skin and she follows the small family through the barn door as if in a dream. The blue glow of twilight has melted into real dark, and the change in temperature outside is as sudden as the change in light. The damp grass sends a chill from the soles of her feet up through her spine. Her nipples harden and goose bumps prickle her limbs. Down the hill, music is thumping, and she can hear the other counselors yelling, singing, can see their silhouettes in the windows of the dining hall, where a dance party has broken out, but up here it is deserted. The man is taller than she is in a way most people aren't, which is to say significantly; his silhouette erases the stars. When the girl named Fern picks up her feet and swings from her dad's arm, he barely seems to notice the small change in weight, in momentum.

Wait a minute, says Cory as they approach the parking lot, I left my shoes.

We'll get you shoes, he says without breaking stride, and she wonders whether she is too high to understand what he means.

A convertible sits apart from the other cars, aerodynamic as a bullet. Are you—? she starts to ask, but leaves her question hanging in the summer air, unfinished. It would be childish to ask him if he's famous.

He opens the passenger's-side door and pushes down the seat so the children can climb into the back. Buckle up, he tells them, and then brings the seat back to sitting and bows to Cory, ushering her in: Majesty.

She stands for a moment, hesitant and barefoot on the dusty gravel. She is listening to a recording of her mother's voice inside her head. *Never,* never *get in a car with a strange man*: it is of course among the first rules drilled into her in early childhood. Seems sort of funny now, the double meaning. Who knew that when the occasion arose the man would be so strange.

Coming? A hint of impatience constricts his voice.

Uh, she says, and glances at the children looking at her from the back seat. The little girl, she thinks. Shouldn't she be in a car seat? But something in his expression cuts short her line of thought. His eyes have a hypnotic effect. She feels at once and overwhelmingly that not to get in would be an error. She slides in and feels the leather seat butter soft on her bare thighs. Then the driver's-side door slams and the small car rocks with his weight, and he cranes his neck to make sure the children have their seat belts on, and keys the ignition and tears off, over the gravel, under the close-knit pines, onto the narrow highway.

Wind freezes her neck, dries her sweat, whips her hair. He turns on the radio and some buoyant fugue rises into the night, strings interrupted intermittently by static. Her heart is beating hard in her ears and it takes her a moment to realize that he is grinning at her, his teeth very white in the dark. She laughs in his direction, but her high has tipped over, as highs always do, into dry mouth and gnawing hunger. The physical discomfort is welcome, in a way. It helps drown out her misgivings.

I'm starving, she says over the noise of the music and wind.

I bet you are, he says under it.

The headlights ripple over the woods. She watches the flickering trees, then lowers her seat back, the better to drink in the leaves above and, beyond them, the stars. They turn off the highway and end up at a strip of low-lying stores: a Starbucks, a gas station, a vacant Panera. A Red Roof Inn, a Motel 6, a combination Pizza Hut/Taco Bell. An all-night diner, chrome and glowing, with old-fashioned lettering that blinks Pluto, Pluto.

Ooh, she says, admiring it.

No shirt, no shoes, no service, he tells her. First things first.

He pulls into a massive parking lot outside a Walmart, passing a klatch of campers and trailers. A dog barks. A man laughs. Despite the late hour there are a couple dozen cars parked near the entrance. He kills the engine. Stepping out of the car in her bare feet, she feels the warmth, baked in over the long summer day, still releasing slowly from the asphalt. As the children scramble out, he approaches her from around the car, swiftly, with intention.

She steps back from him reflexively. What are you—

Before she can complete the sentence he's swung her onto his back and is carrying her toward the sliding doors. She yelps and the kids laugh and she squeezes his broad trunk with her thighs to make herself as light as possible, and throws her arms over his big shoulders. His back and neck are warm and damp with perspiration. His hair is thick and fragrant. Like a two-headed creature attended by imps they galumph across the threshold into the fluorescent lights and air-conditioning. She half expects everyone inside to laugh or clap or otherwise commend their entrance, but the customers slumped over their coffees near the front are in another world and the checkout girls are deep in conversation and the woman sticking price tags on beach balls is focused on her task.

19

You can't make an entrance at a Walmart, he says. No matter what you do, they've seen weirder.

He carries her to the shoes and lets her down. Get whatever you want, he says. What are you, an eight, a nine?

Ten and a half, she admits. Her big feet have always been a source of shame.

He disappears behind a rotating display of flip-flops. Reeling a little at the direction their adventure has taken, she wanders vaguely. A nearby fridge glows with dozens of bottles of water. She opens it like a holy grail and retrieves one. The cold plastic crinkles in her fingers. She untwists the cap, drinks thirstily, and takes a moment to be mind-blown by the beautiful junk of this late-capitalist Earth, overpopulated by a parasitic glut of violent omnivorous primates who have made an industry of scraping up the very stuff of life, repackaging it in plastic, and selling it to one another. Amazing. Weed always has this flattening effect on her attention. Like Google Earth it spins the world and zooms in on its topography unbiased. Everything is equally entrancing-slash-distracting. The world is a bottomless trash bag.

What do you think of these? he asks, stepping back into her field of vision with a pair of espadrilles.

Nah, she says. She likes the sneakers better, mostly knockoff styles—Chuck Taylor–like, Adidas-like. She finds a pair of plain white near-Keds held together by a magnetic alarm-triggering device, lays them on the floor, slides in one foot, then the other, and admires the way the white fabric enhances the deep red-gold of her suntanned legs. When she retracts her feet from the sneakers she sees her heels have left two dirty marks inside them.

Now I guess we have to buy them, she says apologetically.

But he is distracted, flushed: What else do we need? The unflattering lighting makes him look older, more grizzled. Gray stubble frays at his jowls. His teeth are too white, too large. She feels a small twinge of sadness, or is it revulsion, for the way his ugliness undercuts his enthusiasm.

Need? she says. For an hour or two?

He says, You'll want something for the air-conditioning.

As the children set their hearts on other objects—Spenser is begging for a bug zapper, Fern for a tiny succulent in a shot glass—Cory slides her gaze over a display of patriotic summer wear, sweatshirts and tees in all sizes with American flags assembled out of bullets or eagles juxtaposed on stars and stripes; camo patterns in every hue, words in all-caps: HONOR, RESPECT, FREEDOM. PRETTY IN PINK, DANGEROUS IN CAMO—

Ooh, ooh, says Spenser, pointing at an olive-green shirt as large as his person, sporting a graphic of an army tank.

Absolutely not, says his dad.

—and a more evergreen display of women's sweatshirts catches Cory's eye. They are tie-dyed and single hued, cropped and over-sized, adorned with sequins, fuzz, and patches, hand-drawn crosses and kitten ears. There are shirts that read FLORIDA, VEGAS, PARIS, and FIND YOUR HAPPY, NOT TODAY SATAN and ROSÉ ALL DAY. Their insides are heavenly soft and their outsides are insane. She picks a cropped hoodie, bleach stained like cowhide, with appliqué lettering that reads QUEEN. She pulls it over her head and swoons for the fuzzy interior and the made-in-Taiwan smell of chemical cleanliness.

Sticking with the royalty theme, huh? he says. Jungle king turns Walmart queen?

Cory laughs politely, but a candy display beckons from near the registers, and she can't help but answer its call. She is vaguely aware of a spat breaking out between the children and their father—Spenser kicks his dad's shoe; Do that again, Dad says calmly, and you'll wait in the car; Spenser whines, She gets a shirt *and* a plant; Dad tells him, The plant is a gift for Cory, isn't it, Fern?—when she turns back to them, a family-size bag of sour gummy worms and value pack of Skittles under one arm, and says, on cue: Aw, that's so sweet. Thank you, Fern.

Anything else? says Dad. Candy? All right, candy.

At the register he pays with a black card that clangs when the young cashier accidentally drops it. Cory places the tiny succulent—a cluster of blushing globules no larger than a Ping-Pong ball—on the conveyor belt among her candy, and notes with a small laugh what comes up on the screen when the cashier scans its bar code sticker: Jelly Bean Plnt. As the foursome passes through the automatic sliding doors and walks back to the car, Cory thanks the children's father and rips open the bag of worms. She dispenses one to each child and a few to him before stuffing a handful into her own mouth. The sour sugar makes her jaw seize with pleasure.

Thank you, the children sing.

Don't thank Cory, he says between chews. Thank me. I bought them.

Thank you, Daddy.

Daddy giveth, he warns; Daddy can taketh away. At the gleaming car he pauses and adds: Do me a favor, everyone. No worms in the car, okay? It was a pain in the ass to get the leather on these seats replaced. I hate doing business with Italians. Everything takes four times too long.

Pluto smells of decades-old cigarette smoke, stale coffee, and pancakes. Brown-and-gold lamps hang over yellow countertops.

Tabletop jukeboxes cast a low glow in each red vinyl booth. Behind the counter a woman with hair like blond yarn nods at them and in a dusty voice says, Anywhere you want.

Isn't this place great, the children's dad murmurs under his breath, as if saying something nasty, and despite or because of his obvious wealth, Cory regrets not having grabbed her wallet before leaving camp. Fern has brought the shot glass succulent inside. In the booth she sets it down sideways on a napkin, as if putting it to sleep. Spenser reads the extensive menu with intense concentration. *Disco fries?* he says in disbelief, and lets out a high-pitched whinny. You guys, it says *disco fries!*

His dad is laughing, too, a low, amused growl, but not at Spenser.

What? she says.

Nothing. You're cute.

Realizing she's been chewing on the drawstring of her new hoodie, she feels her face flush and drops it from her mouth, wiping away a thread of drool. Fortunately the waitress approaches with ice water and plastic glasses.

He sings: Mona, Mona, from Daytona.

You're back, she observes.

Couldn't stay away.

Hi, cuties, she says to the kids.

Spenser and Fern go shy.

She yours, too? Mona asks, jerking her head at Cory.

Coffee, cream and sugar, he says by way of reply, then turns cursorily to Cory—Coffee, Highness?—and does not wait for a reply. She'll have a coffee, too.

The waitress looks at Cory a beat too long and Cory thinks wildly, *She knows I'm high,* before reminding herself it's all right, it's legal, after all, and they're strangers, and it's none of her business, et cetera. When the waitress has gone the man smiles, as if having watched Cory's internal monologue unfold on her face, and says, Does that happen to you a lot?

What? she says quickly.

People treat you differently because you're beautiful.

Oh—Cory feels her face heating up—I think she just knew I'm a little . . .

You model?

Me?

Your value won't last, you know. Time is money, and time is finite. You ought to get while the getting's good. Young people all think they'll be young forever. But before you know it you're a fat old gasbag like me. *You* could be worth millions—but only for, oh, four or five more years.

Her face is furiously hot, she must say something, but all she can come up with is: My mom would never . . .

And your mother does what, exactly?

Um, agriculture, basically. She runs an NGO?

A far cry from modeling, he observes.

It's called RHEA Seeds, Cory says, and starts to give him the spiel, but he cuts her off.

I've heard of it. He tilts his head at her and gives her a small, inscrutable smile. She is relieved when he drops his gaze, ending the moment, and unfolds the laminated menu to sigh dramatically and say: What are you going to get?

Rather dizzily, Cory laments: I don't know. Waffles look good. Pancakes look good. I sort of want bacon? But, ooh, I sort of want pie. And a milk shake? God, I don't know. What are *you* going to get?

Coffee, he says. Maybe a cinnamon bun. A secret about places like this? Most of the shit they serve is bought in bulk, frozen, and defrosted. The scrambled eggs are powdered. The waffles could be ten years old. Of course, the boy loves them. You love an aged waffle, don't you, Milhouse?

Spenser nods enthusiastically.

But a few things they make fresh.

Like the cinnamon buns, she says.

He taps his nose with an index finger and points at her.

Do I want a cinnamon bun? she asks.

You do.

What about the pies?

Mona has reappeared and is setting sloshing mugs before them, along with a ramekin full of disposable creamers and a glass jar of sugar fitted with a miniature spoon. Depends, she's saying. I'm supposed to tell you they're all delicious, and they are, but what I'm really going to tell you is get the berry-cherry.

All right, says the man. A cinnamon bun, a slice of berry-cherry pie, a side of bacon, a short stack of chocolate chip pancakes—

Fern lights up.

—a waffle—

With syrup, Spenser interjects.

—and two vanilla shakes.

Three vanilla shakes, Spenser says.

Two. You can have some of mine.

You want the pie warmed up, honey? says Mona without looking up.

It takes Cory a moment to realize that she is the honey, another moment to imagine pie, first cold, then warm. Yes, she replies.

Whipped cream or à la mode?

Uh. Both?

You got it.

As she walks away Cory starts to laugh. At first it's just a little bit, but before long it has taken over. Laughter runs through her like a galloping animal. My mom would be so mad, she manages to say at last.

A disciplined woman, he guesses.

Oh my god, Cory says. Channeling all her giddy energy into her mother's low, rapid, urgent voice, she launches into a lecture: *You don't see what goes into this stuff. Most food is literally poison. Microplastics in your hamburger. Mercury in your fish. You think your salad is healthy? That romaine is crawling with E. coli. Corn is basically candy. Nothing is safe!*

The children are laughing, and their amusement eggs her on. She peels open a creamer: *Just* look *at this wasteful packaging. There are mountains of these in the middle of the ocean. Trashbergs of plastic pods that once contained—what? Not* milk. *Milk* ingredients. *Corn syrup and maybe some partially hydrogenated soybean or cottonseed oil, mono- and diglycerides, dipotassium phosphate, casein, artificial color and artificial flavoring* (they never tell you what *that* is!). As a kind of punctuation, Cory downs the stuff like a shot. The children laugh. The man is clapping. He watches her wipe a drop of cream from her lip.

Incredible. How did you do that?

Cory demurs. Most packaged food is basically the same old chemicals and grain derivatives, she starts to say, but her little speech is interrupted by Mona's delivery of the two milk shakes, overfull and perspiring in fountain shop glasses, topped with whipped cream and a cherry each.

Napkins on your laps, he tells the kids.

Spenser puts a napkin on his head and grins broadly.

On your laps, his father repeats sharply. What were we, raised by wolves?

What are we, *aliens*? Spenser riffs.

What are we, *aliens* from *Planet Raised-by-Wolves*? And he pours two fingers of milk shake into water glasses for the kids.

Cory puts her mouth around her straw and sucks. He watches her like an audience of one. He watches her as a man watches a woman, and she is aware that he is watching her, but the absolute heaven of vanilla and sugar and cream reaches her brain before self-consciousness can take over. Oh my god, she says between sips. She can practically hear her dopamine receptors chattering with pleasure.

So, Cory Ansel, he says. Tell us about yourself. What is your life like?

How do you know my last name?

It was on the bulletin board in the Rec Hall, along with what I must say is a pretty gorgeous photo of you.

She knows the Polaroid he's referring to—double chin, frog mouth, crossed eyes—taped onto a blob of construction paper and labeled in Sharpie: *Cory Ansel, New York, NY*, between *Iris Aaron, Albany, NY* and *Adam Diamond, Short Hills, NJ*. She laughs and makes the same face now. What is my life like, she says. God, I don't know.

Sad, he observes.

She looks at him, surprised. I just finished high school.

Private? he guesses.

She nods.

All girls?

Rolls her eyes and nods.

So you're off to college in the fall.

Shakes her head. Gap year.

Didn't get in?

Surprised by his directness, she sort of shrugs.

And what will you do during this so-called gap year?

After these past few weeks at River Rock, where she's been pleasantly insulated from adults and their future-tripping, she does not enjoy being interrogated about her capital-L Life. She shrugs again and looks down at her milk shake to conceal her annoyance. Her mom did enroll her in not one but two short-term programs, without her consent: (1) volunteering with climate refugees in Ecuador, or was it El Salvador, one of those small earthquake-prone countries in the so-called Ring of Fire, she can't remember which, she's the worst, and (2) a permaculture program in New South Wales. But then, what do you know, another earthquake hit South America, and then pretty much the whole continent of Australia caught on fire—she has seen the videos of orphaned children in sports arenas, eating nutrition bars donated by multibillion-dollar corporations so the world would see their packaging on television, of smoke-choked koalas huddled on living room sofas, kindhearted zoologists tending to their burns—so those plans were scrapped. *What's the point of thinking about the future when the world is literally burning?* she demanded, and what could her mother say to that?

Listen, I'm going to suggest something, and I know you're going to hate it, but I'm going to say it, just so that I've done my due diligence. You could come work for me.

To which Cory retorted, You *don't even believe in what you're doing. And you're the* boss.

Get a job? she says now, rather weakly, to Spenser's dad.

Mona brings Fern's pancakes and Spenser's waffle. Their father melts a pat of butter on each and drenches them in artificial maple syrup (corn syrup, high-fructose corn syrup, salt, cellulose gum, sodium hexametaphosphate, sodium benzoate, caramel color). While the kids are absorbed in their food, Mona comes back with the cinnamon bun and the bacon (pork, salt, sugar, sodium phosphate, sodium erythorbate, sodium nitrite, gelatin, cornstarch, caramel color). Cory marvels at the indulgence. There's so much, she says, I don't know where to start.

He cuts a square of bacon with the edge of his fork and carries it over to the cinnamon bun. Laying it on the bun's sticky surface, he slices through the confection around the bacon's crispy edge, piles the arrangement, regular as a petit four, onto his fork, and brings the whole thing across the table to her mouth.

Start with this.

She balks at the intimacy of the gesture, at the black hair on his thick hands and the elastic of spittle waggling at the edge of his lips. Laughing a little, she shakes her head.

Come on, he says earnestly, it's a perfect bite. I made it for you.

Not quite knowing what else to do, she opens her mouth and lets him feed her. The cinnamon bun is pillow-soft and oozes with icing. The bacon is hot and crisp, all carcinogens and salt. Her brief disgust melts away as easily as the sugar and salt and animal fat and sweet, bready warmth on her tongue.

Oh my god, she says, mouth full. This *is* a perfect bite.

Spenser says, Me, me, me, I want a perfect bite, too! and Fern sits up high in the booth and opens her mouth and eyes as wide as they will go, and then Mona arrives with the pie, which turns out to be the real pièce de résistance: a fat purplish wedge with a scoop of ice cream melting on its flaky bronzed crust and a dollop of whipped cream atop that. Cory alternates bites of pie with sips of milk shake and acrid coffee as if in a dream. She can feel her belly stretching to accommodate the volume of sugars and carbohydrates, her jean shorts cutting into her stomach, the lipids leaching into her bloodstream. She knows that she is poisoning herself and she knows she really should stop but she wants to put it off for just one more bite, just two, just three—

You eat like a fucking horse, he says.

Daddy! Spenser is aghast.

I fucking love it.

Daddy, don't *swear*, says Fern.

He pays no attention to the kids' entreaties, but they seem to enjoy the challenge of being ignored. His mouth is open, his lips wet. His hands are under the table where Cory can't see them, and she has a thought about what they might be doing down there, and it grosses her out, and she tries to erase it, but erasing is unnecessary: all her thoughts, dirty and otherwise, are drowned out by eating. Her hunger is violent. One last bite, she bargains with it, then bargains again: Two last bites.

Tell me about your work experience, he says.

Her mouth is too full to swallow so she pushes the food into her cheek to say, What?

You said you might get a job. What do you want to do? What have you done?

Couple of internships? she attempts to say, then chews and swallows.

You don't know what you want, he declares. How old are you?

Eighteen last week, she says, and remembers her small birthday party in the woods: blunts, tallboys, a bonfire; Iris, Dora, and Melissa, Hot Adam and New Jen. They kissed her on the cheek. They ate chocolate cake with their hands. On the car ride back she sat on Hot Adam's lap and, as if unintentionally, he rested his hand on her thigh.

Spenser's dad's eyes flicker over her. You don't look it, he says, and in his voice for just a moment there is a note of tenderness, a note, almost, of regret. He lays his large hand on hers, and she has the brief and eerie feeling that she can see herself through his two potent, inky eyes, and is ashamed for having thought he might find her attractive—*her*, a gawky girl with foolish, Pepto-colored hair; a loser, but perhaps, from the point of view of a magnanimous man, a loser worth saving—and she feels disgusting, and sorry for herself, and flooded, weirdly, with a kind of grateful humiliation, or is it humiliated gratitude, that he has found her. Her stomach gurgles wretchedly.

He lifts his hand, goes on: So your senior year was a bust. Maybe you blew off a few classes. Maybe you smoked a little too much pot. Your mother wanted you to go to, I don't know, Berkeley, Yale? and was disappointed when, let's say, Bard or Pomona ended up being your options—

Those are really good schools, she objects.

Which, even if you'd gotten in, you'd just have been going to school for the sake of going to school, and after a whole life of compulsory school going—of being, I'd guess, the precariously positioned scholarship kid at a fancy prep school—you're sick of it, burned-out and jaded, can't bring yourself to get psyched for your mom's sake about four more years of essays and exams and con-textless information that has no bearing on anything that actually lights a fire under your butt—

Spenser and Fern find this phrase hilarious.

—that piques your substantial curiosity, that actually gets you excited. Am I on the right track?

Being analyzed so breezily is at once flattering and embarrass-ing, means she is both worth remarking on, worth the attention, and totally, dully predictable. Go on, she says queasily.

I'm guessing your social scene was less than ideal. You drifted away from your nerdy old friends, didn't you, toward a quote-unquote cooler crew, perhaps due to a shared interest in mind- and mood-altering substances?

She feels herself blush.

Eventually, though, the honeymoon phase with that clique ended. A girl as pretty and guileless as you, can't imagine you'd last very long among wolves. Maybe somebody's boyfriend had a crush on you, maybe you just got bored, whatever, by then it was too late to return to your old compadres, who were still licking their wounds after your rejection. By spring you were alone and aimless, no real friends, no real plans, no real laurels to rest on, so you went back to work at River Rock, your safety net, your happy place.

How the f— She cuts herself off so as not to curse in front of the children.

But now that's all done with, and you're hardly looking forward to going home. You love your mother, but, I'm guessing, from the food additive recitation, she's exacting, high expectations, low tolerance for fuckuppery, so that maybe you felt, with your pink hair and, pardon me, slacker vibe, you may never be capable of becoming the daughter she wants you to be. Meanwhile, your dad—

He reads her expression.

—is . . . unavailable? No longer around? Never was? And your shame at letting Mom down has come out in all kinds of nasty ways. You've lashed out, she's said regrettable things, blah-blah, et cetera. Long story short, neither of you really wants you to come home.

It is unreal how right he is. He is a kind of genie, maybe. She imagines she could get something precious out of him if she only knew what she wanted, if she only knew how.

Do I have pie on my face? she says, voice cracking, and stands abruptly. Her eyes sting with hot tears, her throat with bile. The children look up at her. I have pie all over my face, don't I. Sorry, I'll just—I've got to go—I have to go to the bathroom.

His head tilts as he watches her. Dizzy with sugar and adrenaline, she squeezes out between the banquette and tabletop and, without waiting for a reply, hurries past the bell jars holding pies and cakes, past Mona at the register, past the griddle where a man in a stained white apron is frying onions and peppers, to the ladies' room. A thousand thoughts have risen up and are clamoring all at once to be noticed, including: (1) she's alone with a strange man and his children, who knows where; (2) she has no wallet or charger or any independent transportation; three, her mother would be so, so unbelievably angry; four, and this one is urgent, she's about to be sick.

She locks herself in a stall and kneels on the tile and lifts the seat and gags and it all comes up, burning and sweet, purple and creamy-acidic. A relief to know it isn't too late, a relief to be rid of the poison. Limbs shaking, nose running, face sweating with exertion, she flushes it down, wipes her mouth and eyes with the back of her hand, blows her nose, and stands on shaky legs. She sits to pee quickly, flushes again, and opens the stall door, and is face-to-face, suddenly, with her reflection.

A tall girl stares back at her. Thin and awkward with a worried expression, cotton candy hair, and a bleach-stained crop top. She looks hard, searching for the girl people say is so beautiful. She wants to believe her friends that she's the prettiest girl at camp, but she suspects, no, she knows, that everyone lies about that sort of thing, and all she sees in the mirror is a giant nose atop a Gumby body, a toddler stretched long in a funhouse mirror, playing at adulthood, ungainly and absurd. Her mother's voice rises unbidden in her head. *You're going out like that? Have a little self-respect, honey, come on.* She shakes her head to loosen her mom from her mind. Runs the tap hot and washes out her mouth. Scrubs her hands and face until they're red. *Never,* never *get in a car with a strange man.* She has always known her mother was right but used to argue anyway, for the comfort of catechism: What if I'm being chased, though? *Use your phone.* What if I have no phone? *You must always keep your phone with you.* What if it's dead? *A charger, too.* What if he steals it? What if I drop it? *Find the nearest grown-up woman.*

What if there is no woman? *Find a crowded place.* What if I'm in the desert and there's no other human for miles?

Eventually her mother would tire of the barrage of hypotheticals, take Cory into her arms, and hold her close as if she'd had a nightmare. *Monkey, do you remember how you used to be inside me? And, do you know, the stuff you're made of is still inside me now? Well, that stuff is like a psychic thread, keeping us connected. Now close your eyes and try. Concentrate and try to reach me. If you pull the thread just right, I'll feel it, right here, where you used to be.*

Cory wipes her face dry with a paper towel. Sticks out her tongue at her reflection. Now is not the time for crying. Now is not the time.

Back at the booth the receipt lies among the detritus of their sugar feast. The family is gone and Mona, the nearest grown-up woman, is walking away from the booth with a tray of soiled flatware. Cory casts about for the kids and their father. Panicking, she looks out the window for the car in the parking lot, but does not immediately see it. She is pulling her phone from the pocket of her shorts, she is Googling rideshares in the area, she is waiting for the page to load, when she hears voices and turns to see the three of them coming out of the men's room.

Everyone had to whiz, Dad reports. As he approaches he looks at Cory with concern. You okay?

The kids climb back into the booth and so does she and they attach themselves to her, Fern in her lap and Spenser draped over her arm. I thought you were gone, she admits, sounding more wounded than she means to.

What, and leave you here? A castaway on Pluto?

His kind humor, and the warmth and weight of the kids against her, is all too much. She dares not speak for fear of choking up again.

Are you angry at me? he asks.

The question surprises her. She can't tell whether he's teasing. Of course not, she says.

You're lying. I can tell. I'm sorry. Sometimes I cross the line. I don't mean to. I'm curious about people. It's who I am.

It's okay, she says reflexively, then adds: I'm curious about people, too.

Are you curious about me? His dark eyes search hers.

Yes, she says, shifting under Fern's and Spenser's weight, avoiding his gaze. I mean, yeah.

What do you want to know?

This guy. This dad. This flirt. This wicked genie. She looks at him straight on and a desire crystallizes in her, clear and smooth and perfectly formed as if it has been there all the time.

I want to know if you'll give me a job, she says.

A broad smile reveals his gleaming teeth. I thought you'd never ask.

He leans forward and takes the pen from the tip tray. On a fresh napkin he does the math, mumbling: Eight-hour days, make that twelve-hour days, seven days a week. Minus a few hours off here and there, TBD, all right. What do you say to twenty thousand dollars?

What! For *what*?

Call it babysitting, if you must. You can be our temporary nanny. Four weeks of childcare, maybe the option to extend into some kind of paid internship or executive assistant deal if all goes well. In September Thing One and Thing Two will go home with their mom. After that, my crystal ball goes dark.

Twenty thousand dollars is more than triple Cory's take-home pay for her weeks at River Rock. With twenty thousand dollars she could rent her own apartment in the seacoast town near Château Relaxeau. She could put down first month's, last month's, and security on a place in the city, and still have spending money left over. Twenty thousand dollars would more than get her started. Twenty thousand dollars is too good to be true.

Don't you want to, I don't know, check my references or something? she says.

I just told you your whole life story. I heard your psychotic recitation of packaged creamer ingredients. I know everything I need to know. I had an instinct about you, Cory. I felt you would be an asset to me. Let's see if you prove me right.

Beside her, Spenser has been watching his father closely. Now his father nods in his young son's direction at last before sitting back, going on:

Anyway, your highest recommendation is that Spenser here already loves you, and let me tell you, this guy is not easy to please. Fern is a dream. She's like a dog in a handbag. The human equivalent of a Pomeranian. You can bring her anywhere and she'll more or less take care of herself. I've brought her with me to meetings all over the world. She's slept in restaurant cloakrooms, in corporate kitchenettes, on planes. She's been taken care of by clerks, cooks, and maids. People go out of their way for her. It's her blessing in life: wherever she goes, everyone loves her.

The child in Cory's lap has taken an interest in the sugar spoon, angling it this way and that, watching the upside-down reflections in its diminutive concavity. Her hair smells like baby shampoo. She is too sweet for this world.

It's Spenser I'm concerned about. He was too young for sleep-away camp and I knew it, but I just couldn't take him all summer. His mother and her, god help me, new husband, they just had a baby, and the old nanny, well. Isn't available. Fuck. *Cory.*

He runs his hands hard over his eyes and his brow and into his thick pewter hair. Leans forward and looks at her deeply.

I saw him crawl into your arms outside the barn this afternoon. I saw you rocking him, singing. That is special, my friend. You're special. Nobody ever treats this kid like that.

Self-conscious, sorry for him, she pulls Spenser close. He rests his head against her.

I'll have to talk to my mom, she says.

The man makes a regretful sucking sound, lips on teeth, and winces apologetically. Afraid I can't let you do that. NDA. Common practice, you'll find, with high-profile public figures, et cetera.

He drops his credit card onto the tip tray and gestures at the waitress. Cory glances at it to see if the name embossed there jogs her memory, but all she reads is the name of, presumably, his company: Southgate, LLC; it means nothing to her.

I have to tell my mom *something*, she says. I can't just disappear. Can't you? He smiles.

Fern lays her head back against Cory's shoulder, burying her nose into Cory's neck, and her father lowers his voice to add: And, listen, wait'll you see the place. Roaring ocean. Soaring cliffs. Complete privacy. Luxury that, not to toot my own horn, I'm going to guess not even a prep school girl from Manhattan has ever seen. You like luxury, Walmart Queen?

She thinks of rich friends' houses. Leon Hunt's two-story Chelsea apartment comes to mind, makes her ill. At Ella Ha's uncle's lodge in Vail, too proud to admit she'd never learned to ski, Cory faked a torn tendon to spend hours alone in the hot tub while Ella snowboarded with her cousins. On her one visit to Iris's grandparents' Connecticut compound, she woke early and roamed the sprawling property alone and unattended as a pet. Chandeliers split the morning light into rainbows. Lush carpet muffled low voices. In places like these she has always squirmed internally with a feeling of shabbiness, has always been perversely afraid of stinking, somehow, of having forgotten to apply deodorant. She recalls the rush of shame when Iris's grandparents' driver dropped her off in front of her building, and she had to pick her way through the trash piled up on the curb to get to her own familiar door. When her mother asked her—brightly, falsely—*Did you have fun?* she had no answer. Does she like luxury? No, she loves it, she loathes it.

He is watching her closely. Tell me one thing you want, he says, that your mother won't give you.

She shifts in the booth, subtly enough not to disturb the children, who seem to have fallen asleep. *A family,* she thinks.

Aloud, she says, Pie for breakfast.

Every morning! he declares warmly, and sits back, admiring Cory and the children upon her: What a tableau. Wish I had a camera.

What about your phone?

I never take pictures with my phone, he says, but shifts to root in his pocket. Very particular about my digital footprint. And don't you go taking any pictures, either, of me or mine, he adds rather sharply. No faces, no location-tagging, no identifying information, nothing.

Wow, o-*kay.*

I'm dead serious. Brandishing the retrieved cell phone, he busies himself looking for something on its screen. It's all in the NDA.

Mona sweeps by to collect his credit card and wipe the table. He ignores her. Half to himself, he is saying, Pretty good deal. Pretty good deal for both of us. I get the childcare, obviously; you get another month to delay the yawning maw of your future. And actually, who knows, a few weeks out there could change the course of your life. Such things have been known to happen. Decisions have been made on those thirty acres of mine that have altered the course of history, no exaggeration. Mergers and acquisitions, business partnerships, offers of marriage, lawsuits, you name it. Anyway, you're eighteen—he hands her the device, looking her in the eye—you can make your own decisions.

She takes the phone. A PDF glows on its screen: Times New Roman and a yellow arrow indicating the empty field that awaits her digital signature. She wants to ask for more time, wants to rewind, but the door to this opportunity seems to be closing, closing ever faster, the longer she hesitates. What's beyond the door does sound tempting, more than tempting, in fact; it sounds like an adventure. Her only concern, really, is her mom, but something the man said during his soliloquy of clairvoyance has stuck in her head and is circling, now, like a gull, around and around in her mind: *Neither of you really wants you to come home.*

Fuck it, she says. And with her index finger, beside the words *Receiving Party*, she draws her initials, noting as she does the name and digital signature that has autofilled above her own, beside the words *Disclosing Party*—Rolo Picazo—and recalling Soul Patch Adam's epithet: *Dude's a world mover.*

Now the world mover takes back his phone, slips it into his pocket, and rubs his hands together like a plump insect. Mona returns to lay the bill on the table and thanks him for coming back in, and he winks. Replacing his card in a leather billfold, he commands: Toss me the Pomeranian. Let's blow this Popsicle stand.

Cory lifts sleeping Fern from her lap and bundles the child onto his shoulder. She picks up the small plant and rouses Spenser as gently as she can. He whines into waking and clings to her as they leave. A bell rings as the diner door closes behind them. In the cool parking lot Rolo puts an arm around her, and she feels both trapped and protected. The weight of it reassures her. Its strength unnerves her. What does she know of big masculine bodies? When's the last time a man held her this way? A dad has never played with her on his hands and knees, or tucked her in at night, or cleaned a scrape until it stung, then kissed it. Fatherless girl, she bends toward his bulk, his warmth, as he guides her toward the car.

Then she hears a voice and they both turn to see Mona flagging them down: Excuse me! Outside the diner in her girlish waitress uniform, she looks smaller, older, drained of some power, dwarfed by the night.

Did you, uh, she says, approaching them with his receipt on the tip tray, looking up at him. Is this tip correct? Didn't want to charge your card before I checked with you.

It's correct, he says.

She says, This is a month's worth of tips.

It's correct, he repeats, and turns away.

At the black car, Cory watches him pull the front seats forward and buckle each of his small kids into the back. Is he avoiding her eyes? She gets in and closes her door, quietly as she can, and puts Fern's little succulent in a cup holder. He starts the ignition and raises the soft top of the convertible, enclosing them under a ceiling so low he has to slouch so as not to graze it.

Why did you tip her so much? she asks him.

He lays his hand on the gearshift. Waitressing is hard work.

She laughs. How do *you* know?

He starts the car. My mother was a waitress. For thirty-eight years.

Are we going back to camp? she asks as they pull out of the lot.

Why would we?

I don't know, to say goodbye? To get my stuff?

He pauses, lit intermittently by the clicking blinker. Do you *want* to go back to camp?

I mean, yeah? she says, and laughs again, because isn't it obvious, but then she thinks, *is* it obvious?

River Rock, he says, shaking his head, and lets out a short, nasal laugh, and the disdain with which he has intoned the alliterative name invites her to reevaluate. The dark and the chill. The Sysco food. The scrabbling of animals, muffled laughter, and metal bedsprings. The too-hot sleeping bag that smells of her own accumulated perspiration. Waking early to stagger down to the dining hall in the mist for a bowl of strawberry yogurt and off-brand Os before roaming the campground with a contractor bag, collecting trash. Does she want that? Does she want any of that?

He pulls out of the lot. At Little Île des Bienheureux you'll have whatever you need, he tells her, and then they are on the road, driving fast, and what is left for her to do but let her seat down a fraction and try to relax.

The drive is long. The kids sleep soundly in the back seat. Beside her, Rolo seems preoccupied. She can still taste vomit at the back of her throat.

At a half-obscured exit he takes a sharp turn, and then they are wheeling quick around the curves of a mountain road. Between thick woods in the dark of night there is no light at all except what the headlights cast ahead of them, a flickering black-and-white film of road and trees, the occasional pair of reflective eyes, real or imagined, and Cory has a sudden wild thought: maybe he is going to kill her. It would not be so strange. Horrible things happen to girls who go off with strange men. *Girls are abducted, raped, and murdered every day. Girls are chopped and cubed and stowed in freezers like beef*—shut up, Mom—

It is a curse of hers, this difficulty separating her mother's voice from her own internal monologue. She has discussed the problem with her therapist, Dr. Jim. Try, he has encouraged her. Imagine your mother within you like egg yolk, encased in the white that makes up the rest of you. Quiet your mind and separate out your mother's voice. Slowly transfer the yolk from shell to shell while letting the white drip into a bowl below. What does her mother's voice say? *Get out of the car, Cory.* What does her own voice say? Unclear. Should she be frightened? Probably. The word *murder* has popped up, after all. But she finds she is not scared, not exactly. Apprehensive, yes. Buzzing, but free.

Murder is improbable, is late-night TV, is camp-wide games of Assassin and tabloids in the checkout aisle. *Murder* is too abstract to be frightening, and anyhow she's no stranger to violence. She has been attacked, slandered, humiliated. In ninth grade at a party a classmate's boyfriend cornered her in the bathroom, held her down, and pressed his dick against her face while his friends laughed. In tenth grade, Leon Hunt—well, she won't think of that—suffice to say, occasional visits by violence are part of the cost of growing up female.

So she examines each thought with curiosity and lets it go, as Dr. Jim suggested she do when meditating: *Thank you, frightening thought, for paying me a visit. I release you now into the glimmering woods. I return to my breath.*

Anyway, they are driving fast in the woods at night and it's thrilling. There are children asleep in the back seat and what killer would bring his kids along for the ride? And he seems relaxed, steering with one wrist draped over the wheel, humming tunelessly, and if he were going to murder her he'd be a little nervous, wouldn't he? Unless he were a psychopath. But he doesn't seem like a psychopath, and surely if growing up in New York City has not prepared Cory to get a decent read on psychopaths, she's basically destined to be murdered. No, Rolo Picazo just seems kind of lonely. Lonely and funny. Lonely, funny, and sad. Okay, lonely, funny, sad, and into her, but not in a rapey-killy way. In a normal way. The way that she—admit it—is into him. Curious. Playful. Up for a drive.

The Wide-Pathed Earth
Yawned There in the Plain

According to Huang, we must see the world's most famous rice paddies, so on our second day in China, Ian and I are driven to a windy, vacant airstrip, where we board a glossy six-seater.

The plane smells faintly of the detergents that were used to clean it. We tear open small packages of cookies. From Styrofoam cups we sip bitter tea. We introduce ourselves to our placid tour guide, Jiao, a representative from the Ministry of Culture and Tourism, and our interpreter, who—smiling, smiling—invites us to call him Toad.

My Chinese name would be too difficult for you, he says with a laugh.

But Toad, I say. Why Toad?

Oh! he says, bobbing with delight. I like this word *Toad* because it is a word from nowhere. Many English words, they come, you know, from Latin, Greek, German, but *Toad*, it has no cognates, no known origin. Its etymology is a mystery. It just popped up in English, in the twelfth century, as a toad pops up from behind a rock! It has not evolved; nor has the animal. It is funny! *Toad*.

Funny, I agree with a smile. Beside him, Jiao watches, cool, benign. On her lap her hands lie curled, one within the other. Our pilot instructs us to put on our headsets. On the bulky headphones I can hear him murmuring to other aircraft.

Do you know *Frog and Toad*? I ask, and hear my voice very loud in my ears.

Frog, says the interpreter. A different but similar creature.

It's an American storybook, Ian tells him, then turns to me to be sure: Right?

Dear Ian: stout and bearded in a pale pink button-down and saffron cardigan. Sometimes, just looking at him, I want, inappropriately, to hug him.

Yes, I say. One of my daughter's favorites when she was young.

Oh! says our Toad happily, and recounts our exchange to Jiao. She nods and smiles and asks something in return.

Toad tells us: She says, *How old is your daughter, Ms. Ansel?*

Please, I say, call me Emer. She's seventeen—no, eighteen, last week.

Toad relays this information, and privately I feel my mood decline. My little girl's eighteen. Can vote. Buy cigarettes, god forbid. My baby's a young woman and I didn't get to be with her when she blew out her candles.

Jiao is speaking.

Toad says: Jiao has two daughters, twenty-five and twenty-eight.

You? I say to her directly, and try not to be astonished. To my eyes, she looks no older than thirty. Toad laughs and tells her what I've said, and she nods and gives me a tiny, closed-lip smile.

Daughters can be difficult, I suggest aloud.

Toad translates.

She breathes in, raising her eyebrows tensely, as if inhaling an acrid smell. The plane begins to move, first slow, then quick, over the tarmac, and heaves finally into the wind. I watch Jiao look out the small plane window at the receding Earth, and wonder if I see, in her guarded expression, something like the desperation I often feel: the hopelessness, the shame, the profound, haunting inadequacy peculiar, I imagine, to us mothers of grown or near-grown girls.

I could ask her, I suppose. I could try, anyway, but so much of what I mean would be lost in translation. All my conversations with our Chinese hosts seem desaturated somehow, drained of the rich hues of subtext, implication, connotation. Without a common tongue, language is not much more than an exchange of information. Like everything, it becomes a kind of commerce.

The paddies are flooded with still water. From high above, the terraced field looks like stained glass. Flat nesting surfaces in brown and green and blue and liquid white seem pieced together with earth-colored glue. Layers of mist hover over the water like scarves, pinned there and rippling. In contrast with the placid pools below, the wind around us seems ferociously alive. I raise my phone to the juddering double-paned glass and take a video for Cory. I want to remind her how much there is out there for her to see. I want to show her how large the world can feel.

Jiao leans forward and begins a history lesson. Her tongue is soft on her teeth. We are close as lovers in the narrow seats.

Toad translates: *It is believed,* he says, speaking sometimes in her pauses, sometimes over her quiet voice, *that the domestication of rice occurred between thirteen and eight thousand years ago, south of the Chang—that is, the Yangtze—River. According to carbon dating, our oldest known paddy field is from the early Neolithic period.*

47

I wonder, not for the first time, coming as I do from a country that's less than three hundred years old, what it would be like to have grown up in this place, in the tumultuous present, with thousands of years of history preceding you. But when I say something to this effect, and Toad relays my words to Jiao, she smiles with some reluctance, and, amiably, he corrects me:

This notion you have of China. It is quite romantic, isn't it? Your thousands-of-years-old China, your mythical China, is, if you'll excuse me, a more or less imagined place. Our modern China, the Chinese nation-state, was established less than a century ago! What *China* means, what *Chinese* refers to, these ideas have evolved countless times, have been evolving, always, and will continue to.

Jiao adds something, and Toad pauses to listen, nodding, before translating with a laugh:

Indeed, indeed! Additionally, as my colleague wisely points out, indigenous peoples in the Americas were harvesting rice, too, wild rice, many centuries before your European predecessors came along and—well! You know this. You see! Every history has its patterns. Every song its chorus, one might say.

Well put, and yes, exactly, I agree—but I cannot bring myself to nod. My face burns with a troubling flush of shame.

When our aerial tour is done, the small plane tilts earthward and we redirect toward Anhui Province, where are clustered what we have been calling *our farms*: those that, according to our agreement with China's government-subsidized agricultural conglomerate, are supposed already to have harvested one season's worth of our proprietary rice. The plane thunks down upon a deserted airstrip, where we are met by an official-looking SUV. We climb into the vehicle and go quiet again as the landscape hurtles by. In the rearview mirror I can see our driver's eyes, bloodshot and bleary, darting back and forth between our reflections and the road. He drives as if hell-bent on escaping something. We must be going eighty on the packed-earth road. When he brakes suddenly for an old woman crossing slowly, I am jolted into the seat back. I brace myself against the door handle. Try to avoid carsickness. Focus on the horizon. There is no vast scenery out here. No terraced fields rise up into the hillsides. I do not glimpse the Yangtze between the great gray hills, flashing bright with sun. There are only dusty fields, the odd high-rise and boxy house, rebar protruding from its roof. Far off, a herd of smog-smudged hills. When I told Cory I would be coming here, she sent me a link to a video: *Chinese Farming Couple Goes Viral, Dances Away Depression.* I must have watched seven or eight linked videos—they kept popping up, one after the next—strangely moved by those two sweet-faced farmers, their synchronized moves, their unself-conscious smiles, the way that, soon as they heard so much as a passing phrase of music, they'd drop everything to perform the Melbourne shuffle in their lonely field.

Our farmer, as we think of him, is a worried-looking older man. He speaks in hoarse spurts to Toad, who nods at him sincerely, then turns toward us and translates with a smile: Farmer Liaoning welcomes you. He says that thanks to your generous patronage he has been able to upgrade the machinery, the—the *combines* that he uses for harvest. He says he is looking forward to using this new combine, except that he has not yet had a chance, as the rice you sent him last year unfortunately does not grow.

What? I say.

Toad repeats: Does not grow.

Has grown, though, yes? I say. He was able to harvest last season?

Toad confers with the farmer, then turns back to us. Does not grow, he says again.

The farmer raises his voice, gesticulates. Toad nods again, then turns toward us: He says he has read the materials you sent about this so-called *magic rice* and, forgive me, it can be difficult to translate these slight variations, but he says it is not white but black magic. Like, you know, *hex*? Like *curse*?

I turn to Ian. Did you know anything about this?

Ian shakes his head. In his dress shoes and impeccable pastels, in this brown landscape, he could not look more out of place. Under his breath, he says, I was told the reason the rice wasn't shipping had to do with the snow disaster.

Snow disaster, I repeat.

I guess this winter they had so much snow no trains could get through.

I muted that thread in October, I admit to him, referring to our emails with the Ministry of Agriculture, heavy with niceties and circumlocution. Addressing Toad, I ask: Are the other farms experiencing similar problems, does he know?

Toad has barely finished translating before the farmer vehemently nods. Over the tail end of his monologue Toad smiles and explains: He says his cousin also signed a contract with your esteemed organization and also received a shipment of your famous seeds. Forgive me, he says they also did not grow. He says he is concerned they ruined his land. He says with his cousin live a wife, two grandchildren, a great-nephew, and the mother of his son-in-law. He says he is concerned that if he does not harvest he will not be paid.

My understanding, I say, is that our farmers are paid in advance. He should already have been paid.

But even as I speak the farmer is talking over me. Toad is looking first at him and then at me, smiling worriedly, nodding: He says there is a small initial payment upon signing and then a larger payment upon harvest. He says that is the way the contract is written. He says it is, forgive me, *despicable*. He says he wishes he would never have signed. He says not only do he and his cousin take a pay cut, they are also hungry, for a portion of the rice they would have grown, they would have eaten.

Jesus, I say to Ian.

He exhales: This is a situation.

Back to the SUV. We drive in silence at top speed along a winding highway. Toad smiles vaguely out the window. Jiao closes her eyes. Ian naps, too, an inflatable C-shaped pillow cozying his neck, but I cannot rest. I try to strategize. I make notes to myself and come up with phrases I might use to explain this to the board. Out the window the farms are closer together, and then they are not farms but factories, vast industrial fields of who knows what, laid out in grids. These transition into the sprawl of Shanghai proper, endless and complicated, the skyscrapers and warehouses of the biggest city on Earth, its elevated highways, homes, and busy streets, its small areas of green, where palms grow cheek by jowl with deciduous flora, all of it veiled in haze. It is that golden hour just before dusk and the lights of the city scatter faintly in the day's last sun.

We exit the highway onto a city street and a fleet of men on motorbikes zips by. I roll down the window and can hear, on one man's handlebar, a plastic bag snapping and rippling in the wind. The air smells like fire. Ian wakes and wipes his mouth. I recall a conversation I had at a fund-raising event last year with our government liaison and one of our board members, a man with a name like a pope, high up in the auto industry, whose company has a big hub here. The senator asked with apparent earnestness about food insecurity in China, then laughed with all her teeth at some joke the auto scion cracked about this country's convenient lack of environmental regulation.

The labs that have been working on our seeds these past eight years are located in an old colonial building. Were it not for the constant flow of language I cannot understand, the smells of peppercorn and ash, I might think I was in Europe. Inside, the halls are dully lit. My heels click on the laminate floors. A thin-fingered scientist, our longtime lead researcher Hong Tao, touches a plant under a grow light. Toad translates, smiling as always. He has no trouble with the dizzying jargon of our industry. They talk of engineered disease resistance, microbial pathogens, plant-pathogen coevolution. Of pattern-triggered versus effector-triggered immunity. Of genes and proteins, RNA, hormone responses, and transcription factors; of immunogenesis and endophytic fungi. I frown and nod and try to look authoritative, but even in English I cannot keep up. I'm ashamed to say I barely know what I am looking at. When we are led to the next room, I say to Ian: What's the takeaway here?

He says, Nothing we don't already know.

I trust him. This is his area, not mine. I hired him in part for his undergraduate background in plant biology. Me, I'm good for two things: managing people and raising money.

Why didn't we know the rice wasn't growing? I ask under my breath.

Could have gotten lost in translation, he says. Could be they've been keeping it from us until they figured it out.

I try not to sound too frantic. Why don't they know?

He says, They have to do more tests. They think it may have something to do with the genetic engineering. You know, you alter a protein here, a protein there, it has knock-on effects.

We've been working on this for the better part of a decade, I say.

He raises his eyebrows, shrugs.

Ian, I say in as low a voice as I can manage. Magic rice is a key talking point in the senator's reelection campaign. We were going to roll it out at the top of Q2. Gretchen already sent around the press releases. I have an appearance coming up on *GMA*.

Well, he says, holding the door for me to the next lab. Looks like that was all a little premature.

By the time we leave the lab, the sun has gone down. We have run late and are to be brought straight to dinner. I ask if I might go back to the hotel briefly, to shower and change, but Toad thinks I mean I want to bow out of the whole evening. The food, he assures me, is very good. With gusto he adds, You are getting the authentic Chinese experience! Too exhausted to make myself understood, I acquiesce.

At the restaurant we are led through a dining area hung with massive chandeliers, crowded and very grand. Passing lively tables, I hear French, German, maybe half a dozen languages. We are seated around an oval table in a private area, separated from the action by intricately carved wooden screens and lit by fat red lanterns. Our party numbers twelve: Toad, Jiao, Ian and me, four senior scientists, a man in a tight belt who turns out to be Jiao's boss from the Ministry of Culture and Tourism, his wife, or friend, perhaps, and a couple who, I gather, owns the restaurant. At the center of our table rotates the kind of disk-shaped tray my mother would have called a lazy Susan. I wonder now, as I settle in between Ian and Toad, about the possibly classist implications of that term.

Several of the party light cigarettes, and the meal begins. As the chef brings out dish after dish, the smells of daikon, pepper, and onion mingle in the smoke. Here are noodles, fatty sausage, vegetables in sauces. Here, sinewy shark fin soup, fragrant roast duck. Pork belly glistens, glutinous red and sweet. A whole steamed fish lies agape behind its veil of scallions. A pair of mitten crabs are plated as if locked in combat, and bowl after bowl after bowl is served of hot white rice. Rice, our common denominator, our old friend, our currency. Not for the first time, and with familiar unpleasantness, it occurs to me: the audacity of our organization. How did anyone think it was a good idea to try to streamline, optimize, expand, and improve on *rice*, of all things—in this part of the world, of all places. My mother used to have a saying: *Don't teach your grandmother how to suck eggs.* I flush again at our colonialist wrongheadedness. Lowering my head I follow my hosts' lead, reaching forward when they do, helping myself with my chopsticks as they do, eating when they eat, losing myself in the deep and complicated flavors, orchestrated to touch every corner of the tongue, and the round tray turns, and with each mouthful I feel afresh how hungry I am. I haven't eaten since breakfast. I have been running on discipline and worry.

A bottle of clear liquor is brought out, and we fill our glasses. Jiao's boss stands and begins to speak. Toad leans toward me to translate: He is giving a toast. He is saying you have honored him, them all, with your presence. He is saying how fortunate he is, and the people of his village, to receive guests as distinguished as yourselves. *Ganbei!* he says: This is like, bottoms up!

I perform humility, smiling and shaking my head, and then he sits, we drink. The liquor is harsh. I cough. They laugh. After a moment Toad leans toward me and says in a hushed voice: It is expected that you will now toast him.

Toast *him*, I say, hoarse from the alcohol. I don't even know him.

You can talk about the excellence of this place, he suggests, of the food, the welcome.

Oh, I couldn't, I wouldn't know . . . do I have to?

The way the question leaves my mouth reminds me of Cory, daughter of reluctance, daughter of squirm.

It would be good if you would toast him, Toad advises. If you do not, it will be considered rude.

So I stand and raise my glass, and fumble through something or other. I talk about how wonderful the trip has been, and how illuminating. I thank the minister of culture and tourism, I thank mild Jiao, I thank Hong Tao and the other scientists who've worked so hard. *Ganbei*, I say, and they all laugh and drink, and I sit down.

Now you drink, Toad tells me.

I can't, I say.

It is expected, he says, and leans over me to get Ian's attention, too. Mr. Iacchos, he says, you, too, must drink.

In reply, Ian raises his glass, and we both shoot the mean clear liquor. It leaves me dizzy, burning. At the specter of drunkenness I seem to be having a response akin to fear. I clear my throat and take a bite of food to chase it. As soon as I have refilled my mouth, Hong Tao's colleague, a stocky man with a boyish haircut, stands to toast us in turn.

He is saying that you are very distinguished, Toad tells me. He is saying he is honored—

I can't keep drinking this stuff, I say under my breath.

That would be considered rude.

I understand, I say, but please, I have a low tolerance. I'll get drunk.

We will all get drunk! Toad replies. He is laughing. All our tablemates are laughing.

I don't like it, I tell him, not knowing how else to describe what I mean.

You cannot hold your liquor! He laughs and claps me on the back, jolly as always, speaking loudly to be heard over his neighbors. It is the same with me, he says. Once I fell asleep on a bench. When I woke up I was in March!

What month was it when you went to sleep? I say, baffled.

He looks at me a moment, then bursts into more laughter. No, no! In *a march*, he says. Like a parade? A protest.

In *a march*. What were you protesting?

Oh, it is not important, he says loudly, perhaps tensely, but smiling. *Ganbei!*

Everybody takes another shot. Toad gestures at me with a look of encouragement to follow suit.

Wild with desperation, I tell him: I'm pregnant.

You? He looks at me and laughs, flushed cheeks, wet mouth.

I feel my expression flatten. Is that so surprising?

He stops laughing. Pregnant, he says. That is very joyful. And Toad stands and announces to them in Chinese the lie that I've just told him. Everyone roars with appreciation, claps and drinks, they are all looking at me. Beside me, Ian leans in.

What did he tell them? Ian says.

How would I know? I say vaguely.

What did you tell him?

I busy myself with my plate.

The restaurant owner stands to toast us now, and Toad translates as he speaks, revealing my fib: He says this is a miracle. He says a good omen that you are pregnant here in China. He says eat more chicken, walnuts, lamb, for warming. Garlic for the liver.

Salmon for the spleen. Carrots and sweet potato to detoxify the body. Spinach for the blood and eggs for harmony. He says it is amazing this American phenomenon. Women get pregnant at forty, fifty, sixty years of age. American women are fruitful, fertile—

A smile has begun at the corners of Ian's lips. His thick brows have lifted. Emer, he says.

What? I say. It's not impossible.

So he believes, Toad says triumphantly, that our magic rice will grow. *Ganbei!*

They all drink. We all eat. With my eyes averted I find, to my surprise, that I wish my falsehood true. My daughter is a woman now, in body if not in spirit. To think back to her infancy makes me queasy with love and yearning.

Now you toast him, Toad reminds me.

The night passes, measured in speeches. More food is brought out, special food, to nourish me and my supposed seed. During a lull I navigate the lavish dining room to the front door and step outside to digest, to pause, to breathe. In the humid evening people pass, lovers holding one another's waists, businessmen looking at their phones. A woman exits a kitchen door holding a headless chicken by its feet, and drains its dark blood into a bowl. A teenage girl chases a small boy, whipping a toy like a glowing sea creature against the backs of his legs. He runs, laughing, from her, and she runs and laughs with him. His head seems too large for his tiny body, and even as I have the urge to reach out, grab him, hold him, I feel myself sink inside. I wonder is she his young mother, older sister, cousin, or caretaker. She glances up at me, acknowledging my gaze, inclining her head politely, midgame, and I recognize something in her glance—some nascent adult manner, the way her attitudes, still young and indistinct, are just beginning to harden like clay in sun—that brings to mind my Cory. A feeling swells inside me, something difficult to name, a cousin of regret.

I look at my phone. Bring up Cory in my texts. Scroll through what is less an exchange than a travelogue. Chronologically from most recent to least: aerial view of the terraced rice paddies. No reply. A dance troupe performing in a Shanghai street. No reply. My face in an airplane bathroom, deadpan, ill-lit, a bean-shaped golden snail-slime mask stuck under each exhausted eye. She did not reply to that, either, but she did take a fraction of a second to double-tap a canned reply: *Ha ha!* in a cartoon balloon. It has been two months since she sent me any words at all, and those were predictably demanding, lacking in intimacy: *can u pick up ice cream / NOT VANILLA! snore / fun flavor idk.* Spoiled girl. Daughter of demands, daughter of hunger. If memory serves, I brought home a thirteen-dollar pint of something outrageous that night, raspberry and chocolate, rivulets of caramel, chunks of who knows what. She took one bite, declared it gross, and closed herself behind her bedroom door.

Now I feel a presence at my shoulder. I withdraw my attention from my phone and reacclimatize, or try to. Beside me: Jiao, tipsy but solemn, brow drawn, eyes wet. She looks at me with gravity and touches my wrist.

Daughter, she says, nodding at my phone.

Yes, I say.

She squeezes my hand tight. Together we watch the passersby.

III

The Sea's Salt Swell Laughed for Joy

Cory's descent into delinquency began with a benign exam in ancient history, second semester sophomore year. For weeks she put it off because it seemed distant and doable. As the time between the present moment and the test began to dilate, she put it off because it felt increasingly insurmountable. When the day came, she went to class having smoked with Ella Ha at lunch, and having studied not at all. She sat down with her favorite pen, and for the duration of the fifty-minute period stabbed in the dark at what felt like could be the truth of history. She approximated the stories she remembered her teacher having mentioned in class, digging up bright details in the backwoods soil of her mind and enhancing with imagination what she could not precisely recall. When she was handed back her exam the following week, on its final page was a big C-plus, in red, with commentary: *Good story-telling, a lot of pure invention, not one correct date. Next time, read.* She chalked it up as a win, but that test was worth 50 percent of her final grade. Where she'd been used to getting exclusively As and Bs, she began to falter, and even to experiment with how well she could continue to do without studying. As she became what was known as a C student, teachers stopped paying as much attention to her. She stopped sharing her report cards with her mother, when she could get away with it. She lowered her standards and she didn't die, wasn't jailed or even suspended. At first, the Cs were liberating.

If at home her mother raged, her concerns seemed to Cory remote, bourgeois. Specifically: college. Why all the panty twisting about higher education? Everyone from Cory's school got into college. No doubt she would, too. Which institution specifically mattered to her about as much as what she ate for lunch. She'd end up somewhere, she'd go through the motions for four more godforsaken years, and then she would be free.

Her mother, panicked, pressed Cory to pad her schedule with extracurriculars, and at first, out of what remained of her habit of obedience, Cory tried. It took less than a semester to systematically eliminate academic activities. Chess was boring, debate confounding. She had a good ear for foreign languages but no head for grammar. She was decent at drawing but the art teacher developed a vendetta against her after confiscating her unflattering caricature of him, jerking off in the direction of a long road disappearing into his obsession, single-point perspective. After much hounding by her mother she did try out for the school play, and was given the smallest possible part in *The Tempest*, just one line and a joke of a stage direction: *Enter mariners, wet*. It was sort of fun at first, but the theater geeks, with their in-jokes and their overdeveloped sexuality, made her uncomfortable. After three rehearsals, freaked out by everyone's enthusiasm, she quit.

Inspired by a friend who'd hired his son as an intern at his law firm, her mother decided that if school was not Cory's thing, work might be. With some finagling, under the perhaps over-valued impression that English was Cory's best subject, she landed her daughter an internship at a publishing company. The editors seemed to find her a beguiling curiosity. They treated her at first as a kind of oracle from the future—or, more accurately, from a present that remained opaque to them. *What percentage of purchases do you make from ads you see on social media?* they asked her. *Do you and your friends use TikTok? Is Facebook still relevant? What can you tell us about Discord?* But then Cory misfiled a tax form, which invited some unwanted attention from the IRS; several times misspelled well-known writers' names; and offended the house's most esteemed author by accidentally leaving him on the line when she meant to put him on hold, thereby enabling him to overhear her mutter, *Okay, butthole.* The writer berated her boss and the boss berated her, and she began to cry. Embarrassed, the boss said, *I am sensing that you're not quite, uh, ripe for the workforce.*

The summer after her junior year her mother landed her another internship, this time in the branded-content department at a public affairs magazine. This went well and uneventfully enough until, after a month of photocopying things and filing things and retrieving things from storage and ordering things for lunch and, infrequently, proofing things, and even writing a few things of very minor importance, she found herself not only stultifyingly bored but also in love with one of her colleagues, a twentysomething copywriter who once, over cupcakes at an office birthday party, referred to her offhandedly as quote-unquote *kind of a babe.* This ignited a benign but thrilling flirtation, which landed her eventually in the office of her superior, a charming man with three last names who sat her down and laid the latest issue of the magazine before her.

What's wrong with this article? he asked. Technically it was advertorial, a piece about the cultural value of vacationing in Key West, sponsored by the Florida Tourism Board. She read through it with as much attention to detail as she could muster, but the fact that he was watching freaked her out and she didn't catch the error, a joke between herself and the copywriter that she'd forgotten to delete from a sentence having to do with a Key West bookstore, replacing the word *antiquarian* with *octogenarian*, left to remain in print for all eternity, mocking the elderly population of Florida and prompting the tourism board to terminate its contract. *We look for a certain level of professionalism in our interns*, her superior told her. He was standing while she was sitting, as if to deliberately emphasize the power dynamic between them. *Do you understand what this is going to cost us? A small joke meant for one can have consequences for thousands. I hope this ends up being a learning experience for you. You can pack up your things.* She stood, heart pounding, eyes burning, attempting to keep her face expressionless. As she left his office, he added theatrically: *Oh, and by the way, Jed's gay.*

The fall of her senior year, her English teacher took pity on her and set her up with a volunteer gig as a reader at a college poetry journal, where she was expected to go through hundreds of poems a week to determine which ones were crap and which were halfway decent. English being the only class, by the end of her pockmarked high school career, in which she remained consistently able to dash off work at the eleventh hour that would earn her a B-plus, she thought she could basically recognize excellence when she saw it. But in the deluge of poems she was assigned to read each week, she lost her bearings. In much the same way that once, years before, she'd forgotten how to spell the word *egg*—*Egg*, she'd thought: *Egg. That can't be a word. Is that a word? Egg?*—she read through the slush pile with a confounding sense of jamais vu. *Quality.* What is *quality*? Is *this* quality? Is there even such a thing as quality? Given the endlessness of the submissions and the futility of the task, she thought it was not totally unreasonable to mull over one poetry packet for a contemplative hour or two before entering her copious, thoughtful, and, she thought, clever yet self-deprecating notes in the submissions system, but after two months she was accidentally (?) copied on an email from the managing editor to the editor-in-chief complaining that she was quote-unquote *inefficient to the point of useless*, which she took as a passive-aggressive suggestion to stop showing up.

Over the course of this series of demoralizing experiences, Cory developed a talent for closing her mind to thoughts that troubled her. Exactly as the ancient history exam had, college applications seemed very far away until everyone around her was suddenly obsessed: not just her mother but friends of her mother, teachers, school administrators, and all her acquaintances and classmates. She was forced to sit for two hours a day with a tutor who drilled her on test prep, math—god, *math*!—and the stuff of various APs, and who coaxed from her a passably starry-eyed college application essay, mostly horseshit, about being the only daughter of a single mother, and how her melancholy about often being left alone was mitigated, as she grew up, by admiration, as she came to understand the nonprofit work her mother did for the good of the world, blah-blah, emotional maturity. But then, early in her senior spring, adding insult to injury, she was suspended. It was just a small amount of drugs (she'd never even *tried* acid, she was saving it), and they searched her locker without warning, let alone a warrant (did she have no rights? and why was *she* singled out?), and the suspension itself was just a few days, but her mother was so inordinately distressed you'd have thought her only daughter had died. The vibe in their cramped apartment progressed from tense to frigid. Her mom reacted to each college rejection letter as if she had been stabbed in the heart.

Cory's guilt and shame at having failed so spectacularly at literally everything was compounded by a growing feeling of abandonment, triggered by the dawning conclusion that her mother's love for her had always been conditional, predicated on her performance. When her choice of college came down to community or nothing, she announced she would not be enrolling in school at all, no thanks. She ignored her mother's desperate suggestions for how she might spend the next months of her life. She kept her bedroom door locked. She spent less and less time at home, killing hours at Ella's, wandering the infinite city alone. Eventually, after a last epic argument, she got herself a job at River Rock. At the end of the five-hour drive, her mother touched her face and cried. Cory smiled cruelly, hiked her duffel over her shoulder, and turned away without a hug.

The highway is winding and the car is quick. Cory opens her eyes. Perhaps, uneasily, she's slept. Where they are and how long they have been driving, who knows, who knows. She looks at her phone. Reception is intermittent at best. During a stretch of a bar of service, though it is very late and she imagines her mother is in bed, face moisturized, breath sweetened, asleep or dutifully reading one of the many thick nonfiction books she never manages to finish, Cory texts: *Got a job for a few weeks. I'll be home in September, probably.*

Her mother texts back almost immediately, and Cory is reminded that she is in another time zone: half a day either ahead or behind, who can remember. *Probably?? / Sept?? / Doing what?? Where?? Since when??* Emer gets prim and imperious when she's angry. She uses punctuation like facial expressions. With every double question mark Cory can just see her raised eyebrows and pressed-together lips.

Internship. Parent of a camper, Cory texts back. *Upstate I think*, and she begins to elaborate—spontaneous decision, et cetera—but thinks better of it and deletes the incriminating explanation. Just as she's tapping send, another follow-up arrives, lamenting their annual postcamp dinner plan: *What about Bella Luna?*

But her mother gives her no time to respond to this reference to their happy tradition. *You think??* she responds on the tail of her last text, and adds: *You'd better find out, please.* A moment later: *Had no idea you were even considering.* Then: *Send information immediately.*

Cory turns to Rolo's profile, and her voice sounds weirdly loud in the hermetically sealed car: What should I tell my mom?

What have you told her so far? he asks calmly, and notes: If you've shared my identity or any contact information at all, this arrangement is null, effective immediately, vis-à-vis the terms of your nondisclosure agreement.

I didn't, Cory assures him. I didn't.

He glances at her and seems to soften a notch, sighing slowly through his nose. Tell her you landed a short-term executive internship with the CEO of a high-profile Fortune 500.

Wait, is this an executive internship?

How pleased would your mother be if you got a job as a babysitter?

Oh. Smart.

Say you can't tell her much more than that, due to having signed an NDA. Tell her there won't be great cell service where you'll be, but once you arrive you'll give her a secure number where she can leave you messages.

Having transcribed his words to the best of her ability, Cory watches the screen. A single exclamation point appears in reply, and for a while service drops again, and she loses herself in thought, watching the yellow double line snake-twist on the road. A deluge of buzzing startles her when the highway's lanes multiply: *I don't know what to say* and *How long have you been planning?* and *I need to know these things in advance* and *September will be too late to enroll in college classes* and *Was looking forward to seeing you, monkey.*

Hate for her mother hardens in her esophagus, indigestible. She wants to write back, Don't call me that. Wants to type out: Release me. Instead she uses the abbreviation her mother hates: *sry,* in casual lowercase. *In a car. Bad service.*

The response arrives immediately: *Where are you*

and a last word follows: *Going???*

an island, I think. And Cory presses send and turns off the screen, afraid she's said too much, violated within minutes the terms of her NDA. But with each fresh thought from her faraway mother the phone lights up again, attracting the attention of Rolo, whose gaze falls without reproach from the road to the rectangle on her lap to her face and back to the road again. Sheepishly she stows the device in her pocket, where she feels it buzz over and over with her mother's concern until they lose service yet again, and it goes quiet.

Then the road is rocky, and the car has slowed. She rolls down her window. The air feels cooler, wetter, and smells of brine and nature-rot. She hears a hush of wind in the leaves above, and the crunch of tires rolling over wet sand and rocks, and a buoy clanging, muffled by a heavy fog that in the headlights goes gauzy, opaque, then gauzy, revealing, then concealing, then revealing the road ahead.

Where are we? she asks.

He says, Almost there.

A single light illuminates the end of the road. They seem to be in an unpaved parking lot. She can make out only one other vehicle. He pulls up a respectful distance from the brown pickup and kills the engine. The damp quiet is cut by the mouth-smacking sound of water lapping land.

Are we at the beach? she says.

He's up and out of the car, unloading Spenser's luggage from the trunk, pushing his seat forward, reaching for Fern.

The fog is so thick and the night so dark that she can't see farther than a couple of yards ahead. Her sneaker sinks into waterlogged sand. She has the feeling that she's forgetting something before remembering she's left everything behind. While Rolo rounds up the kids, she follows the lapping of the water, the clanging of a bell, the crackling give of salt-stiffened seaweed. Then one step lands with a gentle splash and her toes go cold. She looks down and there's the water, petting the rubber and canvas of her new white shoes, approaching and receding as if to say, *There, there*, leaving behind its chill. Nearby, low groves of marsh grass waver in the shallows. A wooden dock tapers off into nothing.

His voice behind her: Ring that, would you. My hands are full.

Ring what?

In the fog and dark, with a child's sleeping head on each of his broad shoulders, he is very other. She knows he is a big man, but he looks bigger here, more sinister. The contours of his face seem unstable somehow, as if his outlines have been drawn with thread.

Turn around, he tells her.

She looks toward the dock and sees, as if conjured there upon a piling, a large brass bell. She pulls the damp rope that hangs from it and the bell clangs once, loud and tuneless, echoing off some invisible geology. The children on his shoulders stir and whine.

Ring it again, he says. With gusto!

To the slow rhythm of the clanging bell, he sings toward the water—*Sherry, She-e-erry bay-yay-bee. She-erry, can you come out tonight?*—and the echo of his eerie falsetto bounces over, then fades among, the quiet lapping of the waves.

Then, in low crescendo, a rumbling.

Ah! Rolo says, and in a voice meant for the kids, asks: Who's that?

From the altered cadence of their breathing, Cory can tell the children are awake, but they stay quiet, listening.

Rolo edges toward Cory. Be a good girl and reach in my pocket.

Cory offers a weak laugh.

Go on, he says.

She slides her fingers into his warm pocket, where they find his billfold.

Feed a twenty into that contraption there, he says, and she becomes aware of an object that resembles one of the coin-operated dispensers at the children's zoo her mother used to give her a quarter for, so she could fill her cupped hands with dusty pellets to feed the goats. She feeds his twenty into the machine, and four large coins drop into the outlet.

I want to feed the dummy, says Spenser suddenly.

You're awake, Rolo observes, as the boy scrambles down from his father's arms.

I want to! Fern raises her head and begins to cry. The rumble grows nearer, louder.

You can both feed the dummy, Rolo tells them. Four passengers, four tokens. Give the knuckleheads two tokens each, would you, Majesty?

Spenser grabs the coins from Cory's hand, runs up the dock, and evaporates. As she's handing the other two to Fern, miserable with exhaustion on her father's shoulder, the fog brightens, securing them all in place. Cory understands the rumble has been an engine only when it goes quiet and is replaced by a disturbance on the water. Then a lamp appears, wagging hangdog from the prow of what might once have been a lobster boat, souped up now with a bolted-in table and semicircle of cushioned seats.

In its illumination the beach and dock take on their familiar textures, sand and splinters. The water shines opaque as foil, and Rolo goes dimensional again at last, just some fattish aging dad holding his tired daughter, sweat darkening his pits, fog-demon no longer.

Under the lamppost in the boat's nose stands a hooded figure, dwarfed by a massive lifejacket and anchoring the craft with a ferry pole. A cigarette glows in the shadow of its hood. It raises its unoccupied hand in eerie salute and, in a wry, time-sanded voice, greets them all: Ahoy.

Sherry, Rolo says. How's tricks?

Business is booming, the captain replies, deadpan, and secures the boat with a length of rope to a piling. Hey, kids.

Spenser says, I went to sleep-away camp.

You're a big boy now, the captain observes.

Snared a new sitter for the kids, Rolo says, indicating Cory.

Great, says the captain without interest, and pulls open a door in the gunwale: All aboard.

Spenser climbs in, followed by Rolo, balancing Fern. The boat rocks. Where the smooth wall in the hull hinges open there has been secured a handmade mechanism: the head of a ventriloquist's dummy. As they pass, the captain pulls it open, and the dummy's weighted eyeballs roll, the better to watch as Spenser, then Fern, deposit their tokens in its mouth. The coins clatter within, metal against metal. When the captain releases the head it snaps shut again, cartoon eyes bobbing.

Rolo extends a hand. Cory hesitates.

His outstretched fingers beckon impatiently, slapping his palm. Come on, he says. Sherry doesn't have all night.

Right. The captain tosses her cigarette into the water and pushes back her hood to reveal a weathered face, delicate bones and deep-set eyes cast in jagged shadow by the amber lamplight. Drily, she adds, Can't keep the other customers waiting.

I— Cory begins, but her voice falters. It occurs to her to run, but running would be futile; Rolo could just drive after her. To jump into the convertible would be stupid; Rolo has the keys, and anyway she's never learned to drive. She wonders if the brown pickup belongs to Sherry. She wonders if she could ask Sherry for a ride back to camp. She pulls her phone from her pocket. No service. This trip is feeling increasingly irrevocable.

If she doesn't want to go, Sherry tells Rolo, you can't make her.

Of course I can, Rolo snaps, then laughs. Jesus, Cory, get in the fucking boat.

Daddy, says the lifejacket with legs that was once Fern.

Don't listen to him, says the captain. Rolo's just an ugly old fuck who can't take no for an answer.

Sherry! Spenser exclaims.

Laughter curtails Cory's hesitation. It comes from Rolo, big, heavy, and real. Then it comes from both kids.

Ugly old fuck, he repeats, breathless. Amazing. He grasps the shoulder of Sherry's life vest but she pulls away, and he slips forward, catching himself with a hand on the rail. Seeing him wipe out on the wet deck, Sherry laughs, too, a weird and high-pitched whinny, and everyone is weakened and bizarre, and with something like relief Cory is compelled to smile. In the fog-pearled light her strange new friends look disfigured by hilarity.

All right, kiddo, the captain says at last. Coming or going?

Her dread diluted, Cory steps into the hull.

While the captain loads their luggage and unlashes the rope, Rolo brings the kids down into the belly of the boat. Sherry maneuvers the craft through the shallows with the ferry pole. The fog lamp swings. Cory watches in silence as the convertible, the beach, and finally the dock all disappear behind them.

Asleep, announces Rolo, reemerging moments later. Both of them.

He swings open the top of the bolted table. Inside is a well-stocked cooler. He removes two beers, pops both tops on the table edge, and hands one to Cory. When she reaches for the bottle it tips and splats on the rocking floor. She drinks. The fizz hits her throat and ears and brain and descends warm into her belly.

When at last they are out of the marsh, the captain cuts the light and starts the engine. Under Cory's thighs the boat comes to reverberating life. As her eyes adjust to the dark she sees the eyeballs of the puppet head jiggling epileptically. Then they are speeding through the water, jumbling its surface in their wake, and then they're flying. Cory leans her head back on the canvas upholstery and looks up into the night sky and is dizzied by a froth of stars. Her eyes drink in the starlight, her mouth drinks in the beer, her mind the moment. If her friends at camp could see her now would they be frightened for her or impressed? And her mother? Swallow the thought. She drains her bottle quicker than she means to and Rolo opens two more. Cheers, he yells, and hits his bottle against hers, and comes to sit beside her.

When they've traveled a significant distance from land, Rolo rises and speaks briefly to Sherry, and the captain cuts the engine. The boat drifts in silence. There is no sound but their own breathing and the gentle slap of wave against hull, nothing to see but the stars and their reflections, separated only by a thin strip of land in shadow.

This is . . . Cory begins, but she leaves the sentence momentarily unfinished for want of an adjective. What word could possibly describe this hushed astonishment, this glory. What could begin to suit the infinity of stars above her and their endless liquid twins that stretch and contract, light-years below, in this black water. There is no word in all the rubbish heap of English for this euphoric awe, this feeling of drowning in an infinitesimal point in time and space, the intersection between unbearable beauty, inconceivable freedom, and heady apprehension.

. . . cool, she says at last.

You're cool, says Rolo.

She turns to him, takes in the whites of his eyes glowing beside her, and searches him as best she can, in the dark, for sarcasm. In her own estimation she has been cool only once, and briefly, for about four months during sophomore year. She was anointed by a boy, a senior, Leon Hunt, don of the rich kids at their brother school, a smart and extroverted textile heir whose parents were never home. Cory was not rich, but she was thin and tall, and back then her hair was blondish, tangled but long. She was inexperienced, though, a slow wit, an ingénue, and Leon treated her at first with a kind of expansive bemusement. *Ansel*, he'd say, or *Yo, Anse is here. Let's play never have I ever. She always loses*. It was on Leon's couch that she first smoked pot, in Leon's kitchen that she took her first shot, coconut vodka, on Leon's Chelsea roof, wedged snug between two taller buildings, that she drank her first forty, first felt that woozy, breezy freedom, vintage hip-hop playing on a phone, Ella Ha making out with somebody by the edge. Cory had a bit of a thing for Leon, mostly a buddy-buddy thing, mostly chaste, not much more than admiration, more wanted to be like him than wanted him, per se. Meanwhile Leon's buddy Jase, MVP of the basketball team, a long-limbed, wet-mouthed colt of a boy, had an unconcealed thing for her. Their crush triangle was just becoming a topic of speculation when one night by the fire exit Jase kissed

her, sloppy, all teeth, erect and breathless with the rush of consum-
mation; the next day at school, everyone knew. *Heard you and Jase
finally sucked face.* She protested, but when school let out at four,
there he was, all six and a half feet of him, waiting for her on the
curb with a Ding Dong and a bouquet of maple twigs. Everyone
said it worked, everyone said cute couple, everyone said it's perfect,
you're the only one tall enough to reach him. She felt weird about
it but she didn't want to argue. She had a B-minus grasp at best of
the advanced social trigonometry of which she'd suddenly become
a variable, but she knew enough to know that dating Jase was good
for her. It set the girls all talking, admiring and inviting. It ignited
the attention of other boys. Specifically it woke up Leon. A hint
of lechery crept into his whole big-brother shtick. Now, when Jase
would goof, Leon would cut him down with subtle cruelty. Now,
when Jase left the room, Leon would lean in toward her, lock eyes,
and make a comment no one else could hear. At a party while the
basketball team was out of town for county championships, Leon
brought her into his bedroom to share his secret stash, top-shelf
mescal and Mexican hash. It was a ritual he performed only for
the most *I* of VIPs and she was flattered, then flattened, by the
potency of both. *I'm too*— she heard herself say, waving it all away,
but he urged it on her, and then he was on her, and she was flat
on the floor, pants down, numb and nauseated, and should she be
grateful, should she be scared, would she be hurt, would she puke,
would she pass out— She woke feeling peculiar and greasy the
next morning in her bra and socks, shoved against the wall beside
his hard twin bed. Crawled over his snoring bulk and picked her
underwear off the floor. Walked home dazed in the too-bright
morning, passing churchgoers and runners, strangers that failed to
see her and strangers that looked too hard, and her only thoughts
were *I'm not a virgin anymore* and *Can they tell*. Not long after that,

Leon told Jase she'd thrown herself at him, so he'd fucked her out of pity, and Jase broke up with her, which would have been more or less a relief except that it was soon common knowledge that she'd slutted it up with his best friend. And everyone said poor, doofy Jase, and everyone called her Whorey Cory, and her brief cool was punctured as thoroughly and irrevocably as her virginity. It took her six months of slipping grades, low morale, and uneven self-inflicted haircuts to disclose the event to her mom, late one windless winter afternoon. When she did, her mother's mouth went stiff. Silently she rose and left the room, leaving Cory alone on her unmade bed in the dark. They never spoke of it again. No charges were filed, no more conversations had, not with Leon's parents or the school administration or even between Cory and her mother. And since then Cory's had neither the willingness nor the opportunity to have sex again.

All of that, though, is long in the past. Now, beside Rolo, the only thing that could make her feel more elated—she thinks, suddenly, thrummingly—would be a pair of hands, a mouth, to hold and be held. Dizzy with awe and beer and, for some reason, shame, she has a weird and unexpected urge to kiss the big old man beside her. The captain's back is to them. She might not even notice. Holding eye contact with Rolo, aroused by the sex-adjacent thought, Cory lets herself go there, just for a moment—warmth, wet, pressure—but the fantasy dissipates before it can coalesce into narrative, swiftly dispelled by a whiff of his beer breath and the hair on his hands that rest so close, one around the beer that hangs between his legs, one on the rail behind her, by the recollection of his eagerness and the spittle on his lips. And Rolo must feel that the moment has passed, too, for when Sherry cranes her neck around he nods at her, just slightly, and she restarts the engine, and Cory breaks eye contact and leans her head way back, the better to feel the growl of the engine in the base of her skull, to breathe in the wind and the night, to devote herself, again, to the stars.

Time passes. Water passes. The stars remain fixed. Eventually an archipelago comes into view, and the boat slows. A dock extends from a white-sand beach, its length illuminated by flat lights embedded in the wood. A shadowy figure walks its length to help secure the boat and hold out a hand to Cory as she disembarks.

Thank you, she says, but the figure merely steps onto the rocking boat and ducks into the berth.

Lit from below like a Disney villain, Rolo performs a one-handed flourish and bows his head. Welcome, he says, to Little Île des Bienheureux.

Island of the . . . good and happy? she says, attempting to show off her eleventh-grade French.

Island, he says, of the Blessed.

The silent staff person passes them, toting the sleeping children to a golf cart parked at the edge of a landscaped lawn. There is a revving and a mechanical groan, and a sailboat the size of a walk-in closet bobs in the wake of Sherry's ferry as it recedes.

Go on, Rolo says, dismissing the golf cart, which speeds up and, with electric grace, winds a graded path between various points of interest cast in soft chiaroscuro by lights in the grass: A gazebo. A greenhouse. A swimming pool as bright and yellow-blue as afternoon. A gleaming machine on a broad tarmac—

You have a helicopter? she says.

—and, above it all, the wedge-shaped house, poised on the edge of a cliff as if contemplating jumping. It is windy—she pulls her new sweatshirt close—and, as the boat recedes, increasingly quiet. Rolo walks ahead of her, and a trio of tawny animals gallops down the hill to meet him, legs like deers' and ears like rabbits', three slim bodies jumping high on twelve powerful legs.

Aw, you have dogs!

These are my girls, says Rolo: Serita, Bertie, Ursula. They're pharaoh hounds.

He crouches down to be licked and jumped up on. The dogs' ears are stiff with anticipation, their jaws wide and smiling.

A cold wet nose on Cory's neck, a tongue on her arm, paws all over her chest and legs. So playful! She squats to rub their ears and necks and they respond sloppily. How old are they? she asks.

Two, two, and twelve, he says— Or twenty-nine, thirty, and twenty-six. Depends how you count.

What?

Clones.

You're kidding.

Not at all. This is my third Serita, third Bertie, and second Ursula. It's astonishing how deeply rooted the personality is in the genetic material. As if their very spirits are preserved. Yes, he says. Yes, yes, you are. Who are my immortal loves?

He stands and the dogs turn their attention to her, and he waits a moment to observe her canine molestation before heading up the hill. Come on, he says. I'll show you around.

A rustling in the nearby trees, a lapping at the shore. The parchment glow of lights behind drawn shades. The panting of the pharaoh hounds that seem to herd him homeward. As they climb the hill the ocean spreads below them, waving like a torn white flag its reflection of the gibbous moon. The wind is cold. Her sneakers are wet. The density of the stars is overwhelming. She hustles to keep up.

At a side entrance through a rock garden the dogs go on ahead, nails clacking on the floors. Rolo kicks off his sandals and steps into a pair of slippers, boiled wool. She steps out of her shoes, too, and hurries to follow him barefoot past open doors to empty rooms.

In a kitchen-dining area the floor tiles radiate heat. A low light shines above a silvery oven. He digs in a canister on the kitchen island, the three hounds behind him, tails whapping at the tile. Turning around he calls the dogs' names and tosses each a treat; one by one they jump on their hind legs to catch their prizes. Opening cabinets, opening the fridge, here in his own world, he seems excited, possibly nervous.

Can I get you anything? Tea? Sparkling water?

I'm fine, she says.

He takes two glasses from a cabinet. From the refrigerator door, ice clonks; a spigot hisses. A woman appears with a tray of cut fruit and fragrant, crustless grilled cheese sandwiches.

They're in bed, Rolo tells the woman.

Expressionless, she replies: I'll just leave it here for you two, then, in case you get peckish.

That won't be necessary, says Rolo. This girl just ate a diner.

The woman nods and recedes with the tray through a hidden door. Cory watches the grilled cheeses disappear with disappointment. Hester, Rolo says, when she has gone. Award-winning chef, noted photographer, style icon. Someday she'll have her own restaurant. For now, I imprison her here.

He hands Cory the water. Tour?

He indicates various elements offhandedly, almost as if they embarrass him. Nodding at a closed door, he remarks: Wine cellar's down there. Waving at a dark alcove, he says, Dining room, and she catches a glimpse of a long tabletop, a light fixture like a cluster of oversized soap bubbles suspended above it. Living room, he notes, and she steps for a moment into a room as vast and unlived-in as a hotel lobby. From its beamed ceiling hangs a chandelier, easily four or five feet in diameter, which seems to be made of antlers. Long, firm couches, punctuated with animal skin pillows and draped with creamy white throws, are arranged around a hearth the size of a pizza oven, and in one corner is a well-stocked bar of glass and gold bamboo. In the study she peruses framed plaques engraved with his name—awards and prizes, marks of distinction for the waitress's son—before following him upstairs.

On the closed doors to the children's rooms their names are spelled in brass lettering. There are two guest bedrooms. The beds are vast and the rugs are plush and the rooms are painted in ultra-saturated hues. Overstuffed leather armchairs sit beside book-shelves and curio cabinets. Marble-topped nightstands support globe lamps. Long gauze curtains ripple in the central air, just revealing the trees that waver outside, in the dark.

The tour ends in the master bathroom. She admires the deep tub, the mother-of-pearl tiles, the golden faucets and showerhead that glow against the marble walls. *Ostentatious*, she thinks in her mother's voice. *Gauche*, she thinks, but she likes it. When he looks at her in here the veins of the stone seem to blush with color. She runs her hand over a cloud-light towel and her curiosity gets the better of her at last.

How did you get rich?

Drugs, he says.

It's a joke, she thinks, and quips: Rolo Picazo, *drug lord*.

Yes. Welcome to the off-the-grid lair of the lord of stool soft-eners, the kingpin of nasal sprays.

She laughs. Oh, *boring* drugs.

He says, You're a breath of fresh air.

In the tiled bathroom his voice is wet and resonant. It fills her ears as if it were inside her: Don't pretend like you don't know the story. Southgate Pharmaceuticals? Granadone? Ring a bell?

She shakes her head.

He sits on the pink marble edge of the bathtub. My company, he says, we manufacture mostly laxatives, fungal creams, unglamorous shit like that. But we also make stronger drugs, prescription stuff. The type of thing you might be prescribed after surgery or something. It's enormously effective. Doctors love it. Patients need it. You know Percocet, right, you know codeine?

When I got my wisdom teeth out they gave me Vicodin.

So this is like that, but better. And in fact we're on the road to FDA approval for a stronger, smoother strain—a highly effective, highly popular, *highly pleasant*, highly *safe*, frankly groundbreaking painkiller. Greater efficacy. Fewer side effects. Longer relief. Plus, you know, between you and me, it's a good time. Not too good. Just good enough, let's say. Granadone is so safe we used it in a cocktail at the company Christmas party. Vodka, soda, bitters, a splash of pomegranate juice, a slice of lime. Tasty—kind of plummy—and so potent you felt like you'd transcended this earthly sphere. We called the cocktail Fruit of the Dead. I mean, come on. Irresistible, right? Plus it's a sustained-release formula, so nobody got a hangover. All to say it's a great product. Doctors are begging us to expedite approval. But, you know. Due to various legal tangles, the current climate, et cetera, that's all been delayed. Prosecution, incidentally, is having a field day with that Christmas party. Trying to drum up a scandal. Frankly I don't think they have anything.

You're being sued?

Don't get me started.

Is it addictive? She examines his expression for structural vulnerabilities, finds none. He waves her question away.

People can get addicted to sex, alcohol, chocolate, video games, you name it. Any sudden infusion of endorphins or serotonin. Addiction is just habitual dependency on the stimulation of our natural reward system. Some people get addicted to work, you know, or fame, or love, or to another person. Whatever your thing is, you can develop a dependency on it, if you're not, you know, wise, if you're not vigilant.

Anyway, he says, and pauses, as if remembering something that troubles him. He looks old again, but in a nice way. Sad, long eyes. A framed photo sits on the edge of the sink: Rolo, younger and thinner, with a beautiful woman in white, both of them laughing, holding each other, on a green lawn. He grasps her by the waist in such a way that her breasts are practically airborne. Her eyes brim with sunlight, her white-blond hair blows in his face. One of her small brown hands cups the back of his neck. His dark eyes take her in adoringly, hungrily. Here is a man for whom beauty is food to be gobbled.

I heard somewhere that seltzer is addictive, Cory says, to cheer him up.

If that's your thing. He smiles.

Her glass is just melting ice. She shakes it a little. The cubes clink. How pleasant is *highly pleasant*? she asks.

His voice is low and musical: Would you like to find out?

The answer is, yes, she would like to find out, she would like nothing more than to get high right now, preferably alone, but if necessary with this strange, somehow alluring, sometimes revolting man. The right answer, though, is: You're my employer.

He looks toward the ceiling. Not until Monday, he says. Tuesday, if you prefer. Your choice, of course. Up to you, always. But, I suppose, if you're going to be working for me, you might as well find out what all the fuss is about.

He keeps them in a corked amber glass bottle, here in his massive bathroom. They are just pills like any other pills, ruby-colored gel caps the size and color of ladybugs. She swallows one with the ice melt and asks, Aren't you going to take one, too?

He says, I'm too old to take drugs recreationally.

This isn't recreation, she says. It's research. She ambles into the bedroom and runs a hand over his suede comforter, feeling the thrill of impending adventure, feeling him watching her. One spring day late in tenth grade she skipped school to eat mushrooms with Ella in Central Park. They got lost, climbed rocks, haunted Belvedere Castle, watched absurd humans do absurd human things. Everything was sunshine, everything belly laughter. A fleet of Spandex-clad recumbent bicyclists sent them into paroxysms. They fed a hot dog bun to a tiny turtle. They ran from a horse that was also a cop. Remembering what Ella said to her that morning, she says to Rolo now, Anyway, it's bad manners to let me trip alone.

He says, If *tripping* is what you're expecting, my friend, I'm afraid you're going to be sorely disappointed. But he uncorks the bottle, tosses one into his mouth, and swallows, no water.

As they descend the stairs she has to hold on to the silk-smooth wooden banister to steady herself. A glimpse at a shadowy clock at the end of the hall tells her night is catching up to morning. She has been awake for nearly twenty-four hours. How long ago yesterday seems: the 6 a.m. wake-up bell, the exhausted procession to the dining hall, the smells of wet soil, damp wood, and unclean laundry, of compost, sour milk, and young unwashed bodies. Though she's never really minded any of it, not consciously, the clean quiet scents of Rolo's house—hyacinth air diffuser, cedar, lemon Pledge—make her dreamy with contentment.

In the living room she lays a hand on the cold glass of a floor-to-ceiling window and can almost feel through her palm the cavernous star-addled sky, the long plane of the sea, and between them, edging up to a razor-thin slice of mainland, a hint of the coming day's light.

Then she feels a tectonic shifting. The glass is sliding and, in her periphery, Rolo is stepping through. Thinking of Alice melting into the looking glass, climbing down from the mantel into another world, she follows her host over the threshold and feels on the soles of her feet the cool Earth in shadow. Looking up, taking in the minute shifts in the blues between the stars—blue-black and cobalt and a thousand shades of gray; *gradations*, she thinks: *gray day shuns*—as she follows Rolo down the hill she can almost hear the edge of the day breathe into being, the light and warmth of the giant star-called-sun like a monstrous exhale on the other side of this shadow-called-night; can almost feel the magnificent bulk of the planet spinning, a thousand miles per hour, spinning, yes, if she stops and closes her eyes and holds her breath and stands very still, very silent, she can feel its vivid revolution—*viva la revolución!*—in the endless, airless oubliette of space.

Her ribs are grabbed and she recoils instinctively, opening her eyes, shocked into a garbled yelp. It is Rolo, desperately terrestrial, and he's laughing; ew, was he trying to tickle her? She skids on the grass, eluding his grasp, and stumbles as she runs from him to where the man-made beach of moon-white sand meets water. With him in pursuit and laughing wheezy-deep behind her, she has only one thought and that is to keep going. As she runs she tries to unbutton her shorts but it's impossible—on this swiftly tilting planet she will lose her balance and he will pounce when she's down—so she gives up and sloshes in fully dressed. The sound of her splashing seems very loud, and as in a nightmare her motion is slowed, her feet sink, an updraft of cold rushes in through her ankles, up her veins, and into her heart and brain, and she can hear him behind her, ugly laughter, happy shouting—*You're a maniac!*—and there's nothing to do but dive in.

Muffled silence. Aching cold. She is swimming before she knows she is swimming, out, out, beneath the swells, away from her pursuer. She stays underwater as long as she can, releasing breath in bubbles as she goes, surfacing only to be slapped in the face by a wave and knocked back under, and then the ocean bottom has dropped away, and her head breaks the surface, and after a disorienting moment—endless water, endless sky, where is land—she locates herself, breathing hard, treading water gracelessly out past the dock, where the waves are still unripe and the ground seems miles down. Now it is the air that is freezing cold and the water that is warm as her blood. She keeps her ears below the surface to protect them from the wind that will freeze her brain. He is bent over on the shore, hands on his thighs, panting, a dark toy of a man in the distance. He is righting himself and saying something, but with her ears in the water his voice is languageless melody. She lets her head fall back, her torso float up, so she is suspended, body in water, *body of water*, and sees that the sky has been brightening, velvet gray paper gray dust gray rabbit gray, vein blue lapis blue and infinite blues without names, and what is a name anyway but an arbitrary enclosure, delineating one small parcel of infinity from the infinity of everything else—and when she bobs up again, ears draining, he is gone, but his voice is wildly close:

Come on, you're going to freeze to death, and then what'll I do. I'll have to take care of my children myself.

She turns, bobbing, to see him on the dock, shaking a big towel as a bullfighter shakes a cape. Her teeth are chattering.

The ladder's over there, he says.

She swims to the end of the dock and puts her hands on an algae-slick wooden rung and climbs, dripping, out of the water, becoming heavier with each step. He wraps her in the towel, which becomes heavier, too, as she soaks it, and he warms her against him, holding her close as they walk together back up the hill, the three dogs trotting along after them.

Inside, he ignites a fire in the hearth with a remote control, and it is reflected in the tall window: a smaller fire, hovering above the lawn. Flat clouds sit like fallen feathers at the bottom of the sky, their fringes blazing. A handful of jagged little birds soar like throwing stars from the bracken. Then the first blinding ray crests the horizon, setting on fire the skin of the sea, and she feels the spear of light in her throat, tight with joy.

Her back to him, she says, If I lived here I would watch this every morning.

He sits, and the dogs gather at his feet like acolytes. You do live here, he says.

She floats to join him, moving through space with all the bulk and heft of dust. At the couch she hesitates—she is soaking wet, surely it is expensive, she does not want to ruin it—but he smiles and arranges a deliciously fuzzy blanket for her on the seat beside him. Wrapped in the towel she curls up, close enough to the fire that she can feel it drying the salt water on her skin, and he reaches down and cups both her heels in one warm hand, extending her legs, laying her feet in his lap. On the coffee table is a children's book, an ornately illustrated abecedarian, left open to the middle of the alphabet:

M is for the Monster that Moves under the bed.

N is for the Negligence of one who did not Notice when we said—

O is for Ouch, which One might cry Out, had he not ripped off One's head.

She laughs at the rhyme, at the sign, at the strange warping of time. She slides back into the couch's elbow and lands on a shaggy pillow. She can feel her diaphragm convulsing against the hard, wet waistband of her shorts, can feel the laughter bubbling from its source, spilling out of her mouth and nose and into the air around them. His hands move over her feet, her ankles, her legs, and it occurs to her that she hasn't shaved in days, but he seems to like the prickling stubble, to linger on it before making his way back down to the soles of her feet, the spaces between her toes, kneading her arches and the tight muscles on either side of her Achilles tendons. A strange, not totally unpleasant idea arises: that there is no real separation between the tips of his fingers and the edges of her legs, between his skin and hers. They are two halves of a collective organism, just as each of his three dogs is a third of the breathing, sighing, intermittently tail-wagging puddle-of-dog below.

Never in my life, she begins to say, but language is exhausting. She lets her head fall into the pillow. Never, in my whole entire life, she tries again, have I ever felt this good. Her eyes close and her hands run over the angora, and she gives herself over to the pleasure of his touch. She can feel his voice vibrating in her feet.

This never happens to me, he is saying, as if to himself. I live alone. I don't trust people. My friendships are more like alliances. But with you. As soon as I saw you. Was it just this afternoon? Singing to my son. Then, later, in a bed of paper flowers. I felt. I feel. Something alive between us. Something that lives in both of us at once.

She barely registers his words. Her eyes closed against the now bright dawn, she registers mainly the light behind her eyelids, the texture of the pillow on her neck and the blanket around her body, the touch of his strong hands on her soles. The thought *A strange man is rubbing my feet* occurs to and disturbs her only in the passive, dissociated way she might half register some faraway tragedy on the news. The sheer intensity of sensation is more than enough to smother the disturbance. She has somehow at once left her body and remained fully, deeply inside it.

All my life, all my work, he goes on—and he, too, seems to be in a kind of trance—has been an attempt to understand people. And I guess I understand people as well as anyone can. Which is to say I expect them to contradict themselves. I don't always understand when they don't expect the same from me. I have trust issues, the ex-wife says, and, sure, I guess, I do . . . approximate. I tell half-truths. I stab in the dark. Sometimes I hit on something true. Other times I'm left outside, shouting nonsense in the shadows. I have been—for many years, Queenie—only half-alive. But seeing you today. Being with you tonight. I've come to life. I feel like I *know* you. I feel like you know me. Like I've found in you a piece of myself—not myself as I am now, but some long-ago, better self, which I'd forgotten. I feel like we've known each other for a very long time. Can you feel it, too?

I did sort of feel—Cory yawns—like I recognized you from somewhere.

It's like meeting a fellow alien, he says. Like inside of us beat twin hearts. Blood of the same color courses through our veins, at the same pulse. The two of us, Cory, we come from the same planet.

Planet Raised-by-Wolves, she murmurs, remembering something—but her voice is so quiet, language so heavy, she isn't sure whether she has spoken at all. Her eyelids, her head, her hands, are leaden. She'd like to keep talking, but she is beyond responding. She has fallen asleep.

She sleeps soundly, long and deep, her body heavy and tingling. She knows that she is sleeping but she cannot wake. She breathes but shallowly, hears but mutedly. Sounds are muffled and obscure. Daylight is less seeable than feelable, deep behind her eyelids. It is as if she were still underwater. Indeed it feels as if she has been sucked below, and one foot is caught now in, who knows what, a reef, a lobster trap. Try as she might to rise, dripping, from this semiconscious pool, she cannot break the surface, cannot make a sound. Subject to its currents and vibrations, she is maybe fractionally aware of being handled, picked up, moved. Or maybe that is just the undulation of her beating blood.

When her eyes blink open again, it is so bright she has to squint. She is tucked, cozy, in a nest of a bed, under a featherlight comforter in a warm puddle of sunshine. She stretches her limbs and feels her muscles release, her joints fall open, delirious sensation. In the daytime the guest room seems smaller, and perfectly quiet. The mottled ray of afternoon that woke her falls in through sheer white curtains past shifting leaves. The walls are the injured purple of a days-old bruise. She props herself up on one elbow to look around without leaving the comfort of the bed and sees herself reflected in a gold-framed mirror between the two west-facing windows: a mess of sea-stiffened pink hair, a bare sharp shoulder overlit by sun, alone among a soft sierra of pillows pressed up against a tiger-striped wooden headboard. Her tank top and underwear are itchy after yesterday's dunk in the sea. Her belly gurgles. She is ravenous.

Rising, standing, her feet land on lambskin. She lets her toes sink into the rug and looks around. Her underwear is embarrassing: a childish pair from a days-of-the-week set her mom gave her years ago. She's lost every day—at sleepovers, in the camp wash, in dozens of rituals of packing or unpacking—except the pair she has on now. *Is* it Thursday? She has to think. No, it's Sunday. Maybe Monday. Could it be Tuesday? More important, has somebody undressed her? Seen her too-small Thursdays? She has a vague sense memory of being jostled, handled, though not violently—but she can't remember. If she tries, she can almost recall undressing herself—but, no, that is not memory; it is imagination. The truth of this morning does not exist.

Does this worry her. It does and it doesn't. She is semi-aware of the same low-key dread she's felt in school, for instance, procrastinating an assignment, or at home, knowing she's kept something from her mother that will soon be found out. But for now she has other, more pressing concerns, concerns of the body: a need to pee, a need to eat. And anyway she is not in pain. She has no new bruises. So she buries the anxiety, shoving it deep and out of sight, in the jumbled laundry pile of her mind.

On the side table she finds a cell phone charger and a pretty bowl of uncooked rice. She dips her fingers into the grain and finds, buried there, her phone. Of course: she never took it from her pocket before last night's impulsive swim. Biting her lip she tries turning it on, and—hallelujah!—finds it functional, though without service; also sees that it's already four o' clock. There are two networks, lilile and lilile_guest, but both require passwords. All right. Her clothes have been laundered, folded, and laid on the seat of a leather armchair. Her Walmart candy has been organized in bowls atop a mirrored vanity. She grabs a handful of sour gummy worms from their jewellike cluster and stuffs them all into her mouth at once, a semi-inedible fruit-and-gelatin glob that makes her drool, which makes her laugh, which makes her drool some more. Wiping her chin with the back of her hand, she opens a door she expects to be a bathroom and finds instead a closet. A few tidy dress shirts hang inside, relics of a thinner Rolo.

Having located the bathroom, she peels off her briny clothes. The toilet seat is warm, the walls white tile that sparkles with mica, the shower a glass box stocked with products in attractive bottles, a natural sea sponge, a matching gold razor and nail brush. Beside the round porcelain bowl of a sink is a tube of toothpaste and a toothbrush still in its packaging. She flushes and brushes and, after some maneuvering, figures out how to operate the shower. An even downpour rains from above.

A hot shower—after weeks of summer camp, where dirt and grime and itch have long been accumulating under her finger-nails and on the nape of her neck, in the crooks of her ankles and backs of her knees, where she's only showered, and rarely at that, in the girls' changing area by the lake, behind a moldy plastic curtain in a stall not much wider than her person, where the floor is slick with accumulated soap scum, and the faucet only runs scalding or frigid, and you cannot so much as steady yourself while shaving your legs with a hand on the wall for fear that a many-legged creepy-crawly straight out of a nightmare will skitter up your arm and into your hair—the luxury of a hot shower, now, is beyond pleasure. She lets the water drench her hair and fill her ears and mouth. She scrubs her scalp with the hair products and every protrusion and cavity with the body wash. She bends to lather and shave her legs and the hot water beats down her back, up her neck. She removes the handheld showerhead affixed to the sparkling wall and tries the different pressure levels until she finds a hard, percussive rhythm that feels almost violent. It beats her shoulders and neck, her calves and thighs. Then she turns its attention to where it will have the most profound effect. Increasing breathlessness. A tightening, a relaxing, a tightening. Concentrate on the pressure, the desire it elicits. Concentrate on the full-body crescendo, a tingling in the soles of the feet. At last, delirious paroxysms, that final sweet release.

Unsteadily, she turns off the water, then sways, dripping, toward the thick towel that waits for her on a heated bar. She wraps herself in it and wipes the condensation from the mirror, where her face, bare and wet, is as pink as her hair. Clean and damp, fresh and fragrant, she dresses in her laundered cutoffs and a button-down from the closet. With the sleeves rolled up and the two sides knotted together at the waist it almost works. She slides into her new white sneakers—they, too, are mysteriously clean—slips her phone into her pocket, though it is only at 18 percent, and opens the door to the hall.

The house's silence amplifies her footsteps. A dog clacks up to meet her at the foot of the stairs and follow her into the living room, inundated now with golden light refracted, flashing, off the ocean. In the empty kitchen, the dog hops up to take her place between the other two, which are waiting limply in a dog bed in the bay window.

The coffeemaker is full and hot. She finds a mug and hunts for cream. On the top shelf of the fridge is a covered plate with her name written on the Saran Wrap in Sharpie. She unpeels the plastic to find a pile of scrambled eggs, a couple of thumb-sized sausages, and a slice of apple pie. Pie for breakfast: he remembered. She is a girl in a fairy tale. Behind a sliding panel, she finds a black reflective box: the microwave. At her touch it comes to life. She puts her plate inside, and it commences whirring. The dogs hop down from their bed and sit upright on the tile, ears erect, noses twitching. She casts about in drawers until she finds a fork and knife. When the machine chimes, she retrieves her food and slides open a glass door at the back of the room.

The three eager animals follow her to a patio nestled in the crook of the house at the edge of the cliff, where she is surprised to smell a faint whiff of cigarettes, and hear fragments of conversation. Two girls sit, smoking, at the strangest picnic table she has ever seen.

Sorry, Cory says automatically.

They are both in flats and short black skirts that reveal their long smooth legs. Their glossy hair is pulled back and their button-down shirts are open at the top. One lowers her lashes and addresses the other: I'm done. You?

By way of reply, the other drops her half-smoked menthol into a coffee can of butts and sand.

Staff, Cory supposes, from the matching outfits. As she is employed here, too, she guesses she should introduce herself. I'm Cory. I'm the new babysitter.

They exchange a glance. The first excavates her glowing cherry, lets it fall into the can. The second stands.

Do you guys work here? Cory asks, flushing as soon as she hears her own voice, unforgivably dorky.

Housekeeping, says the first, standing, too.

Cool, Cory says miserably.

They linger for a fraction of a moment. The second opens her mouth as if she might say something more, then closes it again.

See you, says the first, and then they disappear around the corner of the house.

Upon closer inspection, the picnic table seems to be made of thin layers of poured epoxy, between which are sandwiched a variety of pills: oblong white ibuprofen, little red Sudafed, speckled horse vitamins, two-tone gelcaps, and so on. Its surface is so gleaming clean she can't be sure whether it is furniture or art, so she sits beside it, cross-legged on the sun-warmed flagstone, and attempts to extinguish her self-consciousness with breakfast.

There is no railing at the edge of the patio. It simply ends before a sharp drop to the sea. It is sheltered from the wind by the house

itself, which protects it to the south and west, but she can tell the
wind is high from the choppiness of the water, and the rustling
and weaving of the wild trees that grow nearby, thick as the bristles
in a giant hairbrush. The dogs seem to like it. One makes its way
down a path that leads beyond the cliff face. Another sniffs and
pisses on the gnarled roots of a crabapple tree. The third lays its
long, thin head in Cory's lap, a picture of affection. Cory rewards
the dog for its flattery with a bite of the sausage, which is divine.
The apple-sugar goo inside the reheated pie is hot and melty. The
eggs are salty and light. The coffee tastes like toast and soil.

She is savoring it all and wondering how long she will be
left alone when the dog in her lap perks up and joins the others
to gallop as one down the hill. A figure is approaching, holding
Spenser's hand, Fern riding on its shoulders, a hand on each
ear as if on a steering wheel. As he comes closer she sees he is
good-looking, tall and thin with a head of asymmetrical dread-
locks, in a denim button-down and black denim shorts cut ragged
at the knees. He might be anyone except that he has the children
with him, and from his belt jangles a ring of keys.

Spenser runs up and hugs Cory, nearly knocking her onto the
stone. Fern smiles down at her, bare feet wiggling near the breast
pockets of the young man's shirt. He stands apart from the patio,
eyes bright, head cocked in the sunshine, a smile folding back his
face, revealing perfect teeth.

I see you found your breakfast.

She looks down at her syrup-shellacked plate.

Rolo said we should let you sleep, he says.

Thank you, she says.

Did you sleep?

Really well. Thanks.

Virgil, he says, and steps closer and extends a hand.

At the touch of his dry palm, she goes shy. Cory, she replies, and coughs.

Follow me, he says. I'll show you your new digs.

Oh, she says, I slept in the guest room last night, so.

Yeah, he says, and from now on you're going to be in the shed, so.

Oh, sure, yeah, I'm fine with whatever.

He is already turning down the hill.

I'll just put this in the kitchen, she says, moving to stack fork and mug atop her plate.

Leave it, he says over his shoulder and Fern's leg.

It's no trouble! Her voice is unexpectedly high.

Leave it, he repeats, as if to a dog. Someone will grab it later.

And Spenser tugs her arm and says, Come on! so she does.

On the grassy hill, away from the shelter of the house, she is an easy target for the wind. It blows through the thin men's shirt and makes cold whips of her wet hair. The dogs hang back to lap at her breakfast plate like a single wriggling organism with three heads, three tongues, three sets of teeth. A jumbled singsong bubbles up among her thoughts, in the style of the book on Rolo's coffee table:

D is for the Drove of Dogs that Dances round the Dish.

E is for this Ever-growing F-for-Feeling amiss . . .

G for the Grizzled Genie who Granted her wish.

Where *is* Rolo? she asks.

Virgil glances at his wrist, illuminating a smartwatch. D.C., he says.

Washington, D.C.?

For the next few hours.

Do you think he'll— She hustles to keep pace. Do you think someone will be able to get my stuff from River Rock?

River Rock.

Spenser's camp. I was— All my things are there. Clothes. Wallet.

Virgil taps his watch and speaks into it: Retrieve nanny's belongings from River Rock. Lowering his hand he tells her, It will be taken care of.

Thank you, she says for the third time, but her words are lost in the wind, and despite Spenser beside her and cherubic Fern above, Cory has an almost grief-stricken sense of being quite alone.

On the other side of the lawn sits a squat shed, which looks as if it might once have been a small garage. Two men on stepladders are painting its exterior blinding white. One is middle-aged, in sunglasses and a baseball cap. The other is young and shirtless, burning pinkish in the sun. That's Ray Gray, says Virgil, pointing to the older guy, who waves back with a greeting for the children.

I went to sleepaway camp! Spenser tells him.

Wowee, says Ray Gray. What'd you do there.

Spenser stands there a moment, staring up at him, before replying: I held a frog.

No shit, says Ray.

Spenser gasps and covers his mouth.

And that's Honeybowl, says Virgil.

Hi, says Cory to the shirtless guy, but Honeybowl appears to be listening to music.

Virgil opens the door of the shed with a smile, as if revealing a secret. Cory walks the length of the room admiringly. Where the garage door once was, a wall of glass bricks abstractifies the landscape in shifting swirls of color and light. Floor-to-ceiling bookshelves, neatly filled with books, line the adjacent wall. In the middle of the oil-stained concrete floor, a squat couch and handsome armchair rest on a round Persian rug. Slick magazines lie on a marble-topped table: *The Economist*, *Vanity Fair*. An air conditioner whispers near a minimal collection of kitchen items: minifridge, hot plate, toaster oven. Two mugs hang above a four-cup coffeemaker. From a hook by the door dangles a baby monitor. At the back of the room, a lofted bed makes a low ceiling over a midcentury bureau with a tilted mirror. A chrome sconce at its head serves as a reading light; a wool Pendleton blanket is folded at the foot.

It looks like an ad, she says, and glances at Virgil. In a good way.

Virgil says, It's been a project of mine. There's no bathroom, but you can use the one just inside the basement door, across the lawn. There's a shower in there and no one will disturb you. Everyone else showers in the shanty.

The what? she says.

On the southwest side of the island. Where the rest of the staff sleeps.

Wow, she says, toying with the knot in her shirt. Why do *I* get such luxury?

Virgil gives her a look she finds difficult to read, but resumes his tour. The door locks from the inside, he says, see? If I were you I'd keep it bolted when you're asleep. Just a good habit. What else. Baby monitor loses reception past the tennis court. He glances at his watch. All right, it's five. Kid dinner's at six in the big house. Let me know if you need anything. I'll be around.

He squats, lowering Fern to the ground. She loses her balance as she disembarks, rolls onto the rug, and stays there, petting it contemplatively.

Later, Munchkins, says Virgil, heading out the door.

Oh, says Cory. One thing? Could I get the Wi-Fi password?

Virgil pauses and presses his lips together. I'll see if I can arrange it, he says at last, and then he's gone.

Spenser is sitting in the armchair, reading *Harper's* through his glasses like a little old man while Fern communes with the rug.

Well, says Cory. What should we do?

IV

I Sped, Like a Wild-Bird, Over Firm Land and Yielding Sea

At eight in the morning, Shanghai Pudong is a madhouse. Ian and I perform the complex gauntlet that is international check-in, make our way through the dense crowds to our gate, and are ushered across an airfield and up a flight of rolling stairs. Outside the small plane window the sky is white with smog. During this flight to JFK we will lose twelve hours. Eight thousand miles from now, when we arrive in New York City, it will be Sunday afternoon. I'll get a taxi home, eat with Cory at Bella Luna—provided she deigns to dine with me—then take a pill, sleep twelve hours if I can, and be back at work on Monday morning, dealing with this mess.

The aircraft lifts, nauseating, and we are speeding through the sky. I pull on my supposedly noise-canceling headphones. I wrap a scarf around my neck. I wonder for the hundredth time about the whereabouts of my old Hermès number, splurge of splurges, the Gordian knots of aqua snakes and pigs with jewel-like eyes, my talisman. I bought it for myself when I first landed this job and have worn it on every international flight since. Bad luck to have misplaced it just before . . .

Never mind. Superstition is for the feebleminded. Breathe. Pull on my silk eye mask. Listen to a guided meditation. Intentionally smile. Think of Cory at River Rock, happy and strong, aglow as she always has been after those sun-drenched weeks, smelling of sunblock and lake water, hair bleached, cheeks rosy, an arm linked perhaps with another girl. Daughter of beauty, daughter of sunshine, daughter of ungainly grace. Think of summers past, when Cory was a camper. I'd go up at the halfway mark for Family Day, take her out for ice cream, marvel. Cory at eleven, ice cream on her chin, letting spill all the minutiae of the past few weeks. She became a different girl there.

Of course, she has become a different girl since. Did she speak more than two words to me our whole ride up in the rental? Every attempt I made to draw her into conversation was met at best with grunts. As if my Cory—quick to laugh, imaginative, surprising—were stuffed inside a poorly manufactured Cory suit, too-long limbs and sad expression, sewn in cloths of gray. For years now it has been like that. The way she's shut her door on me has tinfoiled my heart. Though, hey, she graduated, right. Low bar, but what did Dr. Jim say? *The teen years are a time to test newfound freedoms, make mistakes.* Understatement of the century. Can only hope that when I see her, River Rock will have worked its magic on my love, my heart, my daughter, the best girl in the world.

When I say my daughter is the best, it is not because I think she is without fault. Faults she has, and many of them. She can be lazy, distractible, undisciplined. Gullible, reckless, aimless, and naive. She tends to lose herself in thought, in friendships and activities. Still, she is the best, I say, and when I say she is the best, I mean she has remained, retained, so far, what I have lost—what, I daresay, we all eventually lose. Just as our skin in adolescence begins to toughen, pock, our hair to coarsen, eyes to close, our spirits harden. We learn to be critical, mean, and cold. To lick wounds and nurse grudges. We embark on the construction of defenses. My own childhood feels as dim as a horror film half watched long ago and now mostly forgotten, but I know by twelve or thirteen I had become impenetrable. Small but hard. Ramparts of stone. Battlements well defended.

Sweet Cory, though, she has remained an open field, sprawled out green and fresh under all the eyes of Heaven, meeting with equal welcome animals and elements, letting the seasons alter her tone and colors. I have watched her process casual irony with a knit brow. I have helped her save a young brown mouse. Even as a child she could hold a flower petal in her small hot palm so delicately it wouldn't bruise. I won't pretend I am not wholly biased. I know she is the best to me in part because she is my daughter. But there are certain undeniable, objective truths. Cory is beautiful. Cory is credulous. Cory is in tune with the world. Until recently, Cory was happy.

The recirculated air is freezing cold and the blankets they've provided are mere rags of fleece. I suppose if I cannot sleep I should at least attempt to work. Opening my laptop, I locate the PowerPoint I will present at the quarterly board meeting next week.

It starts strong, I think, with a bird's-eye survey of the relationship between Chinese and American economies over the past two decades, interrogating the finer points of cultural and technological difference vis-à-vis agricultural development, and delineating new opportunities for RHEA Seeds. Then an overview of our current programs, for those who may be new or want a brief refresher: credits, farm inputs, extension services for women farmers; education programs, free seeds, improved silos for farms in the developing world; hybrid rice programs in fourteen developing countries. We design, provide the seeds, outsource growth to farmers, and export to the hungry in Yemen, Syria, South Sudan. Over the twenty years since I have come aboard—as development director, then deputy director, executive director these last twelve years and counting—RHEA Seeds has doubled down on, da-da-da, ba-ba-ba, copy-paste, ta-da. Achieved buy-in from top-level hum-dee-hum, insert headshots here. This latest deal with China's government-subsidized agro conglom means our proprietary strain of blight-resistant rice is grown by more than a hundred small farms in the nation's poorest provinces. What did they call it when we shared it with them? What has the press been calling it? *Magic rice.*

Drag-and-drop a photo Ian took of me, Toad, and that pissed-off farmer. Admit that, fine, right now, we have encountered a what, a glitch. Brass tacks, the magic rice: not growing. Don't know what the issue is. The guys at the lab are looking into it. Things will be on hold awhile longer. Let's not linger on these setbacks, though. The future is bright. See: screenshots of my multiple appearances, just this month, on Fortune Online, MSNBC, face contoured, hair shining. See: how we have become a darling org among first-world philanthropists, politicians, grant-makers. So we've run into a little trouble. Nothing we can't overcome. The bigger story is we're making headway. The bigger story is, always, yawn, success.

How long must I keep trotting out this stale old salvation narrative. How long before I can give up. Can't I *retire* already—

I realize I've asked that last question aloud when Ian turns to me, pulling out one earbud with a querying smile. Tell him, Sorry,

sorry. Just talking to myself. He goes back to the four-inch screen embedded in the seat back, blaring chipper Chinese TV.

Give up. Close my laptop. Retrieve my eye mask and my Xanax. Try, at least, to rest.

The parallel that nags at me is this. You plant and tend and grow a thing from seed. You cultivate and usher it into its lush full bloom, and then. Having reached maturity, it does not behave as expected. It falters. It runs wild. Is infringed on by more aggressive flora. Is blighted, stunted by environmental factors or disease. Worst case, it simply does not grow.

When we are alerted that we may connect to the in-flight Wi-Fi, I lift my mask and take my phone off airplane mode. It buzzes immediately. A text from Cory! A little fish within me leaps, then sinks, as I read:

> Got a job for a few weeks be
> home in September probably

Probably?

Ian turns my way again. What's that? he says.

Sorry, I say, and tap it out instead, with two question marks. She does not reply. *Sept??* I reiterate. *Doing what?? Where?? Since when??*

What's up? says Ian.

What do you mean? I say, still looking at my phone.

You just said *what the fuck.*

Did I?

He is drinking from his plastic cup, regarding me with amusement as I type.

101

It's Cory, I tell him. She says she got a job.

Well *that's* great, he says. Right?

Really fucking short on details, though. Oh, here we go:

> Internship. Parent of a camper. Upstate I think

I show Ian the phone.

Upstate she *thinks*? He laughs.

A flight attendant comes by to take our drink orders. Ian asks for coffee; I, black tea. When she moves on I tell Ian, It's 10 p.m. there.

So? he says.

So how the hell is she just coming up with this, at ten at night?

Maybe she got to schmoozing with a camper's parent.

Ian, I say, texting, texting. You know my daughter. Cory doesn't schmooze.

She's beautiful, though, he says. That goes a long way.

A long way toward self-destruction.

The phone buzzes again:

> Short-term executive internship w CEO of
> high-profile Fortune 500. Signed an NDA

Ian, looking at my phone screen: Fuck me!

Can you believe? I type a single character—*!*—and say, Do you see what I'm dealing with here?

It's a good sign, though, Ian says.

Is it?

Emer, Ian says. With all due, you know, et cetera, by eighteen I was going to clubs, hooking up with who knows who, using my yaya's as a crash pad.

By eighteen, I tell him, I was already halfway through college.

Of course you were.

I refrain from returning his smile. He does not, cannot know how desperately relieved I was to escape my mother's house, the hunger, secrets, violence. Hysterical midnight games of drunken cat-and-mouse—*I'm gonna eatchoo*—my stepfather's fingers, the teeth of his dog embedded in my thigh. My stepdad was a monster and my mother was a gray stone wall. Ignore Ian's friendly teasing. Text, instead:

How long have you been planning?

But Ian persists: And look at us now. We're *fine. She* will be fine. Cory is a grown woman, almost.

Almost.

All I mean, he says, is you can let out the leash a little.

Was looking forward to seeing you, monkey.

I'm just worried, I tell him.

sry, comes Cory's maddening reply. *In a car. Bad service*

Ian goes quiet. The flight attendant returns with coffees. Excuse me, I say to her, before she can move on. I asked for tea.

Two coffees, she replies with irritation.

Ian lays a hand on mine, sensing, I suppose, my inchoate rage. She asked for tea.

The attendant moves on, and he calls, Thank you!

Thank *you*, I say to him. I look down again at my phone and type: *Where are you*

You're just shaken up, says Ian. It'll be okay.

But what if it isn't.

Ian sighs, as if with me, as if for me.

Going??? appears on its own line.

I tell him, Her therapist calls this stage *individuation.*

He laughs. I've been in that stage my whole life. Individuation, baby.

I smile vaguely, half ignoring him, texting her, getting no reply. Frustrated, I open social. A four-second video has appeared on her account: a paper flower falling, casting rainbows, from between a forefinger and thumb. I have known this flat-tipped thumb since it was a half inch long, these ragged, poorly painted nails since they were no larger than sequins. The flower falls and falls again, twirling, shedding glitter. The video cuts off before it lands. Location tag: *Never-Never Land.* Eye roll. And yet. Rereading her totally uncharacteristic text—*Short-term executive internship w CEO of high-profile Fortune 500*—I dare to hope. Possibly Ian is right. Possibly, invigorated by her time at River Rock, away from her despised old mom, my wayward daughter is finally taking her fate in her own beloved hands.

Is Cory— Ian begins, but interrupts himself. You don't have to answer this, he says, but—did you have, you know, a donor, or . . . ?

I look at him.

You've been single as long as I've known you.

I must be making some kind of taken-aback face because hurriedly he qualifies: I only ask, he says, because, you know, it's been on my mind. Hasim and I . . .

You are?

He smiles.

Ian. I squeeze his hand. You two will be such good parents.

Thank you, he says, and sips his coffee and looks at me, querying.

It was a fling, I say. Nothing more.

*   *   *

In those months, in my memory, it is always raining. Rain glazes windows, rain beats down on roofs. We met in the rain. A garden party, Montauk. During a toast, when the others' attention was directed elsewhere, he grazed my bare back with a knuckle. When I turned he raised a brow at me and headed up a garden path. I didn't think. Just followed him from under the tent into the drizzle. Droplets in my eyelashes, mist on my skin. In a screened-in gazebo, dry and dark, he didn't bother to kiss me. He turned me around to face the dripping roof and party tent and murmured, *You're the lookout*, then lifted my skirt. I was the lookout so I looked out, breathing, at all those acquaintances and strangers in the tent, at the finches loudly taking their own hedonistic pleasures in the birdbath, at—kid you not—two garden snakes, intertwined and writhing in the grass, half obscured by the white blossoms of our host's hydrangea. I laughed at that—so on-the-nose—and felt his erection growing, and then the band recommenced and he thrust in, fat drops and jazz and those lithe green snakes, and I came unexpectedly, pulsing with the music, heady hemiola. The affair lasted only a few months, but in that time I lost myself in a way I never had or have. I became, temporarily and despite myself, another kind of woman, the kind who lets herself believe a man can be good, can be kind, can somehow make it through a lifetime of masculinity unpolluted.

The pregnancy was a surprise. To let it unfold was a choice. By that time I'd been engaged for years in a serious process of what I thought of as informed deliberation. I had frozen my eggs at thirty-eight. I wanted a baby. I loved babies, their sweet warm scent, cartoonish proportions, mysterious neurology. Meanwhile I assumed I would make a better-than-average parent. I was reasonable, patient, sane, and adequately resourced, and therefore more capable than most of giving a child every advantage in this broken world. Pregnant—albeit plagued by heartburn, swelling, and sciatica—I felt assured and luminous. My lips were full, my hair was thick, my complexion bright, high contrast.

But in the days and weeks after the traumatic rupture of her birth, in the place where she was gone from me, a kind of illness began to grow. Empty of Cory, I was emptied, too, of all that beauty. Bleary bloated weeping leaking haggard chapped and sagging. All my life I'd been a competent, imposing, young, then youngish woman, but face to tiny screaming face in the forlorn hours after midnight with this preconscious, deeply freaked-out little life, it became clear to me the persona I'd taken for granted all those years was really no more than an elaborate decision tree, a series of choices, of shallow roles, each with her own costume, character, and skills; each, in her way, limited; all of them middle-aged. I was not reasonable or patient. Certainly, in those desperate screaming hours, I was not sane. I was far from adequate.

For many years I did my best to keep her safe and nourished, to keep her company, to love her harder than anyone has ever loved before—harder at least than my mother loved *her* daughter—and, though she may tell another story, I did all right, I think. I succeeded at least in seeing her not as I wished her to be but as she was—in all her half-cocked brilliance and imprudent beauty—and isn't that, for most of us, enough? But the failure I'd expected of myself since her beleaguered infancy nagged at me, insidious prophesy, even at the best of times—and, sure enough, when she was sixteen, my darkest fear for her came true. After months of bickering, weight loss, and declining grades, late one winter afternoon she let me into her laundry basket of a room to tell me how some boy, some fucking animal, had hurt her. I listened to her story, enraged by its banality. I watched her sweet face crumple. But where I should have felt sympathy I found I had gone cold.

I tried to lay a hand on hers but, no, I couldn't move. I couldn't feel a thing.

Problem was, I was broken, too, long before, and worse than she was. Problem was, I couldn't stand that she'd been broken, too. Daughter of ignorance, she'd willfully ignored the statistics with which I'd armed her, the history in which I'd tutored her. Daughter of frivolity, when I'd tried to warn her she'd treated me as if I were a stick-in-the-mud, a prude. Daughter of neglect, she let herself be wounded—my baby girl, born tender, didn't get why the mean kids laughed. She chose to forget that boys rape, men rape, it happens all the time. They're monsters, undersocialized, poisoned by testosterone and millennia of power. They'll kill us if we let them. I'd told her so dozens of times.

So anger grew, quick as a cancer, around my grief for her. Anger at the boy who'd broken her. Anger at her for being arrogant, beautiful, and dumb. Anger, most of all, at the man I never told her about, the man who, once upon a horror film, broke me. Anger, hard and keratinous as fibroid, confined my sympathy. It muzzled me. Sitting with her in the waning winter light, upon her unmade bed, I could not speak.

Though what could I have told her. Should I have shared with her the violence that I endured before her. Could I possibly have said, *This sort of wound, it will never heal. It will be there all the time but you will cease to feel it. The nerves will be killed, the muscle atrophy, all your blessed tenderness, my baby girl, will go*—? I didn't want her to harden as I have. But because I had, I could not feel for her. I could not even look her in the eye. The second-worst thing that could ever happen happened, and, forgive me, all I could do was stand and leave the room.

*   *   *

The plane lowers unsteadily through violent wind, hits the ground, and thunders over blacktop. When it comes to a stop, a round of weak applause goes up around the cabin. I do not join in. My attention is diverted by some activity outside the window. A couple of men unloading luggage have paused to watch a woman in a reflective orange vest pursue something across the airfield. At first I cannot tell what she is after. It is just a smudge of white on black. Putting on my prescription sunglasses, I see a milky swan, big as a lamb, hurrying across the runway.

Call Cory while shoving out of the plane. Call Cory while waiting in line at customs. Call Cory while jostling through the crowd. Call Cory at baggage claim. Get the same message every time. *You have reached— Cory?* That voice. That intonation. She says her own name like a question, her *name*, for god's sake, her identity, have a little self-respect, honey, come on. Then the inevitable error message: *The mailbox is full and cannot accept any messages at this time; goodbye.* Ian and I part with a brief hug and I watch him peel off his cardigan as he goes in search of the subway. Me, I have a rule. On my own dime I'll do the subway, fine, but coming home on business, I exclusively take cabs.

Outside the air is damp and heavy and smells of exhaust and trash. Wait in line for a taxi. Slam, slam, *Where we going, ma'am?* From the back seat I study the wallet-sized photo of a young boy—fat cheeks, neatly combed hair—tucked into the elastic in the visor above the driver's seat. I watch the city spillover pass us by: apartment buildings and row houses, bodegas, auto shops, and chains, billboards hawking in English, Spanish, and sometimes Russian the questionable services of real estate brokers and personal injury lawyers. New York, New York, America the beautiful. Home again, home again, jiggity-jig.

At 86th Street I pay and tip. Slam, slam. Our doorman, Giovanni, stands stoic just outside the door. Septuagenarian widower, father of two, grandfather of four. Two years ago his wife of almost fifty years, dear Sheila, died. Pancreatic cancer, sudden, ruthless. Diagnosed in March, she was gone by May.

Gio, how are you? Good?

Ms. Emer, he says, how was your trip? I got some mail for you.

Seen Cory, by any chance?

He shakes his head, regretful.

Trying to hide my worry, I say, See you soon, all right?

Call the elevator. Dig for my keys. At the fourteenth floor, open the apartment door, breathless, in case of a miracle.

It is clear from the quality of the silence in the apartment, and from its tidiness, that Cory is not home. She is not sprawled like an opium fiend in front of the TV. She is not sullying the daybed with her big and always dirty feet. She is not leaning into the fridge or charging her phone at the kitchen counter before heading out. She is not at her desk, nor curled among the blankets in her chaotic bedroom. She is not in my home office; why would she be. She is not asleep in my bed. She has not trespassed in my closet to rifle through my clothes. Only a memory of her hides here, aged four, crouching gleeful among the hatboxes. Daughter of reminiscence, daughter of carelessness, daughter of unwelcome surprises.

Days go by and do I get a text or call? Do I receive the promised number where a message can be left? Does a cow walk on its hind legs. Does a house cat read the Bible. Daughter of negligence, daughter of fibs.

Here is what I do: fumble through a catastrophic board meeting. Endure and lead a dozen useless discussions. Leave early every morning and come home late each night to this apartment, where I can hear the neighbors' children stomping, shrieking, laughing, above and below and on all sides. Minutes and hours and days my girl is gone, and every moment is a seed, and every seed grows into brambles, a tangled thorny knot of love and panic.

Ian continues to tell me I should not give her so much thought. He reminds me that at Cory's age, he was shacked up with some closeted widower in Hell's Kitchen.

To which I reply, That's all well and good, but what about your mother? Did she pace your Astoria apartment into the early morning, praying to Saint Anthony, wearing soft as cotton the pages of her Rosary Novena?

If he admits it is a mother's curse to worry, he tries, too, to help me lift it: *Emer, breathe in, breathe out. Repeat after me: individuation. Make it your mantra.*

Which, fine. All right, I guess. But God help Ian if he and Hasim have a daughter. Help them doubly if she turns out to be a beauty.

When she was a little girl my Cory's beauty was so extraordinary it was almost frightening. Semiprecious eyes and hair as light and fine as memory. Glass-blown lips that shattered easily into wide-open gusts of smile. Strangers gave her gifts, free samples, opportunities. Maître d's comped her desserts. At a Paris boutique she was given sample-size dresses. At an aquarium in Florida she was chosen from the crowd to feed a killer whale.

Her beauty has been for me a source of pride, anxiety, and, yes, envy. Girls who are born with the misfortune of being average or even homely: I know them. I have been them. The pains they take to camouflage their acne with concealer, to tame the hair their hormones ruin with grease and frizz, the volume of their sad false laughter, the way they shrink into the furniture—their insecurity leaches into the air around them, into the groundwater. As someone who's worked for what beauty I now have—which is to say for an approximation of it, for poise and style—I admit that at my worst they inspire a pity in me akin to loathing.

Since Cory, though, I've learned true beauty is a mixed blessing. Cory has done what she can to muffle hers. Her ill-fitting mismatched outfits are the stuff of sitcom clowns. Her posture is a master class in spinal contortion. She does not wash her face. And yet, as smog and atmospheric detritus amplify the colors of a sunset, in spite of her best efforts at self-pollution, her beauty shines perversely brighter. Under her iridescent eyes day-old mascara smears look high fashion. Slicked with a sheen of oil her skin looks only more taut and poreless.

Picture her now, in threadbare tee and Spandex shorts, scrolling through her phone in the window seat. Afternoon sun, squeezed through the buildings on the west side of the street, makes of her unbrushed hair a wispy nimbus. Sweet otherworldly girl, as alien as she is angel, leggy love child of Ziggy Stardust and the Faerie Queen: my Core, my Corazón. My girl, my life. Where have you gone?

V

And the Heights of the Mountains and the Depths of the Sea Rang with Her Voice

Babysitting is chaotic mornings, whining and sleep-smelling heads, food spilled or stuck in nostrils, when everything—clothes, language, the children themselves, but, most of all, time—is always slipping away. Babysitting is a juggling act performed poorly behind the back or under the nose or in absentia of the resident ringmaster, in whose presence Cory feels by turns exceptional and unremarkable, thrillingly adult and embarrassingly childish, as if she should be not the babysitter but the babysat.

The kids get up before seven, which means she is out of bed by six. She wakes to the beeping of the coffeemaker in her shed, walks across the lawn in a towel, and showers in the windowless basement bathroom, the only place on this pristine island that smells of mildew, and where the water never gets really hot. Then she crosses the lawn back to her temporary home, with its coffee and siren song of a bed and her duffel full of clothes, which has arrived, as promised, from River Rock. After toweling dry her hair, dressing, and returning to the big house, there's usually enough time before the day really begins to finish her coffee looking out over the lawn and the sea, where the gulls make wonky carousels in the wind, laughing sharply, and the starlings dive-bomb the grass, then rise in erratic flight toward the sun, before she has to head upstairs to get the kids.

The children's rooms are beautifully decorated but strangely lacking in character. It takes her a few days to realize what's missing: stuff. The detritus of childhood. Here the toys all look unused. The books are new. She visits Fern's bedroom first, small and pristine. The pale green wallpaper features a pattern of birds and insects in foliage, delicate and wild. The twin bed is half concealed by a decorative mosquito net and populated by a motley crew of stuffed animals. A lamp shaped like a goose glows in one corner. It is always dusk in here, just as for its occupant there seems to be no clear distinction between sleeping and waking. Her eyes are often already open when Cory walks in. With a serene smile she holds out her arms to be lifted from bed like a royal, but Cory learns after a couple of days she should pick up the girl gingerly; as often as not, she's drenched in night pee. So Cory runs a bath and peels off Fern's wet pajamas and, while the water is running, strips the bed and tosses the sheets and clothes into the laundry. After the child has been soaped and toweled and dressed, she can be brought along to collect her brother.

Perhaps because he is nearsighted the boy always seems to startle when Cory comes in. He launches immediately into a list of urgent concerns. What are they doing that day? What is the weather going to be like? What's for breakfast? Sensitive to the textures of different fabrics, he dresses with persnickety anxiousness, trying on outfit after outfit before deeming it inadequate and throwing it, in a fit, onto the floor. How did this child survive even a single day at summer camp, she wonders, before recalling he wore the same filthy clothes every day—and, indeed, nine times out of ten he ends up in that very ensemble, sometimes washed, often not: a pair of too-short shorts, his five-inch Teva sandals, and a too-large pink tee sporting a big Star of David that reads in splashy gold lettering, *I Got Spoiled at Ruby's Brat Mitzvah.* Who's Ruby? Cory asks once, but the question seems to confuse him, so she lets it go.

Trying to figure out what to do with each day after breakfast gives her hives. Spenser hates sports because he is puny and uncoordinated. He hates board games because he's played them all. He hates swimming because the chlorine makes his skin feel weird. He hates being outdoors because, though he likes bugs, he freaks out when they bite him. Meanwhile, Fern wants nothing more than to climb boulders and trees, revel in the mud, splash in the sea, collect wildflowers and press them between books, and swim, and sing. Babysitting is decisions, negotiation, staying in motion, thinking fast, acting immediately.

To mollify Spenser they tend to spend mornings indoors, reading in the living room or lounging in his room, which is papered dark blue with a pattern of planets, suns, and spaceships, and whose walls and ceiling are stuck with glow-in-the-dark stars. Among the sheets of his bed lie approximately half a dozen books at any given time, a flashlight, and three lifelike stuffed animals: a leopard, a lion, and a wolf. The former two look new, their plush thick, their plastic eyes smooth, but the wolf stirs something in Cory. It looks old, hugged lean, its fur matted in some spots, sparse in others. One of its eyes is missing. The other is nicked and scratched to opacity.

What's this guy's name?

Shewolf, Spenser tells her.

It's a girl?

It's a *wolf*.

Cory picks the creature up, says: She looks like she's been through a lot.

He's had her since he was a baby, says Fern.

Kelly dried her on hot, Spenser adds. You're not supposed to dry them on hot.

Sounds painful, Cory agrees.

Spenser shoots her a concerned look.

Who's Kelly? she says.

Our babysitter.

Kel-ly. Fern's quiet singsong, from the depths of a beanbag chair: Kel-ly.

What happened to her? Cory asks.

She went away, Spenser says.

She was an orphan, Fern sighs.

She was not, says Spenser.

An orphan princess.

She could do magic, Spenser says.

Toying with Spenser's battered animal, Cory thinks with a mild pang of her own well-loved Bunnydog, the stuffed cat she slept with into early adolescence, when an acquaintance at a sleepover made fun of her. Back home the next morning, her skin still crawling with shame, she inhaled its grubby fur one last time, then threw it down the garbage chute.

What do you call a female wolf? she muses now. A sow? No.

A bitch, Spenser says, his voice high and nasal.

Lunch is at noon, served buffet style in silver chafing dishes in the empty kitchen, as if left there by fairies. After they've eaten, Cory and Fern lure Spenser outdoors, alternately wheedling, whining, and promising adventure. Cory soon learns he'll often relent if she gives him a time limit—Just half an hour, she might say—and,

116

conveniently, he has no sense of time. Once they're outside it's anyone's guess how long they'll spend climbing and running, spying and collecting, swimming in the pool and wading in the ocean, lying on the lawn and finding shapes in the clouds.

The island is not large but its geography is confounding, and they often lose their bearings. Somewhere deep in its woods, for instance—where, exactly, they cannot be sure, they have to hunt for it every time—is a high curved wall of gray rock. The question of what it encloses becomes a topic of heated speculation. Cory thinks at first that it walls off the back of the island, where dead logs and splintered two-by-fours, shards of plastic and bleach-white bones, have washed up among the weeds and jagged granite. But Spenser and Fern maintain—fervently, spookily—that it encircles something, that something or someone is inside it. Another house, says Fern, like Daddy's house, but smaller. A minotaur, Spenser suggests. A monster! Tracing the rocky shore one day they find they can scrabble like goats all the way around the island—no wall prevents that—so the children are right about its shape, at least. Another day, after a storm, when the woods are wet and fresh and dripping with sunshine, they manage to trace it nearly all the way around, save a couple of sections where the overgrowth is too dense. Running their hands along the damp stone, they find a spot where the moss-bearded rock recedes an inch or so and gives way to weather-grayed wood. A door! They try the handle but find it locked. They attempt to peer through the keyhole, but the lock being a modern one, they are unable to see. Little Île des Bienheureux is full of secrets.

She learns quickly to set an alarm for kid dinner in her otherwise useless phone, after, once or twice, they miss it and raid the pantry, to the chagrin of Hester and her line cook, a slight person with hooded eyes people call Spider. (Did you think those cucumbers were just sitting around? Hester snaps. They were for my gazpacho.) When Rolo joins them, he makes cocktails for himself and Cory, and everyone stays up late, and the vibe is celebratory. When he doesn't, they stick to the script, eating early, just the three of them, on high stools in the kitchen, then have baths and bedtime stories until sundown casts its spell and they begin to whine, slump, and veer from dangerously manic fits of laughter into tears, or to call her Mom by accident, which tightens her insides with a seizure of something like homesickness, something like guilt, like a stolen glimpse into another world. They rarely ask for Rolo.

Bedtime happens in Spenser's room, because his bed is bigger than Fern's and all three of them can fit in it, smashed together on his pillow. She reads to them from their overflowing library, alternating Spenser's choice, then Fern's, occasionally overriding them with a choice of her own, and she is surprised by how long she can spend reading aloud, how much she enjoys revisiting the tales of her youth. The kids are in no way invested in finishing anything—they treat story time like a sampling platter—so she gets to dip in and out of dozens of books nightly. A boy receives alien transmissions in his dental work. A girl befriends a spider and a piglet. A new kid in an elementary school class turns out to be a dead rat in a raincoat. A girl walks through a wardrobe into snow-blanketed woods. She reads until she's hoarse and the children are nodding off, urging her to keep reading even as their eyes roll behind their lashes.

Spenser sleeps soundly, breathing heavily, emanating heat. But though Fern's eyes close, she never quite shuts off. Night and day, Fern seems to live comfortably in the borderlands of consciousness. So when her brother's breathing slows, and Cory has removed his glasses from his bath-damp head and brought Fern to her own bedroom, as she lowers the child onto her pillow, the eyelids part, and the small arms stay locked around Cory's neck.

You want me to lie down with you?

Fern nods.

The comforter cover is velvety and smells like lavender. Fern snuggles up to Cory like a cat. There is still a hint of light in the sky, but it is a hair before nine, and Cory hasn't felt until now how tired she is. The day has drained her. She closes her eyes and squeezes the small body beside her own, and though she doesn't mean to, she drifts, she dreams.

She had babysitters herself when she was a little girl, maybe a dozen of them, but her favorite was Katya, a friend of her mother's: overalls, hair out to here, flappy wrinkled arms, a thousand years old. On nice spring days after school Katya might bring her to the Museum of Natural History to stare up, awestruck, at the bones, or to Central Park, where Cory would climb the Alice sculpture and watch the toy boats. It was there that once, aged four, she kissed a snow-white goose. Is it memory or imagination? She can't be sure she did not daydream it, but if she did, the fantasy is elaborate, complete with picnickers and sun worshippers, past whom she chased the grand animal off the Great Lawn. At a path it paused, as if to let her come close. She reached out and the bird, nearly as tall as she was, stepped tentatively toward her, then hurried into the mouth of a cave and hid behind a stone. She followed it in without a second thought. The space was dark, the damp wall scrawled with graffiti. She heard Katya's onion-and-sour-cherry accent, resonant and close: *Gentle, my love.* The goose let her stroke its tough, vinyl-like feathers. It did not move when, gently, she held it. She brought her lips to the down at the base of its lissome neck and, for one vivid moment, all was still. Then it panicked and flew off gracelessly, a mess of pillow stuffing. Katya ducked in, and the cave became small. Together, who knows why, they lifted the goose's stone and rolled it over—cool and dry on top, it was all green slime on the bottom—and then their shoes were wet and the soil floor was flooding. The stone had been acting as a kind of plug for some plumbing. As they laughed and ran, splashing cold, the cave became the mouth of a stream.

She is awoken with a start, who knows how long after lying down, by the feeling of someone watching her in the dark. She grips the edge of the bed in disoriented panic before she remembers where she is. The sleeping girl is beside her and the child's large-bellied dad is above, close enough that she can smell his breath, liquor-warm. He is rocking a little, back and forth beside the bed, the reflection of the dim goose lamp rocking, too, in his eyes, its light passing across his wet lips. Lifting her head, she pulls off the blanket and inadvertently pulls up her skirt. It bunches briefly around her belly, revealing her underwear. Her heart speeds up. She yanks it down, gets up, and leaves the room.

Rolo follows her out, closing the door behind them.

Sorry, she says quietly, wiping her mouth, fixing her clothes. I guess I fell asleep.

He does not reply. He leans back against the wall, breathing slow but noisily, taking her in: wrinkled clothes and sleep-rumpled hair, neck breasts legs. Is there a kind of sorrow in his bloodshot eyes, his open mouth? She feels consumed. She envies him his stupor. She has a sudden urge to press her body against his and, here in the hallway, let her weight become his weight, to breathe his heavy breath and feel for herself his evident desire for her. She wants to go back to his marble bathroom and take another Granadone and swim again among the liquid stars.

Instead, buzzing with adrenaline, she whispers good night and walks quietly down the stairs, through the kitchen, out the sliding door to the patio, and across the grass.

Midlawn, she pauses to breathe in the wind, the dark, the fragrant night. Awake and alive, wretched with shame and desire, and receptive to it all, she hears, mingling with the pulse of ocean waves, what sounds like the beat of far-off music. The shanty: Did Virgil say it was on the other side of the tennis courts? She walks the lawn, past the gazebo and greenhouse of imprisoned plants, its glass walls dripping. She enters and crosses the tennis court through its chain-link gate. Beyond it, a path leads into the woods. She ducks under branches and is scraped by shrubbery. The music becomes both louder—deep bass beat and harmonic falsetto chorus and intermittent rapping, layer upon layer of sound—and polluted by muffled conversation and laughter. Then the flora opens, the path ends, and she is face-to-face with a white flaking clapboard wall and unbuffered wind.

The shanty is patched in spots with plywood. Towels dry on the railing of an exterior stair. A window is propped open with a shoe. A dilapidated porch hangs over the rocky bluff, thumping. It feels like the edge of the world.

The music turns out to be emanating from a crappy Bluetooth speaker set up on a three-legged chair. Cory doesn't recognize the musician, but she likes the strange, elated feeling of it, the airy chorus, *Come find me, come fiiind me*. The hot maids are dancing under a net of Christmas lights that swings dangerously, and their long hair is dancing, too, made animate by the wind. Hester is smoking a cigarette with someone Cory doesn't recognize, leaning over the porch railing, their backs turned to the party. Virgil is standing by a waist-high tree stump dangerously close to the rocks, with Spider, the line cook, huddled in a hoodie, and the house painters, middle-aged Ray Gray and young Honeybowl. They are playing a kind of game, taking turns passing a hammer around, throwing it behind their backs, catching it in midair as it spins, and attempting to bring it down on the head of a nail in the stump. The young men are ribbing Ray Gray, who is compelled to yell out, Nailed it! every time he does.

Cory stands and watches, smiling when they laugh. Eventually Virgil seems to notice her. Nanny!

Hi, she says gratefully.

You found the secret bar. Grab a beer. He nods toward a well-stocked cooler under the porch. She reaches in and takes a chilly bottle. You want to play? he asks. We'll teach you.

They open her beer for her. They show her how to toss the hammer up, past her back and over her shoulder. They watch her practice, laughing when she drops it, clapping when she makes it. They seem glad to have a protégée, but she is no good, and the game is soon abandoned. The group ends up just sitting around, smoking, drinking, chatting. Virgil becomes absorbed in his phone, choosing songs. Conversation between small groups gets overheard and adopted by the larger gang, then splinters again, recompartmentalized. Ray Gray calls it a night and disappears into the shanty. In a second-floor window a light comes on and then goes out again. Virgil unhooks his phone and turns in, too, leaving her all the more unmoored. The music silenced and the group reduced, the porch feels less like a party. The maids compare handstands against a peeling wall. Spider joins Hester for a cigarette. Honeybowl slouches, elbows on knees, on a log by the porch railing, his longish hair lashing his face in the gusty wind. He keeps pushing it back, half absent, half irritated. Now and then he glances at her, the swinging lights reflected in his eyes. Too uncoordinated to approach the maids and attempt a handstand, too intimidated to join the kitchen staff, Cory sits down next to him.

Hey, new nanny, he says.

Hey, she says. Honeybowl?

He tilts his beer at her.

How did you get that name? she asks.

Just my last name, he says. Trevor Honey-Bowles.

Which parent is Honey, and which one's Bowles, she asks.

He laughs as if that is a joke, which mystifies her. He is in his early twenties, probably, with the twisty smile, too-loud laugh, and avoidant eyes of a person who is both playful and shy, the brawn and sunburn of a naturally pale guy who spends his days doing manual labor out of doors.

What do you do around here? she says.

Maintenance. Buildings and grounds. Whatever needs to be done. He looks around as if hunting for something to show her, then nods toward the woods. I roofed the gazebo, he says.

It looks good, she says, though she didn't notice.

He laughs, knows she's humoring him, and looks down at his work boots, big dirty round-toed things. Takes a sip of his beer, then looks up again and smiles at her sideways. You want to go for a walk?

They amble slowly, drinking their beers, up the path and out onto the lawn, swinging their arms in the wind. They talk about their lives, about her life mostly, though he tells her about himself, too, his brothers and dad in Nantucket. He is the black sheep, he says, and with some relief she says, I'm not going to college, either. Oh, I go to college, he says. You gotta go to college. Which leaves her mute. At the gazebo they pause so he can show her the interior of the roof, the way the beams hold up the slats and meet in the shape of a star. It's dark and she can't make out his face exactly, but she likes his low voice, his awkward bark of a laugh, and the way he keeps asking about her, even when she doesn't know what to say. When he kisses her it is sloppy and weirdly soft, his breath IPA-sweet, like making out with a Starburst, but it's a relief to be kissed, a relief to feel wanted by someone like him—which is to say someone normal, hot, young—a relief to feel that she may end up having a role to play in this strange, audienceless theater in the black Atlantic, after all.

He leads her back around the island and up a different path, this one over the rocks, through a maze of windblown shrubbery, back to the shanty. The Christmas lights are off and a threadbare cloud does little to veil the moon, whose light makes a white flood of the porch, whose echo swims on the shining water. He leads her up the creaking exterior stairs to his room on the second floor. Inside is an unmade twin bed and a scuffed dresser that looks like it used to be nice. Everything else is on the floor: a couple of paperbacks, a laptop, a backpack, a pair of sneakers, an alarm clock, a whiskey bottle, and a mostly empty case of beer. The ceiling is low and the open window is undressed. She leans her hands on the sill and inhales the wind and waves and salt. She can't see anything but water and sky and, so far from everything she knows, looking out from a strange boy's room, the expanse fills her lungs, dizzies her head, threatens to pop her heart. He gives her a shot of whiskey in a Listerine cap. She drinks, coughs, and laughs, then feels something like panic.

From the edge of the bed he looks up and watches her. How old are you? he says.

Eighteen.

Oh, he says. You got time.

She looks back out the window, her heart pounding. Is this a good feeling or a bad one, anticipation or fright? She can't tell.

I took two years off before college, he tells her.

What did you do? she asks, but finds, a few sentences in, that she is not listening to his answer. Despite herself she is thinking—kill the thought, kill it quick—of Leon Hunt. The crush of his weight. Her paralysis on the floor.

And yet, when Honeybowl rises, she stays where she is. When he reaches under her dress, she doesn't stop him. When he pulls down her underwear and begins to touch her, she closes her eyes and breathes. When he leads her out of her dry puddle of clothes and into his boy-smelling sheets, she follows, pounding inside.

You have a bush, he observes.

I've been at a summer camp, she says apologetically.

I like it, he says, and lowers himself into it, face-first, as if to illustrate.

She knows people do this—she wasn't born yesterday, she's seen it on Internet porn, she's heard about it through gossip—but no one has ever done it with her, and it takes her a few minutes to get over the weirdness of it, the sea slug feel of his tongue, the self-consciousness, the sound of his breathing, which seems very loud in the small room. Eventually, though, she gets into it, moves her hips slightly, and—there, yes—she gets why people like this. She grips his strong shoulders, his hot neck, and he holds her butt cheeks, one in each hand, and keeps at it, and she remembers Rolo, mute with desire and liquor, looking down at her undies, and then her whole body is a neon light, a sign on the fritz, blinking. A series of shivers begins deep within, then spreads out, finally reaching her skin. She can feel her skin prickling and, with every lick, more shivers, and he's going faster, and she's thinking of her boss, her hands on the back of this stranger's perspiring neck, and then she can feel it everywhere, through every inch of her skin, every nerve ending and synapse, her whole body about to come unglued from the middle, he's squeezing her butt and she's losing her breath, and then her feet stiffen, her skin flushes with goose bumps, and from her mouth comes an embarrassing sound, and she is unraveled. From her scalp to the soles of her feet she is flooded with tingling bells, and for one short, miraculous moment she knows what it's like to be weightless, and there's nothing at all—

And in the blissful ear-ringing quiet Honeybowl gets on his knees, straddles her, and jerks off. She watches with curious detachment as he handles himself with urgency, then lets out a series of shuddering sighs, spews all over her chest, and collapses.

Afterward he pulls a couple of tissues from the kind of travel pack her mother carries, and wipes her off with an air of chivalry.

Your tits are adorable, he says.

She is weak with release, but the compliment draws a smile. The bed isn't big enough for two people, really, and he only has one pillow. He gives it to her, balls up a sweatshirt for himself, and lies on his side, turned away from her. She considers leaving, going back to her pretty bed in her pretty shed, but would she even be able to find her way, who knows. So she faces the wall and closes her eyes. Somewhere nearby in the shanty, a toilet flushes, a sink runs. He turns over again to spoon her; she can feel his breath, warm and steady, on the back of her neck. And then he is asleep, one arm thrown heavily over her body, and then so is she, lulled to unconsciousness by the ocean's perpetual sigh.

They wake to his alarm, shrill and mechanical, two bodies too long for his crappy twin bed, and covered inadequately. The red numbers on the windowsill read five thirty. Seagulls hiccup and whine in the pink sky.

So early, she complains.

He slams the clock, sits up, rubs his face. Other alarms are going off, too, in the neighboring bedrooms, up and down the length of the shanty. He stands to pull up his boxers. The number of boy butts she has seen she can count on one hand. His is narrow and muscular, moon-pale, and stippled with zits.

I gotta run, he says. Gotta get to the coffee before Spider does. He always nabs the first cup before it's done brewing.

See you later, then, I guess, she says.

He kisses her forehead. You're kind of a fox, you know that.

Her smile remains, long after he's left.

Babysitting is an exhausted, underslept morning, going through the familiar motions while running on fumes. Babysitting is pitting the children against each other to see who's the best fake-sleeper, so she can sneak in a five-minute nap. Babysitting is a sunbaked afternoon, lying in a recliner beside Rolo by the pool in a too-modest two-piece her mother bought her years ago, ostensibly watching the children attempt underwater handstands, actually watching Trevor Honey-Bowles, shirtless in Carhartts, replace a loose board on the dock.

A Fruit of the Dead for each of them becomes an afternoon ritual when Rolo is around. After their initial adventure, mixed into a drink is the only way he'll give her any more Granadone. He makes them extra weak, he says, no big deal, the equivalent of smoking a joint, he'll even have one himself, and though they don't feel much like a joint to her, she doesn't argue, she likes them, she wants them.

Queenie, Spenser calls from the shallow end. The children have adopted their father's nickname for her as naturally as they'll adopt his other affectations one day. Watch this!

Fern climbs onto Spenser's shoulders and slips off with a splash.

Cory gives them a thumbs-up. Despite her dowdy swimsuit, she feels queenly indeed, blissfully glamorous, enjoying the first woozy dance steps of intoxication as the Fruit of the Dead slips down her throat and into her blood. The day is languid and happy, sexy and murky, cloudy but bright.

They love you, Rolo says. He is in his usual ensemble: linen shirt, khaki shorts, leather sandals, silver aviators that read, in the corner of one lens, near his brow, *Cartier*.

I love them, she replies.

He snaps his fingers, suddenly seized by a great idea: Let's have an Easter egg hunt.

It isn't Easter, she says. Her voice in her head sounds constricted and guttural. She clears her throat. Is it? she adds, just in case.

His laugh always takes her by surprise. Is it? he says. Who knows? How long have you been here? What is time?

Shut up, she says, smiling.

We can do an egg hunt whenever we want, he says. Who needs Easter? Do you believe in the Resurrection?

What? Oh! No.

Nobody died for *my* sins.

We're sort of Jewish, she says. Not super Jewish. We don't go to . . . She can't think of the word, so she tries from another angle: They didn't give me a . . . whatchamacallit.

A yarmulke.

A what?

For the top of your head.

No, no.

A yellow star for your coat.

Jesus, *no*.

No Jesus: check. Me, neither.

You're evil, she says, laughing. She can't tell what face he's making. His eyes are obscured by his mirrored lenses, in which recline two small, convex reflections of herself, a skinny doll on a chaise longue.

Where were you last night? he asks in a friendly tone.

Her belly drops. The skinny dolls' twin smiles fade.

Spenser had a bad dream, he says. Didn't you, Milhouse?

The boy in the pool is towing his sister from side to side, not listening.

It was actually useful, Rolo says, to be interrupted. I should have been done working anyway. I have to say, though. I don't know what to do with that kid when he's whining. He gets so *pathetic*, you know.

He's seven.

Yeah, yeah. I know. But, see, that's what I mean. *You're* the freak whisperer, right? That's what I hired *you* for.

Down at the dock, having finished his work, Trevor Honey-Bowles stands, stretches, and crosses the lawn. The blood-colored drinks sparkle and sweat. The lawn and hedges pulse electric green. The pool is Lisa Frank blue. As the kids trouble the water, its grid of tiles warps and wiggles. When Honeybowl disappears beyond the tennis court, she realizes with a cramp that Rolo has been watching her watch him.

She gives her employer a weak smile. An egg hunt would be so fun, she says.

He leans forward to unbuckle his sandals. Perspiration falls from his forehead, leaving a dark spot on a paving stone. He unbuttons his shirt to reveal a taut, ovoid belly.

Come on, he says, holding out a hand. Let's show these losers how to dive.

Then time speeds up like a film reel in fast-forward, and the hours pass, buzzing and breathless. The cold rush of diving into the pool, the confused splashing and goofing. Trying to run from him when he chases her in the water is like trying to run in a dream, heavy and slow. When he catches her, he holds her under just long enough that when she surfaces again she is sputtering.

The children laugh but she can't get her breath and the mood shifts briefly to worry. They all go back to the house wrapped in too-large towels, and she and the kids are installed on the patio. They sit at the pill-studded picnic table as the sun falls, winking through the trees at the edges of things, and the lawn goes bluish in the dusk. Spider comes out to arrange sausages and vegetables on the grill, and then Rolo's ignoring her and the kids, pacing the lawn, a towel hanging over his shoulders, belly hanging over the lip of his swim trunks, talking loudly into a phone in one hand, a sausage piled comically high with peppers and onions in the other. And then Virgil has disappeared with the kids, and indeed all the staff has gone, and the dinner's cleaned up, save for a plate on the table before her, a single bronzed sausage gone cold in the dark, and she's alone again on the patio, wrapped in a towel the size of a bedsheet under the stars, drips of pool water tracing the back of her neck like cold fingers. She is conscious enough to hobble barefoot back to her shed, but barely.

Babysitting is waking just minutes, it seems, into her own deep sleep, to wails of terror on the baby monitor. Is lying in bed for a long moment, the comforter over her face, before stumbling groggily on a midnight trip to the big house to soothe a kid damp and haunted by nightmare. She murmurs as she enters so as not to freak out the myopic boy—for it is always Spenser—but nevertheless he calls out, Who's there? with quavering theatricality.

It's just me, she says. Just Cory—

Who?

Queenie; it's okay—

And when he protests—I want *Mama*, he says, ramping up again, I want to go *ho-o-o-me*—

she agrees with him, a hand on his tangles: I know—and you know what, back at home, your mama just woke up, too, wanting you.

130

How do *you* know, he snuffles, but he lets her pet his head.

Can't you feel it, she asks him. Deep down in your belly, here—

That *tickles*—

What, here?

Stop!

Jeez, I was just trying to show you.

She lays her own head on his pillow and looks up at the faint outlines of the zinc sulfide stars on his ceiling, their phosphorescence faded to near invisibility. What would her mother say to this sad child beside her?

You know how before you were born you grew inside your mom?

Spenser says, Yes.

Well, the stuff that you're made of still lives in her, she still knows you deep inside, and when you are scared or crying she can feel it, no matter how far away she might be.

No way, he says. That's just DNA. Even plants have DNA.

Plants can feel each other, too, she says, even miles and miles away. If one tree is cut down, its pain is communicated to all the other trees through the root system. It's like a super slow, underground game of telephone.

Mama *sings* to me when I have trouble sleeping, he says, petulant, uncharmed.

You want me to sing?

He whimpers, The one from camp.

She starts in on a camp song, a rousing oom-pah march, but he whines and hits her face. Hey! she says. Watch it.

The one you sang on the last day, he pleads, and she senses she doesn't have long, he's catching hold again of his freak-out, recalling whatever disturbed him, his tenuous whining is dissolving into real tears, so she begins to hum, at first nothing at all, quiet

131

and atonal, petting his hair in time to some rhythm stored deep in her own roots, an almost tuneless tune. And as his lids grow heavy again, she remembers rocking him outside the barn, and the rhythm and intervals sneak in, and the words come back, picking up where they left off, summoned by the tune, bounding home like a dog whistled for in the dusk:

> Hail, dear children, whoe'er you are,
> bright eye and ruddy cheek:
> I will answer best I can
> who I am and what I seek.
>
> My name my dears is Doso and
> I rode aback the sea
> on a swift ship sailed by pirates fierce
> who overpowered me.
>
> We landed on the shore among
> the women and the swine
> who gathered in a hungry throng
> to dance, rejoice, and dine.
>
> But in my heart was freedom, dears,
> so furtively I fled
> through this country dark and strange,
> a price upon my head.
>
> I wandered days and then came here
> where I know not sacred from sin,
> what land it is, or who you are,
> or if you'll take me in.

So pity me, my children, with
but water and some bread,
and I will rock you in my arms,
and put you, safe, to bed.

Doso's song: how she has remembered the words, who knows, but remember it she does, and probably will, forever. Indeed, the grooves and crevices of the simple tune are stored in her mind, like metadata, hundreds of memories of hundreds of nights. The yellow pallor and traffic noises and neighbor smells of her stuffy little bedroom on 86th Street. A wicked virus, a basin beside the bed. Her mother's cool hand, her mother's smell, her mother's voice. The fiber fur of Bunnydog against her cheek.

And here is the boy, asleep at last with his mouth hanging open, looking very small and unprotected without his glasses, and here is she, a grown-up now, more or less. Gingerly she draws her hand from his head. In silence she rises, closes his door behind her, creeps back down the stairs, and crosses the lawn under the lurid embarrassment of stars. She can still feel the drug, if slightly, in the gaps between moments, in the way the Earth tips toward her, friendly prank, at the base of the hill, in the immensity of her nostalgia and loneliness, in the lump in her throat and the expanse in her head. She'd like to cross the tennis court and scramble through the dense wood and end up in Honeybowl's bare-walled room. She'd like someone, anyone, to curl up with. She'd like another ruby pill and a deep glass of wine. Is this what it is like, she wonders, to be an adult; is this what it will be like from now on; will she always be so sad, so alone; will she always yearn this way for comfort, or for company, or—? What *does* she yearn for?

A silhouette with hair like strokes of Magic Marker is crossing the lawn.

Virgil, she calls, and trots to catch up with him.

He pauses in the chain-link gate of the tennis court. What's up?

She wants to say, *Could you tell Honeybowl to come find me?*
but, looking at Virgil now, she can't. Under his closed-mouth,
professional gaze, she feels suddenly childish, wary of drawing
him into her drama.

Instead, she says, Any chance you've been able to get me the
Wi-Fi password? I should probably call my mom, let her know
I'm okay.

Virgil sighs through his teeth. Yeah, about that, he says. So the
password here is encrypted, and it changes daily. The tech team
sends Rolo a new one every morning.

The tech team?

Down at Southgate HQ. Couple of nerds in a windowless
room in Connecticut. It goes straight to his devices. Not even
they ever know what the password is out here. Neither do I, to be
honest. For interisland communications I use the walkie-talkie. I
make my calls from the mainland. You could ask him yourself, but.
Personally, I wouldn't. He can get kind of paranoid about security,
for obvious reasons.

Right, Cory says, though nothing about it is obvious to her.
Well, maybe I could go with you to the mainland someday, she
says. Make a call.

Maybe, he replies. May. Be.

He turns to go, but halts, snapping his fingers a couple of times,
as if weighing whether or not to say something. Then he half turns
back in her direction, and says, Word to the wise, Nanny? Maybe,
I don't know, lay off the Granadone. I mean, you do you, but if I
were you, I'd, you know. At least hydrate.

He walks off, still snapping, and she feels a burning shame,
thinking of how he took over for her with the kids when she got

too high, thinking of how she must have looked, wrapped in a towel next to her uneaten sausage, and was she falling asleep?

To push the thought from her mind, she takes her phone from her pocket. The screen glows and one bar of service disappears, then reappears. She tries her mom. The call fails. She tries walking around a little, staring at the device as if panning for gold. Service seems stronger near the beach, that one bar more stable the closer she gets to the sea. Near the foot of the dock she tries again. Nothing.

Holding the phone like a talisman she lowers herself onto the dock's far edge. Her legs swing in the wind and the nearby sailboat creaks, and if she holds her head just right she can see almost nothing, no lights and no beach, no greenhouse, no gazebo, no house, just water and space. She imagines the conversation she might have with her mother, the way it might go. Her mom's exhausting worry. The way she'd focus on the job. The way Cory might say, *It's good. I'm learning a lot. I can't, you know, tell you details, due to the NDA, but I think this is going to turn out to be a great experience for me.*

As she imagines bullshitting her mother, blah-blah-blah-ing in her mind about professional skills, college readiness, and other such nonsense, she can feel herself closing up. The mother she has now is so far removed from the mother she used to have, the mother she wants. How stupid to expect this mother to behave differently. Listening to the slap of the waves against the boat hull, to the straining of the rigging, she feels her throat tighten. Strangled out of her by anger, self-pity, and homesickness, tears fall. She shoves the useless device back into her pocket, and days go by.

She is wading in the shallows with the children, catching hermit crabs, when Virgil appears at the top of the beach.

Hey, Nanny, he says. It's not quite the mainland, but a few of us are going to hear my buddy Pete play a show tonight on Coeur Brisé. Me, Hester, Angela. *Honeybowl.* Come if Rolo can spare you. Meet at the dock at eight.

Flushing, she picks up a crab in a snail shell and lets it crawl up her wrist. What's Coeur Brisé?

He points to an island the size of a thimble on the long liquid shelf of the horizon. He says, They have an open network there, if you need to make a call.

Cool, she says. Thanks. Should I ask for the night off? I think I'm supposed to get a couple nights off.

Virgil raises his hands. That's between you and your boss, he says.

My boss, she says.

Yeah. *My* boss does not keep me on the clock twenty-four/seven. Whatever your arrangement is with *your* boss is your business.

So she does not ask if she's allowed to leave. After dinner and bedtime she runs back to the shed to change. At ten to eight she pulls on a fluttery dress with crisscross straps, a neon sports bra, and the once-white sneakers. Quick quick she pulls a brush through her dumb pink hair. It fluffs up like a clown wig. Frustrated, she roots around in the duffel for something to fix the problem. A scarf of her mother's surfaces, an old silk thing she borrowed without asking, with a strange and murderous pattern of blue-green snakes, mouths open wide to reveal their fangs, coiled around one another, strangling a trio of fat pink pigs. Cory ties it around her head like a headband and knots it at the nape of her neck. At five to eight she grabs her phone, tucks it into the back of her bra, and runs down the lawn.

Sherry is waiting in her strange boat, smoking. Hester is smoking, too, in silver sunglasses, with one of the housekeepers. They are both in jeans. They glance up at Cory but do not say hello. Cory stands foolishly for a moment, unsure whether to watch them, to listen, to try to join in their conversation, highly self-conscious, foolish even, wearing practically nothing, a scarf around her lame pink hair.

You guys going to the party? she says eventually.

They look at each other.

Yes, Hester says.

Are *you* going to the party? says the housekeeper.

Cory hugs herself in the chill. I guess.

Fortunately Virgil, in a backpack, crests the hill with Honey-bowl, who, freshly showered in a white tee and flannel, gives Cory a private smile. Sherry starts the boat engine. Everyone climbs in. The wind picks up—cold, quick, and salty—and Cory has to tuck her hand between her legs to keep her dress from flying up. Honeybowl chats with the housekeeper in the prow while Hester and Virgil watch the island recede behind them.

Thanks for bringing me along, Cory says to Virgil, who is leaning against the gunwale.

Virgil leans toward her and taps his ear, indicating that he didn't hear her in the wind.

Thanks for bringing me, she repeats.

You brought yourself, he tells her.

After a moment, Sherry turns on the radio, and classic rock clangs from the seacraft's tinny speakers. The sun is sinking behind a long bruise of cloud. The sky's a mess of fire. Virgil joins Honey-bowl and the maid, and Cory sits on a cushion wishing she had a sweater.

Hester leans toward Cory. Don't be jealous of Angela, she says.

Who? Cory says.

Hester nods at the trio in the prow, sharp and striking in the angled light. She says, She's had a thing for Honeybowl all summer, but he's not into her anymore.

Anymore, says Cory.

Hester lowers her sunglasses. Honeybowl is kind of a— I'll just say he's kind of a snob. Angela is—she pauses, squinting—not his type. He wants someone he can bring around to parties on the Vineyard. Rich kid seeks rich kid.

Oh, I'm not— Cory says, then laughs quickly. I'm, like. We're, like. You know.

Hester's eyebrows rise. Aren't you from Manhattan?

Yeah, but I'm poor. I mean—she rushes to clarify—not, like, *poor* poor. But, like. It's just me and my mom. We're fine. But we're fine because she's a workaholic. We don't have real money.

Well. Hester pushes her silver glasses back up her nose. Don't tell *him* that.

Coeur Brisé is bigger than Rolo's island, with more forest at its edge, and a small marina in a cove with room for multiple boats. They pull in and disembark. Honeybowl holds Cory's hand to help her out. His palm is warm and damp. They follow a path through a grove of trees and wait. Cory pulls out her phone. Its glass is smeary with the oils of her skin. She connects to the island's Wi-Fi, but replaces the phone in her bra when the headlights of a golf cart wobble fast over the path, then pull up quick.

The driver welcomes Virgil: Look who brought the party!

Pete, says Virgil, and they hug.

Pete is good-looking, with a thick, dark beard, lean-muscled in a sleeveless shirt and red winter hat with a pom-pom. He enumerates each member of their group by name: Hester, he says; Angela. Honeybo-o-owl! To Cory, he says, New Girl!

Cory's our new Kelly, Virgil says.

Pete says, Why don't you sit up here with V and me.

So Cory squeezes in up front, next to Pete and half on top of Virgil, who smells like sage and coconut. The temperature has dropped with the sun. The wind gives her goose bumps. The golf cart lurches away from the sea.

You know Kelly? Cory says after a moment.

Pete nods once and glances at Virgil, but Virgil avoids his eyes. Those kids giving you hell? Pete asks.

They're sweet, says Cory.

She's still honeymooning, says Virgil.

It is a beautiful *ar-chi-pe-la-go*. Pete's left hand taps a rhythm on the wheel, and he draws out his syllables in time to it, and conversation falters, and the trees part, and she smells weed, rank and sweet, on the breeze.

A couple of dozen people are gathered around a keg on a swath of field under strings of lights that stretch out in a sunburst from a cylindrical water tower. Pete parks and Cory half tumbles out. Hester and Angela light cigarettes. Honeybowl goes for the keg. Virgil becomes engaged in conversation with a girl in a jumpsuit, and gets lost in the crowd. Pete, too, has disappeared.

Everyone looks beautiful under the rope lights, under the stars. While Honeybowl waits his turn for beer, Cory stands alone. A joint is passed, and she takes a hit. She pulls out her phone again and is dismayed to see that she has twenty-six unread messages: twenty-four from her mother and two from Ella Ha. She opens her conversation with Ella and sees an invitation to hang out followed closely by *O right I forgot ur in nevrnevrland.* She is considering how/whether to respond when a guy in a Polo shirt approaches. He says he's the owner's great-nephew. Owner of what? Cory asks, and he opens his arms to the trees, the sky, the water tower, the lawn, and faraway lights—the house, presumably—twinkling through the trees.

Then there is the sound of a great bell ringing. The very air around her chimes. She follows the crowd into the water tower through an unexpected door. Inside it is very dark and the walls are corroded as a shipwreck's with a greenish, marbleized patina. Pete and his synth and a couple of speakers are installed on a stage above the crowd. It is an almost religious setup. Below, the murmuring of his disciples' voices resolves, briefly, into recognizable words and phrases—*Genevieve said they had a good time . . . my brother up in Ithaca . . . business here, she has no business here . . . needs to chill*—before fading again into the purling sonic texture of the crowd. The bell reverberates.

Slowly, the clanging becomes a harmony, a rhythm. Up on the transparent stage, bent over his electronica, Pete tinkers, the pompom on his hat bobbing with the beat. Around her, people sway, brushing against her. A heavy bass note fills the space and seems to stretch and warp, and she closes her eyes, the better to feel the sound. Her heart submits to the rhythm. New pops and hisses, distortions and overtones, weave subtly into the rippling fabric of the tune. She feels the click and crackle of an analog tape recorder in the backs of her ears. Above and below and through the music come the same voices she heard moments ago—*Business here, she has no business here. Needs to chill*—and Cory has the brief, paranoid thought that the conversations were staged, and hidden in them is a message meant for her and only her. She has no business here. She needs to chill. She tries to push these thoughts away and distract herself by listening. The words are distorted, the bass joined by a treble melody. At last, in a quiet, bronchitic growl, Pete begins to sing. The recordings repeat and stutter: *Genevieve said they ha— Genevieve said they ha— Genevieve said they ha— ad a good time. My brother up in Ithaca*—and through their looping and fracturing she is relieved to find the words losing their meaning, becoming mere music.

After the show, the audience seeps out into the dark field. Cory stands at the crowd's edge watching its currents, eddies, and knots, small confrontations and emboldened flirtations, keeping an eye out for Honeybowl. Now is a good time to call her mother, she guesses, and takes out her phone a third time, but is startled by an ear-numbing explosion. A blinding peony shatters, outshining the stars. Fireworks!

Enjoying yourself?

She smells body odor, miasmic and male, and turns to find Pete holding two beers. She takes one, and thanks him with a compliment: Your music is amazing. I felt like there were hidden messages in it, meant just for me.

His smile looks woven into his beard. He says, There were.

She laughs and, as if summoned by her laughter, there is a smattering of blasts. Half a dozen glowing white mandalas unfurl in the smoky sky.

Virgil's really hitting it out of the park, Pete says, nodding at the heavens.

Virgil's setting these off?

His whole rig is set up in a clearing out there. Want to see?

She follows him into the trees. The foliage closes around them and for a moment she loses Pete in the dark. She calls his name and is embarrassed by how close his voice is when he says, I'm here. A warm hand lands on her arm and feels its way down, slides its fingers between her own, and leads her to Virgil and his explosives. Honeybowl is beside him, holding a flashlight, and Cory drops Pete's hand quickly but, she hopes, casually, as if to touch her hair. He looks at her with a question. Before she can acknowledge his glance they are both flattened by the bright ray of a flashlight.

There you are, Honeybowl says, and swings his arms wide, splashing beer from his cup, as if he's been looking for her.

Honeybo-o-owl, Pete sings in falsetto. The guys touch knuckles.

Great show, man, says Honeybowl. I don't get it, but I like it.

They all watch in the flashlight's glare as Virgil lights a series of fuses, and orange bolt after orange bolt zooms up and cracks, loud as gunfire, into a million points of light.

You want to try?

Really? Cory asks, turning to Virgil from the sky.

He holds out a firecracker and explains: It has two charges in it, the lift charge and the burst charge. The lift charge does the launching. It's in the bottom, closest to the fuse. The burst charge is above that, inside a shell of stars.

A shell of stars, Cory repeats, savoring the phrase. He hands her the paper cylinder and a lighter, and she hands him her beer to free her hands.

No, thanks, he says. I don't touch substances anymore.

So Pete takes it while she ignites the fuse, and they all step back and watch it spiral up into the dark and shoot out a spherical cacophony of red sparks, each of which opens up into smaller explosions of blue, then breaks into a yet smaller explosion of green, and at last gives rise to a blast of delicate yellow. Beyond the trees, the crowd applauds.

The ride to the dock is quiet. A charm has been cast over the golf cart, a light organic glamour that dispels Cory's anxieties and makes her feel that she belongs here, in this precarious vehicle, with these new friends. Sitting in back, between Honeybowl and Hester, she lets her arm press up against Honeybowl's as they pass the owner's residence at the top of the hill. A long stone staircase leads to a broad patio where two wings meet around the glowing water of a still, flat pool. It is a kind of castle.

When Pete drops them at the dock she waves goodbye with the others, then pulls her phone a last time from her bra and skims her mom's texts, which have accumulated over the preceding days with increasing dread:

Call when u can

I want to know more about this job! Exciting :)

Cory call me when you get a chance please

Honey I've tried u four times. call me back

Cory where the hell are you

I'm so worried, monkey :(

How dare you disappear like this

I'm not angry I'm just worried

That's a lie. I am so ducking angry how could you disappear without telling me anything about where you were going anything about your new employer anything about anything I don't even know what kind of work you're supposedly doing for all I know you could be ducking dead

Nanny. You coming?

Virgil's voice shakes her back into the present. She looks up from the screen and feels the chill of the night air, smells the trees and salt water, sees the others in Sherry's ferry, waiting. As she follows them to the boat she makes the call.

143

Her mother picks up on the first ring. The connection is terrible. She is yelling but her voice is like a whisper. Cory? Cory! Oh my god, Cory, thank God. Cory?

Mom? she says, trying to raise the volume. I got your texts. I'm not *dead*.

She climbs into the boat and, as her mother launches into a furious monologue, smiles at Honeybowl and rolls her eyes at the phone. Sherry starts the engine, drowning out her mother's voice, and Cory leans over the stern, her back to the group. The wind is quick and cold and the engine is loud. She pulls her dress tight.

Mom, she says, as loudly as she can without embarrassing herself, I'm sorry, I can't hear you—

Cory, I can't hear you, comes her mother's voice, ghost faint.

I'm on a boat.

A *what*?

A *boat*!

Where?

I don't know. The Atlantic? You're stressing me out.

The boat is bouncing, the spray wetting her face, and she hears very little except, Come *home*, Cory, please, come home *now*—

And then Sherry accelerates, and the boat heaves over a wave, and the sweat-slick device slips from her hand and is gone in the spume without so much as a splash.

The loss of it feels at once shocking and so unsurprising as to have been preordained. She is foolish to have leaned over the side of the boat in the first place, phone in hand, foolish not to have called her mother earlier, foolish not to have brought something warm to wear. As the boat speeds on she watches the spot where it fell recede until she loses track of it in the vastness of the sea. She is a foolish, shivering girl, and she is all alone.

And then she isn't. Honeybowl has come to stand beside her. You must be freezing, he says, offering her his flannel.

She puts the shirt on gratefully and wraps it around her.

Tough call with your mom?

I dropped my phone.

In the *ocean*?

She looks at him, wiping her eyes.

He laughs. That sucks, he says. You can use mine when we're back.

Woefully she says, There's no service.

Sure there is. You think any of us would come out here for months without Wi-Fi?

I thought— she says, then starts again. Virgil told me—

I set up a hotspot at the shanty. It was like the first thing I did. Don't tell Picazo.

Does Virgil know? she asks quietly.

Honeybowl laughs. Of course.

The thought of having service again, the feeling of being let in on the secret, cheers her some, and she lets him put his arm around her, but uneasiness lingers in her muscles, in her mind. Why would Virgil have kept the hotspot from her?

When Sherry pulls up to the dock, Honeybowl walks with her up the hill. The night is clear, the stars like a sheet of sparkling mesh thrown across the sky.

Never gets old, Honeybowl says.

And she laughs and replies, There's nothing older.

A long light cast from the side entrance of the house interrupts the hill's shadow. A door has opened. A figure appears against the light, enormous, imposing, in its hand a glass of wine. The pharaoh hounds hurtle toward them.

I'll see you later, says Honeybowl quietly, and jogs toward the tennis court.

The dogs reach her, paws and tongues. Rolo crosses the lawn. He stops close enough that she can feel his warmth and smell the wine on his breath.

Beautiful night for a party, he says. His voice is low and hoarse, as if he hasn't spoken in hours.

Yeah, she says uncertainly.

Did you have a good time?

She senses another question buried underneath his question, something more menacing, but can't detect his meaning. Sort of, she says.

He chuckles. He drinks.

Did *you* have a nice night? she asks.

Did I have a nice night, he says. Huh. No. No, I have to say I didn't. Cricket really picked a shit time to have a baby.

Who?

The kids' mother. I'm a generous guy, you know, I told her I'd take the kids while she and her husband acclimate, reacclimate, to early parenthood. Two born-agains with a newborn. There's a joke in there somewhere. Problem is, I don't know if I've mentioned, but I've been prepping for an appearance before Congress.

Congress. Why?

So I don't really have time, Cory, to deal with the two energy-sucking demons she pawned off on me.

He drains the remaining contents of his glass.

I'm sorry, Cory says. You mentioned . . . I mean I thought I could take a night off.

With permission.

I waited until they were asleep.

You waited until you *thought* they were asleep. But for the last—what has it been, four hours?—it's been Daddy this, Daddy that. Daddy I had a bad dream. Daddy I can't sleep. Daddy I have to pee. Daddy I want Mama. I want Kelly—

Kelly?

Queenie.

They said that?

It doesn't fucking matter what they said. They're children. They don't get to choose who's there when they have a nightmare. Their lives aren't up to them. Fucking *that's* fucking *why* I *fucking*. Hired. You. Not to go gallivanting around the archipelago, not to fraternize with my staff. To take care of these fucking kids while I work through what has become the biggest, most career-defining *headache* of my life.

He drops his wineglass in the grass and turns away. The dogs nose it, then follow him to the big house. Midway, he swings back at her with a pointed finger.

Never again! Will you leave without permission.

I'm sorry, she whispers.

Sorry is valueless to me. What I need is for you to do your job. The job that I am, I'll add, compensating you for *generously*. And just in case there's any misunderstanding about what that job is, let me explain: your purpose here is to make it possible for *me* to do *my* job. Everything else is secondary. Being good with the kids, having fun with them, making sure nobody drowns in the pool or falls out of a tree? That's all *fucking secondary*, okay?

She nods. Her whole body is the lump in her throat.

I am docking your pay. You did not do the work. You will not be paid for today. And I am putting you on probation. One more screwup and you're on the next boat back to the mainland. It'll be up to you to find your way home.

The door shuts. As she trudges back to her room, her tears fall freely. She is tired. She has to pee. At her shed, the A/C seems to have fritzed out. She stands in the middle of the thermos-hot space, holding her toothbrush, wiping her eyes and nose. The last thing she wants to do is go back to the big house right now and use the second-rate bathroom assigned her. She goes outside and rounds the corner so she can't be seen, then pulls down her undies and squats by the wall. She goes to sleep without brushing her teeth, exhausted, beer on her breath.

VI

Tell Me Truly of My Dear Child If You Have Seen Her Anywhere

I wake from fitful dreams in the middle of the night to my phone buzzing, and pick it up with desperate, fumbling relief: Cory? Cory!

Amid a slush of background noise, one magic syllable solidifies: Mom? Her voice is quiet as a secret. I got your texts. I'm not *dead*.

My body lurches up, wide awake and overflowing with reproachment. What am I saying I don't know, but the words are tumbling out of me.

I hear: *I'm on a—* and then lose her again.

I yell, as if by raising my own voice I can raise hers. A *what*? You're on a *boat*? Fury snakes in: Goddamn it, *where*?

Static overtakes her. I hear, *Atlantic*. I hear, *Stressing me out*.

I realize I must convey my message as directly as possible. Come home, I say to her, come home, come *home*, Cory, please, come home *now*. Come home, monkey, and we'll start over, I'm sorry, have I said that yet? Hello—

Hello?

Have I said too much have I frightened her off have I confirmed her worst suspicions. The line's gone dead and dialing her back

I reach no one, nothing. The phone just rings and rings before clicking over again to dreaded voicemail—*You have reached— Cory?*

Feel it in my gut: panic. Something is not right. Try to breathe; panic. Miss Clavel turned on the light. Shake the rhyme from my mind. Rise and pull the curtains open. It's still dark outside but I know I will not sleep. Instead I go to the kitchen. Boil water. Grind a cup of oily coffee beans. Try to breathe. I cannot fill my lungs to capacity, cannot drink enough air.

I have tapped into my phone's web browser search bar, almost without realizing: *Fortune 500 CEO private island.* I scan the results as the French press steeps:

As Airline Wobbles, CEO Looks to Private Island for Collateral

Billionaire Reveals Plans for Utopian City in the Sea

The Demanding Travel Habits of the Superrich

Nic Cage's Tropical Oasis: Private Island Magazine

New Accusations Come to Light for Beleaguered Southgate Exec

People Also Ask:
Who owns the largest private island?
Which islands are privately owned?
List of privately owned islands

Pour black coffee, sit, and drink. Panic tingles in my stomach, in my hands, but as I scan the search results I begin to feel my heartbeat settle into a more regular rhythm. I retrieve my laptop from its place on my desk. At the kitchen table, I open Excel. I am not the ED of a multinational nonprofit for nothing. I am a woman who loves a spreadsheet. Copy-paste, copy-paste. There are hundreds of privately owned islands in Asia, the Caribbean, off the coasts of Canada and western Europe. The sprawl is daunting, but she said Atlantic, so I'll start there. Islands owned by cruise lines can be eliminated from the list, presumably. Likewise those owned by actors—although on second thought I suppose the asshole could be bringing her to someone else's home. Stifle the panic. All I can do is all I can do. Perhaps color-code those. Copy-paste, and add them to the bottom of the list.

What else. Check my texts. She mentioned he was a parent of a camper. That's a big clue, isn't it. Type into the search engine, *River Rock Junior Camp roster*. The camp comes up: an out-of-date WordPress site, of course. How this janky operation has become a cult favorite among the privileged is beyond me. Scroll briefly through the featured photos: children tie-dyeing, playing Red Rover. Teens hand-in-hand at a bonfire. A group of kids cross-legged in a circle on the grass. Recall Cory's story, a couple of years ago, about a ruthless camp-wide game of Midnight Manhunt, which left multiple kids and two staff members in tears. Since she was a little girl she'd return every summer with an enthusiasm that bordered on zealotry. I trawl the whole disorganized site, but cannot find a list of this year's campers. A privacy issue, I suppose. I do however find the main phone number. I'll call. Of course: I'll call! Why haven't I already called? I'll call—but not until the start of the business day.

The sun has come up without warning. I glance at my phone and find to my surprise that it's past time to leave for work. I am not dressed. My coffee has gone cold. Tap my calendar: I have an 8 a.m.

with the scientists in Shanghai. My 9:15 with the senator has been canceled, she always cancels. Breakfast with our new chairman, the tedious John-Paul Ferrari. A check-in with Ian and, at noon, a working lunch with Gretchen and her dizzy chickens in publicity. How frivolous it all seems, how hopelessly deluded our lofty mission. I send a note to Ian, et cetera, to let them know I'll join the Shanghai call from home. I reschedule with John-Paul. He writes back immediately, agreeing, *Today's a fuckfest*, and sending a new calendar invite for next week. Great. At two to eight I throw on a blouse, check my background, and log in.

Minutes into our conversation with the scientists it becomes clear we have no new information. I let Ian take the lead while our stoic intern—what's her name?—takes notes. We're going to be here for a while. I continue working on my spreadsheet, stone-faced and busy, as they talk.

They are all men because of course they are all men. Add a column, call it *notes*, for information on the private islanders' biographies. One needn't delve too far into the search results to find: the millionaires and billionaires who own these islands, not one of them is guiltless. Impossible to become as wealthy as these men are without a little blood on the hands. Fraud is the most common crime among them—tax fraud, bank fraud, market manipulation, securities, commodities—but there is also evasion, embezzlement, falsification, kickbacks, laundering, racketeering, sedition, insider trading. Then there are other accusations, not directly related to the accumulation of wealth and/or power, but perhaps products of it. Narcotics. Sexual assault.

Sexual assault.

I hear my name. Irritated by the interruption, I toggle back to the video call. Ian—freshly showered, Polo shirt, striped white and powder blue—is asking me to verify something.

Sorry, I say, my video must have frozen. Can you repeat that?

Ian says: Hong Tao was just explaining the reasons they are requesting *increased funding* for this stage of research.

By his tone I know he can tell I haven't been paying attention. From his expression I can tell he does not want me to approve the scientists' request.

Right, I say, I got that part (I did not).

Ian goes on, I was explaining to him that we won't have a clear idea of our *own* funding streams until the top of Q3.

Right, I say, that's accurate.

Behind Hong Tao there is little identifying information, just white wall and closed door, but when he unmutes himself I can hear children in the background. It is evening where he is; he is dialing in from home.

Pardon me, he says now. Are you saying we are hog-tied for the summer?

I'm sorry? Ian says.

Hong Tao: Without funding now, we have not the ability to research for the duration of the summer. We will lose valuable time.

Ian says, You have other funding streams, though, right? The government—

The party appreciates your project and we are honored to participate in this collaboration, but our priority has to be work that we do on behalf of the Chinese people.

I glance at my phone. It is not even half past eight. I know from experience this conversation could go on for an hour or more, cyclical, useless, interminably polite, and, meanwhile, *sexual assault*—

I interrupt: We'll see what we can do. We need to huddle here, circle our wagons, revisit our positioning. We'll get back to you within the week, let you know if it's a possibility.

Ian is looking on with wide eyes. I am not usually so curt. Nor is it our custom even to consider quote-unquote *extending funds* we do not have.

I'm sorry, I say again: I have to run, I have an urgent matter to attend to. Don't let me end this conversation. I'll catch up on the notes later in the day and touch base shortly. Thank you, as always, for your dedication, and for joining this call at what I know is a late hour for you.

And I log off.

Moments later, a text from Ian: *What's going on?*

Ignore.

Ian texts again: *Are we still on to check in this morning*

Note his passive-aggressive lack of punctuation. He's salty. He resents it when I punt managerial work his way, and I get it, understandable. Will text back in a minute. Right now I have to make a call.

I dial River Rock and the phone rings, but a machine clicks on. A recorded message informs me that the camp is closed for the season. I can leave a message. Someone will call me back in the next few days. Minutes and hours and days she has been gone—

Hello, I say after the solicitous beep, this is Emer Ansel, I am Cory Ansel's mom, she was a counselor at Junior Camp this year. I'm calling—

And I am paralyzed momentarily by two conflicting feelings: on the one hand, self-conscious embarrassment—I am being crazy, overprotective, Cory is eighteen, a high school graduate, no longer a minor, doesn't need me checking up on her—indeed, hates me, she has told me so—and, on the other, flailing helplessness, wild-haired and moaning fear: my baby's gone without a trace; *help,* you dizzy crunchy Kumbaya idealists, help me, please— I watched her sweet face crumple, then, muzzled, stood and left the room—

I'm calling, I say aloud at last, because I believe Cory left something behind, something of value, and I, I need to bring it to her, I need to know where she has gone. If you could call me back, please, that would be very much appreciated— And I leave my number and, trembling, hang up.

How late is too late to file a missing person report? How early is too early? Am I being unreasonable? Should I call my lawyer, talk it out? That's an idea. Oh wait, what's this, a text—has she—

Bueller?

Ian. Right. Of course.

He picks up after one ring. Hey, he says. You okay?

Stand up. Pace. Say, I need to take a personal day.

Today? We're sort of in a crisis.

And I won't be any good at tackling it if I don't take a day off. You can handle it. I have complete confidence in you.

It's not that I can't, he says, then tries a different tack: This is about Cory, isn't it.

I'd prefer not to discuss personal matters right now.

Emer, he says, with all due, you know, this is going to sound harsh, but Cory doesn't need you right now. *We* need you.

Just handle it!

I have snapped at him. Reeling, I disconnect.

Should I call the police?

I should call the police.

155

What do I, just call 911, or . . .

I'll call 911.

I'm transferred to my local precinct. An officer picks up, with a voice like a rumbling engine.

Hello, I say, I'd like to file a missing person report.

Is the individual eighteen years old or older? the officer responds mechanically.

I say, Eighteen two weeks ago.

This individual's disappearance. Was it possibly not voluntary?

I let out an anxious laugh. Do you *know* any teenagers? She doesn't know what she wants.

The officer replies, If she's eighteen and left of her own volition there's not much we can do.

I have reason to believe that she left under coercion.

What evidence do you have?

She isn't responding to my texts.

A pause. Then: Have you tried calling?

I've tried calling, texting, I've tried fucking *waiting*. She went off with someone Saturday night and I haven't heard from her since—I just want to know that she's all right—

Look, ma'am, says the rumbling voice. I can hear that you're distressed, but I'm sorry, if she's eighteen and left of her own accord there's just not much we can do but advise you to remain calm, keep the faith, and wait for her to contact you. Why don't I take down your name and number, and if I hear of anything, I'll be in touch.

I—thank you, but—

Again I cut myself off. A word has risen to the surface of my mind, a cynical word, a practical word. The word is *optics*. Imagine the field day the media might have. *Magic rice fails to grow. Director's daughter disappears. RHEA Seeds in shambles.* The hit to our reputation could be insurmountable.

That's all right, I say at last. Thank you for your time.

Do not think of blood on tile, wrists tied with rope, young hands bloodless blue. Do not type into search, despite myself: *How many girls go missing every year?* The numbers are mind-boggling. How could it have taken me so long to let myself react? The statistics get more desperate every day. Do not think. Everybody sings some version of this hateful recitative: she's eighteen, she will be fine. *Individuation, baby.* God help me, either I am wrong to be concerned or I am being gaslit by the world telling me to calm down, keep the faith, or whatever placating bullshit. Have held on so far but not with fucking faith. Have held on with—what is it called when you don't believe it but you do it anyway? Obedience.

I need to breathe. Need to get out. Grab keys, grab wallet. Need pants. Retreat. Unbutton this fucking blouse. Pull on a tee, leggings, sneakers. Pull back my hair. Grab keys, grab wallet, phone. Feel my belly rise as the elevator descends.

The day is still fresh, bright and breezy. Here's Gio. Beautiful day, he says, and in his stiff shoulders, pressed uniform, and blessed haggard face, broad and squashed as one of Cory's troll dolls', I feel the grief of the world.

Walk fast, uphill, past strangers, backed-up traffic, trash. What is there to do I do not know but I cannot do nothing. Can't go back to work, can't go back to life. What can I do but, I guess, try to find her. Would it be crazy. It would be crazy. But I could do it. Correction: only I can do it. I'll just take a little time off. Ian will cover for me, if grudgingly. Family emergency, I'll say—no, family obligation. I'll just be out of pocket for a few days, whatever. Would people understand, what do I care, I'm the boss. I can take off when I want to. No reason necessary. Let them speculate. Handle it, I'll say.

As I loop back toward home a plan's fomenting. When Giovanni's wife Sheila died she left behind a car. I saw it once, before she passed, parked illegally, shiny and pink as a giant child's toy: a Honda Accord, fifteen years old but pristine, the kind of car Barbie might drive if she could age into a grandmother, downsize, and move to Jersey, the poor immortal bombshell. Gio told me Sheila loved it but never drove. He told me it was mine if I ever needed it. Just don't tell your neighbors, he said conspiratorially. If word gets out I'll be lending it out every other weekend.

At the Italian coffee cart I stop and get a paper cup of light roast, milk and sugar, and a clamshell sfogliatella. Coming back I see him in a shaft of morning light, head tilted upward, ancient and beatific in his epaulettes, admiring a roost of pigeons clustered deep in the sill of a window many stories up.

Pastry?

He turns as if from a dream.

I hold up the paper bag and cup: I have a favor to ask, so I thought I'd bribe you.

Come on, he says, reproachful. What's all this.

Still got that cute pink car?

This is how the hunt begins. An hour before an August sunset in Sheila's pastel Honda, whose interior smells of talcum and Jolly

Ranchers. The floor mats are clean as place mats. An air freshener hangs from the rearview like a paper doll's bouquet. My travel mug of Zabar's in the cup holder, phone charging in the cigarette lighter, I breathe in the old lady smells of her. Hi, Sheila. Thank you for driving an automatic.

Gio hands me a rabbit foot key chain through the passenger's-side window. I squeeze his palsied fingers and pull into the street all jerky and ungraceful. I've neglected to check my rearview; a cab swerves past, honking, Doppler portamento. The look on Giovanni's face! Avoid the speeding cyclist, lumbering bus, jay-walking teens. Drive with caution, halting, braking, through these familiar blocks. Relax. I hang my left arm out the window. Feel the warm wind and blaring afternoon. Here's the on-ramp to the West Side Highway. Direction: north. Pace: quick. Accelerate into the blazing end of day, over bridges, up highways, through tolls, and under overpasses, into glowing night. Change lanes. Pass trucks. Radio on: static, music, ads, fervent monotone of prayer. Radio off. Remember how good it feels to drive. Remember another life, a life at once close enough to touch and so far away it feels like somebody else's: fast cars and parties in the woods. Feeling of power. Feeling of freedom. All of life ahead.

Drive and drive and drive and drive. Past gas stations, strip malls and their town-sized parking lots, the raised beds of mulch and sometimes boxwood that separate each big-box store from the next. The landscape recalls Cory. Everything recalls Cory. At eight or ten she developed this weird romance with the suburbs. I tried to talk her out of it but there she was, in the back seat of a rental, forehead against the glass: *Like dollhouses*, she murmured, passing a travesty of new construction, but give my city mouse a break. She'd only ever seen peaked roofs and clapboard, porches, lawns in picture books.

It wasn't just the aesthetic that charmed her, though. She had a real flirtation going with middle-class consumerism. Cory, eleven, accompanying me on a work trip, begging to be taken to the mall, waiting at a register on tiptoe for a gingerbread candle or rhinestone headband, indulging at last in a long-awaited cup of Dippin' Dots. The disappointment on her face when she said, *They don't taste like anything*, poor kid. I tried to explain about quality and craftsmanship, offshore production and cheap labor, ethical consumerism. Gave her a lecture, me and my hypocrisy, in a J.Crew outlet somewhere in Connecticut: When we spend our money we have the opportunity to advocate for certain practices, to support companies that are doing good in the world, et cetera. She clutched a gaudy fascinator to her chest and told me gravely, *Mother, money is meant to be spent*, my capitalist baby, oh— This time, baby girl, I won't just stand and leave the room. This time, I am coming for you.

Drive and drive and drive and drive. Up highways, past swamps and lakes, through mountains, in deep night. Endless road disappears below the car, endless memories circulate within. They appear not as montage but as heaps of unsorted images: Cory at three at the arts-and-crafts table, mouth full of plastic flowers. Infant Cory swaddled and asleep on a couch cushion. Cory at seven, in tears on Halloween, a Tootsie Pop stuck in her Pippi braids. Newly vegetarian Cory at fourteen, scowling in eyeliner at a plate of coq au vin. Cory at the shoe store, ten, begging for a pair of glitter jellies. Cory behind her bedroom door shouting, Stupid, stupid, stupid, stupid, after she is mocked at school. Cory at sixteen, first day of spring, walking off without a kiss. Cory at two, rosy with flu, hair damp with perspiration, big eyes shining. *Will I die?* she asked me, and I tried to hide my eyes. No, I told her, not for a very very very very very very very long time, and silently I added, *Please*, to make it a prayer, to quell the debilitating fear I've carried since those earliest days, when she was just six pounds of warmth and hunger, sleeping nerve-rackingly still in a bassinet next to the bed. My fear has always been a precondition of her life.

VII

But No One Heard Her Voice, Nor Yet the Olive-Trees

Cory. Hey, Queenie. Highness? Rise and shine.

Waking in the shed is like having been killed in a video game and being forced to restart from the top. She has the feeling that she, that time, that this very world she must navigate, has reset. The light is early and still pure, having not yet soaked up the sins of the day. She hears Rolo's voice and the voices of the children. She feels a wave of dread.

Yeah, she says, disentangling from a veil of sleep.

Muffled, melodic: I have a surprise for you.

She nearly falls out of the lofted bed, changes quickly, and opens the door to see Rolo and the kids heading back to the big house. The heady fog of last night's cocktails lingers in her mind and body, leaving her floaty and unbalanced. She drifts up the stairs on the wafting smell of coffee like a Saturday morning cartoon.

The family is in a sunny mood. An attractive spread is laid out on the kitchen island: bagels and schmear, fat caviar, a pitcher of juice, a cut glass bowl of tangerines. Cory joins the kids on barstools at the kitchen island. Spenser is in his Brat Mitzvah shirt and Fern is in pajamas, cats and rainbows. Rolo is in a suit and reflective black dress shoes, humming to himself, peering into the refrigerator.

We seem to have run out of eggs, he says, his back to them. They watch him.

Huh, he says, and turns to them with mischief in his eyes: Yes, we are totally, one hundred percent out of eggs.

In there, says Fern, pointing at the fridge. Cory reaches for a bagel and the cream cheese knife. Spenser has gotten his hands on a Sharpie and is drawing faces on the tangerines. There's eggs right there, says Spenser without looking up.

Cory sees it, too, clear as sunup: a brown paper carton.

Rolo closes the fridge. Nope, he says. No eggs.

This rouses Spenser. There *are*.

Didn't see any.

Both children are enjoyably outraged now. What? they yell. Open the door! We saw them! Open the fridge, Daddy! The eggs are *right behind you.*

You're telling me if I open this door I will see an egg just sitting there? This door? Right here?

Doubt creeps in. The kids hesitate, suddenly unsure.

Yes, Cory says.

He opens the refrigerator door, but from the other side, this time, and to her astonishment the interior of the fridge looks entirely different: shallower and empty, save for a few bottles of sparkling wine, a jar of mustard, and an egg-shaped object the size of a football that is suddenly being chucked in her direction.

Think fast! he shouts, and Cory drops her bagel facedown on the floor to catch the thing, which slips out of her grasp. She picks it up. It is light as air and its vinyl exterior is refrigerator-chilly. On the bottom is a plastic valve.

Spenser nearly falls off his chair with laughter. There was an egg in there, all right! he says, corny with amusement. That's one *big egg*!

Cory gives eager Fern the inflatable toy. The three pharaoh hounds congregate around the fallen bagel.

Come on! Rolo says. There is no time to lose! There are a dozen eggs hidden all over the island, and only *you* can find them.

Cory helps the kids down from their stools to follow him out to the patio.

Go on, he says, get cracking! So to speak! The island is your oyster!

Is this one of the dozen? Spenser asks. Is it a baker's dozen, or twelve?

A good question, egghead! That's for you to find out!

Where are they? says Fern, hugging the inflatable.

Who knows, Tinker Bell. May be a hard egg to crack! Rolo winks at Cory.

Give us a hint, Spenser demands.

No hints! Just hunt!

I thought with a scavenger hunt— Cory says.

But Rolo is walking fast in the mist toward the helipad, where Virgil stands waiting as the giant vehicle's rotor begins to whirr and thrum.

A scavenger hunt is different! he yells as he goes. Hints and clues and whatnot! We're talking a degree of sophistication your average Easter egg hunt cannot claim! The egg hunt is pure! No games, no rules. Just twelve hidden eggs and three hunter-gatherers.

In the gusts from the blades above him the egg slips from Fern's grasp and blows across the lawn. Spenser chases it into a hedge. Rolo is waving a hand in the air as he walks into the wind, unflinching. Use your instincts! he yells over the noise of the machine. Virgil hands him a pair of ear protectors and he yells something in Virgil's ear. Looking at Cory, Virgil nods, and paranoia bucks in Cory's belly. Rolo puts on the headset and climbs in.

Daddy, says Fern, holding out her hands.

See you in a couple days!

And Rolo retreats into the helicopter, whose violent pulses send minute debris whirling, as it rises with a ruckus into the overcast sky.

Fern collapses like a dropped puppet. Daddy, she mourns.

Having retrieved the inflatable egg, Spenser offers it to his sister. She sits on the dewy grass in her pajamas, resting her face against it, letting the side of her warm cheek adhere to the vinyl, then removing it slowly, feeling the way it comes unstuck, watching the helicopter fly off.

Cory scoops up Fern, puddle-eyed and light as air, and throws her over one shoulder. The child lets out a belly laugh as Cory walks with long swooping strides like a Seussian pack animal, dipping low, rising up, bending from side to side with each step, so that Fern's upside-down hair brushes the backs of Cory's legs. Spenser runs after them, joining in the hilarity. All right! Cory says, turning this way and that, flinging the child behind her. If you were an egg, where would you be?

They spend the morning indoors, as is their custom, but hunting. Behind toilets and under chairs, in cabinets, beneath ottomans, and between couch cushions, in closets, barrister cases, and cedar chests, behind open doors and under the lips of carpets. She suppresses the guilt she feels at the trail of chaos they leave in their wake for Angela and the other housekeeper to tidy—books removed from bookcases, curios toppled onto the floor, the contents of a medicine cabinet scattered all over the bathroom. She hates to leave a mess behind, but it is all right, she tells herself, this is work, too, this manic rummaging is part of the job. In a steel toolbox left suggestively open at the door to the basement stairs, they find a bejeweled egg, its shell squiggled with filigree. The kids fight over it until Cory suggests making a nest for their prizes. So they get to work weaving blankets and scarves into a big droopy bowl in an armchair, leave the inflatable there alongside the quasi-Fabergé, and keep hunting. Under the lid of the record player they find a Hanes L'eggs pod and yell wildly; in the bowl of a spoon in a silverware drawer, an ovoid foam makeup sponge. In the temperature-controlled wine cellar, nestled between merlots, they spy through a pastry box's cellophane window an oversized chocolate egg with white chocolate inlay. It takes all Cory's willpower to resist devouring it with them on the spot.

Fortunately, by then it is lunchtime: tomato soup, grilled cheese, and deviled eggs: a joke. Fern soaks her PJs in soup, so they take a break for a birdbath before coaxing Spenser outside to resume their search. They pry open the door of a rarely used storage shed. They leave pool floats strewn over the lawn. They crawl under the umbrella of a weeping willow and scramble into the nooks of climbable trees and root around in the mulch near the tomatoes that hang like wet kisses in the kitchen garden. When Cory lifts Fern to peer over the lip of a dry fountain, they find a plush speckled egg the size of a softball with a bulbous stuffed dinosaur inside. Under the steps of the gazebo Spenser finds a velveteen box containing a smooth, fist-shaped egg of lapis lazuli. In a tackle box in the sailboat they uncover an egg-shaped paperweight enclosing the fetus of a real baby chick, bedraggled and inert.

Who did all this? she wonders aloud, but they don't seem to register the question. Did your dad just have these things lying around? To her, a middle-class kid in cheap clothes, the Easter egg hunt seems like a beautiful dream, but these two seem to take it for granted. They are used to magic, she gathers, to strange and extravagant surprises, but as far as she can see, they haven't been spoiled by it. In fact, because of their flickering attention to and carelessness with their treasures, because of the way their father comes and goes, rising into the air like a wizard—*People come and go so quickly here*—these kids must be used, too, to gifts melting away, quickly and inevitably as ice.

They take the long way down to the shore through the woods, descending the slope sideways, half surfing rubble and shale, avoiding rocks, plants, and stumps, letting gravity be their driving horse. Daylight glows in the white cloud around them and they seem to glow, too, pink with exertion, hair tangled, knees filthy, mouths hanging open, wet and happy as pups. The only sounds, here at the back of the island, are the rhythmic crashing of waves, buzz of insects, slow wicked laughter of gulls, and susurrus of wind in the trees, which grow right up to the water's edge, long black logs falling in and decomposing, reclaimed by weeds and creepers. Seasons-old leaves among the seaweed make a limp salad along the shore. An old beach chair lies in the rot like a picked-over skeleton, bits of woven fabric unraveling from bolts in its metal frame as muscle from bone. They heave over an ancient rowboat in the growth to find underneath only a clew of earthworms, but the kids soon forget the egg hunt in favor of splashing, no regard for their clothes. In the white fog, water drops seem to hover like crystals. Cory wades into the shallows and sloshes, making herself big and ogreish: I'm gonna get you! The children scream with laughter. I'mmmm gonna get you!

But the membrane between fun and danger is flimsy and easily torn. Eventually—inevitably—Spenser gets carried away and shoves Fern, who falls hard on her butt into cold water that comes up to her chest. Bruised and shocked, she screams fiercely until Cory lifts her up and holds her close—the wet seeps through both their clothes—and they slop out to turn inland.

But here Cory looks at the dirt and shale and considers. It is not possible to climb back up. The incline is too steep, the terrain too unstable. I guess we'll have to go around the long way, she says. Annoyed, Fern squirms from her arms, falls, and scrambles into the path of a tidal stream. Cory takes Spenser's hand and they follow the child's brown legs and wet clinging dress. The overgrowth is thick. Fern slips between trees. They lose track of her. Cory calls: Fern, where'd you go? But it is dark in the tangle of underbrush, her voice strangely muted, and there's something disorienting about the way the meager light shifts in and among the leaves. After a moment, Spenser drops Cory's hand and clambers through a crevice between boulders the size of a doggy door. She exclaims, calls his name, but he doesn't hesitate, and she is too big to follow him. She tries to climb up and around the rock, to get a better view, but halfway around it she loses her bearings. She cannot tell which trees she's already passed and which she has yet to reach. The ground seems uphill in every direction. She can't even hear the ocean to find her way back to shore.

She calls for Spenser, then Fern, then Spenser again. She says, Come on, guys. Kids? Come out. Now! The woods reply with drips and drops and mysterious rustlings. Underfoot, wet leaves squish obscenely. Day-old rain falls into her hair and runs down the sides of her head. The fog is thick as language. It hangs in the air like phrases unspoken, heavy and dense, full of insinuation. *Come out, come out, wherever you are*, she sings, *and see the young lady who fell from a star*. Rustling, sniffling. That's right, she says, come on out! But when the shrubbery parts, she freezes, two yards or less from a raccoon, large as Fern, having halted midwaddle, sitting up, holding something bright and dripping in its furtive little hands, maneuvering dexterously, fixing her with a frank stare. It has gotten hold of one of Spenser's tangerines, god knows how, and is unpeeling it now, before her, shredding the fruit's Sharpie smile and eating the pulp without taking its eyes off her.

When it has finished devouring the fleshy insides, it casts down the rind, falls to all fours, and seems to grin or grimace. It takes a step toward her. She steps backward, loses her balance, puts her hand on a tree trunk, feels slime, gasps, and retracts her hand so suddenly that she slips and falls with a shout. When she looks up from the ground, the animal's gone. She is struck on the shoulder with a pinecone. She scrambles to standing, turns, and turns again, looking into the woods on all sides. Another pinecone hits her square in the back of the head. She hears heavenly laughter and glimpses four dirty feet disappearing.

The relief is dizzying. Oh my *god*! You two! She gives chase, and in just a few steps she is coming out into the familiar landscaped world of the lawn, two grubby children scuttling, shrieking, over the shorn grass ahead of her.

The fog will dissipate. The sun will fall low. The sky's edges will singe with sunset. Blue shadows will fall across the lawn through the rot-addled woods. The ocean will stretch out like Baba Yaga's mirror, concealing under its glass all the death-rich muck underneath, and then, when night falls, turn dark and shimmering as oil. When they wake the next morning the nest of blankets in the armchair will be disassembled and the eggs will all have been thrown out or put away. She will spy the chick in resin days later on a shelf in Rolo's office. The makeup sponge will appear in the medicine cabinet in her basement bathroom. She will find the inflatable egg again the next time they're rooting around for pool toys. The chocolate eggshell will end up in shards, scattered over sundaes.

Meanwhile, while Rolo is gone she will experiment with his fixings for cocktails. She will take the pills he keeps in the amber bottle in his private bathroom—cautiously, infrequently—rarely at first, and only while the children are sleeping. Eventually, in the taffy-pulled time warp of night, she will creep back past the tennis court, through the woods, to the shanty, and open the door to her lover's room to find it empty: twin bed stripped, belongings gone, ocean wind rattling the windowpane like an animal. Weirded out, she will hover there a moment, feeling as if she might have dreamed him, dreamed it all, until she feels someone close by, and turns to see Spider in the folded shadow of the hallway, watching her from under his hoodie.

Looking for Honeybowl?

I guess, yeah.

He was next-boated.

What?

Fired. Sent back to the mainland. Surprised you didn't know.

I had no idea, she'll say.

Yeah. Fucking sucks. He took the Wi-Fi with him.

Rolo returns on a cloudless night. A cool wind gathers the ocean's surface like silk under a full-to-bursting moon. After putting the children to bed she finds him at the living room window, hands clasped behind his back.

Have you ever been sailing at night? he says.

She says, I've never been sailing.

What! He turns toward her. Unacceptable! But when he sees her face his expression changes. You look wary, he says. Are you receiving me warily? Am I picking up on some wariness here?

Uh, she says, and tries for a laugh. Just . . . what if the kids wake up.

He tilts his head, pleased. Look at you. The very picture of responsibility. Not to worry. Virgil will keep an ear out.

He brings her down to the dock, where the sailboat self-soothes, rocking on the restless water. Two champagne flutes and a bottle in an ice bucket mysteriously precede them. If she didn't know better she'd think he was wooing her. But he is unromantic, paternal, even, in his concern: You must wear a lifejacket in the catboat. I saw you splashing around your first night. I know you can't swim.

I can swim, she says.

He retrieves the bulky thing and fits her into it. What, all that flapping and gasping, out at the end of the dock? I was getting ready to fish you out of the water myself. Trying to remember how to give mouth-to-mouth.

She is fidgety with discomfort. The vest, she knows, will look absurd.

Don't be embarrassed, he tells her. New Yorkers can't swim, none of them, not really.

He unlashes the boat from the piling and helps her in. The sail snaps as it rises, sudden violence, and the small boat rocks with drama. A freezing wave splashes up, and he curses as he manipulates the rigging, yells at her to avoid the boom, for god's sake. But then the sail seems to catch, the craft rights, and they are skimming easily over the water, Little Île des Bienheureux shrinking behind them. Relaxing against the mast, he pops the cork and fills the two glasses. He is in a talkative mood, waxing philosophical at the stars, one hand on the tiller, the other holding his flute, but she isn't listening. She is attempting to loosen her anxiety, to let it fly from her into the wind, fizzing, like the bubbles that effervesce even now, incipient sneeze, in the back of her nose. But then he is looking at her, expecting an answer, and she must rewind to understand what he's said:

You, at your age. Surely you have been in love.

No, she says.

Never?

She shakes her head, thinking first of Honeybowl, wondering if she might have fallen for him, if she'd had time, then of Pete, the bard of Coeur Brisé, his hand on hers in the thicket.

Really, Rolo says. I'd have thought. A girl like you.

What's a girl like me?

Never mind, he says. Someday you will fall in love. And then climb out again. And in and out, and out and in, like an ocean diver in and out of the bottomless sea, ears popping, no life vest. And one thing you'll notice is how quickly you will establish various patterns. The world is chaos, Cory, it is pain and trash and death and shit—

Wow.

—and we are meaning-craving creatures, so we find patterns, and where no patterns exist we create them. Our patterns in love are established young. My ex-wife for instance is attracted to larger-than-life, spiritually minded narcissists. Her first lover was her mother's priest. Now she's with a pastor. I was in some ways perhaps a departure from her general pattern, but then again when she met me I was on kind of a Buddhist jag, so, perhaps not.

Are you calling yourself a narcissist? she says.

Nobody's perfect.

He lets out the mainsail until it begins to flap, then brings it in again, taut, full of wind.

Besides, he says, every so-called flaw in another context can be a strength. Only a narcissist for instance would ever try to save the world. When she fell for me I still believed that I alone, my operation and none other, could heal people's pain. I thought we'd made a miracle. A lot of other people thought so, too.

What's your pattern? Cory asks.

Me? In love? He is so large that when he reaches for the bottle the whole boat tips. I like a certain depth of flavor, he muses, like a well-mixed cocktail, of innocence and know-how. An old sinner like myself is looking for absolution, too, I guess. At heart, I'm a romantic, and romance is a kind of optimism, I think. I want to believe love can save me.

The drink, the wind, the slapping of waves, the jangle of stars in the water, all of it emboldens her. That kind of sounds like bullshit, she says.

He laughs, a giant ha-ha-ha from deep in his round belly that bounces away on the water like a skipping stone. Amazing, he says. Thank you. You're absolutely right. Hold out your glass, Queenie, and I'll pour you the last of the Bollinger.

She reaches his way, and he aims the bottle. When the boat rocks, part of the stream is rerouted onto the sea-slick floor.

What I'm trying to say in a roundabout way, he goes on, is lucky you. You're young. Your patterns have not yet calcified, as they have in old fuckers like me. You have a chance to begin your life with your eyes open. To live consciously, awake to yourself and your vagaries of spirit, aversions, and predilections. You don't have to get stuck. You don't have to default. You can start out free and stay that way. That's why I brought you here, Cory, you know. Most people, they go their whole lives craving only contentment, undelayed gratification: the comforts of fictions, falsehoods, and consumption, the dull blank of satiation. But you. You struck me from the moment I saw you as someone born hungry, who's remained curious, and unafraid of the dark. Is this making sense? I didn't bring you here just to babysit, is what I mean. I certainly didn't bring you here so you could get involved with a B-minus like Trevor Honey-Bowles.

The tripartite name between his lips comes as a shock.

You fired him, she says—and the anger in her voice surprises her as much as the realization—because of *me*.

Her employer's face in the moonlight is suddenly unsmiling. That kid was, he says, but halts suddenly, searching for the word. After an agonized moment, he completes the sentence: *tragically mediocre*.

She begins to reply, but in struggling to articulate herself, she reaches the limits of this tipsy boldness.

I'm trying to help you, Cory. Do you get that?

In his voice she hears urgency, maybe a kind of pleading. He seems so unguarded suddenly, so real, a worried dad on a rocking boat—a *dad*, after all, with a daughter of his own, who wants to protect her. And the memory rises again to the surface, as it too often does: her mother's dark eyes, set mouth, and silence, the way she left the room when Cory finally told her why she had lost ten pounds and failed two classes. No complaint ever filed. No one ever called. Her mother simply closed up.

By contrast, here before her, gripping his glass, searching her with his eyes, is someone who will literally fire a boy for fucking her. No matter that her experience with Honeybowl was actually, privately, kind of nice. Queasy—seasick, maybe—and flattered, if fearful, she has the impression that this man wants a more glittering future for her than she's ever wanted for herself, the suspicion that maybe, if she's good, he will escort her to it. She feels at once a kind of gratitude and a kind of power, and the heady rush conspires with the rocking of the sailboat to knock her back against the boom, and the whole boat dips, and as she clambers out of the way, into the prow, he rushes to right it. Cross-legged on the deck, wet-bottomed and bulky in her lifejacket, she watches him maneuver the small craft with grace and strength back to his home.

VIII

Strange Woman, I Went Out Wasting with Yearning

I arrive at River Rock long before the sun. In the parking lot beside the pond, I crack the window and am met by a cacophony of bugs and the relief of organic smells: lake, leaves, dirt. It is so dark here under the country sky. If I look up I can just see the silhouettes of trees swaying. I lower my seat back, try to sleep—

—only to wake with a start from restless semidreams to wind and birdsong. Step out of the car, stiff and itchy, bug-bitten, sour-mouthed, and stretch. The summer mountains and the sky, the air around me, everything, is green, pale blue, and yellow-white. The place is vacant, the office locked. I walk downhill breathing the fresh air, feeling the weak sun on my neck, the dew soaking into my shoes. The door to the Rec Hall is locked, too, but I can see the counselors' photos on a bulletin board. There's my girl, strabismus frog face, second from the left. Daughter of goofing, daughter of grief.

Back uphill, I duck into the barn. Particles of dust float in shafts of morning light. The lost-and-found box is at the end of a downstairs hallway, nestled between two bathrooms whose gendered demarcations have been replaced with hand-painted signs that read simply, ALL. Its contents smell of children: dirt, scalp, feet. Unearthing a stained sweatshirt, several hats, and half a dozen filthy socks, my fingers alight on a strange material. A Birkenstock of poured elastic vinyl, light as Styrofoam and lavender as fog: one of a pair I gave Cory last summer, when she turned seventeen. I trace the imprint of her long foot on its sole. I dig around briefly for the other sandal, but can't find it; landing on a pair of stiffened boxers, I recoil and give up.

The girls' cabins smell of wet wood and hair conditioner. The cots are stripped, the closets empty, not even a crumpled sweatshirt shoved into a corner. I take my tour and step outside again onto the carpeted earth under the pines. Memories of Cory, summers past, sit sullen on the step outside a cabin, sprawl among friends on the sunny hill, play HORSE on the cracked basketball court. Daughter of splendor, daughter of elusion. Swatting at mosquitos with the purple Birk, I return to Sheila's pink car, smooth and incongruous as a Jordan almond in the dappled woods.

Inside, my phone is buzzing with notifications. Pick it up and scroll. Ian. Ian. Gretchen. Jesus. Reflexively, I reach for my coffee: empty, of course. I cannot look at these messages, not now. I need caffeine.

Drive and drive over roots and rocks, a road that curves under dripping trees, past farmland, horses, the earthy stench of cows. Eventually I come to a highway, strip malls, an intersection with a light, familiar chain stores, a diner that looks as if it has seen better days.

A bell rings when I push the door open. Inside it smells of ancient carcinogens. Morning sun falls across Formica tables and illuminates Tiffany replica lamps. At this hour, on a weekday, the patronage is meager. A woman with yellow hair and a face like a Parker House roll nods at me from across the counter. Anywhere you want, she says in a damaged voice.

I take a seat at the counter and she brings me a plastic cup of ice water. Coffee? she asks, and I nod, and she pours it into a too-small mug. I am overwhelmed by the menu, its photographic illustrations of pancakes, topped with square pats of butter and drenched in syrup, stiff, ancient omelets, and sweating shakes.

It's a lot to take in, she says, observing me.

I look up. Could I just have a couple of eggs, I say, and toast?

Scrambled, over, sunny-side, or poached, white, wheat, or rye.

Poached. Rye.

Anything else? OJ?

Is it fresh?

Freshly mixed. She gives me a fraction of a smile.

No, thanks.

The coffee is awful but highly caffeinated. I absorb myself in my phone. It is not yet ten and I have two hundred unread emails, forty-seven unread texts. The sheer quantity afflicts me with paralysis.

You don't look like you're from around here, the waitress says.

I look up to see my eggs in a stainless bowl alongside triangles of buttered toast. I ask, What gave it away?

She laughs, hoarse and wheezy. Your hair. Looks expensive.

Thanks. I laugh. It is.

What brings you to the area?

I'm looking for my daughter.

She squints. Her smile fades. I tell her what I know. At the words *River Rock* she nods, she is familiar. I am encouraged. I say, I haven't heard from her since . . .

But, interrupted by the buzzing of my phone, I trail off midsentence.

When it lights up she glances at it, asks, That her?

The wallpaper photo on the locked screen is a picture of Cory, one of my favorites, now a few years old. Last day of her freshman year I took her out, she ordered cake, the server mistook the occasion for her birthday. She posed because I asked her to—sweet smile, good posture, looking at the camera, waiting to eat—the bright candle in the slice of chocolate velvet illuminating her nose, her chin. Poised and pretty in a floral dress she'd soon outgrow, her cheeks still rounded with childhood, daughter of warmth, daughter of sweetness, daughter of mine—

I say, A couple years ago.

She looks at me for permission, takes the phone and frowns at it, tapping it after a moment to keep the screen from going dark. I spoon an egg onto the toast and press with the fork until the yolk floods through. The food, thank god, puts the coffee here to shame. Toast, real butter, two hot eggs, faint tang of vinegar, mouthwatering dose of salt. Eventually she makes a small noise of recognition and hands the phone back to me. Each of her press-on nails is decorated with a tiny firework.

She says, I can't be sure, but a teenager came in last weekend with a guy and his grandkids, I guess. She was older than the other two and didn't look like them. Tall, pretty. Beautiful, actually. The kind of beautiful you can't look away from. Pink hair.

Pink hair, I say. Not impossible. Who was the guy?

His credit card, it said something on it . . . South . . . bridge?

Southgate, I say—

That's it.

—and then I hear myself utter another word, which stems from the first, organically as a head from a neck: Pharmaceuticals. She's nodding. He gave me a whale of a tip.

The bell on the door rings and a couple shuffles in, silver-haired and stooped. As she goes to help them to a booth I look again at my phone. Ignoring the unread emails and texts I search the phrase: *Southgate Pharmaceuticals.*

The company's figurehead pops up almost immediately. Rolo Picazo: in images he is a substantial man, fleshy, vainly dressed, thick silvering hair tucked behind his ears. The headlines are recent. In an ongoing investigation into his company's role in a national crisis of addiction he is facing indictments of criminal wrongdoing. He has been called to testify in two separate congressional hearings, and is to appear before another panel soon. He is defendant in at least one class action suit. With a little digging into my search results, I can reverse engineer his fall from grace. See: *The Case for Prosecuting Southgate and Other Pharma Operations,* published last month in *Vox.* See: *Southgate Settles Out of Court, But Fresh Charges Loom,* two years ago on NPR. See: a *GQ* profile, twelve years old: *The Bad Boy of Pharmaceuticals Settles Down.* See: a cover story, *Forbes,* several years before that: *The Gatekeeper: The Unprecedented Ascent of Southgate Pharma and the Unconventional Man Behind It.* Notifications keep popping up, work messages all, ignore, ignore. My heart knocks queasily inside of my chest. No man is good, but Rolo Picazo seems deeply bad. His addresses, of course, are all unlisted.

Tell me everything, I say to the waitress when she returns, and, reading the engraved name tag pinned to the tight fabric at her breast, I say her name: Tell me, Mona.

She brings out the cook, a craggy New Englander, and repeats her brief story. The cook says right away he thinks he knows the guy we're discussing. Says his nephew's buddy did some landscaping for him—some off-the-grid mansion, ocean views, hedge maze—the cook isn't totally sure where.

He gave me an outrageous tip, Mona tells me again. The kind of money that makes you wonder if you owe him something.

Meanwhile he stiffed my nephew's friend, the cook says.

No, says Mona.

If it's the same guy, yeah. Lolly did three weeks of work, never got paid.

The percolator bubbles. A griddle spits.

Can you ask Lolly where this guy's house was? I ask.

He frowns at me, reading my face. Sure, he says, I'll text my nephew, and he disappears through the kitchen's saloon-style doors. Mona says she'll fetch the check. We all wait in the tense quiet while she taps at the register. Then the cook reappears, holding his phone and leaning against a swinging door.

He says, Lolly isn't sure, it was a few years ago, he works on a lot of high-end properties, most of them along the coast, he's based in Maine. But he thinks you'd better check Beulah Bluffs, a couple hours east.

Thank you, I say. Thank you. I will.

The cook acknowledges my thanks without a word, recedes again. Mona comes back and, along with the tip tray, lays down a Styrofoam clamshell and a plastic fork. Pie, she says in her sandpaper alto. On the house. The berries are from his garden.

Thank you, I repeat.

An attempt to enter Beulah Bluffs into my maps app fails. A search for it online yields very little information. Here's what I can tell. It is a private community a stone's throw across an ocean inlet from Acadia National Park. The only images are taken by satellite. Information on its residents is purposefully scarce. Public records note home purchases only by various LLCs. An island of tax shelters. I enter Acadia into my GPS and drive and drive. Over and eventually off the speeding highway. Across matte tar and through the fragrant shade of spruce and pine. Around sharp curves and past brief views of blinding ocean. Into the intricate maze of back roads that falls over the coastline like lace, the box of pie on the passenger's seat beside me.

The road to Beulah Bluffs is like the path from Looking-Glass House through the garden of talking flowers: somehow it keeps looping me back to where I began. It is afternoon by the time I arrive at what seems to be the correct bridge. It extends from a cliff-side promontory perhaps a hundred feet above the ocean, high on the eastern edge of the continent, open to pedestrians on both sides but closed to traffic with a heavy iron gate. Gulls circle a lighthouse. Waves crash against gray rocks. A white-haired guard reads a newspaper in a booth made to look like a tiny house: peaked roof, clapboard walls, small window left open to frame his lipless frown. I roll down my own window, and the wind gusts in.

Is this Beulah Bluffs?

I am used, in situations like these, to coming off as an authority, but, reading his skepticism, I surmise these eighteen hours in a midrange sedan have left me rumpled and suspicious.

I'm here to see Rolo Picazo, I tell him.

Puh-kahtz-o. Don't know anyone by that name.

The salt air blows. I push back a loosened hair. Mind if I just drive around?

Can't let you do that, he says. You can park over there and walk, though. Island's open to pedestrians. Up the bridge and around the promontory's not a bad hike. But there's no one here by the name Puh-katz-o.

He seems honest, but I have no other leads. I have to try. Leaving Sheila's Honda at the side of the road in a spot of mottled shade, I cross the walkway that stretches over the water, narrow and improbable. Only a low wall of crisscrossed steel separates me from the beating sky and restless sea. Looking down I can see the waves foaming, embracing, licking the rocks. Walking across the gap I am suspended in the crash and sparkle of the desperate afternoon.

On the other side: sounds of surf, of wind in trees, rude calls of gulls, sweet calls of songbirds. A path is worn into the earth beside the road. A tall boxwood hedge, squared off and fragrant, conceals a property beyond. Now and then, tended shrubs part to reveal a house of showstopping extravagance. A white clapboard leviathan seems buoyed upon its mown expanse, Palladian glass eyes blinded by sun. A shingled mansion hulks among its hedging, all peaked roofs and darkened porches. An incongruous Federal brick box nests in a bed of roses.

Then, around a bend, snakes a single-story stone construction, like a creature formed of, then half escaped from, the cliff-side bedrock. Gusts of sea wind riffle a birdbath. On a gravel path a seagull poses, staring down the sun. One groundskeeper kneels by the edge of a crushed shell driveway, tending to a bed of lavender and lupines, while another trims the leafy exterior wall of a hedge maze. Recall the phrase *hedge maze*, the diner cook, his nephew's friend. My hand lifts to my abdomen: Cory. Passing through the trees, approaching the stone serpent on the hill, I imagine she's been calling for me from behind those concrete walls. She's here, she's here! And, oh, she needs me—

There is no gate around the property, but when I step onto the lawn I understand my presence has set off some kind of alarm.

A golf cart rolls over the hill, empty of golf paraphernalia. The groundskeepers turn to look as it slows and loops around to keep pace with me. The man at the wheel cranes his neck to take me in.

Lost? he says. I hurry toward the house. His arms are tanned, sun-spotted, and sprouting fine bleached hair.

I tell him I am looking for my daughter. Tell him she is five eleven, gawky-thin, and the kind of beautiful that breaks your heart. Tell him I must speak to the man who lives here. He laughs without friendliness. Insist: I must speak to Rolo Picazo.

Rolo Picazo, Rolo Picazo: the name becomes a chant, and he chants back, You've got the wrong place, and the more he denies me the more convinced I become that he is hiding her. At the entrance to the house I ring the doorbell, knock and knock, try the handle, knock again. I become aware that the man in the golf cart is talking on the phone, that the groundskeepers have followed us, and one has raised his phone in our direction like a warning—is he recording? When the door opens I try to enter, but my way is blocked by another man, younger, bigger, stronger, dressed in black. He closes the door behind him, grasps my arm with one strong hand, and directs my body with the other. Thanks, Phil, says the golf cart. I say, Let me in— but the lug has my arm and is escorting me to a black car. His hand is tight, will bruise. Ma'am, he's saying, you got the wrong house.

Resist. Explain. Attempt to break free. Tell him she is only just eighteen, still a child in many ways, still needs me. Tell him: I will not be handled. I must speak to Rolo Picazo! Ro. Lo. Pic. Ah. Zo. I'll call my lawyer. Say: I'm not some vagrant, Phil. You don't know who I am. I'm Emer Ansel—

Emer Ansel, Emer Ansel, little Emer Ansel. Her stepfather was a monster and her mother was a gray stone wall. She enclosed him, neat, so that no one but us could see the beast. Emer was

185

the baby he threw into the air. Emer was the animal he chased up the stairs. Sought refuge in the bedroom closet where she cowered in the dark. He roared outside the particleboard—*I'm gonna eatchoo*—all in good fun.

One man presses my head down to force me into the car and gets in to drive. The other restrains me in the back seat as I fight to open the door. Then we are heading toward the writhing road, and I am yelling, and then—

A woman, maybe sixty, gorgeously fit, in headphones and designer Spandex, is running on the side of the road, white ponytail swinging. As she comes toward the car my abductors raise their hands to her in greeting, and she stares at me with a frown of incipient recognition, and quickly, instinctively, I turn away, for I know her, too—Kahn? Kohn? It will come to me—her wife, years ago, was briefly on the board of RHEA Seeds—and as she opens the door to, presumably, her summer house, my head drops with despair.

I was wrong, of course, my god, so wrong. What have I done.

My protest halted, the car is silent save for the two men's breathing. Ahead of us the bridge is suspended in sunlight, gate at the end, to keep out intruders like me. It swings open to let us exit, and there is Sheila's car. The guard named Phil escorts me out of the vehicle, informing me that if I come back, they will call the cops. The black car turns, gleaming, onto the bridge, and I hear the men laughing as the gate closes. How the fuck did I think I would find Cory so easily. How the fuck will I go on.

Inside the pink Honda is stiflingly hot and smells of dough and boiled berries. Taking in at last the state of myself I notice I smell like body odor and am trembling with hunger. My face is wet with sweat and perhaps tears. Start the engine—hot air blows hard from the vents—and reach for the Styrofoam box. Inside, the pie is melted, a limp triangle of dough half sunk in a purple ooze of sugar-jelly. Utensil-less, I eat it with my hands.

A knock on the window startles me midbite, mouth full and fingers smeary. I roll down the window. The gatekeeper leans down to face me through the gap in the glass. Ma'am, he says, and takes me in.

The pie is sweet and viscous. I swallow hard.

You can't stay here. You know that, right? He glances at my things in the back seat. There's a few hotels up the road a couple of miles north, he says. A Red Roof Inn, a Motel 6. The old Starlight; that one's worth a visit, if you have the cash.

I need to find my daughter, I tell him.

He nods, squints into the sun, says, Everyone needs a little rest, now and then.

Do I rest, though. Can I rest. How could I rest. I am mad with motherhood.

In a Friendly's parking lot just off Route One I set up a phone alert for news of Rolo Picazo. I needn't. The bastard is all over the news. He is issuing statements. He is claiming zero personal responsibility, the coward. He is hiding behind his colleagues and peons at Southgate Pharma, the wretch. He is appearing at a congressional hearing just days from now, what do you know, and I, mad mother, I am following him.

Except that when I arrive in DC, rumpled and bleary eleven hours later, I have tremendous difficulty locating him. These are closed hearings. Not even a press pass would get me in. No high-end hotel is at liberty to disclose its guests, so instead I ask around. At the Willard I overhear a lawyer talking on his phone about the trial, and I park myself under a blue umbrella at an outdoor table, watching the hotel door, until I am convinced he is not there. At the Conrad a bartender tells me a man who matches my description has recently checked in, and I haunt the lobby until I'm asked to leave. Outside the Four Seasons I wait among a clot of paparazzi for over an hour, convinced they must be there for him, only to catch a glimpse of the softball-sized sunglasses and false hair of a celebrity I am too old to know. When my phone buzzes with an alert—a photo: *Rolo Picazo Leaving Hilaria Maxwell's Annual Cancer Research Fundraising Luncheon, Bridgehampton*—I drive all night to Long Island just to lurk outside the private airports. I flag down every driver of a luxury black car. Rolo Picazo, I say. Rolo Picazo. They roll their windows up. They drive on in. He is everywhere and he is nowhere.

When Cory was a little girl she used to bait me into telling stories by pretending she'd forgotten them. *Mama, how does it go, the one with the girl and the storm and the beast? Mama, how does it go, the one about the girl in the tower with the long, long hair?* I tried to get her into tales of swashbuckling heroines—*Why don't I tell you about the wild swans, and the princess who saved her brothers from a curse cast by an evil queen?*—but to my dismay she always loved best the girls in peril: the imprisoned and the orphaned, the captive and enslaved. Because her pretense of forgetting was a game, it was impossible not to play along.

If our relationship can be characterized in any one way, it is this: I can't keep up with her. An early walker and late talker, she ran fast, fell often, threw tantrums when she could not make herself understood. In elementary school she seemed both genius and vacant, magic almost, full of brilliant irrelevance. When she was a preteen, dangerous moods began to overtake her. As a teen she learned how to lie, to brush me off, affect false dignity, conceal her pain or shame, to disappear. To shrug on whatever persona suited her, moment to moment, leaving her discarded selves, along with all her clothes, in rumpled piles on the floor. Eighteen years I've spent pursuing this maddening girl, but like a creature in a fairy tale she's metamorphosed even as I've taken aim. The deer shrinks and rises, flapping, soaring: a seabird. The seabird dives into the ocean, swims away: a fish. Well, let my bow and arrow become a harpoon, then. Let my harpoon become a net. Let me, her mother, be the hunter who saves her from herself.

At a second-rate chain hotel outside New Haven, the gender-indeterminate front desk kid barely looks at me, typing my information into the outdated PC. Beneath their thin green hair, long lashes half conceal their pretty eyes.

You remind me of my daughter, I say, perhaps too warmly.

They acknowledge this with a minute lift of the eyebrow.

She's the best, I say.

They hand me a key card with an ironic, corporate-issued smile: Enjoy your stay.

Shower, scrubbing hard. Lie on the bed in a bleach-stiffened towel. Finding the remote, I turn on the television and am met with *SVU*. Mariska Hargitay and company discuss a victim's wounds. No. Scan to a commercial: two parents and two beaming children enjoy a precooked meal. No. Girl-child plays with Barbies. No. A prestige show whose premise involves a girl found dead in a river. No. No. Turn it off. How many gone-girl stories have I consumed over the years. How could I have given no real thought to any of them until one of those girls was mine.

*　　　*　　　*

I wake with a sharp intake of breath upon the polyester coverlet. Past the slatted blinds, morning, pale and blue, illuminates the fast-food joints and parking lot. Rise. Dress. Locate key card, glasses, wallet. Enter the world. Surely this place puts out some kind of subpar continental breakfast.

In the lobby several plastic bistro tables are arranged in a half-assed implication of a restaurant. On a TV mounted above the concierge a newscaster drones on in flairless cadence. Laid out on the sideboard: boxed cereal, five green bananas, a plate of pastries drizzled in a glaze of diabetic sweat. Danishes—though god knows any self-respecting Dane— A box of Raisin Bran, then, in a paper bowl. A paper cup of coffee.

Did someone just say my name?

I rotate in the empty lobby. Is this an auditory hallucination? Am I cracking up? The concierge is absorbed in his computer. On the TV, images of children are broadcast one by one, emaciated participants in the world's saddest parade. The news story seems to be about the hunger epidemic. What do you know: my wheelhouse. Watch, a moment. Wait. I have seen these images before. Wait, wait. I have *used* these images before. In presentations to the board, fund-raisers, media decks. These are *our* images. RHEA Seeds holds copyright. That kid in the doorway, distended belly, that photo was shot in fact by what's-his-name, the long-haired prick, refused to do the job as an in-kind, even with all expenses paid, though the pictures did come out great, by any standard—look at them—who wouldn't want to buy that poor child a sandwich. Meanwhile, these dented Danishes, the waste, enraging—wait—

What did she just say—? *Hunger is a silent killer.* That melodramatic phrase, that one's all Gretchen. *In a time of unprecedented first-world prosperity, global food shortages in the third world have reached pandemic levels:* better. Less poetic, more alarming. Mine. So, what, did Gretchen land this spot at last? Morning news on a weekday: not ideal. Certainly *I* did not give the go-ahead. What network is this, anyway, not a local station, is it. Should write to Gretch— Hang on. What's this: another sort of body. White woman, aging but stately, red lips, red carpet, fuck—is that *me*—? Well, fuck. That *is* my name they're saying. *Emer Ansel. The New York socialite—as if!—and face of global nonprofit RHEA Seeds has gone AWOL. This at a pivotal moment when, sources say, the blight-resistant rice she has long claimed will solve the hunger crisis just. Isn't. Growing. The executive director of the high-profile organization disappeared just days after visiting the farms in China where her so-called* magic rice *was meant to grow.*

And there, onscreen—how the *fuck*?—our own disgruntled farmer. What enterprising journalist could possibly have found—? An overdubbed American voice recites his frustrations: *They told us that we could have a significant percentage of the rice ourselves. For me and my family that was a not insubstantial factor. But the rice does not grow. If we do not harvest we make only a fraction of the promised income. What do we eat. How do we live. It is worse than an embarrassment. It is our livelihood, our lives.*

Cut to the newscaster, blinking her false eyelashes regretfully: *More than a hundred farms signed the contract to grow RHEA Seeds's proprietary strain of rice. Of those, only* two *have managed to attain harvest. So how did a disaster of such monumental proportions come to pass? Sources say the org's executive director, Emer Ansel, may have a history of mental illness, pointing to an episode of postpartum psychosis after the birth of her daughter. Ansel has been missing for over a week.*

But a video we have obtained through an anonymous source seems to show her in an altercation with security at a private residence—on the coast of Maine? Let's take a look.

A shaky, vertically oriented video appears onscreen. This time I recognize immediately my own flat ass, my bony legs. The audio is blustery, my voice half drowned by the low frequency of wind against mic—*Ro . . . Pic—! —lo Pic— speak to—* And then she, I, implores, imperious, pathetic: *. . . not some vagrant . . . Emer Ansel—* And bulky Phil presses on my head to get me into the car, and then the newscaster reappears, silken hair shining, shuffling her notes, already onto the next item of the morning:

This is a developing story. We'll keep you in the know. And with a swirl of animated graphic, the broadcast cuts to commercial.

Paper cup and bowl have fallen from my hands. Mental illness. *Psychosis!* Milk and coffee are absorbed into the ugly rug. Raisin Bran wilts at my feet. Look, warily, heart pounding, at the concierge—did he happen to see—no. Thank god. And *sources say.* What sources, who on Earth . . . who on fucking Earth—

Ian.

On my phone, hundreds of unread messages—email, text, and otherwise. Scrolling, I look, finally, at the thirty-character preview of each desperate note. *The scientists, they need more time. The deal with China is falling through. The scientists, they need more money. The deal has fallen through. We are back to the drawing board. The fate of the org hangs in the balance, and the fate of this failing planet's hungry millions, no pressure. Emer, where the hell are you. We're concerned. I'm concerned, professionally and personally. Don't know what you expected, disappearing like this.*

A single ring and there is Ian's voice, deceptively warm: *There she is.*

You threw me under the bus.

We tried to involve you.

Not even a bus. A fucking semi—

You've always said stop at nothing. You've always said play dirty if we have to.

How dare you use my own words against me.

Today's media cycle is about five minutes long. It will be old news by lunchtime.

Postpartum *psychosis*?

You were gone for a year.

It was four months!

You were institutionalized.

I went to a *goddamn spa*.

It's a precedent.

What the fuck do you know about any of it, anyway? It was eighteen years ago. You were an *intern*. You'll never work again.

Are you threatening me?

I'll never work again . . .

You've had one foot out the door for years.

You fucked me.

Wait, I'm sorry. Are you embarrassed?

Embarrassed? I'm *livid*.

Because, in my opinion, in this case, Emer, embarrassment would be appropriate. You have been the face of this organization for twenty-five years, rubbing elbows with celebrities, hobnobbing with senators, spouting, I think we can both agree, some pretty ethically dubious shit—and, yes, raising funds, fine, but, let's be serious, spending nearly as much as you've been raising—

Oh *please*. I have expenses. I've had a daughter to raise—

And, sure, that's all been, what, that's all been status quo. I *like* you, Emer. You've been good to me, professionally and personally. Honestly? You're iconic. But have you ever once stopped to interrogate our project, here? Have you ever even stopped to acknowledge your whole *performance*, your *costume*—

My *costume*.

You've gotten so comfortable you forgot you've been running around dressed head to toe in white savior drag.

Wow, Ian.

And, now. Just recently. When shit hit the fan. Where did you go? When the *magic rice* you have been peddling for a decade did not grow. Where did you go?

My daughter disappeared.

Your *adult daughter* got a *job*. And, news flash, you lost one.

What?

Ian's breath, digitized, translates into static. Emer, he says, the board has passed a motion of no confidence. They've already launched a private search for a new ED. They all agree there's no choice here but to rebuild the org from the ground up. I tried to tell you. I *did* tell you. I emailed, texted, called.

I've devoted my life to this project.

You lost faith in RHEA years ago.

And *you* still believe in it?

Listen to him breathing. I've known him his whole adult life, this boy. Since he was twenty-two and thin and starry-eyed and still a smoker.

I believe it has potential, he says at last, and his voice is the voice of a middle-aged man. Complacent, used to compromise. New leadership will help, I think, he says. And scaling back. Focusing on what's really achievable. Maybe working more locally. Starting in our own backyard. For what it's worth, the senator agrees.

Yeah, I say. You know what, maybe start with the bum outside the deli. Maybe give *him* some fucking seedlings. Maybe start a fucking rooftop garden at a public school.

You know what, those aren't such bad ideas.
Oh, grow up, Ian. The world is beyond saving.
Goodbye, Emer. I hope you find her.

In the hotel bathroom I find an electric razor with beard-trimming attachments. Pushing my hair back flat against my head, I look unflinchingly at my own unmade-up face. Skin: the texture of dead leaves. Hair: coarse and gray. My roots are growing in, a quarter-inch stripe at the scalp, chasing back the treated auburn. Don't think. Don't think. Got to stay under the radar. Under the razor. I secure an attachment and plug the trimmer in. It buzzes hard against my head. Yank hair tight. Drag the droning thing across. Snakes of hair fall upon the tile, leaving behind a shorn, ash-colored lawn. Buzz buzz. The vibration, hard and mean against my skull, shakes loose tears. Don't think. Ignore the swell of throat, the sting of eyes, the bits of hair in my lashes. Buzz buzz. Squint. Finish the job half blind. Grip, drag, repeat. Sharp hairs under my collar, on the nape of my neck, stuck to my chest. Grip, drag, repeat. Pull shirt over head. Step out of pants. Buzz buzz. Stand naked in the puddle of cloth and locks, bareheaded animal blurred by tears.

Well, hello, gnome-face. Someone has become quite the crone. What's your name, old lady. Baba Yaga? La Befana? Whose body is this anyway, still long but warped by time, flat from collarbone to breast and hilly at the middle, curved spine shoving one sharp hip inches higher than the other, old pale scar of dog bite on a thigh. Whose pubic hair is this, so gray and sparse, whose thin-lipped scar where they pulled the baby through. No, that one's mine, puckered now like a disapproving mouth, and I said, *Mother, mother,* when they cut through and yanked my Cory out. After all these years it is still tender to the touch, pins and needles where the nerves were sliced, and then my body was two bodies, and they laid the baby on my breast, her eyes squeezed shut, all tiny kitten howls, this living world's raw and only miracle: Cory.

Run the shower. Wash this crumpled skin, this Brillo pad hair. Let the water heat up, hot as hell. Step in and let it scald. This soap smells like nothing found in nature. Rinse. Turn the knob. Step onto the bathmat. Dry with yesterday's towel. Take in my reflection in the mirror, skeletal witch. Not Emer, not I. This woman shops at Trader Joe's, wears Danskos, drives a Subaru, maybe with a bumper sticker or two. A fish with feet drawn around the word EVOLVE. A Democratic candidate for governor. This woman kayaks. Gardens. Composts her coffee grounds. Probably she has a couple of cats. In short, she is nothing like the Emer Ansel I have cultivated all these years. Dry her violently. Dress her quickly. Repack her clothes. Heave up her bag. Wallet, key card, sunglasses, phone—which—

Ah. A new alert.

What do you know. Rolo Picazo has been dining with a state legislator in Portland.

Back to Maine with you, skinny old witch.

IX

And She Yet Beheld Earth and Starry Heaven, and the Strong-Flowing Sea Where Fishes Shoal, and Still Hoped to See Her Mother

Hours pass, becoming days. Days pass, becoming weeks. Time flows on in its usual way, still as ice and quick as current, fading into the background as easily as the rhythm of the waves. Cory's main evidence for its passage is the subtle change she observes in her own body—sunburn darkening to tan, the contours of new musculature emerging, teased out by all the running around, climbing trees, lifting kids—and in the blistering of the island's more sensitive trees into parched reds and waxy yellows. A row of smoke trees has gone cloud-purple at the edge of the lawn. Her brief thing with Honeybowl is no more than a half-remembered dream. Tyler, Taylor, Trivet, Troy? Cory can barely remember his name.

Cricket and her husband, Pastor Paul, are coming to spend the weekend on Little Île des Bienheureux before bringing Fern and Spenser home. Then Cory's work here will be done, and she will go home, too—to what, exactly, she hates to think. Her schoolmates will all have left for Cambridge and New Haven, Providence and Palo Alto. Her nights will be short and lonely, her days long and dull. The idea of staying with her mother in the apartment on 86th Street—her stuffy room and twin bed, their circular arguments, her mother's work spread all over the kitchen table—makes her itchy with restlessness. The idea of her mother at all makes her sick with resentment and guilt. Of course there is the possibility that with all her babysitting cash, she could rent a place of her own. But to think of herself living alone, or even with roommates— stylish twentysomethings, she imagines, with job titles like *content creator* and *social media manager*—makes her lonely and insecure. The option of moving in with Dora and Iris and Garrett Pollack and whoever else is crashing at Château Relaxeau this year, feels worlds away now, faint as fantasy, and anyway she wouldn't know how to reach them. Her phone is no more than a smooth black stone on the ocean floor, its information extinguished by the sea. Without it, these past weeks—and with the increasingly frequent help of Granadone—Cory has been left suspended in a kind of eternal present.

When Spenser spies the helicopter, they have been sitting on the man-made beach, coming up with similes. Cory is still in the shirt she slept in. Hungover this morning, she broke her rule—no drugs during the workday—and took half a Granny a few hours ago. Now she's feeling happy, dreamy, slow.

The sea is like a field of diamonds, she suggests. The sea is like frosted glass.

The sea is a gray rainbow.

Nice, Fern.

The sea is like a big hand petting the shore.

Ooh, Spense, I like.

The sea is a gigantic grave, Spenser shouts, for a bazillion dead crabs and fish and whales!

Fern says, The sea is a secret you can't understand.

Then Spenser's pointing at the sky: Mom! he shouts. Mom! Mom! Mom! Mom!

They run to the helipad. The helicopter blows back their hair. Spenser is breathless, fists clenched, jumping, Fern all but airborne in the thumping wind until the rotor slows. Rolo in his silver aviators comes out with the dogs, which galumph over the landscape and, when Cricket appears in the doorway—long skirt alighting, hair coming loose, metallic sandals flashing—throw themselves at her with slobbery canine love. The kids yell, Mom! and run toward her, and Rolo is drawn toward her, too, as if by magnetism. Cory stands apart, having suddenly gone shy, as Cricket greets her former dogs—Hello, babies!—and, with a smile like daybreak, stretches out two bare arms to hug her children.

Cricket is more than beautiful. Her richly toasted skin exaggerates the brightness of her long, white-blond hair. If her arms and midsection are still thick from pregnancy, her features are delicate: clear eyes, high cheekbones, a tender chin. She is shorter than Cory by nearly a foot, but she is regal. Her children devour her, and she them, gobbling their fingers, burying her nose in Fern's neck, then Spenser's. A beaming pinkish man stands at the top of the stairs behind her, pale infant in noise-protective headphones strapped to his front. The man nods stiffly at Rolo, who nods back, illegible behind his sunglasses.

When the children have been sufficiently squeezed, they move on to greet their new half sibling. Cricket saunters over to Rolo, approaching slowly, playful and theatrical. Rolo kisses his ex-wife on one cheek and then the other, lingering. Cory looks at her feet.

Hey, Ro.

Hello, Bug.

Cricket turns to Cory, takes her in with a cockeyed smile, eyes narrowing: Kelly, right?

This is Cory, Rolo says.

Cory shrugs in a way she means to be comic but is immediately afraid seems dorky. Sorry, she says. Not Kelly!

Cricket smiles at her, holding eye contact a beat too long, and Cory feels as if her whole life story, all her buried insecurities and private anguish, has been unearthed and left to sit exposed upon her stupid face.

All right, Not-Kelly, Cricket says at last, and starts toward the house, calling behind her without looking back: Let's get this party started.

The children scramble after her. The pastor follows. Rolo turns to follow, too.

Do you need me? Cory asks Rolo before he goes back in.

Desperately, he growls, mournful.

It takes her an embarrassing moment to realize he's teasing, and laugh, and say, I'm going to go take a shower, then.

Don't stray too far, he tells her. You're on the clock. Besides, he adds, turning away from her: I want to have a little fun with you tonight.

At worst, it is a threat. At best, she is invited to the party: not just as the help but as a guest again, at last. She showers in the basement bathroom, sudsing, shaving; dries her hair with a hand towel. Wiping the condensation from the mirror, she regards herself. She is tanned and strong, if tired. The skin under her eyes is fragile. Her lips are pale and her hair is ragged, the cotton candy color faded to a stain of salmon, half an inch of dirty blond growing in at the roots, like shadow. She narrows her eyes in the mirror, mimicking the look Cricket gave her on the lawn, mimicking beauty. *Let's get this party started.* She crosses the lawn in a towel, waving tentatively at Virgil, who is directing several others in setting up a long outdoor dining table, decorated with lace cloths and what seems like far too many place settings.

In the hot shed she unearths her mother's scarf from a pile of laundry and ties it around her head to conceal her ugly hair. The only clean thing she's got to wear is a chambray romper, badly creased. She puts it on and tries to smooth the wrinkles, but they are stubborn, so she goes back to the bathroom and stands for a moment in what remains of the steam, alternately pulling at and smoothing the fabric. Cricket is laughing, muffled but melodic, through the ceiling. Rolo is laughing, too. She can hear his low, wicked rumble, and it troubles her, the whole scenario troubles her, the shifting dynamics, the ultraflexibility of her role, Rolo's unclear expectations. There is an ancient bottle of jojoba oil on the side of the tub and she rubs it over her legs in an attempt to soothe her worried mind with vanity.

When she comes back, the living room is bright with sun. She hesitates in the doorway, unsure whether she is welcome. Cricket is on the couch, holding forth, Spenser nestled in the crook of her arm and sucking on a lock of her hair, Fern in her lap, thumb in mouth. The pastor is standing at the window, looking out at the ocean, still wearing the baby, one plump hand cradled in the other at the small of his back. A record is rotating on the record player, something low-key and flirtatious, and Rolo is mixing drinks at the bamboo bar. Cory takes a seat on a chair in the corner.

Cynthia from church comes by a few days a week, Cricket is saying—or Rosemary or Meaghan. They have a whole network, you know, for childcare. It's really something. We've been given so much food I've had to throw some out. I've never been so well taken care of.

Rolo glances at her and she smiles quickly.

By a community, I mean. You should come to church sometime, Ro. I mean it.

Not my thing.

You might like it, says the pastor, turning around.

Cricket says, Everyone would love you.

Pastor Paul smiles in her direction. With his round pink face and shined shoes he looks as if he's here for a job interview.

How did you find Cory? he asks, ostensibly to include her.

I found her, Spenser says.

Technically that's true, Rolo says.

Well done, babe, says Cricket. Her breezy tone, her beauty; the way her white-blond hair falls over her brown shoulder; the way she inculcates her seven-year-old son in the ways of power, of dominance; it is all hypnotic. Feeling Cory staring at her, Cricket narrows her eyes again, half playfully, half daring, and Cory, blushing, hugs one shaved and oiled leg to her chest, letting the other fall open from the seat of the chair. Cricket looks away but Rolo notes the gesture and seems to nod—does she imagine it?—with appreciation. He licks his lips as he turns away, rattling the ice shaker: Want a drink, Queenie?

He has given her many drinks, but she finds herself surprised that he'd offer her one in front of other adults—surprised enough that when she attempts to accept, she inhales her spit or something, and the words get lodged in her throat, and she starts to cough, not hard but persistently. Cricket and Paul turn their eyes away politely to watch Rolo drain the shaker into four coupes, hazy with frost. When Cory has recovered she feels the need to say something, to make conversation, to show them she's in the know. Trying for a low-key, chatty tone—and yearning, too, for another dose of the drug that by now is wearing off—she asks:

You making Fruit of the Deads?

But the question seems to backfire, setting off an inaudible chain of alarms. The pastor tenses and looks at Cricket with concern. Cricket widens her eyes at Rolo. Rolo glances at Cory, quick and mean. A wave of nauseated recognition rises up in her—she's gone and done it, said the absolute wrong thing, so lame—and wildly she attempts to save herself:

Kidding!

At this, Rolo bursts into jolly laughter. *This* fucking girl.

The other two join in, relieved.

Dad, say the children in shrill duet.

Pastor Paul quips: No wonder she's good with the kids. You've been drugging the babysitter.

Cricket says, I know I'd do better with them some days if I could take the edge off.

Smiling, shaking his head, Rolo walks the tumblers across the room. Fruit of the Dead, he repeats, chuckling, and when he hands a drink to Cory his voice is warm but his eyes are cold: Sorry, kiddo. Just your garden-variety Sazeracs here. Cricket's favorite.

Cricket says, I like a drink that's all booze, no booze mitigation.

The afternoon winds on. Another round is mixed and drunk, then another. Stories are told and laughed about. Conversation is mostly easy. If moments of complication arise between them, to her they are aloof but charitable. Eventually Spenser nods off, more contented in his mother's arms than Cory's ever seen him. Fern, bored, gets up to tug Cory toward the sliding glass door that separates the living room from the grass and, beyond it, the sea and sky.

The kids like you, Cricket observes, and is there a hint of sadness in her tone. Cory sits on the floor in the doorway, the sun hot on her bare legs, while Fern makes a game of roaming the windless lawn, collecting the coin-sized purple leaves that have

blown off the smoke trees and arranging them in a kind of man-
dala on the floor. Nobody says close the door, you're letting out all
the air-conditioning. Nobody says put on sunscreen, you'll burn.
Nobody says stay outside, Fern, you're tracking in dirt. Nobody
cares here about carbon emissions or electricity costs, skin cancer
or mess. Rolo's is a world devoted foremost to pleasure, and it feels
right to Cory that she should be here, where inside meets outside,
neither child nor adult, both caretaker and, sort of, almost, part
of the family, the glue between generations, the
imagines, to two younger kids, with a pretty, cool
fathers—one conservative, measured, and dorky; the other fun,
dangerous, and touched, slightly, by madness—*two* fathers, can
you imagine.

When the windless day begins to turn a corner into suffoca-
tion, Spenser wakes and whines. Cricket stands, stretches, and
yawns loudly. Three dog tails thump the hardwood. I could use a
dip, she says.

Joyful clamor. The children run upstairs to change into their
swimsuits. Never, not once since Cory's employ, have these kids
been excited to swim.

Take an hour, Cricket says to Cory. We've got this.

The pastor rises, and he and Cricket follow the kids. Cory stays
in the track of the sliding door, drowsy with drink, eyes closed
against the light. Then she feels something cold and wet against
her forehead and opens her eyes to find Rolo, hovering with a
refill. Smiling, she takes it, and watches him cross the threshold
and lower his bulk down onto the grass several feet from her. He
closes his eyes and balances his own fresh glass on his sternum,
where the condensation begins to seep into and darken the fabric
of his shirt, whose hem has ridden up to expose an inch of hairy
flesh where belt meets belly. Ordinarily the sight might repel her,

but in this moment it attracts. What is his girth but the embodiment of his love for consumption; what is his flesh but mortality. And perhaps he feels her watching, for, without opening his eyes, he reaches out and pats the ground beside him. She comes and lies down, too, balancing her own glass in the grass. Presently the family tumbles through the back door onto the lawn and down to the pool, followed by the dogs, panting with joy, Cricket's laugh bouncing away behind them.

I think I have a crush on your ex-wife. Cory looks up at the sky, which has gone pale with heat. She feels pleasantly heavy. Down at the pool the dogs are barking, the family shouting, splashing. An insect nearby saws a song.

Welcome to the club, says Rolo. Me, I achieved platinum VIP status before being demoted to a basic gold card. But, as a new member, you will still be able to enjoy, for instance, sporadic words of affirmation—better than consistent ones, of course, because in between they leave time for you to build up a craving for more—and a few good looks at the most beautiful woman alive. Clothed, of course. Only platinum VIP members get to see her naked.

And there can only be one platinum VIP member at a time, Cory says.

He yawns. His eyes are closed. Not necessarily.

She looks through the grass at his great dark head resting beside her. What would it be like to kiss those dry lips of his, she thinks, imagining their crinkly, caramelized surface giving way to his tongue, his teeth. He opens his eyes and lets his head fall toward her. She wants him to reach over and grab her, to pounce on her, and for a moment, gazing back at her, smiling with only his eyes, he looks as if he might. But then he resettles his head and closes his eyes again. Nearby, a gull hugs the wind with both wings, settles down on the lawn, and turns its face to the sea.

So, Rolo says. What are you going to wear to the party tonight? The *party*.

I wouldn't have Cricket visit without throwing her a party.

Cory gets up on one elbow and looks down at him. He squints at her, half shielding his gaze with one hand. I don't really have anything nice, she says.

There will be people here, Rolo says, people on whom you might want to make a good impression. As a young person, beginning your life, you should be thinking about these things.

Cory looks down at her bare feet, dirty with soil and grass, her wrinkled chambray, the sweat that has darkened the fabric at her pits. Has she ever thought about these things? Her adolescence has been so constricted by resistance to her mother for making similar suggestions there's barely been room to stretch out and consider what kind of adult she wants to become. Now that the question's arisen again, this time with what feels like the freedom to answer, she tries to imagine herself in the future. She'd like to be like Cricket, she thinks. Languid, clever, magnetic.

Why don't you wear something of Cricket's? he suggests, as if reading her mind. She's got a whole closetful of clothes here she's never bothered to take.

No way. Cory says. For one thing they wouldn't fit. I'm like a giant compared to her.

You're thinner, he notes. She's gained fifteen pounds since our wedding. Probably ten more since the new baby. Not that I'm criticizing. I've gained sixty. But I've always been a fat man in spirit. What do they say, inside every thin man is a fat man waiting to get out?

Isn't it the other way around?

She used to love lending out her dresses.

Cory wonders if she can detect a certain wistfulness in his tone. She imagines the lonely island house as it might have been when they were married, full of Cricket's beautiful friends, dresses strewn upon the furniture, glasses of champagne abandoned for mirrors and silks.

Rolo stands, brushes the grass from his backside, and extends a hand to help her up. They're great clothes, he says, they deserve to be worn.

Without the children and dogs, the house is near silent, save for the low whir of the central air and the occasional far-off clang in the kitchen. She follows him up to his bedroom. When he opens the door to the walk-in closet, a light inside turns on automatically. He goes in and beckons her. It is big enough for them both, but barely. She stands beside him admiring the rows of rich leather shoes, the silks, cottons, and linens on velvet hangers, the fine merinos and cashmeres. She can feel the heat of his body, can smell the fresh tang of his deodorant, or maybe it's cologne. He gives her a smile she can't quite read, and riffles through the hangers on the far end: all women's clothes. This is beautiful, he says, removing a narrow red dress. She wore this at a friend's wedding. Oh, look at this, I love this one, it's Indian silk.

He hands her the clothes and she takes them, because if she doesn't they'll fall onto the floor. When he's piled six or eight dresses in her arms he climbs onto the bed, leans back on the pillows, and stretches out his ample legs, sipping his drink in a shaft of sun that falls through the thick curtains. Try them on, he says.

Now?

The dogs barrel in, wet and breathless, and jump up to join him. He doesn't seem to mind their damp fur on the sheets, doesn't seem to notice their smell. One rests its chin against the inside of his thigh. He strokes its long head, and its eyes slant with pleasure. The other two watch jealously from the foot of the bed, panting.

Change in the bathroom, he says, if you're going to be a prude about it.

She retreats, attempting to close the door behind her, but finds that the door does not actually close all the way, something's wrong with one of the hinges. She tries to push it closed but it won't go and she doesn't want to shove it, to *be a prude about it*. Leaving it open a couple of inches, then, she tries to shrink from his line of vision, undressing awkwardly behind the door, practically pressed up against the wall.

The first one is hard to get on. She can't get the zipper all the way up her back. She looks at herself briefly in the mirror and flushes with embarrassment. Everything about her is oversized and clumsy, strong hands, bony shoulders, big nose, like a child's drawing: *Giraffe in Blue Silk*. She tightens the scarf around her stupid hair. Lifts her Sazerac from where she left it, beside the photo of Rolo and Cricket, young and beautiful, and drinks. Cricket's beauty in the picture is unreal, destabilizing: the fullness of her breasts, the gloss of her hair, the delicacy of her fingers, the intelligence of her smile. Cory emerges from the bathroom tentatively, barefoot, self-conscious, one arm contorted behind her back as she pinches the fabric together with her thumb and forefinger.

He is expressionless, mechanically stroking the dog. Turn around, he says.

She obeys. The drinks have left her light-headed. Has she eaten today? She can't remember.

You can't get it zipped all the way?

She faces him. No.

It's too roomy in the ass anyway. Try the jumpsuit.

She returns to the bathroom and takes off the blue, keeping her eyes on the opening between door and jamb. The jumpsuit is absurdly sexy, flesh-colored bodysuit underneath and black lace on top, but the pants are too short and the neckline's too low. Cory tries to smile at her reflection but the expression looks forced. In the photograph, Cricket's daylight smile mocks her.

It's too big at the top, she says through the door, and too small at the bottom.

Let me see.

It doesn't fit, though.

Let me see.

Back in the bedroom she stands at the foot of the bed, holding the jumpsuit up at the shoulders. Rolo regards her, same as before. The dogs have nodded off.

Turn around, he says again.

She does as she's told and waits.

Face me.

She obeys.

Put your hands down.

I have to hold it up, she says.

Let me see.

It'll fall, she says, shaking her head.

He makes a small sound, something like a long hum, scratching a dog's head with his fingers. The dog lets out a sleepy groan. Too big and too small, he decides.

That's what I said.

Try the white one.

She returns to the bathroom and finishes the Sazerac all at once. It goes right to her head and she loses her balance trying to step out of the jumpsuit. Catching herself with a hand on the doorknob and the garment down around her knees, she glances in the mirror to see whether Rolo can see her stumble. From her awkward position he is out of view.

The white one clings, very tight and short, though she can tell it isn't meant to; the waist hits only an inch or two below her breasts.

She tugs at the hem and smooths it over her butt. Compared to Cricket she is a scarecrow: bad posture, mismatched features, pink straw for hair. When she finds herself this ugly, the self-loathing runs so deep it feels like grief. Opposing thoughts nag at her simultaneously: that she wants Rolo to want her and that she wishes he'd never look at her again. Tears threaten to well up but she forces them down, forces her face into a grimace-like smile.

His voice from the bedroom: Well?

She stands a little straighter, tightens the scarf around her head again, and steps back out, mugging dumbly, throwing her hands in the air, making herself into a joke: Ta-da!

A smile spreads over his face. Surprise, surprise: he is pleased. He hums and raises his glass and swirls it, signaling to her to turn around. She spins slowly. One of the dogs hops down from the bed and stretches, emitting a high-pitched whine. Rolo gets up, too. Suddenly he is standing very close to her.

You look good, he says, his voice deep and quiet.

Her belly twists and her face heats up. No, she says.

You do.

A current runs between them. She feels his breath on her neck.

Why do you insist on wearing this old lady scarf around your head? His voice is very low, very close. Do you think it makes you look sophisticated? Bohemian?

The touch of his fingers prickles the skin down her back, electric, eliciting concentric ripples of goose bumps as he unties the knot at the nape of her neck. She closes her eyes, whispering: I don't know.

He breathes two words—*So dated*—and lets her mother's scarf drop to the floor. He runs his hand through her hair, pulling at it, tracing her hairline where the fabric pressed. She loves having her head touched, always has, since babyhood, when her mother

210

would put her to sleep petting her hair, singing softly. Woozy with pleasure, she feels a weight on the bridge of her nose and crests of her ears, spindly as a bird alighting. As she opens her eyes she hears him say, Better, and sees him in sepia, through the sunglasses he has perched upon her face, to complete the look.

He's laughing.

What? she says, worried.

You look great.

She brings a hand to her head.

Don't touch your hair. Your hair is terrific. Very Madonna, circa eighty-four. *Like a Virgin. He-e-e-ey.*

She rolls her eyes and laughs at the falsetto of his final syllable, at his dorky vogueing, but can feel herself blushing under his flattery.

Learn how to take a compliment, he says. Without warning he brings his cold glass to the spot on her bare chest where her cleavage would be, had she cleavage to speak of, and leaves it there a moment, looking right in her eyes. The condensation drips down the inside of the dress, and she stifles a gasp.

And then he steps back, suddenly friendly, matter-of-fact, unflirtatious, breaking the current. The dress is a gift, he says.

I thought it was Cricket's.

The sunglasses are on loan. *Don't. Lose them.* Now. I've got a party to host.

And, whistling Madonna, followed by his three brown hounds, he leaves.

A chill lingers where he held the glass against her skin. She touches it and turns back toward the bathroom mirror. She looks changed. Tall and flushed, lips open. His Cartier glasses exude glamour. The dress is like nothing she's ever worn, nothing she'd ever have the guts to wear, but somehow it is flattering. She studies herself, pulling the glasses down the bridge of her nose, turning to the side to examine her silhouette, craning her head around to check out her behind. With her face mostly hidden by the sunglasses, if she ignores her broad shoulders and bug-bite breasts, if she focuses mainly on her collarbone, hip bones, and the small convex cheeks of her ass, she does look kind of hot, actually, in a mismatched, color-by-numbers sort of way. Madonna/whore, as her high school English teacher might have said. More like Madonna/horse, but still. She is turning and turning again when she notices, in the mirror over the sink, that even with the door as closed as it can be, she has a clear view of Rolo's now half-flattened pillows and headboard. Which means from his seat on the bed he almost certainly had a clear view of her in her underwear.

Back in her own clothes, carrying the dress to her shed, she sees Cricket at the dock, talking with Virgil and some people who have arrived early on Sherry's ferry. Cricket looks up and waves and Cory waves back, reflexively stuffing the dress under one arm to conceal it. Cricket motions for her to wait, and comes up the hill. Her hair is wet, and as she approaches Cory sees her face is bare. Without makeup she looks older, her eyes tight and discerning, but when she reaches Cory her head falls to the side and she smiles. So! How are you liking Little Île?

It's fine, Cory says, holding the dress to her body. Seeing that Cricket is waiting for more, she elaborates: I mean, it's amazing, obviously. Definitely the most beautiful place I've ever been.

Yeah, says Cricket, looking around. Yeah. She closes her eyes, breathes in, breathes out, and Cory is mesmerized by her naked face, her expression of bliss. Opening her eyes again, she says: He bought it for me, you know.

He bought what for you? Cory says.

I grew up around here, did he tell you that, on the mainland. I'm a seacoast girl. Not a lot of money, but my dad had a little sloop and I grew up sailing around these islands. On weekends we used to lay anchor nearby at sunset and watch the archipelago come alive: the lights, the parties.

Sounds nice.

I told him it always bothered me I couldn't dock at any of the landings, since the islands are all private. So as a wedding present he bought me Little Île. Cricket smiles. It was my favorite.

What happened when you got divorced? Cory asks.

Oh, I signed a prenup, Cricket says, and though she remains pleasant, a fraction of a frown appears, adjacent one eyebrow: I got nothing. I mean, I got *something*. I got alimony. I got the kids. Which, you know, is all I really need. I don't believe in regret.

Cory looks out at the vast mirror of ocean. It is difficult to imagine having all of this, then losing it. More difficult, though, to imagine having it at all. The ability to buy an island. The absurdity of *buying* parcels of the planet.

Cricket says, You're how old?

Eighteen.

I was seventeen when I met him. Nineteen when we got married. I have our children now, a good husband. I walk with God. I've worked to forgive Rolo, and to forgive myself. But it was a mistake, you know? I gave him my twenties. I gave him— It fucked me up.

Oh, I'm not— Cory shakes her head. We're not—

I'm not assuming anything. I'm just saying. He likes you.

You think?

You're a pretty girl, Cricket says, but her smile has faded.

Thanks, says Cory, squirming. Rolo's advice—admonishment?— is still with her: *Learn how to take a compliment.* So are you, she adds, and in Cricket's smile is something like a warning. Who is this baffling woman who gave Rolo so much of herself?

You're born-again, right? Cory says after a moment.

Cricket nods.

But you, like, curse and drink. You're fun.

Cricket laughs. Is that a question?

No, Cory says. I guess my question is . . . can you really just *decide* to believe in God?

No, Cricket replies slowly. You don't just decide to believe. It's more like you start to look, and when you're really looking, you start to find God, inside of you, at first, and then outside of you, in other people, say, in . . . this . . . in everything. And when that happens, you begin to understand that God has been there all along. It's just that now you're listening. Paul always tells me: if you're searching, you're with God.

I think I'm always searching, Cory says. But I'm pretty sure God isn't real. No offense.

Cricket touches one cool hand to Cory's. Looking into Cory's eyes, she says: Just listen.

When Cory emerges from her shed in Cricket's dress, having packed up all her grass-stained clothing in advance of her departure the following day, it is late afternoon, and Rolo's staff has proliferated. The island is busy with dozens of efficient people she has never seen before, all dressed in jaunty vests and riding pants, like jockeys. A bar is set up near the pool, a dining table on the lawn, a band in the gazebo. Music swings on the wind and lights swing from the trees. The helicopter lands, and party guests descend from it, laughing, clutching at their clothes, accepting champagne flutes from a steady-eyed caterer, and then it rises and flies away and lands again an hour later. Boats arrive, drop anchor, and sit rocking on the water, reflections of their lights glimmering back up at them, and people row in on rowboats, climb out unsteadily, and help each other wade up onto the sand. The men are tall and loud in sunglasses and sandals or unnaturally clean sneakers, their hair too long and pomaded or short and balding, helping themselves to passed hors d'oeuvres. The women are beautiful in wide-brimmed hats, sleeveless silks, and shoes like jewels. Some are nearly as young as Cory, tall thin and alien, eyes as far apart as fawns', mouths long and shut as zippers. Others are older, louder, freer, chatting, hugging, laughing, exchanging secrets. Cory watches one—ankle-grazing dress and lipsticked mouth, treated hair pulled back—bend toward her interlocutor and touch an arm, engaged in urgent dialogue. The intensity and elegance of this older stranger, the wrinkles at her elbows and creases in her neck, bring Cory's mom to mind, and she is momentarily unbalanced by homesickness.

The only pair of shoes she has are the knockoff Keds, which, after weeks of chasing after Spenser and Fern, are soiled beyond presentability. It could send a strange message, she reflects, not to wear shoes at Rolo's party. It could say, *I am part of the landscape, I belong here, belong to him,* just as the outrageous picnic table does, or the trio of dogs. On the other hand, perhaps there is something brazen about being barefoot, something almost territorial. Perhaps, she thinks, it will say not just *I belong to him* but *He belongs to me.* So she approaches the party shoeless, emerald toenail polish half cracked off, in Cricket's dress and Rolo's sunglasses. Women behold her briefly, size her up. Men drink her in. At the bar, feeling rather dizzy, she orders a Malibu and Coke and is given it in a beveled glass. From one caterer she takes a burger the size of a golf ball, from another two figs wrapped in bacon whose warm interiors ooze tart, semiliquid cheese. From a third she snags a palm-sized nest of fried dough with a marbleized chocolate egg resting in the middle. Cocktail napkin laden with snacks, she stands at the edge of the cliff, where the glass of the house reflects with blinding symmetry the late-afternoon sun. She sets her drink on the grass and devours all the food hungrily, watching the crowd.

A small group has gathered around a handsome if ragged man who is telling a story. Something in his gestures, his cavalier delivery, is familiar to her, redolent of adolescence: defrosted pot pies eaten with her algebra homework on lonely weeknights in front of the TV, reruns of syndicated sitcoms, the exploits and misadventures of families larger, happier, and more charming than her own. She is midway through her inhalation of the fried dough when the wind carries toward her the ragged man's laugh—his hand grasps a woman's elbow, pitch-perfect—and in his masculine staccato she practically hears one of these old shows' theme songs. What was his character's name? Uncle something. Uncle Perry? Uncle Mickey? She knows she knows it, but she can't quite get it now—

Startled by a hand on her elbow, she coughs out a puff of powdered sugar and turns to see Cricket, transformed. Her long hair is a braided crown, her dress a lavender cloud, her face painted with a perfect mask that looks just like the face underneath but smoother, rosier, and more clearly contoured, with sharp-edged lips and eyes and unreal lashes, as if seen through a photo filter.

Wow, uh— Cory wipes her mouth, swallows prematurely. You look amazing.

Where have you been? The severity of Cricket's tone is at odds with the sweetness of her expression. I've been looking all over for you. There are kids here that need looking after.

I'm . . . supposed to be working?

Did you think you were a guest?

Chastened, Cory follows Cricket to the kitchen garden, where a selection of too-small furniture is set up like a garden party for gnomes. Balloon animals lurk among the pepper plants. Five other kids have been penned in with Spenser and Fern, and their nannies are gathered by the picket fence, chatting intermittently. They are, all of them, exceedingly chic. Though it is hot, not a one is perspiring.

These are the other kids, Cricket says, ignoring their caretakers, and rattles off the children's names. A boy named Willie or Billy looks like a three-foot-tall stockbroker in his suit and tie. Harriet, a bucktoothed redhead, is built like a linebacker. A freckled pumpkin called Vito is stuffed into a high chair, eating rice snacks by the handful. A couple of homely twins in puffed sleeves, Grace and Joy, stand side by side under a trellis, straight out of *The Shining*.

Cricket turns to leave, then hesitates, looking her over. Are those Ro's sunglasses?

Cory takes off the glasses, and the day is suddenly brighter, harsher. She looks at them dumbly, as if she hadn't noticed.

Is that *my dress*?

The nannies turn to watch.

Rolo, uh, suggested—

That's a four-thousand-dollar dress. He just loves a new Barbie, doesn't he?

I can change—

No, you can't, you're watching *these* losers. The way Cricket indicates the hapless crew of young misfits with an ironic jerk of her head is exactly like Rolo. She lets out a quick, irritated sigh. It's fine, she says. It looks good on you. And in a whirl of lavender, the matriarch is gone.

The compliment, swallowed whole, sticks in Cory's chest like a lozenge. Fractionally more confident, she turns to the nannies and says hi.

They stare back at her. One says, Do you have a cigarette?

Cory shakes her head, and they go back to their conversation, in Italian or something.

Fortunately Grace and Joy are way into ghost stories, and spend the better part of an hour entertaining Harriet, Fern, and an increasingly concerned Spenser with bone-chilling tales from beyond the grave, while Cory is led around the garden by Billy/Willie, who tells her about the vegetables in incomprehensible babble, like a tour guide from space. After less than an hour, Harriet announces threateningly that she has to pee, and then so does Billy/Willie, and then so do the twins, so Cory, in an attempt to ingratiate herself with the nannies, volunteers to bring the whole troupe into the house for a bathroom break. The children collect at the door of Cory's basement bathroom and play I Spy while taking turns in the facility. When it is Billy/Willie's turn he drags Cory in because he can't yet go alone. Reluctant to leave the others to their own devices, she puts Spenser in charge. It is dim in the bathroom so she sets Rolo's sunglasses inside the medicine cabinet for safekeeping. When she and Willie emerge they find that Spenser has taken his job seriously: all the kids are lined up against the wall in order of height, chins tucked, eyes goggling expectantly, plump Vito, who can barely stand up, laughing uncontrollably on the short end. I spy the Seven Dwarfs, she says, and begins to name them: Grumpy, Happy, Doc (that's Spenser), Dopey. The last three proceed to clamor: Which one am I? Which one am I? but Cory can't remember any other Dwarfs' names except Sneezy, which doesn't apply, so she points to the twins, says, Creepy, Kooky; and, hugging Fern, finishes with Altogether Spooky.

When they return to the garden the nannies are nowhere to be found. It's all right, though; the trip to the bathroom has generated some camaraderie, and by the time dinner is served, the kids seem glad to tuck in. The caterers bring them dumbed-down versions of the adults' food. Spenser holds forth about global warming. His tablemates mostly ignore him, though Harriet, suddenly adversarial, turns out to be a climate change denier. It is perfectly fine, as babysitting goes, there are no major squabbles, but even as Cory half listens to the kids' demented conversation and attempts to keep at least a fraction of Vito's food inside his mouth, she smells cigarettes and sees the nannies perched like models on the rocks just over the cliff, smoking and gossiping; hears laughter, rising and dispersing like pollen on the wind, and cannot help but keep glancing down the hill at the party guests, among whom she was so looking forward to being included, conducting their own dinner at the long table where the setting sun flashes and refracts, splitting rainbows through crystal glasses. The alcohol of the day has left her brittle. A headache expands at her temples. In the kitchen garden, situated beside the south edge of the house, the acoustics are such that the music and adults' voices bounce right off the wall and windows. Cory can hear fragments of their conversation as clearly as if she were at the table herself.

At one end, Cricket and Pastor Paul are seated side by side, a couple of benevolent monarchs. Cricket is nursing the baby, one full breast frankly exposed, chatting with the aging TV star, who sits near the head of the table like a high member of the court, the jack to their queen and king. Which makes Rolo, at the other end, what? The fool, Cory supposes bitterly.

Eventually the old fool stands and taps his knife against his glass. The musicians pause, lay down their instruments, and go off in search of drink and food. Rolo waits, looking west, as if for the sun itself to quiet down. Conversations fade. The diners' heads turn in his direction.

Thank you all for coming, he says, and the last of the talk dies out, with an audible groan from Cricket:

Here we go. Get comfortable.

First and foremost, Rolo says, ignoring her and the laughs she's generated, I want to congratulate our Cricket and Paul on their beautiful son. I couldn't be happier, Bug, that you've decided to have another baby. This time with a partner who actually deserves you. Truly it's a miracle *this* gorilla ever got the opportunity.

Mild laughter.

Seriously, though, Reverend, you are a man of exceptional goodness. I have witnessed Spenser and Fern developing into wise, kind little souls, under your influence. And Cricket? Cricket. Beautiful, magnificent, confounding. If you know Cricket Caldwell, and most of you do, you know that as a philanthropist and friend, as a partner and mother—fuck it, as a *woman*—she is a force to be reckoned with. Your kids are lucky sons of bitches.

Clapping, laughter. Rolo raises his glass in the direction of his ex-wife, who regards him with a look that means *You shouldn't* and *I love you, too, You scoundrel*, and *Whatever*. The pastor brings his hand to hers and squeezes. Rolo adopts a contemplative posture, surveying his guests. The man was born to give a speech.

I want to say a few words, while I have you, about loyalty, he says. About loyalty—and pain.

Some of you know my history. It's a downer. Let's not get into it! But let me just say that for years, for decades of my life, I labored under a burden of excruciating pain, physical and metaphysical. I simply lived with it, as a man with chronic migraines lives with the constant threat of blinding pressure building up behind his eyes, or a gimp— I'm sorry, that's not PC, but I knew a man once, a blacksmith, who called himself— It doesn't matter—as a man with a bum leg must drag his useless limb around behind him. Pain is a curse, I know firsthand, and my life's work has been to lift it.

He looks around and smiles. Look, I'm a sucker for pleasure, okay?

His tablemates laugh and clap.

It is *human* to seek pleasure! *Human* to avoid pain. Human, even, to try to help another human achieve a state of deep relief. Relief is what the humans wanted, and relief is what we engineered. But, you know—and I don't think there's a single human being on this godforsaken Earth who *doesn't* know about the absolute shitshow that has been going on for me lately—sometimes relief comes with complications.

And, look. It is a tragic, painful thing. Off the record—and I know you all signed my documents to be here tonight, but listen, *off the record*, okay—I think about those poor fuckers every night. I do. It's fucking tragic. Perhaps the greatest tragedy of all is that it's no one's fault. Nevertheless, eventually, the powers that be are doing their damnedest to ensure that someone pays. And smart people, you know, can sense that. What I'm getting at is I've lost friends. Good friends. Dear friends who have looked at me and thought, *Not my problem.* And I get it. I really do. *Mi casa es tu casa,* okay, but *mis problemas no son tus problemas.*

Do you all know what the word is for scapegoat in Greek? *Pharmākos.* From medicine, of course, and charm. It's a good story. Maybe you're familiar with the ancient festival Thargelia? No? I'll jog your memory. The two ugliest fuckers in this town—a woman and a man—once a year, these two were wined and dined, paraded around, *beaten*, and *stoned to death.* Special care, incidentally, was taken to make sure they whipped his dick. For what, you may ask? Aha: for *luck.* For the good luck of the town, they sacrificed these poor dogs. Well. *Plus ça change.* Those bastards in Congress, they're champing at the bit, aren't they. Can't wait, can they, to parade me around and whip *my* dick. Pharmākos. Ironic, right? I mean, I'll fight it. I got the best people on the planet fighting on my behalf. Some of them are here tonight—and for you, words cannot express my gratitude—but we all know how this story ends. They want someone to stone to death. And me? My ugly mug?

He holds up one hand to half frame his own rueful smile: Ought to do.

The diners are quiet. The sun has slipped into the foliage. The mood at the table has darkened, too. Two light-footed caterers shimmy in between the guests, reaching between shoulders with long-necked lighters. A flame dances into being, then another and another, shrinking and warping the table, pulling all the focus inward, to the plates and shining cutlery, the jewels and drinks. The intensity of Rolo's expression is exaggerated by the flames. He brings his glass to his mouth and drains it. A server emerges from the dark to refill it.

Well! says Rolo, watching the black liquid pour. As usual I've gone and made tonight all about me! Sorry about that, Bug.

Cricket, at the end of the table, barely seems to be paying attention, tucking one breast back into her dress, shifting the infant over to her other.

I just want to say, Rolo goes on. At the risk of sentimentality, and I'll make this brief: the only real emollient for pain, really—besides the shit *I* manufacture—is loyalty. When a man is in his darkest hour he needs to know he's got his people on his side. If you're here tonight, you're inner circle. I don't trust anyone, but I am trusting you.

In the absence of sunlight and sound, the insects have come alive. The lawn hums. A staff person plugs in a web of paper lanterns, which hover now above the lawn like UFOs. Abruptly, fat

Vito begins to cry. His nanny approaches, a glossy woman with sharp elbows and lips of wax.

So! Rolo raises his glass and his voice: Because I don't know how many more parties like this we will have, this one's for you, my friends. To loyalty!

The diners raise their glasses, too, and a few repeat: To loyalty!

To pleasure! he shouts.

A few more join in: To pleasure!

He growls, Let's burn this party down.

Applause. The musicians, having resumed their places in the gazebo, start up a dervish of a song. Vito's nanny is hissing something at Cory, but Cory can't hear. The sky is afire in the west and gray-blue in the east, and nobody cares about the crying baby in the garden.

What? Cory asks Vito's nanny.

Did you. *Feed* him. Baklava.

Uh, I guess, Cory says.

God, Kelly!

Was that wrong?

Vito's nanny unstraps him from the high chair and pops him out of it like a cork. Babies can't *have* honey, she snaps.

I'm sorry, I didn't know—

But explaining herself is a lost cause. The caterers are back to clear the table, the nannies are wiping faces and hands. A few wine-drunk grown-ups come to collect their progeny. Grace and Joy are ushered toward the helipad. Billy/Willie is brought down to be put to bed on his parents' boat. Harriet is to stay in a sleeping bag laid out on Spenser's floor, so Cory takes the three remaining children upstairs and guides them through the usual ablutions. The kids are dazed and docile. During story time Cory is charmed to note that puny Spenser is holding big Harriet's hand.

When she comes back downstairs the party is in full swing. The kitchen is a crowded hot box of grassy smoke. Just outside the sliding doors a couple of long-legged girls lie on the epoxy picnic table, arms raised, taking selfies with the pills. The lawn is scattered with large and small groups in conversation. Piles of desserts are laid out on the tidied table. The bar is crowded with thirsty men making demands, and she stands for what seems like fifteen minutes before somebody notices her. It is the TV star, his shaggy face flushed and laughing. Putting his arm around her, he demands the bartender pay her some attention.

What'll you have? the bartender asks briskly, but face-to-face with her quick eyes and tense, impatient mouth, Cory chokes.

She'll have what I'm having, the TV star declares. The armpit of his shirt is damp on Cory's bare skin.

Scotch, neat? The bartender looks at Cory with a near-imperceptible frown of doubt.

Make them doubles, he calls.

You're— Cory says, but again the name of his longtime TV character eludes her.

Call me Uncle, he tells her, and winks, and his hand travels down her back.

As she maneuvers, carelessly as she can, away from his touch, Cory feels her youth betrayed by her eyes. With a pang of anxiety, she remembers Rolo's sunglasses in the medicine cabinet, his words of warning—*Don't. Lose them*—and resolves to go and get them as soon as she can make a graceful exit. The drinks are handed over and the TV star touches his glass against hers, leaning in too close. This is the good stuff, he tells her. Sip, don't shoot. She's never liked whiskey, but this *is* good, smoky and warm. It reminds her of bonfires at River Rock, and wool slippers, and mushrooms on the side of a tree. As it slips down her throat the party seems to melt away, the volume of the voices to dim.

And then there is Rolo's voice behind her: Oh, god, not *him*. Of all the bad influences here.

She and the TV star turn to see their host, flanked by two laughing women, both of them tight-skinned, white-toothed, and silky-haired in a way that belies their age, one in a dress that seems to be woven of flaxen rope and pearls, the other in leopard print, one eye half-closed.

Girls, says Rolo, biting into a thumb-shaped sponge cake: You know this bastard.

Hi, they sing.

And this is my friend Cory.

Cory smiles at the word *friend*, but her smile is short-lived.

Oh, says the one with the permanent wink. Is this the girl you keep in the shed?

The one in the elaborate dress laughs and riffs, a hand on Cory's arm: Careful of this man, she says. He's a butterfly collector.

Is he feeding you? the first goes on. Is he treating you all right? Does he make you clean the cinders from the fireplace? Blink twice if you need help.

Cory looks at Rolo.

Oh no, says the dress: You've offended her.

Stockholm syndrome, says the winking one.

Rolo says: Queenie, show them your party trick. What's in this Twinkie?

Flushing, Cory says, I can't.

This girl is like Rain Man for food additives, Rolo tells his friends.

Go ahead, says the TV star. Dance, monkey, dance!

Flour, sugar, water, eggs . . . Cory trails off, embarrassed and distracted by the star's unexpected, out-of-context usage of her mother's nickname.

Come on, says Rolo, a warning of impatience in his voice.

Is it a real Twinkie, Cory asks, or homemade?

A real Twinkie. Isn't she adorable?

She feels her face get hot. Animal and vegetable shortening, she says quickly.

What's *in* the shortening, Rolo says.

Tallow, she says. Cottonseed oil. Mono and diglycerides, Polysorbate 60, soy lecithin.

And the flour? he demands.

Niacin, ferrous sulfate, thiamin mononitrate, riboflavin, folic acid.

The women are clapping.

And now, for her final trick, he says: Contains two percent or less of the following!

Cory hesitates.

Come on, Rain Man, he shouts. Don't crap out on me now!

Baking soda, cornstarch, whey, salt, glycerin, agar. Calcium carbonate, calcium sulfate. Modified cornstarch, corn syrup solids, of course—

Of course, say the women, laughing.

Go on, says Rolo, mouth full, having stuffed in the rest of the Twinkie. Go, go!

Sodium acid pyrophosphate, disodium phosphate, monocalcium phosphate.

Yes!

Cellulose gum and xanthan gum and maybe some locust bean gum?

Yes, yes!

Sorbic acid, potassium sorbate, *to retain freshness*, natural and artificial flavors, yellow 5, and probably red 40.

They are all clapping now.

The TV star says: Teach her how to do that with pharmaceuticals, and you'll have yourself a protégée.

Rolo winks at Cory. That's the idea.

Cory shoots the rest of the Scotch; it burns. She turns to hide her coughing, and the women laugh. Oh no, one of them says. Breathe, honey, says the other. Wicked Rolo, says the first, and the women close in on him, and Cory is left unattended, clearing her throat.

She sees an opening at the bar and signals to the bartender she'd like another; the bartender supplies her. She needs to retrieve the sunglasses. The glasses will protect her. She makes her way back up the hill, but is halted again by another voice: Hey, Kelly! She keeps walking but hears it again, closer—Kelly!—and turns to see a youngish guy, scrawny, long-haired, hailing her like a taxi: Remember me?

You remember *me*? she replies.

He says, Eddie! Eddie, remember? Hey, how was Venice, huh? Sorry, is that—you were in Venice, right? Did I remember wrong?

No, yeah, she says, confused, then not. Yeah, I mean, it's sinking, so.

Funny, I remember that. You're a funny girl. Listen, he says, do you still have access to—you know—

She watches him fumble, or act like he's fumbling.

He says, Come on. You hooked me up last time.

Yeah, well, she says, pretending herself into the skin of her predecessor. Last time I got in a lot of trouble, so.

I thought you had like a whole thing going on out here.

That's all over now.

No way. Why, uh. Why are you still hanging around, then? After the way he—? Sorry. None of my business.

Tell me something, Eddie, Cory says, for inspiration has hit. What do you remember about me?

Eddie demurs. Oh, he says, uh, you know. Not much. I know you were Rolo's girl. But we had a good time, I remember that. He lets out a harsh, monosyllabic laugh.

She does not smile. She waits. Lowering his voice, he elaborates: You and Virgil and me, we got fucked up, we climbed down the rocks and went swimming at night? After everyone else went to sleep? You let me, uh . . . I mean, it was chill. We talked, mostly. After Virge passed out you told me about how Ro—

Eddie searches her face. She tries to keep her Kelly mask on, immobile, and he seems to sense that in some way, for his tone changes.

Sorry if I'm overstepping. I'm just surprised you'd want to come back out here, after all that. I mean, if I were you, I'd never look back. I'd take what I got and get the fuck out.

I'm not looking back. I'm looking *inward*. Know what I mean?

She herself has little idea what she means, she's just improvising, trying on for size the role of Kelly, an attitude, a tone of voice.

The guy's eyes widen and then his mouth widens, too, and breaks, once, into another strange laugh. Oh, he says. I got you. Looking inward. That's chill. And he lifts his hand to touch a fist to hers and, strangely enough, ambles off.

Thank god she finds the sunglasses where she left them, between a paper box of Band-Aids and a bottle of ibuprofen in the basement bathroom. A few bottles of other pills attract her, but there's nothing really good down here, in the bathroom meant for the help. *A is for the Aleve that will Allay an Ache. B is for Benadryl, which will Befuddle you to sleep. C is for the Claritin that clears up Congestion. D is for the Drug upstairs that Demands her full attention.*

She puts on the glasses and closes the cabinet door. In the mirror she is beautiful again, anonymous, and safe. The Scotch has tipped her over the edge, warmed her veins and made her rosy, stirred up in her a buzzing, breezy vibe, an appreciation for herself, a feeling that here in the mirror is a girl worth loving. She makes a little face, drawing her lips together and sucking in her cheeks, and is amused by herself, by the ease of her glamour, the way the narrow face partially visible below the glasses invites speculation on the beauty of the eyes. Then she is half stumbling out the basement door to the lawn, knocking into somebody on her way out—she can't see who, it is very dark behind the glasses—and without the benefit of sight her other senses are heightened, the voices and music are louder, richer, the sea-salt night chillier.

She walks the length of the mostly deserted dining table, selects a macaron from a glass basket. A small group still sits at the table, ashing cigarettes in a plate of half-eaten cake, talking about—what—real estate, sounds like. Blah-blah, the dull topics of the middle-aged. She pours the dregs of a bottle of red into a cleanish water glass and wanders downhill with her head tilted back, her eyes on the stars that seem to have come unfixed from the sky, to slide in a great clockwise slump toward the Earth.

A lone figure stands at the edge of the beach, hands clasped at his back: the pastor. She comes to stand beside him and look out into the night at the stars' southward skid, the wobbling lights of the anchored yachts.

He acknowledges her with a nod. Having fun?

She has to keep blinking the stars back into place. Kind of, she says.

Not really my scene, he says. It's strange to me to witness all this. Like being a tourist in Cricket's past life.

You think less of her, Cory observes.

No, he says, taken aback. No, no. It's not for me to judge.

She considers this. All the adults I know, she says, being judgy is their whole deal. It's like how they prove their worth.

Well, he says quietly, I believe judgment is up to God.

I'm not a Christian, she says.

No, he says.

But all this, like, this—Cory gestures at the sky, the light-jumbling waves, the wind, and stumbles a little in the sand—this is God, right?

She tries to fix her eyes on him and sip her wine. His expression is earnest. His jowls are soft, his hairline receding. What does Cricket see in him?

Some people would say so, he replies. But I believe all this is merely God's creation. Evidence of his greatness. However awe-struck we might be by it, if we were to look upon him, our awe would be amplified infinitely. It would be unbearable.

She considers this a minute, or tries to. The idea of this hope-lessly earthbound man, with his heavy cheeks and long forehead, in thrall to divine infinity, she can't help it, makes her laugh. She tries to apologize, afraid her amusement will offend him, but he laughs along with her, and his laugh changes everything. In its light, his doofy glumness dissipates, replaced by something warm and free and truly lovely. This must be what Cricket sees. A kind of sweet-ness, of ingenuous credulity, that cynical old Rolo will never have.

She drains and raises her glass at him, taking her leave. She staggers, weaving, up the hill. The Earth has conspired to join the stars in their slippery spin, and she has to keep crisscrossing her legs to counteract its momentum. At the patio she joins a group, some sitting, some standing, at the picnic table, and laughs at a joke she hasn't heard. Someone shoves over so she can sit on the edge of the bench. Someone refills her glass.

Laughter everywhere, revolving with the trees, the house, around her. Harsh mean laughter above her, deep reckless laughter beside her. Everyone holding their glasses out, cheersing, everyone giddy and glamorous, spinning. She finds herself laughing so hard she can't breathe, though she doesn't know why, her cheeks hurt, she is breathless. She has to get up, has to get out of here, has to take a breath, to breathe, but there are people around her, people behind her. Still laughing, she says something that should be *Excuse me* but comes out like burbling, and there is more laughter. She attempts to push herself up, glass in hand, and sort of swing one leg over the picnic bench, but the gesture is clumsy, her limbs aren't behaving, and she topples—someone says, What the fuck?—and then she's on the ground, her nose having slammed into the lip where flagstone meets grass, and nothing is where it should be.

Wind on her face and wind on her legs, but no wind in her lungs, the wind's been knocked out of her. Fireworks kaleidoscope in the dark behind her eyelids, fireworks of pain at the front of her head. A ringing in her ears mostly drowns out the voices: a dismayed Oh my god! through the ringing, a laugh. Faces above her, bonkers mirages, fade in and out of the dark. She attempts to push herself up on an elbow, but the ground slips sideways out from under her, and she falls up the avalanche, and someone catches her head.

She's bleeding.

She's wasted.

There's blood.

Somebody grab a towel or something?

We need ice. Where's Rolo?

Hey, Rolo? You'd better come deal with your, uh, domestic.

She can't tell who is holding her head. She has just enough time to take in the Florida-shaped red wine stain that's appeared down the front of her, nipple to rib cage.

Oh no, she says aloud, and begins to cry: No, no.

Stay still, kiddo, says the person attached to her head, and then: Fuck! Towel, please? She's bleeding all over my jeans.

Sorry, she tries to say through her tears—

And then the hand is replaced by another hand and a towel is applied to her face, and the new hand is Rolo's, Rolo is here, and he's squatting beside her, he's helping her sit, he's telling someone in a low voice that there should be an ice pack in the freezer, and retrieving his sunglasses from the grass, he's singing quietly—*I wear my sunglasses at night*—and smiling at her in a private way, and she's relieved, she's so sorry, Sorry, she tries again, but it comes out all weird, and a small alarm goes off in her brain, reminding her that a consequence of having had too much to drink can be vomiting, and she lurches forward and gulps and everyone steps back, and time slows, giving the strangers an opportunity to disperse, and then she's on her hands and knees, puking into a flower bed, and it feels like the heaving will never let up, the moment she thinks she's done it starts again, but his hand is on her back, he's got her, thank god, and eventually, ears ringing, eyes streaming, muscles trembling, nose bleeding into her mouth, she is done.

Kneeling bare-legged on the flagstone in the stained dress, wiping her eyes, wincing when she grazes her nose, she looks up at him and is relieved to see he's still smiling, is relieved to see they're alone.

Hold your head back, he tells her, and press this against your nose, hard.

She obeys, taking the ice pack, looking up at the old blurry stars.

I fucked up Cricket's— She is shivering.

Forget Chekhov's white dress, he says. You fucked up your face.

I'm sorry, she says, and begins to cry again.

Head back, he reminds her. His smile is so warm she wants to crawl into it. You're a hot mess, he says. Let's get you cleaned up. And he helps her slowly to standing.

I have to pee, she whispers.

All right, he says, come on.

With an arm around her waist he leads her in through the kitchen door. Her feet have become marionette feet, they keep getting tangled and falling in the wrong places. The faces of a few stragglers follow them and he waves, calling: As you were. Nothing to see here.

Sorry, she repeats, but he doesn't reply. He leads her up the stairs and into his bedroom. She's relieved when he opens the door. Quiet sanctuary, velvet blue, cedar. I'll wait, he says, closing the bathroom door behind her as far as it will go. She nods and makes her way to the toilet, where what should be a familiar process seems hopelessly complicated, but the relief of finally emptying her bladder is so deep it's almost erotic. She stands, woozy, a hand on the sink, and looks in the mirror at her bloodshot eyes, her nose beginning to swell, the blood on her face and the grass in her hair, the shameful stain, and as she tries gingerly to clean the crusted blood she recalls how stupidly hot she felt just hours ago, and shame springs up around her, squeezing then puncturing her, a corset studded with nails. Suffocated by shame, she begins to cry.

A knock on the door. Rolo's voice is followed by his reflection behind her: Queenie.

She turns toward the door. Sorry, she says for the thousandth time. I'm an embarrassment.

He laughs. You sure are!

Her face crumples, ouch, hideous shame.

Oh, please, he says. Pull yourself together. Everybody out there has been eighteen and had too much to drink. Everyone's been an embarrassment, if they've ever had any fun. Okay? Maybe they'll gossip about you. Probably they'll take the opportunity to say a few nasty things about me. But I know every one of those assholes personally, and I can tell you right now, they've been right where you are, every single one, some of them a lot more recently than they'd like to admit. Let he who has never been a drunken idiot cast the first stone. Know what I mean?

She tries to frown and shrug and nod all at once.

He comes toward her, wipes her eye with his thumb. You're pretty when you're drunk.

I'm pretty when *you're* drunk, she slurs.

His laugh echoes in the marble room.

My nose hurts.

I bet. You may have a concussion.

I should go to bed.

If you have a concussion, he says, you gotta stay up.

Pain comes in fierce waves. She raises a hand toward her nose. Touching it is a mistake.

Reading her expression, he makes a sympathetic face. You want a Granny? he asks.

She nods.

Good girl. Let's take a couple Grannies and run you a bath. Don't worry. I won't look. I've got to stay in here to make sure you don't fall asleep, but I promise I'll face the other way the whole time. I won't look unless you want me to.

E is for the Ease with which she slips into Euphoria. F is for this Finite moment of Excelsis Gloria. G is for Guiltlessness and Gratification. G is for the Granadone that's like a divine vacation. She lies in the tub for who knows how long while he sits with his back to her on the closed toilet, telling her about what he calls his misspent youth. He likes his tales like he likes his women, he says, beautiful and tall. She plays a game of submerging her ears so the hard edges of his consonants melt away in the hot water, draining his words of meaning, leaving only the cadence of language behind. When the bath goes cool and her teeth begin to chatter, he leaves her a folded towel and his own silk robe and retreats while she dries off. When she comes out she finds the bedroom empty. He has disappeared. A game? She makes her way back down the stairs—each step feels steeper, longer, taller, than the last—and from the quiet and the bluish light outside the windows she deduces more time has passed than she might have guessed.

The house is like a castle under an enchantment. In the living room, sleeping forms are sprawled on all the couches. A middle-aged man is chin up in a chair, snoring. On the shag rug, two people are quietly fucking. In the kitchen, three women laugh mutely but hysterically, taking turns stacking crackers on the face of a fourth, who has passed out with her head on the tabletop. Somebody's curled up in the bay window dog bed. The floor is sticky and littered with crumbs and Cory's clean feet curl against the spillage. She runs the kitchen tap and the water stretches from it like chewing gum and she watches, entranced, for too long before remembering that she's thirsty and finding a glass to hold under it. When it begins to overflow she removes it and drinks it all in one draft, feeling the liquid glug through the valve of her throat and down into the long biotic siphon inside her, feeling it fill her belly and hearing it gurgle there, slosh, and be absorbed through her stomach. She is a jug with sponges for walls. The water's still running, cold current of glass, so she refills the cup and stands at the open door, regarding the sky that's just beginning to lighten, listening to someone humming under the crabapple tree.

She steps into the night, into the earliest traces of day. He is lying on a tablecloth, reprising a song the band played hours ago.

Without looking up he pats the fabric beside him. She comes his way and lies down. She feels deeply and all at once that this is where she belongs, on her back on a swath of lace, wet hair, silk robe, bare feet, black leaves rustling overhead, gray-black sky lightening beyond them, and Rolo's bulk, weight, and warmth beside her. Yes, this is where she is meant to be, Queenie; queen of this moment, at least.

His face is dark with a hint of beard, his long lashes still against the curve of his cheek, his humming accompanied by the morning's earliest birds. She lies there listening, becoming slowly aware of the proximity of her hand to his, the fine tickle of the hair on his forearm against the bare skin of hers as the sun rises, ever so slowly and then all at once, rendering in flat strokes the dark vertical woods against the sky. A thin blade of light cuts across the grass, and then all the lawn is illuminated, and the swallows mosh, airborne, around them, and the planet spins imperceptibly quickly, and she gets that ancient, Jurassic feel, the elemental thrill of bearing witness to the planet's gazillionth sunrise. She cannot bear to think of her belongings, all packed, by the door of the shed, of the helicopter ride she is to take, just hours from now, with Spenser and Fern, Cricket and Pastor Paul. There have been a finite number of moments in her life so wretchedly beautiful, so saturated with possibility and even with love, that she has wished time would stop so she could live inside them forever. This is one.

Stay, Rolo says.

His eyes are still closed. His hand lies close, but he does not touch her.

He says, Our story isn't over yet.

She smiles at the leaves, the sky.

What else do you have going on? he asks.

She thinks reluctantly of her so-called responsibilities. She has a college essay to revise? The very idea seems quaintly ridiculous, out here, on this island, beside one of the richest men on Earth.

He takes a long breath. There's nothing easier than staying where you are, he says.

He tells her it will be like a vacation. He says he won't always be here, he's got business, of course, but Queenie, you'll have the run of the place, while you are here you will rule all that lives and moves. Look at you, he says. The pink in the sky matches the pink of your hair. It's as if you're meant to be here. I want to come home to you—

And he's getting excited, he's sitting up: This is a great idea, he's saying, eyes wide, smile wide. He cups her face in his warm hand, and brushstrokes of sun stretch across the trashed lawn like epiphanies, sketching lateral blades through the trees and flooding the grass and casting everything in pearly light, upturned glasses and forgotten silverware, plates like smeared palettes, the pharaoh hounds by the garbage cans, reveling in a trash bag of chicken parts, and she feels she can see the kid in him, chubby, crinkled, and bristly, but hopeful as morning. He needs a shave. He is lovely.

Okay, she says.

Okay? He laughs.

Okay, yeah, okay! I'll stay. But I really have to call my mom. She'll freak if I don't come home.

You are home. You are my home. He runs a finger along the edge of the robe, where silk meets skin. Planet Raised-by-Wolves.

She shivers at his touch. I'm serious, she says.

Anything you need, he says, and produces his Cartier sunglasses from his breast pocket, and replaces them tenderly, avoiding the gash, atop her ears and nose.

She floats back to her shed in his silk and silver. She curls up for what seems like just a few minutes of sleep, and dreams she is buzzing her mother far away, across the ocean, down innumerable highways, and through the jagged city, ESP bouncing like sound waves off steel and glass to land, thrumming, in the embodied receiver. The tug of the psychic thread is as deep and elemental as current—and surprisingly persistent, surprisingly loud, in fact— indeed so persistent and loud that when her eyes blink open again in the afternoon, it remains, she can feel it in her bones and blood, and it takes her a moment to put together that the dream was no more than an intricately imagined scaffolding around a sound, and the sound is the helicopter, bringing guests home to the mainland.

Her mouth is sour. She digs in her just-packed duffel and finds a wrinkled excuse for a shirt and a pair of skintight exercise shorts. She puts them on sloppily, tottering, before stepping back out of the shed into the butter-colored afternoon, hot now and banal, so different from that mystical first light of morning. The staff roams the lawn like beachcombers with trash bags, collecting party junk. Guests, washed and dressed for travel, mill about near the dock, drinking bloody Marys and coffees, the pastor and Cricket among them, chatting in straw hats. Rolo lies a few feet away in the sand, letting Fern and Spenser crawl over him. The sight of the kids there, about to leave their dad, hurts. She does not want to show her face among the adults, does not want to invite any censure of last night's drunken foolery—or to remind anyone, if (one can pray) they have forgotten—but she does want to say goodbye to the children, to give them each one last hug.

In the basement bathroom she brushes her teeth, turning her head from side to side to examine her swollen nose. It is bigger than ever, purple and dappled as shadow, but strangely enough it is less hideous than intriguing, has a certain dignity, maybe, like a battle injury. She looks sort of pretty, actually, despite it: fragile and cavernous, with her unwashed hair and sleep-swollen lips. Her breasts seem weirdly big. Her skin shines. Thin and mysterious, tragic, victorious, bruised and still barefoot, she approaches the group. People complain about hangovers but she doesn't understand why. There is freedom in this unsteadiness, in the unfiltered flow of her thoughts. Her limbs are loose, her legs sharp with stubble, her belly empty. Rolo's sunglasses slide down her nose. She feels sloppy-glamorous, like a pop star on E! *Cory Ansel shows up to work a mess! Is she still drunk? On drugs? Will she fuck her employer? Stay tuned!*

At the beach she kneels and holds open her arms for Spenser and Fern.

I thought you were coming with us, Spenser says. His eyes squint with concern behind his glasses.

Cricket turns, overhearing, and gives Rolo an inquisitive look.

She decided to stay, Rolo tells his ex-wife. A vacation. Who was I to stop her.

I need a little time to myself, Cory tells the boy. You know what that's like, right?

Spenser nods. Fern kisses Cory's thumb.

Cory helps herself to a mug of coffee from a copper urn set up on a table by the dock. She is admiring the bright confetti of sun in the waves when she feels someone beside her. Cricket: barefaced in the harsh light of day, despite her sunglasses and scarf dress, she looks tired and wan, cleavage crinkled, hair dry.

Hi, Cricket, says Cory sociably.

Cricket faces the water, her back to the others. Look, she says. It's none of my business, but I think you should leave with us.

Cory turns to her, surprised. She can't decide whether to say *Why?* or *It isn't* your business, or something else, so she says nothing.

I think you should go home to your mother.

Cory mimics Cricket's slight smile, raised chin, and faraway squint. She tries for a tone that's warm but haughty: You don't know anything about my home, or my mother.

Cricket turns toward her and says, in a low, rapid voice, I'm not saying you don't know what you're doing. I'm not saying I don't love Rolo, or see how he loves you.

Cory raises the mug to her lips, attempting to conceal the smile that the word *love* pulls from her lips. Coffee burns the roof of her mouth.

I know you, Cory. I *was* you. I would have done the same thing. I *did* do the same, at your age, and worse. I'm just saying. If you were my daughter I'd want you home.

Cory touches the growing blister on the roof of her mouth with her tongue. You're jealous, she observes.

Excuse me?

No offense.

Light flashes in Cricket's sunglasses. Are you serious?

Something in Cory's belly seizes and drops. She has overplayed her hand and regrets it. Nothing to do now, though, but commit. She keeps her face placid, stares back.

Whatever, Cricket says. I guess I misjudged you. Stay, then. The fuck do I care. If it weren't you it would be some other idiot girl.

She goes back to her family.

Heart beating hard, Cory walks, slowly as she can manage, to the pool, and dives in. The cold water is a shock after the hot sun and she stays below as long as she can, buffering. When she resurfaces she glances down at the beach and sees with satisfaction that she's being watched. Heads turn away when she looks, so she keeps to herself as she climbs up the ladder, wet tee clinging, nipples hard, flips her hair, and lies down on a chaise, dripping. She can hear the party passing, the helicopter starting up again, can feel the edges of its wind. When the kids call to get her attention she waves but does not go over to them. They look a little disappointed, maybe, but she is determined to remain self-possessed. She turns her face to the sun, ignoring the heat that's burning her outsides, ignoring the dread within.

X

Disfigured by Grief Terrible and Savage, I Sat Near the Wayside Like an Ancient Woman

I have traced the wild eastern edge of this vast country. I have trespassed on private cliff-side driveways and been aimed at with a gun a hundred feet above the sea. I have slept in Sheila's car. I have spent sleepless nights in Sheila's car, on open Wi-Fi networks in the parking lots of large high schools and little libraries, running down the battery, reading on my glowing phone every available document about Rolo Picazo I can find.

I have learned by heart the number of deaths by overdose, the details of the lawsuits, the ins and outs of his ongoing hearings. I can recall verbatim his clever testimony quoted in the *Times*, down to when and where he paused to cry his crocodile tears, but I still know almost nothing about who he is behind closed doors—and I'm sure that is intentional. A man like him, he must be followed all the time by digital janitors, scrubbing his footprints from all the Internet's labyrinthine, ever-branching corridors.

And then. Today. Going sixty on the highway. Something popped and began violently to wobble. A flat. Only just managed to get off at this random exit, to wheel the pink Honda, wompy-jawed and thunking, into a spot in front of a Dick's Sporting Goods. Now I sit at a derivative bistro table at a Starbucks somewhere in rural Maine, forehead on forearms, bent by hopelessness. How long have I spent hunting her down, daughter of evasion, daughter of evaporation, daughter of god help me. And I am still all but lost, and I still know next to nothing.

Somewhere behind my left shoulder a voice comes into focus, high and bright as lens flare: *Ma'am?* I raise my old head, bleary, and look up. What do you know, I am attended by four cherubim. The elder three are Caucasian as Creamsicles; the youngest, who is maybe three, is Asian. All four are squeaky-clean up top and dusty at the bottom, with brushed hair and cheap but pretty clothing, scuffed knees, dirty sandals, and silver crosses at their throats. Each holds her own icy, sunrise-colored drink: water, sugar, grape juice concentrate, rebaudioside A, I'd guess, or some other steviol glycoside, coconut cream, and months-frozen strawberries . . . all of them Cory. None of them Cory.

It is the eldest who's been speaking, air kissed by pubescence, blond hair parted in the middle to reveal pink scalp. On her thin lips, a tinted gloss, a hint of sparkle. On her chin two spots of grainy concealer barely mask two painful-looking pimples. Do you need a doctor? she is asking. We could call someone?

I see myself for a moment as if through her worried eyes: aging woman, gray hair short and sparse as an invalid's, apparently passed out in a strip mall coffee shop. Fragment of an old song skips in my head, some strange ballad my mother used to sing to me:

FRUIT OF THE DEAD

Good my mother, whence are you
of folk born long ago?
Why are you gone away from all
you ever seemed to know?

Shake it from my mind. Laugh a little, to illustrate the senti-
ment: I'm all right! The younger two look frightened. My laugh's
high-pitched and strangled and the adults at the register are turning, looking. Explain: I'm just having a rough day. A rough few
days. A few rough weeks.

Can we help? the child asks. *Bright eye and ruddy cheek.*
Come home with us, the smallest says—
and who am I to resist the call of angels?

Out of the Starbucks, past Sheila's gimpy car, to the highway they
lead me, talking all at once. They are fourteen, eleven, nine, and
three. Their names are Callie, Carly, Katie, Kai. They walk on the
shoulder of the road like ducklings. Callie takes the lead and dark-
haired Kai rides piggyback, holding her strawberry lemonade in
both hands so its condensation drips upon her sister's head. Pale
Carly in her pink glasses holds apple-cheeked Katie's hand. They
are unbothered by the cars that vroom past, the occasional big
rig leaving us in a wake of exhaust and dust, drowning out long
sections of Callie's rambling informational monologue. I gather
they have brought home other strays, that they are Christian
charity enthusiasts. I am grateful for the way the girl's soliloquy
streams on, without inviting response.

At a bend in the highway, Callie ducks right through a curled
opening in a chain-link fence and leads us through tall grasses,
probably overpopulous with ticks, up a street whose asphalt is

buckled by the roots of trees. A pit bull springs up barking behind a chain-link fence to shadow us. A motorboat sits rusting in a yard. Then we come to a lot where a sign staked into the dirt reads LILY DELL: LUXURY HOMES NOW SELLING, and the developer's 800 number. Half a dozen driveways lead from a cul-de-sac to half a dozen identical garages attached to clones of the same large house: turrets at the top, arched windows looking into empty rooms. We process up a path of pale shells, crunching. Callie opens the door. Kai jumps from her shoulders and runs out of her shoes and up a staircase yelling, *Mama!* The word weakens my knees.

Inside the McMansion it's immaculate. Neo-midcentury furniture is clustered around an eighty-inch TV. Throw pillows on a green velour couch read HOME IS WHERE THE COFFEE IS and GOD'S GOT THIS. Scent diffusers on the sideboard do little to mask the deeper smells of new construction: sawdust, latex paint, chemical adherents. On the wall by the front door hang constellations of framed photographs: contemporary candids, school photos, black-and-white ancestral portraits. In a large recent photo—aesthetic: JCPenney—the girls are arranged against blue satin like Red Rose Tea figurines, Mom and Dad behind them. He: an aging Ken doll in tight sleeves and a shapely helmet of brown hair, determined smile; she: a buxom overtreated blonde, powdered and bloated, in false eyelashes and the wrong hue of blush. Her ruddy hands, heavy with rings and long white nails, rest upon two daughters' shoulders, and though she is smiling her lips are closed, her expression stiff.

We're a shoes-off house, Carly tells me, so I leave my dusty running shoes on the rack alongside dozens of other shoes in all sizes: matte Uggs and soccer cleats, sneakers with lights embedded in their soles, loafers the size and shape of madeleines. Cory, Cory, Cory. Weakly I lower my bones onto the interior step. Katie, pink apple of the four, sits down and lays her head against my arm. The scent of her shampoo is a sweet hex. Upstairs, a baby screams. An adult coos. I hear Callie's voice among the racket: *We found her at Starbucks. She was all hunched over. She looks like she hasn't eaten in—*

Then an adult voice: *Can't just go picking people up at Starbucks, Cal.*

—needs our help.

It isn't safe, it isn't . . .

The voices drop off when their sources come into view. The woman from the photograph stands before us in full maquillage. She is maybe forty-five and big, with a heavy step, blond hair extensions, thick hips camouflaged and cleavage revealed by a summer dress in a pattern of pineapples and toucans. Callie is beside her and little Kai hangs on to one pink arm like a swing. Settled in the other elbow is a brown baby in a white diaper, clutching the strap of her dress and wailing rhythmically and without urgency, as if he's been crying so long he's forgotten how to hush.

Katie nestles closer. Carly sits down on the other side so I am flanked, protected. I am their stray and they are telegraphing *Can we keep it?* I try to make a face to Mom that says at once *I'm sorry* and *Don't ask* me, *they're* your *kids*, but looking up at this Target Madonna I am seized by grief, guilt, envy—Cory, Cory—and my lame attempt to telegraph polite apology ends in crumpled face and blurred vision. I try to stand, to detach from Katie, Carly, to say this was a bad idea, turn back. But they grab, I stumble—Girls! the mother snaps—and, on impact with the floor, a painful spark ignites in my coccyx and burns through my spine. The woman steps close, reaches toward me—You okay?—but it is too much. A fat, wet drop falls from my nose. The *shame*. The *shame* of losing her. The baby's long, bored cries come from its belly, unadulterated by meaning or intention. Cory, Cory.

Then a hand is helping me up, accompanied by a voice: What can I get you? A glass of water? Cup of coffee? Wine? Come in, come in, take a seat. Carly, bring her a cookie, will you, and a glass of milk. Is whole all right? You're going to love these. They're vegan, but I swear you'd never know. Callie found the recipe online.

I am installed on the couch. A pillow is stuffed behind my back. Against the backdrop of the house's scent my own smell rises, rank and jagged. Two substantial cookies are laid before me on a Happy Birthday napkin, and a tumbler of milk so thick its sloshing leaves white residue on the inside of the glass. Nod in thanks. Stay silent, eyes downcast, for fear of what sound might come out if I attempt to speak. The girls stand around, watching. Their mother sways in time to the baby's wails. I cannot bring myself to touch a cookie.

From upstairs comes a digital tune. The mom perks up: Hold the baby for a minute, would you? I just have to restart the dryer.

Startled into receptivity, I raise my eyes and hands to take the wailing boy, who, weirded out by me, at last goes quiet. Black hair curls from his shapely head, thick lashes from his eyelids. His hand curls, too, small and plump, around my thumb. Tears begin to dry in the creases below his inky eyes, and in the stillness of his searching gaze I feel a memory: how, even in the flattening throes of postpartum motherhood, a quiet look from Cory could amaze me; how I came to depend on my baby's dependence, smiling for her when I could not smile for myself. And sweetness, I recall sweetness by the gallon, our mammalian games, how we hooted like apes, the throaty abandon of her belly laugh. Now this other baby blinks, awakening from a kind of trance. Drool floods his inch-long chin. I realize I've been smiling at him only when he smiles back, gummy mouth opening wide, big cheeks shoving up to crinkle bright his eyes. He lets out a sound that is part squeak, part sigh, the progenitor of a laugh, and his heavy head bobbles

FRUIT OF THE DEAD

back. His sisters laugh and call their mother back: Mommy, look, Demi is laughing!

He is in the doorway of hysteria: on one side is that cozy interior, laughter, on the other side the wilderness, distress. My job, I see, is to keep him in the laughter, and it all comes back to me, the tone of voice, the gestures, the *Who's a bun-bun? Yes, who is a sweet potato?* With each rhetorical interrogation, I lift him so his round belly is level with my lips, blow a raspberry on his covered button of a navel. With each rude noise he throws back his head and emits his goofy bark again. With each of his near laughs, the girls laugh, too, a high-pitched chorus.

You have a way with him.

Their mother's voice reminds the baby that he is not in her arms, and his lip starts to tremble. Distract him with a loud, wet kiss.

I'm Metta, she says. This is Demian. We call him Demi. You've met the girls.

A beat. I know I am expected to give a name, perhaps a history. Think of the buzzing phone, the blighted rice, the news report. Think of Cory.

And you are? she says.

The song that has been record-skipping in my mind reveals itself on cue: *My name, my dears, is Doso and I rode aback the sea—* Aloud, I reply: Doso.

Doso. What kind of a name is that?

It's from a song.

Huh, she says. Well, Doso. Would you like to stay for dinner?

Thanks. I think I would.

Chatter and bustle of dinner preparations, scents of butter and onion, chicken and potatoes. Metta, baby on her hip, supervises children chopping carrots at the kitchen island, pulls a sunflower cloth over the dining table, pops open a paper can of biscuits. She pours herself a glass from a Bota Box and offers one to me: *Doso? Vino?*

Dare not. Tipsy, I am liable to revert to Emer. Instead, watch the way she floats from child to child, lays a hand upon a back, helps guide a knife. Admire the apparent ease with which she loves them.

Metta drinks with dinner but she drinks alone. The children's father enters, to much rejoicing, takes my hand in his—Welcome, he says—and pours himself a glass of milk. We sit at the oblong table, dinner steams, and we all take hands as the father of the house settles into prayer. With his eyes closed, brow furrowed, and attention directed to his god, Metta's Ken doll is embarrassingly handsome—younger than her, I think, and perfectly groomed. His demeanor is gentle, almost shy, his voice soft as lambswool. Lord, he says, thank you, et cetera, and the family recites: *For food in a world where many walk in hunger. For friends in a world where many walk alone. For faith in a world where many walk in fear.* Demi and I are the only ones who keep our eyes open.

The biscuits are grabbed and torn, the chicken carved. The girls ask me questions. Where I come from (here and there). If I can drive (yes), cook (yes), swim (yes). Whether I have been to the nearby amusement park (no), play double Dutch (no), Ping-Pong (no). What I've done for work (this and that). Nobody asks how long I will stay. Nobody seems to wonder where I will go next. Perhaps they assume I will become a family member, adopted as Kai and Demi have been—and several beloved, tragically temporary pets and injured wild things, about whom they tell me in detail: a rabbit with a bum leg, an ill-fated sparrow chick, a neighbor's puppy. And as I listen they grow bolder, developing perhaps their own idea of who I am or Doso is. So, over the course of dinner with this family, as I build up and manipulate my mask, does Doso begin to take on a life of her own. She is invited to stay over.

After dinner and cleanup, after scrubbing a pot and sitting with them in the buggy yard as dusk falls over the lawn and its contents—a plastic slide, a kiddie pool, grounded toy boats and shipwrecked Barbies—while the girls run around playing some vigorous game, and Metta bottle-feeds the baby, and the Ken doll asks polite questions intended to gauge the degree of my relationship with his Lord, I lie among redundant pillows in the air-conditioned guest room. Where am I. Who am I. What have I done. My eyes seem to be stuck open, my ears attuned to the house's every murmur. Again the baby's crying. I hear Metta wandering the hall with him, shushing, bouncing, murmuring. Giving up on sleep, I venture downstairs and find her on the couch.

She turns quickly, warning, *Shh*, wiping her eyes and pointing at the rug by the coffee table. Coming quietly toward her, I see little Demi, in a diaper and one sock, asleep on the living room floor, both hands holding one bare foot. As he drifts off the foot drifts toward the floor. Each time it breaks from his grasp he startles, nearly wakes, and clutches it to his chest again.

Almost inaudibly, she whispers, He hasn't slept more than forty-five minutes at a stretch in days. She drops her head into her hands. Without her extensions her blond hair is shoulder-length and stringy. She says, I'm losing my mind.

I bring a hand to her back. Rub it in light circles. You're tired, I say.

Tired! Metta smiles, crazed: I don't know whether I'm awake or dreaming, except that I'm never awake, and I'm dreaming all the time.

I remember that feeling, I say. I used to hallucinate. I'd see rats running across the room out of the corner of my eye.

251

Yes, yes, she says urgently, I keep thinking my phone is ringing, but when I pick it up there's no one there. I love him, I think. No, I know I love him. I thought caring for him was what I was meant to do. But maybe it isn't, maybe I misunderstood. I don't know if I can do it. I don't know what to do.

Go to sleep, I tell her. I'll stay with him.

Really? she says, so pitifully I almost laugh.

I can't sleep anyway.

She hugs me and I stiffen against the give of her, her smells of hair conditioner and night breath, and then, consciously, I try to relax, and feel almost as if I could melt into her, as if we could become one woman, our edges dissolved. She gets up. Climbs the stairs. The baby drops his foot, begins to cry. I pick him up. Tell him: I know. Tell him: We're in this together. Walk him to the kitchen. Bounce him. Sing. Match the rhythm of his wailing. Add to it a tune. He wails along halfheartedly, lowering his volume to listen. Decrescendo tentatively. Savor one desperately sweet stretch of silence. The hum of the fridge, the tick of the novelty wall clock whose face reads TAKE YOUR TIME, which is a full four minutes faster than the microwave clock, which is two and a half minutes faster than the digital clock over the oven. He sighs, and then, as if remembering his old complaint, revs up again, his engine roaring.

Browse the contents of this foreign kitchen for things that might distract him. A bottle top, a lemon squeezer, a collection of souvenir matchboxes in a cookie tin. Strike a match. He goes quiet, entranced by the flame. Watch it waver, bright, in his reflective eyes. Let him reach for it. It goes out. He cries. Strike another and he quiets, smiles, laughs and reaches. It goes out. Grimace of frustration, howl of loss.

They say when you're burned very deeply, because you lose your nerve endings, you feel not heat but chill. Think of it, the sigh of it, cool breeze, relief, raw skin. Licked as if by cats' tongues. A kind of baptism, a kind of pickling. Strike another match. Let the baby bring his unsteady hand toward the flame. Say, reassuring him, that we can do this all night. Like a sleazy comedian tell him, I'm here all night.

Cory's infancy. An eon of eerie, lonely months. A letting go of any semblance of routine. Showering if at all in seeds of hours pared from the cores of nights. Sleeping almost never; almost always half asleep. The struggle, in those brief moments when she slept, between working and rest, which is to say between selfhood and erasure. How slippery and futile it seemed—seems, now as then—to try to remain the woman I'd always assumed I was, the woman I would ever be.

That loss of self, it frightened me. My resentment of her plagued me. And the way she'd reach for me, despite me. Her innocent dependency. From the outset of her life, guilt had already begun to taint my welling love for her. Guilt's constant sour flavor in my mouth, my mind, my breast milk. I'm sorry, I'd whisper as she sucked, feverishly, painfully, depleting me. Tears and sweat and floods of milk trickling down the folds of my belly, staining the silk pajamas I'd foolishly bought in advance of the hospital stay, staining all my clothes. They called her fussy, *fussy*, which struck me as a terribly effeminate word—a word for a prima donna, for a fastidious grandmother, perhaps, not for anyone so terrified and alien as a baby. Her cries were furious and agonized as if she'd witnessed the end of a world. They drew milk from me in prickling waves of pain, they ignited in me the unhinged urge to hurl her like a bad cat against the wall. I never did, but, so help me, I wanted to. She humbled me, she crumpled me.

Now, patting, soothing, singing to another woman's child, I collapse, again, inside. Cory, my core, I feel you in my bones, feel how I have failed you. I miss you so much that all the babies in the world are crying.

I wake with a sharp inward gasp, neck stiff and crooked, in the glider in the nursery, to a morning dull with drizzle, smells of bacon, butter, coffee, and for a moment I am anyone: grandmother, kidnapper, mourner, god. The baby is awake, happy, feet up, babbling and grabbing at the silver clouds that hang from a mobile over his crib. The door opens and, as Metta's face peers around it, I register having just heard the words *Knock knock!*

Sunday morning. How long have I been here? If it's been twenty-four hours it could be a week.

Metta hands me a mug and picks up Demi. He smiles, laughs, she coos, I sip. The coffee is unforgivably hazelnut.

Thank you for letting me sleep, she says. I am a whole new woman.

I try to smile, but my grief won't have it.

She brightens. Come to church with us this morning!

I'm not— I say, but before I can speak the word *religious*, I halt, feeling like a hand around my throat the grief that has tagged along with me on this whole reckless trip. My grief, she is a woman with a torch in either hand, raging and aflame. I do not want to go, but my grief insists I take Metta's invitation as a sign.

So I thank her. Accept. Confess: I don't have anything to wear.

I'll lend you something, she says, and, seeing my expression, laughs. Don't worry, I'll find something that suits you.

The church is the size of a department store and shaped like a great white ship. We pull into a parking lot crowded with cars.

Metta and her Ken doll introduce me to their friends, but I hang back like a sullen teen, tiny raindrops collecting in my woolly hair. I envy them their hugs and laughter, their community and comfort. I envy them their daughters. I shiver in the sanctuary air-conditioning. The pastor steps up to the dais and a hush of anticipation falls over the congregation, with the exception of Demi beside me, in a snap-on bow tie. Metta bounces him, smiling determinedly.

The pastor talks about a girl he met. A lost girl, he calls her, who nevertheless saw God in the sea, the stars. The pastor says that seeing God in the world around us is what makes us human. Although, he says, he does wonder about his cat, who gets a funny far-off look sometimes in the sunshine. The congregation laughs. Demi is on the edge. The pastor says it is a commonplace mistake to confuse God's work with God. He says just think how silly it would be to confuse a masterpiece, no matter how magnificent, with its painter. He riffs a bit on this idea. Demi starts to really cry. From somewhere in the depths of the building, I think I hear another baby crying, too, as if in answer. The pastor says that we are all lost children. He says that God will find us if we let him. But the spell that he attempts to weave, because of the crying, will not be cast.

I reach for Demian, offering to take him, and Metta gives him to me readily. I sidle out of the pew and carry him into a hall. The echo baby cries nearby. Its howl is different from Demian's. Where his is rough, the other's is smooth. Where his is throaty, the other's is nasal. Following it, I understand it's rising from a door that leads down a flight of stairs. The steps are concrete, the walls beige, glossy. My footsteps echo, and then we are in a basement play space. Half a dozen children rummage in toy kitchens and stack blocks under the dubious authority of a teen in braces. On a two-foot plastic chair a striking woman rocks an infant. Her skin is brown, her waist-length hair bright blond, her baby swaddled in a cotton cloth. Beside her, two children look on: a girl of maybe four, who's mostly tangled hair, and a boy in wraparound glasses, who is singing.

Demi, alert now to the activity around him, squirms from me. I put him down on a tumbling mat and he crawls like mad. The teen flaps a hand at me: Don't worry, I got him. The child's song is barely audible amid the other kids' commotion. Strain to hear it. His voice is high and bright, the tune familiar. Am I having some kind of hallucination? Minor key, iambic rhythm, melancholy chantey:

> We landed on the shore among the women and the swine
> who gathered in a hungry frong to dance, rejoice, and dine.

My vision is unclear and blotchy. Tears conspire temporarily to blind me. The air seems thick and wavering with heat, though the church is thoroughly air-conditioned. The small boy's reedy voice goes on, though the words seem strange and warped:

> But in my heart was freedom, dears, so for TV I fled
> through this country dark and strange, and rice upon my head.

The woman looks up at me with something like dismay, holding her baby close—her beauty is unnerving—and I understand I must seem unsettling if not altogether menacing, but I have to ask:

Where did you learn that song, little boy?

The melody breaks. The boy looks up. His mother watches me.

Queenie sang it to us.

Who's Queenie? I ask, kneeling, trembling.

Our babysitter.

And was she tall? Long legs? Eighteen? Pink hair? I say, remembering.

He says, Are you the lady from the song?

She's Queenie's mama, says his sister. I take her little hand.

You know her, I say, you saw her. Is she okay? Where is she? Where is she now?

Thank god. Thank whatever. Thank the livid hag that is my grief for leading me here.

Their mother, understanding me, explains: A couple of hours northeast of here and eighteen miles off the coast, she says, is a shoal of private islands. There's Coeur Brisé, Île des Grenadiers, Belle Île en Mer, and Little Île des Bienheureux. That's where your daughter is.

With Rolo Picazo, I say.

The two words darken her expression. My ex, she murmurs.

How do I get there? I ask.

Do you have a boat?

Do I have a boat. Do I have a car. A job. A name.

Nor a helicopter, I'd imagine, she says.

Her son pipes up: You can take Sherry's ferry.

Where do I find that?

The boy gives me an elaborate shrug. I turn to his mother.

I'm sorry, she says, I don't know, I've only ever sailed or flown.

Google it, the little girl says.

Okay, I say.

I stand and squeeze their mother's delicate hand. Thank you.

I'm sorry, she tells me, and—standing, too, lowering her voice— she says: I tried to get her to leave with us. She wouldn't come.

Did she seem okay to you? I say.

She's as bullheaded as I was. God knows at eighteen I didn't want to be anybody's daughter, either.

Drop her hand.

I'm sorry, she repeats. I wish there was more I could have done. The truth is, despite everything, and I mean everything, he's been good to me. He's been good to the children.

Open the church door to the warm wet day. On my phone, look up the child's clue. I find a simple webpage, just a clip-art boat and crude logo, two words stretched into an arc—*Sherry's Ferry*—and below, an address and a hand-drawn map: a star resting on a shoreline.

Thank coincidence. Thank the little boy with rumpled hair. At the side of the hot highway, stick out a thumb. Wait for a ride.

The truck driver looks like death, but he kindly stops for me. He keeps his old eyes on the road. Chews Nicorette. Swigs from a sour-smelling travel mug. Not one for conversation. Nor am I. The day is rainy gray and I am dressed in Metta's paisley and I've left most of my things in a three-wheeled Honda in front of a Dick's Sporting Goods, but I am, for the first time in a long time, optimistic, lulled by the rhythm of the windshield wipers, the pull of the highway, the angry voices on his radio, staticky as polyester, punctuated by lies. We drive. He knows no haste.

At a lurch I startle, dry-mouthed, and wake. We have stopped on a stretch of wooded road. The rain has crystallized to mist. He reaches across my body to open the passenger's-side door—my belly flips, sick with dread, at his inadvertent touch—and gestures to a dirt road that branches off the highway into woods.

Trust him, my grief tells me. Trust him, I reason, because what choice is there. Light-headed with apprehension, I walk into the forest.

The trees drip. The ground is spongy, matted down and puddling where tires have depressed it. The smell is rot and salt. One bird calls. Another answers. After ten or fifteen minutes the road opens onto a lot with an unlikely collection of cars: a rusted pickup, a workaday sedan, and a licorice melt of a Cabriolet. A security camera stares down from a fence post. At the shore extends a dock; at its foot, a bell. I pull the rope. I wait as clang of gong melts into fog.

And then a lamp wags forlornly from the prow of the strangest boat I've ever seen. A dummy head stuck on the gunwale rolls his eyes above a piggybank slot mouth. At the helm its shrunken, wrinkled captain, smoking in the shadow of a stained sou'wester, loops a rope around a cleat.

She drops her cigarette butt into the seawater and looks me up and down. Where to?

Little Île des Bienheureux.

I take it you're not headed there for a meeting.

I'm looking for my daughter.

Tapping a fresh cigarette out of a creased box, biting the paper end between her yellowed teeth, she says, It was only a matter of time.

My token clatters in the dummy's maw. The captain unravels her rope. I step down into the boat's belly and we glide, guided by her ferry pole, through reeds. I try to ask about a pink-haired beauty. She replies, Sorry, friend. I'm not at liberty to say.

So I turn toward the prow, and as the bay fans out into choppy open water, the fog clears, and I can see far out to the half-erased horizon. Sky rests on sea as gauze on steel. The captain starts the engine. Standing, despite the bouncing, I face the spray and breathe the wind, and feel myself come alive again, on my way, at last, to Cory.

XI

From the Misty Gloom, in His House upon a Couch, His Shy Mate, Much Reluctant, Yearned for Her Mother

Without the children to take care of, Cory becomes accustomed to sleeping in unpredictable intervals. Six hours in the sunshine. Three hundred minutes in the night. She bathes. She sleeps. She masturbates. Takes walks. Loses her way. Tries on clothes she finds in long-untouched closets, scavenges for food in the miraculous refrigerator, helps herself to Rolo's ruby pills. She has nothing she must do anymore on Little Île des Bienheureux, nowhere to show up, no time to keep. She wakes dazed, unremembering, as if for the first time, every time. She gets used not to waking up so much as to materializing from nothing, in this room or that one, smelling sometimes of booze and often of sweat, throbbing with headache and woozy, but light. Rolo comes and goes. The sun rises; the sun goes down. Darkness gives way to day; day fades, replaced again by darkness. Time passes, has passed, is passing, as it must—the planet spins—but each small symbol of its passage comes as a vague and somehow contextless surprise, an incidental experiment in art direction, an alteration to the intricate light and set design on this ever-changing island. It is a great relief to give herself over to lost time.

As responsibility and routine fade, the physical landmarks of Little Île become increasingly familiar. The manicured beach with its imported sand. The catboat tied up with rope. The temperature-controlled greenhouse and its collection of unlikely cactuses, the rock garden's bed of black stones, a palatial birdhouse built into a death-smoothed tree trunk. It is the wilderness she likes best, though: the overgrown woods that sprawl and clamor, extending from the lawn to the island's savage edge. She spends long afternoons exploring the deciduous overgrowth, letting her feet sink into black mud, peeling curls of bark, examining worms and maggots, startling toads. For hours she does not eat or drink. Thirsty, hungry, she craves neither food nor water. She wants only Granadone.

Strange, this urge, this thing that is happening to her. Her body and mind are being warped around and up and past something. She recalls an illustration that her physics teacher drew on the blackboard in white chalk: a small body in motion altering its course around a larger body, the latter's gravity having dented the fabric of space-time, causing the former to veer off course. So has the Granadone altered her course, so has her fabric wrinkled, stretched. Dr. Jim used to like to talk, in their sessions, about *framing*. Through one frame—gilt and driftwood, Cory imagines, embedded with sea glass—she is having the time of her life, she is free, she is adventuring, Dorothy in Technicolor, Wendy in Neverland, Alice through the looking glass. Through another—her mother's frame, maybe, dented metal, heavy as the past—she is lost, sad, and unaccompanied, except sometimes by a wicked old man.

The staff no longer speaks to her. When she stops to say hello they lower their eyes, make busy. The brass bulb at the end of a curtain rod wants sudden polishing, a rug to be vacuumed, a waste basket to be emptied.

What's up? she says, raising a hand in Virgil's direction one crisp morning. You doing anything tonight?

He raises an index finger as if he'd love to get into it, but pauses and pretends to take a call on his toy boat walkie-talkie.

It didn't even go off! she says, and gets up to pursue him, barefoot in her bathing suit, until he reattaches the object to his belt and turns around. It is only when he looks at her that she realizes she has nothing to say.

You know you don't have to stay here, he tells her sadly. Say the word, I'll call Sherry, and she'll swing by with the boat. You are not trapped.

I know, she says with unintended petulance. She resents the way he's speaking to her, as if she were stupid, or a child. Why do *you* stay? she asks.

Me? His face changes. He gives her a kind of defensive squint, then laughs, showing all his perfect teeth. I stay because I am compensated handsomely. I stay because this is a good gig for me. There's a difference between being a guest, if that's what you are, and having the keys to the castle.

He lifts his key ring and jangles it.

Let me tell you something, Nanny. I started here more than ten years ago. I was a chem major at college. Summer after my senior year, I landed an internship at Southgate. We were trying to come up with a cure for cancer. Noble shit. I was sitting in on a meeting one day, taking notes—they always have the lowest guy on the totem pole sit in the corner taking notes—and the Big Guy was coming in. That's how they talked about Rolo in the office. *Ooh, the Big Guy.* Quaking in their New Balances. We're sitting in this conference room waiting for, like, forty minutes. Everyone's rearranging the doughnuts. Looking at their phones. Then this guy, this huge-ass guy, comes in, sits down at the head of the table, rubs his hands together, all schmoozy-schmoozy, all, *How's the wife, how's the kid*, all, *Happy birthday, Cynthia*. Got a personal comment for everyone—except for me. He'd never met me. Then Marketing gives a presentation about how they did that quarter, line graph here, pie chart there, and it's clear that the whole fucking business is being driven by sales of painkillers. Keep in mind this is years ago. Granadone isn't even a twinkle in anyone's eye. These painkillers were more basic. Like, hospice pills. Like, Grannys' Grannies. Anyway, they zoom in on this slice of pie, and break it down demographically, as you do, and what do you know, business is booming in what they call *the Black community*. Tens of thousands, hundreds of thousands of Black people are being prescribed these very potent pills very fucking liberally. So: Huh. This is interesting. Everyone sort of thoughtfully leans back in their chairs. I'm maybe one of two people of color in that room, and I am the only Black man. One guy fixes his gaze on me—me, who no one's looked at in, you know, the whole four months I've been there—gives me this encouraging, disingenuous smile, and says, like, *Huh. Why do we think that is?*

Everybody at the table turns around. Everybody—including Rolo Picazo, president, CEO, and billionaire—is waiting to see how I'm about to respond. What I'd like to say is: *You really need me to spell this out for you?* What I'd like to say is: *Turn the fuck around*. But, as it happens, at the time, I do have a family member who's hooked on the stuff, an aunt of mine, I love this woman, one of those people so sweet it's like the world was bound to break her. In and out of treatment. Kid got taken away. She's my grandmother's deepest source of pain, and that's saying something. So I'm thinking about her, and I'm looking straight at Rolo, and I'm like, *Some people, they're just not fit for this world*.

And Rolo, he gives me this, like, nod, and they go back to their meeting, and the moment's over. But a day or two later my supervisor lets me know the Big Guy wants to see me. They fly me out to San Mateo in a private plane. A Maserati picks me up. He tells me he looked at my résumé, says he was impressed. He needs someone discreet. Offers me a hundred grand a year, out the gate. And you know what else? He'll put my aunt up at the world's ritziest luxury rehab. He'll fly her to Thailand himself.

How did he know about her? Cory says.

Come on, Nanny. In this world? You can find out anything you need to know about anyone in thirty seconds.

If you have Internet, Cory mutters.

Yeah. Virgil sucks a regretful breath through his teeth. Sorry about the whole Wi-Fi thing. He didn't trust you.

He *told* you to keep it from me?

You know how people his age can be. They think anyone under twenty-five is a compulsive exhibitionist who can't survive without social media on intravenous drip.

A seagull alights on a chaise and stares into the pool. A herd of flat-bottomed clouds ambles across the sky.

How's your aunt now? Cory asks.

Virgil's face shuts like a door. She's dead, he says.

He walks back toward the house, detaching his walkie-talkie from his belt on the way. The seagull lifts into a sudden gust, and only a syllable or two of Virgil's conversation floats briefly back to her, scattered by the wind.

In Fern's room she finds the Walmart succulent Rolo bought her that first night, its once plump leaves desiccated now like scraps of wrinkled paper, and her eyes fill with heat. She wanders, high and tipsy, that cloud-white afternoon, into the woods, a couple of pills in her pocket and a bottle of wine in one hand, the lifeless jellybean plant in the other. She finds again the high rock wall, spattered with lichen, furred with moss, and what do you know, the door is open, just an inch, enough for a slip of brilliant green to leak out. If she hadn't been looking for it, she never would have noticed it. Tentatively she pushes it open and steps in.

The enclosure seems bigger on the inside. Behind her, in the woods beyond the wall, there is birdsong and chatter, dripping and creaking, waves crashing and wind in leaves, but when she pulls the door closed behind her the volume drops. The sky glows pearl. A cool breeze only lightly troubles the fine young grass that spreads like a broad carpet, wall to wall. The only object that interrupts the vacant landscape is a single, well-kept tree. Its bark is white and its leaves are green on one side, silver on the other. She sits, her back against the wall, takes a pill, and finishes the bottle. She sings that song her mother used to sing. She cries, and laughs a little at herself, and cries some more.

Either the Granny is kicking in or the field is breathing. Maybe a little of each. She stands woozily and steps out of her sneakers. Her feet sink into the grass and spongy soil. Crouching, she lays a hand on the earth's belly, to see if she can feel it inhale and exhale. When she touches it, it's still, but when she rises again it sighs. The clouds crack open and the sun streams through, illuminating countless jewellike drops suspended in the grass. She bends again to touch one, but the earth rises up and she is lying in the chartreuse carpet, damp and sweet. Another attempt to stand only brings the field lunging back up to meet her. Her head thuds against the soil. Rolling onto her back she sees the clouds have been sorted into formation, periodic tufts lined up and set alight by sinking sun. How long has she been in here, who cares. On her hands and knees, holding the wrinkled plant, she searches for and finds the tree in the center, sun blazing through its empty spaces, its edges golden bright. She crawls up the path of a long shadow the tree has hospitably extended toward her. The crawl's a trek. Her bad balance is a bother. There are innumerable side plots along the way, investigations to be made into the nature and construction of, for instance, a dandelion's waxy orange floret, the moist metamerisms of an earthworm curled from soil. By the time she reaches the tree, half the sky is drenched in pink.

With a great full breath of inspiration, she finds a spot in the knee crook of a root, and digs with her fingertips in the damp earth. She upturns the tiny pot and shakes out the jellybean plant. The old dry soil rains down. She nestles the roots in the divot and, humming a little, tucks it in. You'll be more comfortable here, she tells it, and realizes: I'll be comfortable here, too. She is deliriously sleepy.

Having ensconced the poor succulent in wet new earth, she pulls her sweatshirt around her and curls up between the tree roots. Her brain is slow. Her eyelids and limbs are heavy. Blue night snuffs out sunset's fire, and the leaves above her shiver in the moonlight, concealing then revealing the ancient blazing stars. Everything is breathing, everything whispering. Lying on her back on the grass, she thinks the allure of the drug and the drinks and even of Rolo himself is like the allure of a cave full of diamonds, a glorious, luxurious, protected place she can crawl deep into, out of the moonlight, out of reality. The air may be stale in there, the light false, but it is beautiful and she is beautiful, too, inside it—and completely, deliciously, fearfully alone.

She wakes dry-mouthed, thirsty, and chilled, in the blush of dawn. Her neck is cricked, her bare legs covered in goose bumps, her feet inflamed by insect bites. Some bird virtuoso drills études nearby. The field feels smaller in the morning. The dark woods peer over the edge of the wall.

She sits up and digs sleep from her eyes. Rolls her neck to ease the cramping. Scratches at a welt, releasing her mother's voice inside her: *Don't scratch, you'll make it worse.* Glancing down, she finds—small miracle!—during the night, the succulent has come back to life. It is not yet what it was, of course—a few of its leaves are still no more than scraps of wet brown paper—but it is standing unmistakably taller, craning its three inches toward the rising sun. A joyful sound escapes her, frightening a bird, which takes to the sky with clumsy panic. Nothing, she thinks, has ever made her so happy. A daydream knocks on the open door of her mind, something about the life that lies ahead of her, in this magic garden and others like it. For the first time, perhaps ever, she has an idea about what she wants to do, to be—and isn't it etched, now that she thinks of it, in her genetic material, foretold in her prehistory, in her mother's life and work? She wants to plant things in the earth and watch them sprout and reach for light. She wants to help bring things to life.

Thirsty, happy, letting the daydream in, seeing herself in her mind's eye—a year or several years from now, bent over a garden row in mucky boots, her face in the shadow of some nerdy, floppy hat—she gets up and reaches on tip-toes to hang from a tree branch. Maybe when she gets home she will swallow her pride and ask her mom to hire her. Maybe she can be one of those people who grows a pot of basil on the fire escape. Leaning her head back as far as it will go, she takes in the flushing sky, the tree's duotone leaves and its long trunk, and she sees that in the bark is etched with penknife,

KL + RP
FOREVER

Below, the wood has grown into and around a jagged heart that bulges in the tree bark like a scar. The carvings below look newer, though: two dates, connected by a dash—one of them twenty years ago, the other just last year—and a full name, *KELLY LIGHT*, which she reads aloud—

And in its alliterative syllables she hears Fern's beanbag sing-song, *Kel-ly, Kel-ly*. She hears Cricket's dismissive name for her, *Not-Kelly*, and Virgil's introduction to Pete: *Cory's our new Kelly*. She hears the voice of everyone who has mistaken her for this name on the tree: strange Eddie the party guest; that wax-lipped nanny. And she hears Spenser's insufficient, three-word explanation—*She went away*—and drops, heavy with revelation, to the ground.

An image of Rolo has come to mind, unbidden: stout and tall but stooped, chin on his chest, alone. He has stood at this memorial a hundred times, she thinks, reading to himself the name of his dead beloved. Morning sun shimmers through the foliage beyond the wall and her heart bends for him, even as she feels a chill. Wind blows. Her stomach growls. She scans the wall that encircles the field, turning her whole body slowly and mechanically, and sees herself as if through the cyclopean lens of a drone, trapped and spinning as a jewelry box ballerina, suddenly foreign to herself, and she is struck by a strange and unnerving fancy: perhaps she *is* Kelly. It's plausible enough. Everyone else seems to think so. What makes Cory Cory, anyhow? A name? A life? A brain? She has lost these, all of them, or compromised them beyond recognition. And wouldn't it be just like old Rolo to fashion of her malleable self a replica of her predecessor, just as he has cloned his dogs.

And wouldn't it be just like poor, stupid Cory to show up for an adventure and end up somebody else, somebody dead.

She has to get out. Not seeing the door she came in by, she rushes to the edge. Lays her hand on the wall and walks the perimeter, running her fingers over the stone until they sting. Toward the sun, away from the sun, and toward the sun again. Strange: the wall is all just wall. She slows her pace. Caresses every divot. Feels the texture of the earth on the undersides of her feet. Away from the sun, toward the sun, and away from the sun again. She thinks of Virgil's words, *You are not trapped*, yet trapped she seems to be.

The sun has risen, the shadows receded, the sky gone purely blue. There are no landmarks to determine when she's completed her disorienting orbit. Hungry, thirsty, sore, with each rotation she becomes increasingly panicked. From which direction did she enter? Why didn't she leave the door ajar? Where are her shoes? Where is she? A pill will calm her, she thinks, and digs in the pockets of her shorts to find just one tucked in the lint and sand. She dusts it off, a ruby in the morning light, works up a meager ounce of spit, pops it into her mouth, and swallows.

The wall breathes and rocks. She has to work to steady herself amid the rush of warmth and wonder. She becomes invested in a patch of lichen. Worlds within worlds within worlds. Everything is alive, everything breathing. Only she is dead. Then the sun is all the way up. Her pits are wet. Her shirt is wet. White stars float in her field of vision. She is mind-bogglingly hungry. A sudden worry bobs to the surface like a long-dead fish: How long has she been in here? Hours? Days? Eternity? Is she Kelly? Is she dead? Hello, she wants to say, but her mouth is so dry. She paces the perimeter, half wild, hoarsely barking Hello! hoping that anyone will hear her. The wall shifts under her hand. It seems to be composed of thin layers, like pastry dough. Her belly snarls.

Perhaps if she unpeels the layers she will find the door. She digs at the stone. Hello! It is the only word she knows. She hears a murmuring. It rises in volume, and then subsides. Someone is there. She can feel it. Just on the other side of the door. Somewhere there's a latch. She kneels and feels into the cracks between the stones. Murmuring becomes chattering. Hello! Chattering becomes laughing. Someone is there, listening to her, maybe even watching her. A new word issues from her: Help! Precious fluid spills from her dehydrated eyes. She bangs on the stone. She looks up, loses her balance, and falls back onto one elbow. Pain thrums like electricity. Among the branches and leaves that reach over the wall is a monster, black as shadow, with spindly claws and two sky-bright eyes blinking at her meanly in the breeze. A giant gobbling mouth comes into focus and recedes, rudely laughing. *Cory!* It shouts her name in a sharp voice. She half scoots, half crab walks away from the frightening wall. Her heart is pounding. Tears spill into her ears. All at once, as if on sped-up video, she is grabbed from behind and held. She screams. Roughly she is whipped around, face-to-face with her captor.

A big, fragrant countenance. Smiling face and gleaming teeth, smells of laundry, cedar, Listerine. Rolo, thank god! She puts her arms around his neck and feels him chuckling.

Scared yourself, did you? he is asking kindly. Are you a little stoned? Did you have a psychedelic time in here, all by your lonesome? Get turned around? He rubs her back with a big warm hand. The rhythm of it helps. Eventually her breathing slows. When she's finished snotting the shoulder of his cream-white cotton shirt, she lifts her head and wipes her face. The field is, yes, much smaller than she thought it was, and the door's right there—how did she miss it?—open wide to the woods. Her discarded shoes lie, laces splayed, on the grass just inside it.

You're filthy, he murmurs. When's the last time you ate?

Her eyes go wide. He laughs at her.

He says, Let's get some food in you.

With Rolo beside her, a path appears through the woods that she'd have sworn wasn't there before. It is mere moments before the trees clear and they step onto the lawn. There is the gazebo and tennis court, the greenhouse and the pool, there the white beach and blue ocean. The day is bright and clean.

She sits on a stool at the kitchen island running her hands over the marble. Light falls in through the massive windows, over the floors and gleaming countertops. Her brain hurts. She remembers a YouTube science video she watched once about what happens to the brain in a state of hangover: dehydrated, it pulls away from the sides of the skull, tugging taut whatever veins and vessels connect it. Her poor brain is an ugly, thirsty, three-pound animal, afraid to snuggle up against the walls that contain it. She presses her index fingers against her temples.

You're a real pain in the ass, you know that? he says, but he's smiling. He pours her a glass of lemon water and she downs it in moments, cold trickling over her chin and neck. She wipes her face and he pours her another. He is happy, yammering on about something or other while he fills the kettle, ignites the burner, turns on the oven, grinds coffee beans. Only half of what he says makes any sense to her, but when, from nowhere, he produces a white paper box, she tunes in:

I brought treats. Fresh baked this morning.

He opens the top to show her a dozen gorgeous doughnuts, each slathered in icing of a different color, this one sprinkled with lavender, this one with chocolate shavings, that one with candied cardamom. She reaches for a rumpled cruller, its edges stiff with sugared glaze, but he says, Uh-uh-uh, and waves an index finger at her, and puts it in the oven alongside a maple glazed.

Have you ever had a doughnut-egg-sandwich? He is pouring hot water over velvety coffee grounds.

She begins to shake her head, but has to stop midgesture for the way it rattles her brain.

Amused, he points at her. Somebody's hungover.

I don't know, she says. She squeezes her temples to keep the brain inside from rattling. This feels worse than a hangover. I feel like I'm dying. Like I have like some Victorian illness that should not exist anymore.

Consumption, he says. Dropsy.

The fuck is *dropsy*?

He laughs. He peels strips of bacon from a plastic package and lays them in a hot pan, where they pop and hiss. He sets out a liquid prescription for her beside her glass of water: a cup of coffee, a bottle of beer. Drink this, he says, drink that, and then drink this. Trust me.

She drains the water glass. Her hands are shaking. She tries the beer but it nauseates. The coffee prickles her brain.

He cracks a couple of eggs into the pan, then drops two curls of cheese to melt on top. He takes the doughnuts from the oven, slices them horizontally, and lays the halves facedown on the griddle, pressing them with the spatula, waiting contemplatively.

How did Kelly die? she asks.

Who? he says. She waits. The food on the griddle whispers. The bacon smells like everything she's ever wanted. He plates the halves of maple doughnut, grilled side up, piles upon them cheesy eggs and bacon strips, and tops each with half a cruller. His face is long with concentration, or is it anger, or is it grief.

Without looking at her, he says quietly, Kelly just had a little too much fun.

He looks so very old and tired. It makes her want to cry.

You loved her, she says.

He sets the plate and silverware before her. With a half-assed flourish he dismisses the conversation: Breakfast is served.

What before seemed playful strikes her now as tragic. She sees he wants to please her very deeply, very badly. With a steak knife she cuts a bite of the vulgar sandwich. Yolk dribbles out, melting and mingling with sugar glaze. He watches her bring it to her mouth. It tastes like their first meal together at the diner. It tastes like romance. It is so delicious that every muscle in her body slackens.

Oh my god, she says.

He says, Never say I wasn't good to you.

The rest of the day is intimate. They walk among the spined and velvet limbs in the greenhouse, and he holds her hand. They nap side by side on chaise longues under a pool umbrella and, though she could swear when she fell asleep she was on a separate piece of furniture, somehow when she wakes up, chilled in shadow, he's beside her. For dinner he sends someone to the mainland for Chinese. They dine on chow mein and crisp Riesling. On the patio he lights a cigar. When he kisses her, she understands it is the price of admission and always has been. She tries to lose herself in the sensations of the moment, but his breath is nauseating, cigar-sweet, his lips fat and slick with fry oil. She closes her eyes to avoid his face. Her ears ring as if to help obscure the sounds of his heavy breathing. She wants a Granny. She doesn't want a Granny. She wants a Granny. She never wants another Granny again.

Can I have a Granny? she says.

He brings her upstairs and shakes four pills from the bottle. Take two, he says, and she downs them as if swallowing God's name. She feels her pulse in her temples, in her heart. She concentrates on breathing, on feeling her old friend, the drug, set in.

The room is dark. He sits down and pats the mattress beside him. She considers saying, You know what, I'd rather stand, but she feels she cannot. She has been so cooperative, so far. When she sits, due to his weight her body slants in his direction, an endless dance move, a letting go, a swimming with the current of the Earth. He catches her, puts an arm around her, pulls her close. He is talking but she cannot hear him for the ringing in her ears, her brain. He touches her thigh, releasing prickling. She tries to push his hand away but her fingers end up intertwined in his. His palm is hot and damp, his fingers thick and curious. She tries to make a kind of game of keeping his hand in hers, preventing it from crawling up her leg. Her pulse is quick. She is afraid that she might cry, or yell, or vomit. Recalling an exercise of Dr. Jim's, she tries to focus on the here and now, the physical details she can smell and feel and hear and see.

Coarse oiled hair. His ubiquitous cologne. His body's warmth, the heavy breath that troubles the dark hairs in his nose. His skin, its bristles and pores. The exercise is backfiring. *Mindfulness* was Dr. Jim's word for it, but mindlessness is what she needs. The drug ebbs up in her, a nauseous tide. Looking at his skin she thinks she has seen such a texture before—but where?—and what springs to mind is a long-ago vacation with her mom, when Cory was very young. The sand was just like this, each pore a tiny hole bored by a tiny translucent crab. With every wave that came in, all the holes would fill, only to drain and bubble when the tide retracted, setting crustaceans scuttling. The itch of sunburn, the clump of wet sand in her bathing suit. How she marveled to think of the gazillions of them, digging always digging below the surface. What microscopic creatures live in Rolo, she wonders now; what teeming hordes call home this man who sits beside her in the dark, hand on her leg, breath heavy on her neck? She imagines into being several dozen microscopic crabs scurrying from the apertures of his big face, and breaks into a laugh.

He smiles, too, confused: What? he asks, eagerly, but guarded—and she can tell he is afraid of being humiliated, even now, when he's all but won, which makes her laugh harder. How men fear humiliation! Of all the things to be afraid of. Laughter is a discovery, a relief, the pleasant involuntary convulsions reminiscent—ugh—of sex, but even sand crabs mate, she thinks to reassure herself; even, in their way, plants. The whole living planet spins by means of encounters chance and planned, sex makes the world go round, or, no—sex makes the world go *thrum*, go *hum*, go breathing darkly—

Rolo's halting syllable hangs like an odor in the air. How long has passed, is passing?

What? she asks, then laughs again—she is losing her grip—at the absurdity of two English-speaking primates, sitting in the dark, repeating a single syllable signifying only their confusion. It must strike him as funny, too, for he collapses sideways on the bed, bringing her down with him.

I meant, he says, and his big warm hand is on her, moving, shoulder elbow rib cage belly ribs, I *meant*—through heavy breath—what were you laughing at—?

Touch makes the world go thrum, she thinks thickly, as a comfort to her rapidly beating heart, but fear has joined the party of thoughts and feels inside her, let in by his touch, his tug, the way he has destabilized her and is now somehow pinning her down.

Fear is bristling within her, beside hilarity and recklessness, and the persistent impression of imminent revelation. Something tells her if she answers the wrong way, his fear of humiliation may combust into violence. She sees it in her mind's eye like a diagram, as she's drawn simple molecules in chemistry, how elemental the construction: fear, reversed, is rage.

You, she says, but her capacity for spoken language is as weak, suddenly, as her thoughts are quick. You, she says again, hoping the rest will follow—

And he draws toward her, he is above her, his hope repulsive, and for fear of him she forces on: You're a— It's not a bad thing, she says to assure him. Just a *thing*, a . . . truth, a . . . what's the *word*?

She sits up, hoping to break the web that's fallen over them, and at first it seems to work—yes, even now the silks are fraying—his hand falls away. She shakes her head. She cannot retrieve the thought. *Water* is what she needs, she realizes with sudden urgency. Her mouth and throat are parched, as dry as—*oh*. She looks at him and sees it all again—but the notes of fun and whimsy in the idea of tiny crustaceans scampering from his pores have shifted to some weird diminished key, dream become nightmare—

I'm a what? he asks, voice low.

An *ecosystem*, she says at last, throat cracking.

His countenance changes. He brightens. Then begins, heartily, to laugh. He gathers her whole body in his arms, kisses her neck, gropes at her back, her tits, and desire, panic, and repulsion all flare up, incongruent, incompatible, unwelcome.

You're amazing, he murmurs. She can hear the smack of his lips. Amazing, he repeats to her hair, her collarbone. You are such a good time.

I'm super thirsty, she whispers, but her voice, croaky and quiet, is drowned by the eddies of his breath and hands. He will not hear her. She will be sucked down into the twisting sheets. She closes her eyes and lets the thirst and dizziness overtake her. Her head falls back, and the world spins.

To think this is what she wanted, if just now and then, if just in theory. To find in practice that it's painful, dizzying, and gross. You like that, he tells her, but she does not like it, she is not a good time, she is having a bad time. He holds her by the hip bones, he holds her by the ass, he pushes into her—it hurts—mutters into her hair his incantation: *You like that*; it is not question but command. *You like that*, gripping her ribs, *You like that*, holding her throat. He pushes faster and deeper, ow, fuck, holding her by the neck, tight, gasping, *You like that*, his fleshy back, tight grip, he's dripping, heaving, threatening her with more. It hurts and she says stop but her protest only reenergizes him. *Stop*, she says, and he growls, *Say it again*, and tightens his grip. *Stop*, she pleads. *Again*, he says, and thrusts harder. *Again:* his weight on her throat and inside her, his sweat in her eyes. It lasts for an hour it lasts for a minute it lasts for days. It lasts for eternity, for she is Kelly and she is dead. She squeezes her eyelids shut, stinging, and tries to will herself to shrink inward, away from the container that is her skin, away from her organs, far from him. With pressurized willpower she forces everything that makes her Cory deep inside, then deeper, until her self is nothing more than a hard clenched stone inside a lifeless body: densely compressed, tiny, and far away from the living world.

She wakes to light. A whole-body ache. The smells of sex and perspiration. The sound of him breathing, slow and labored as a failing engine. His body beside her, creased and damp. The tug of sheet against her skin. Her cramped hand still clutching the side of the mattress, even through those lost hours of unconsciousness. Dizziness and nausea. Has she slipped again outside of time? Is this forever? Her breasts ache. Her stomach aches. Her eyes ache. Her calves feel as if someone went in during the night and cranked them each six notches tighter. Sunlight makes the curtains into a rippling scrim for shadow puppetry, casting upon their surface the inscrutable narrative of the leaves. Through a square of stained glass high up in the wall, the sun casts colored light over the bedsheets and what lies on the floor: a white shirt, a pillow, her wrinkled clothes. She is damp and smelly. Not dead at all. A living, sweating animal, pubes stiff with dried-up fluids.

Beside her: a throaty noise, a shift in weight. He turns, heavy with sleep, to face her. She examines him with curiosity drained of affection, drained even of revulsion. The bulldog folds of him. The open lips and too-white teeth, the sour breath. An arm lands on her belly, pulls her closer. His penis is a purple sausage. She will vomit. She *will* vomit. She breaks free, struggles to stand on tingling feet, scrambles to the bathroom, forces closed the door behind her, and pukes. Tears of effort. Acrid odors. She flushes the toilet, runs the tap, and drinks cold water. A shower of stars appears in her vision and momentarily her image in the mirror is obscured. She loses her balance, catching herself painfully on the tile with the flat of a forearm.

She finds an emerald bottle of mouthwash and swishes as long as she can. Shards of light float. Her limbs are tingling. Her center of gravity is out of whack. Her insides feel clenched and aching. She expels a stream of orange pee. When she wipes she finds blood: her period. She begins to laugh, and laughter, crying, what's the difference, it's all the same. Tears roll. Snot drips. The body and its effluvia. What could be funnier. She's nothing but a *sieve*. Just a poor, embattled sieve with, unfortunately, a brain.

Way in the back of the cabinet under the sink she finds a cardboard box of tampons that looks about a decade old. She slides one in and winces at the pain. Naked on the tile, legs splayed, cotton string hanging out, she closes her wet eyes and leans back against the cabinet door, queasy again, hilarity replaced with something darker, bleaker. She feels so *bad* for her body—the frightened sponge in her head, the bloody membrane between her legs, the bruised organ that holds her together—feels *bad* for her thick tongue, cracked lips, and inflamed, star-blinded retinas. Her skinny ass, which has begun to ache, pressed hard against the tile below her, her stubbly legs, her liver, her still-beating heart.

Behind her: a gentle knock.

Queenie?

She reaches quickly to lock the door.

Another knock, less gentle. Hey. Highness. You fall in? If you're upset, we can talk. Nothing's off-limits. You can talk to me.

With the back of a hand she wipes her nose and eyes.

Listen, I don't know what you remember about last night, but I'll tell you what I remember. Best night of my whole godforsaken life. No exaggeration. I've wanted you for so long, and then. My god. The satisfaction. Please don't ruin that.

It is no use. The tears keep coming.

Please. It's all right if you're upset. Just let me in and we can talk about it.

She stands and crosses to the sink.

I don't know what you remember, he says again, but in case there's any confusion you were into it, okay, you were very into it. So if there's any question about the, you know, mutuality of what occurred, let's just address that directly, off the bat, okay. I mean, come on, this has been building for weeks. That look in your eyes?

The night you decided to stay? I can take care of you. I've been taking care of you. I want to keep taking care of you.

The photograph of him and Cricket still sits beside his toothpaste. She picks it up.

Look, Queenie, here's the situation. Here I am, in absolute misery. Having the worst goddamn year of my life. Lawyers hounding me on one side, media on the other. All my best people quitting on me. Backs turning, left and right. Hundreds of lives on my conscience. Not that it was anyone's fault. Top it all off, my ex-wife, thriving, just gave birth to another man's child.

She brings the frame down, glass first, hard, against the faucet. It shatters in the marble sink. The photo inside is damaged, its surface crinkled, the two smiling faces abraded.

The fuck was that? he says.

After a beat he says: Are you okay?

She waits, immobile. She hears his body shift on the other side of the door.

Let me tell you a story, he says, conversational again. Do you know the guillotine was intended as a more humane form of execution? Sounds counterintuitive, but it's true. Before the guillotine, they'd just fucking torture you. Don't get me started on the breaking wheel. But then this guy, Dr. Guillotin, came up with the idea of chopping people's heads off more neatly. The device caught on. It seemed effective. Painless, even. He was so proud of his invention he named it after himself. But, you know, you can't tell a whole society to practice moderation. Moderation, that's no fun! The Reign of Terror was one year long, and during that one year they beheaded *seventeen thousand* people. Crowds would gather to watch and cheer as heads rolled in the streets, and you know what, for at least a few seconds after decapitation, those heads, they'd keep moving. The face would grimace, the eyes would roll, the lips move as if they were trying to confess or plead or tell you all their secrets. There was no way to know, because they couldn't speak, but they certainly didn't *look* as if they weren't in pain. Beheadings became a spectator sport, and Monsieur Docteur was horrified. He tried to get people to stop using the device, or, barring that, to rename it. But guillotine stuck. His name, forever associated with this exquisite miscalculation of human nature, this unquantifiably fatal mistake; his very name, the name of his children and his children's children, his legacy.

Can you imagine? Being haunted by all those dead? I'll tell you what, Queenie. You're too young to know what it's like to wake up every day and want immediately to die. You're too young and too fucking beautiful to be able to imagine the self-loathing. But this is my brutal legacy. I am Dr. Guillotine. I am the tragic fool.

His voice is very close. He must be leaning his forehead against the door. She picks up a shard of glass and tests its sharp edge against the soft skin of her arm.

So that's my fucking year! he says with a bitter laugh. And then. And then I end up at this excruciatingly boring play, at this middle-class wet dream of a summer camp, because who knows why, because the ex-wife says I'm supposed to bond with the kids, and I'm sitting there, just stewing in the heat, you know, stewing in my loathing, and I look up and I see—God. I'd never call you anything so trite as an angel. I've never believed in anything so offensive as love at first sight. But, my god, Queenie. Your legs. Those cut-off shorts. Your pink hair in the sun. When you dropped those paper flowers, it was as if we were in a snow globe, all that glitter in the air. And your laugh. Fresh air in a stale room. Cold water down a parched throat. I mix my metaphors. You are an oasis.

The glass slices. Pain and blood well up and drip onto the marble. The dumb body's predictable response is a relief. She has just one reflexive thought, the same thought she's had forever, whenever she's been hurt. *Mom.*

I'm not an idiot, he says, I don't believe for a minute I'm the kind of guy you imagine yourself with. I'm too old, too fucking ugly, I come with a shit-ton of baggage, it's not like we'd be starting fresh. But here's my value proposition, okay. Be my oasis. Be the girl that I come home to. Get your bloody noses on my patio, go night-swimming off my dock, sleep in my bed, eat at my table, drink at my bar, and the island's yours. The house is yours. *All* the houses can be yours—San Mateo, Rome, Manhattan, Aspen. The drugs are yours. The helicopter's yours. Virgil's yours. You can even fuck him if you want to. Fuck anyone you want, as long as I can fuck you, too. I'll bring you to all the parties, dress you in Gucci, Prada, Louboutin. Where do you want to go? The Oscars? The Met Ball? The inauguration? You'll outshine everyone. You'll make such a splash. The world will love you the way I love you—and I do love you, Queenie. Fuck it: be my wife.

Blood on the marble, blood on the bath mat. She lets it drip and stain his blushing bathroom. She likes the way it hurts. She turns on the faucet in the marble shower.

Queenie, he says, a last time, through the door.

And she lets the beating water fill her mouth, swallowing again and again; she lets it fill her ears; lets it beat against her face, her head, her neck. She watches the blood wash down her body and around the drain. She scrubs her hollows and the cut, hard enough to sting. She stays under the hot water until she can no longer feel him on the other side of the door. Then she gets out, dripping, and surveys the bathroom for what other havoc she may wreak.

On the windowsill behind the toilet there is an orchid in a round metallic pot. She picks it up and drops it. Dirt and flowers fall on the wet marble, muddying the floor, but the flowerpot just bounces. She climbs up onto the sink itself, the better to dent the metal against the counter, and there she is, her whole long body, tampon string and, oh look, bloody arm, face blank and humid. Having caught herself, unaware as a raccoon in a garbage can, balancing over a sink of broken glass, she pauses.

Destroying his shit will not affect him. He can get a new print made of his wedding photo. He can buy a thousand orchids. He can have anything, everything. The only way to really hurt him, she understands with sudden clarity, is to deprive him of herself.

She opens the door quietly. The bed is unmade but he is gone. She puts on her clothes from yesterday and goes back into the bathroom, where she takes one Granny, for the pain, and then empties the whole amber jar into her pockets. They bulge. Leaving blood in the bathroom, she goes downstairs and out of the monstrous house.

The sky is breathing. The sky is gulping. High above and yet somehow almost reachable it moves in giant pulsing slugs. At once physical and metaphysical, beyond space, through time, it gropes for her to come inside. It wants to swallow her. She has the urge to climb and knows what tree to tackle. She hacks her way through the crosshatched woods like an explorer. A voice in the back of her mind murmurs a monologue in a hushed Australian accent, narrating her progress: *Observe our young protagonist . . . breathless, she struggles on . . . unsettling a pair of sparrows . . . startling a vole.* When she comes upon the stone wall, she touches its surface with great concentration. Circles its exterior. Searches for the door. Finds nothing. But wait: a giant tree bends one thick branch over the edge. If she jumps she can just reach it. She leaps and grasps and hangs from stinging hands to swing up her lower half, folding her legs around the branch as she used to at the playground jungle gym, and shimmies, hand over hand, foot over foot. At the top of the wall she pauses and looks up. It won't do: the hungry sky is still obscured by layers of leaves. *She will not be thwarted or distracted . . . labours bravely onward . . .* She lets down one leg, then the other. Gathers her breath and releases, to fall onto the grass below.

She lands on all fours like an animal. The impact of the ground sends a seizing up her palms and heels and through her wrists and ankles, but she crouches, breathing, and it dissipates. She is back in the elusive field, with no one but the ghost of Kelly and her poplar tree. It is not yet noon. The wall casts a misty shadow over the east side of the enclosure, while sunshine sets the dew-soaked west half sparkling. She is not so incapacitated that she cannot walk across the grass, stride, even, float: every step she takes feels like soaring, her legs are longer than they've ever been. In a moment she reaches the tree and is ensconced by it. Hey, Kell, she says. How you doing, girl? Still dead?

In the wind the poplar's leaves whisper and flip, cream-white to green, reflecting then glowing in the sun. Its trunk is imprinted with marks the shape of diamonds. When she grips a branch with her soil-stained hands its bark seems supple and scarred as skin. She brings a sneaker to a crook where branch meets trunk and hoists herself into the shimmering leaves. Up she climbs, until the branches are too thin to hold her weight and she is hovering there, sitting on a limb that presses uncomfortably into her ass crack, one arm clinging to a branch above, the other clinging to its trunk.

Though the view is intermittently obscured by leaves and boughs, from up here she can see the whole island. Her internal narrator babbles on—*high at last above her usual terrestrial perspective . . . she finds her island prison cannot be more than a mere few city blocks around . . .*

From up here the wilderness looks no larger than Union Square. The beach umbrellas are garnishes discarded from tropical drinks. The gazebo is a cake decoration, the helicopter a children's toy, the green field below her no more than an area rug, her own footsteps having left a soft impression in its pile. Far off, other islands sit and glimmer, treasures punctuating the expanse, and all around the ocean glows, an endless blinding field. Underslept and empty-bellied, light-headed, euphoric, high, she closes her eyes to the warmth of shifting sunlight on her eyelids, and feels as if she could ascend. The earth has had its way with her, it is the sky's turn now, the sky will take her! She loosens her grip. The wind wraps around her like a sling. She lets go and raises her arms to the sky and everything is glory, glory—

and then: a gust. The branch she's on heaves over, unbalancing her. Her eyes pop open, her lungs fill with air, her heart seizes, her arms scrabble and cling. She is wide awake, her heart beating so fast it hurts, her face smarting, having smashed against the tree trunk. All the muscles of her body have been switched to vibrate mode. She tastes blood inside her cheek, and that primal thought appears again, as if spelled out by the stinging. *Mom.*

Eventually, she knows, she will have to climb back down. But she has to wait for her body to stop shaking. She tries to focus on breathing through the panic, on letting her body relax against the solid tree, and on the sun that shines, slow but sharp, through mottled cloud. Her heart thudding, eyes leaking, body trembling:

FRUIT OF THE DEAD

if any moment was right to try her mom's old psychic trick, she thinks, this would be it.

The clouds shift. She pulls at the wind as if at a thread unraveling, catching at the current. She yells, yells loud into the current the oldest word she knows.

And, as if in response, so far off to the west it's hardly even visible, a boat cuts the water.

287

XII

Go Now, He Urged, to Your Dark-Robed Mother, Go, and Feel Kindly in Your Heart Toward Me; While You Are Here, You Shall Rule All That Lives and Moves, Queen of the Land of Sweet and Sea-Girt

At the dock, the captain lights a cigarette. She'll wait. I thank her and walk up the beach to the perfect grass. This place is like a mausoleum for a goblin king, meticulously still. In a greenhouse, cacti stiff as corpses strain toward the heat-fogged glass. Above a pool of false blue water, steam rises untroubled in the chill. The shapely trees are coppering.

A peal of barking startles me. Three aerodynamic animals—ears of rabbits, speed of racehorses—sprint toward me down the hill. Sudden fear reels a loud sound from my open mouth—turn back, run—my stepdad's dog, my thigh between its jaws: *I'm gonna eatchoo . . .*

But when I reach the water I realize, though the wild sound persists, their galloping has subsided. I stop, panting, doubled over on the sand, and hear the captain's voice: Shoulda warned you about the dogs. A few feet from the beach the animals have halted and are jumping, dropping, nosing over, and circling one another. The way they churn, there on the lawn, there could be six of them, or nine; there could be one, alone but monstrous, with a dozen whipping tails and drooling heads. Despite their hyperactive dance I see their collars, smooth black tech, are blipping red. They've hit an invisible fence.

A young man approaches in cutoff jeans and high-tops. A walkie-talkie and a key chain jangle at his belt.

The nanny's mother, says the boat captain behind me.

He gives me a charming smile. She'll be glad to see you, he says. Come with me. I'll let Rolo know you're here.

He snaps his fingers at the dogs. They fall in line and so do I. The path offers a view of the house as we approach. I understand it is a multimillion-dollar estate, but also that the owner would likely refer to it as rustic. On one side, a well-tended garden overflows with late-season harvest. A couple of black trash bags wait by a door, and I wonder if he is short-staffed. How many people have seen and even met my Cory here, and, like his beautiful ex-wife, done nothing, or next to nothing?

We enter through a side door. The floors are glossy, the furniture designer, the art on the walls by artists I recognize and mostly loathe. He leads me to an office, rich woods and leathers. His voice muted by the rug, he asks, Can I get you anything while you're waiting? Coffee, tea, sparkling water? Something stronger?

No, I say, reluctant to accept anything in this evil place. He nods and leaves, pulling the door almost closed behind him. I smooth Metta's church dress, whose polyester spandex blend looks particularly cheap in this environment, and listen to the sounds of the house that contains me: low male murmuring, the clack of dogs' nails on the floor, the quiet breathing of the air-conditioning.

Around me, among the books on the floor-to-ceiling shelves, plaques and awards congratulate Rolo Picazo on his philanthropy, and I think I will not stay and wait for him, as if for a favor. I open the door and set off up a hall to look for the asshole myself: in a living room among the animal skins, below the chandelier of bleached white antlers; in a dining room as clean and affectless as a page in *Architectural Digest*.

I find him standing at his marble kitchen island with an empty mug, an open checkbook, and a newspaper: an ogre of a man. His hair is gray, thick, and too long. His face is bloated, weary. His robe is silk, with a pattern of black rams against an emerald ground, their nautilus horns interlocked in combat. Behind him, a glass percolator drips coffee into a carafe. In his hand rests a fountain pen.

He folds the paper, looks up at me, and smiles. Mama bear!

I have just three words for him: Where is she.

I've heard so much about you. All good things, of course! Guess I expected eventually you'd find your way here. A mother knows, they say. Hey, listen, I read about your, uh, expulsion in the business section. Pretty dramatic fall from grace. You and I, we have that in common, in a way. I'm currently midcatapult myself from heavenly Olympus, and for reasons not unlike your own. Two products, both alike in dignity . . . one severely blighted, the other dangerously profuse.

Where. Is she.

Different business models, of course, different issues, different projects—you wanted to cure the world of hunger; I, of pain—but both of us are scapegoats, aren't we? Just a couple of scapegoats who flew too close to the sun. If you'll excuse the mixing of metaphor. Funny story, actually: Do you happen to know the word for *scapegoat* in Greek?

Where—!

Whoa, now, mama bear! Slow down. Not in the mood for chitchat, you know what, that's fine. Fact is I'm not sure where she's got to. She's around here somewhere. If you'd called, I could have had her ready for you. *If I knew you were a-coming I'd have baked a cake! Hatch-e-doo ah-hatch-e-doo ah-hatch-e-doo.*

His cutesy little dance, his atonal falsetto, grotesque, he is grotesque, but lunging at him backfires. Immediately the dogs are on me, paws jaws breath tongues. And the sound that issues from my throat is pure fear—*I'm gonna eatchoo*—tongues nails breath barking, and he is laughing, laughing.

All right, all right! he says when I've been adequately frightened. Easy, girls! He snaps his fingers, and the animals retreat to a dog bed. You know what, he says, filling in the blanks on the check, ripping the paper from the book, why delay the inevitable? Let's find her.

He slips the check into the pocket of his robe and steps out a sliding door into the afternoon, and what can I do but follow him.

The day's gone dark and wet with drizzle. Gulls make hurtling loops on the wind. The dogs follow but he keeps them close, thank god. I become aware I'm weeping. I am so tired my bones ache.

Queenie! he yells toward a tangle of woods. Queenie? You have a visitor.

I want to call her, too, but I do not want him to hear me. So I whisper, Baby girl, into the wind, and wipe my nose. I breathe, Monkey, Cory, honey, Mommy's here.

See her at first without seeing her. Feel her somewhere near, and turn, and look. Somewhere, a disturbance in the trees, the sounds of breath caught quick in a throat, of feet running on grass. Turn, and turn, and then—

it's her at last, long, pink, and real, mouth open, yelling Mom!
and running, Core, my girl, my god, my heart. Who knows what
words are tumbling from my mouth, who knows how I've scrambled up from stumbling. She is in my arms, all five eleven of her,
baby girl or giant, and I'm laughing, digging my nose into her
shoulder, grabbing fistfuls of her shirt, kissing, and she's holding
me and laughing, too, embarrassed now, letting me hold her out,
arm's length, to drink my deepest look at her, to say, What's this,
baby, what are these scrapes and scratches on your arms and face—?

She looks down, and says, I climbed a tree

                              All these spots and bruises

          I don't know, bug bites, clumsiness

                    And what's wrong with your eyes

     What do you mean what's wrong with my

                    They're all bloodshot, monkey, it's

     I'm just tired I just woke up I've been

                    like you're looking at me through frosted glass

roaming around

                              Did he hurt you

     in the sun all day

                              Did he hurt you

     I'll be fine, I'm fine

                              I'll fucking kill him

     He loves me

He doesn't *love* you, Core

His voice, like poison: She came of her own free will.

The fuck

What, did you forget I was here?

She's a fucking child, you—

She's eighteen. She can make her own—

Don't fucking speak

Mom

I'll kill you

You can try.

Mom, what the hell, you are so

Where are your things, Core

What happened to your hair, your

We need to go

whole, like, vibe

I've been looking for you

Where did you even come from

Searched the whole coast

How are you here

I lost my job

How did you find me

left people to starve

Did you come because I called you

Called me? Do you mean

The psychic thread, Mom, remember

the call that dropped, that night, is that

I ESP'd you from Kelly's tree

Who's Kelly?

Can't believe it worked

Focus, honey, where are your things

Can't believe you don't remember

We're leaving, baby girl, you're safe

Of course I'm safe

What if she doesn't want to go?

Go fuck yourself

Mom! What the

Do you *want* to go?

Don't talk to her

You know you don't have to.

Don't speak to her

You can stay.

You know what, forget your things, let's just—

Ow! Mom

                          The boat is waiting

Let go!

                  What's gotten into you, you're so

I've never seen you like this,

              different, so, I don't know,

so different, it's like you're

              blurry around the edges—

the most yourself you've ever been—

She is pulling Cory down the hill, this woman who's unmistakably her mom—same eyes, same nose, same voice and phrases, same gestures, expressions, touch, smell, kisses—familiar as comfort, more dear and real to her than her own mind, but, stumbling along behind her, half resisting the viselike grip on her wrist, Cory thinks this mother is also not at all the mother she remembers. This mom looks older than her mom, at once homelier and lovelier. Her shorn head exaggerates the delicacy of her aging face. Without the coiffed and treated hair, her ears protrude, her brow goes on for miles. Her lips are thin, the skin around them drawn and lined; her bare eyes droop a little at the lids. How ordinary she looks, and yet unreal; how much more like any middle-aged woman, and yet how frightening. She will not be disobeyed. Who is this fierce and violent woman who has replaced the poised and uptight mom Cory has always known? Where her mom was tame, this mother is wild. Where her mom was smoothed and buffed and contoured, this mother is all jagged lines. When this mother glances back at Rolo behind them, Cory relishes the murder in her eyes.

Down at Sherry's ferry, the dummy's eyes are wiggling. The old captain in her beat-up vest has started the engine. Emer descends into the boat but Cory pauses. Rolo is watching. Indeed, several of them are watching her, in the dark, wet afternoon: Ray Gray is peering over the long-handled net with which he has been skimming leaves from the pool; Spider is looking on from the garden, where he's been loading bags of trash into the golf cart. Even Virgil has paused, mid-lawn, to observe the goings-on at the dock. Under their observation Cory realizes she expects to be embarrassed—saved by Mommy, after all—but, in the care of this formidable new mother, she feels not shame but pride.

Do you want to stay? he asks. His face is loose and old, his voice weak. Where is the man who seemed so powerful last night, who hurt her so demonically? This man is an emptied sack. In him, she thinks, is a loneliness so complete he cannot feel it, a loneliness whose shape she has grown to fit.

You don't have to answer him, says New Mother from the boat.

Don't you want to stay? he asks, revising slightly.

You're coming home, New Mother says.

Let her speak for herself. Rolo bows his head but keeps his eyes on Cory, his chin tucked, doubling.

Cory waits, suspended.

Stay, he says, quiet as the rain on the leaves. Oasis, he tells her.

Taking in the sad old dad before her—face flushed, hair wet with mist, expression at once doubtful and hopeful—she tries to hold all the Rolos she has known in her mind, together. Rolo in the sailboat: *I'm trying to help you.* Rolo under the crabapple tree at dawn: *You are my home.* Rolo in bed: *You like that.* Unthinkable violation. She shakes her head at him so subtly that she can feel the vertebrae in her neck click like gears in a watch.

His eyes fall. She feels a flood of power.

She despises him. She adores him. Despite herself, she pities him.

He hands her a folded square of paper from the pocket of his robe. He says, Come back, then. Sometime.

Cory takes the paper and sticks it into her crowded pocket, between the pills. In her stained sneakers with their shitty treads, she slips on the sea-soaked step into the hull. Her mother catches her. Rolo stands on the dock with his arms crossed. Sherry takes a last drag and flicks her cigarette butt in his direction.

He leans a little to the side to dodge it. Cunt, he says sadly, without malice.

She shifts gears and maneuvers the boat out into the open water.

As they pull away from the dock, the old man's great bulk shrinks. In a matter of moments he looks very small, standing there against the fire-colored shrubbery, despite his wild hair and flapping silk. If he says another word, she does not hear it. His voice is out-rumbled by the boat. At last she turns away, toward the mainland and the sea that separates them from it, toward the force of a woman her mother has become, standing tall in the narrow prow.

The wind is chilly-quick. As the dark water parts, two angel wings of spray shoot up on either side of them. Cory puts her arms around her mom, for affection and for warmth. This body—aging and a little crooked, thinner than she recalls—has, her whole life, been both object and source of all her love.

Emer's thin lips are set, her eyes narrow. She says, You're going to need so much therapy.

Cory digs her nose into her mother's home-smelling head. You just send me to therapy when I do things you don't like.

Her mother grips Cory's hand and smiles, though her face is sad. *I'm* going to need so much therapy. I already do, she says, and adds, Core, I'm sorry.

For what?

There are things I should have told you. Ugly things . . . which it might have been useful for you to know. I thought keeping them from you would protect you. As if you could ever be protected.

The boat begins to speed. Its engine roars. Emer looks toward the mainland. Cory hears just fragments of what she says:

It took me a long time to . . . I'll tell you all about it, sometime soon. I just . . . Core, it took me many years . . . I think . . . years ahead of you.

Cory nods, but she can barely hear, and anyway is barely listening. She drops her mother's hand to reach, instead, into her pocket. There is the paper Rolo handed her at the dock. She unfolds it, taking care to grip it tightly in the wind.

A check for twenty thousand dollars. No more nor less than what he promised. Her smile is involuntary. Her laughter is confounding.

Her mom turns toward her, hopeful, relieved: What?

They are going fast enough now that when Cory speaks again her mouth fills with wind. She yells, He'll write me a glowing letter of recommendation!

The sun breaks through the cloud cover and elastic light swims, blinding, on the waves. The island behind them is no larger than a lozenge. Rolo has disappeared. Cory feels a tightening in her chest, a heat in her eyes, and wonders if, in some way, she loves him—or if she loves the island, or the drug, or the person she's beginning to become.

299

This is how the story ends, Emer shouts, and grips her daughter tightly. This is how the story ends.

But even as she incants this six-word mantra, Cory senses its inadequacy. *The end* is for parables and fairy tales. *The end* is no realer than a lullaby. Lifting her head, replacing the check in her pocket, Cory toys with the ruby Grannies that will last her, who knows, a few months, a season. The island shrinks to nothing, but Rolo's invitation lingers. *Come back, then. Sometime.*

She expects she will.

Acknowledgments

This book would never have become what it is were it not for several other works of art, and many people.

The general story and several specific passages, including Doso's song and all the chapter headings, are adapted from Hugh G. Evelyn-White's translation of *The Homeric Hymn to Demeter*, published by the Loeb Classical Library in 1914. A few lines throughout the book are adapted from passages in Louise Glück's *Averno* and Rachel Zucker's *Eating in the Underworld*. For the pastor's homily on master versus masterpiece, I drew on C. S. Lewis's *Mere Christianity*. Pete's show on Coeur Brisé was inspired by the work of the musician Wren Kitz, and the abecedarian on Rolo's coffee table by Hasanthika Sirisena's illustrated series "Abecedarian for the Abeyance of Loss," published in *Epiphany* in 2019. Thanks to Star Island and my friends there for inspiring details of this world, including the Shanty on Little Île, the staff's game of nails, and Château Relaxeau. Thanks to Lauren Hilgers, Anne-E Wood, and Athena Wrann for speaking with me about their experiences as Americans working in China.

I am unspeakably fortunate to work in a community of wise and generous people who have been willing to read and/or offer feedback on this project, including Clare Beams, Max Bean, Sarah Bridgins, Jessie Chaffee, Zhui Ning Chang, Amanda Dennis, Lota Erinne, Molly Gandour, Rachel Glaser, Manuel Gonzales, Zack Graham, Eva Hagberg, Rachel Hinkel-Wang, Juhea Kim, John Kleber, Ben Lasman, Danielle Lazarin, Chris Leslie-Hynan, Mojo Lorwin, Chris Lyon, Kyle McCarthy, Kate McQuade, Wah Mohn, Keija Parssinen, Debra Pearlman, Alexis Schaitkin, Lena Valencia, and Anne-E Wood.

Meredith Kaffel Simonoff, thank you for your faith, your nerve, and your immeasurable grace. Thanks to the whole excellent team at the Gernert Company, especially Nora Gonzalez, Rebecca Gardner, and Will Roberts, as well as to the team at Abner Stein, Rachel Clements in particular.

Kara Watson and Sophie Missing, thank you for your sharp edits, wise counsel, and bighearted support. Thanks, also, to many other wonderful people in this business of bookmaking: at Scribner US, Nan Graham, Stu Smith, Katie Rizzo, Jaya Miceli, Math Monahan, Georgia Brainard, Ashley Gilliam Rose, and Sabrina Pyun; at Scribner UK, Ella Fox-Martens, Genevieve Barratt, Amy Fulwood, Rebecca McCarthy, and Matthew Johnson; and, at Simon & Schuster more broadly, Wendy Sheanin and Hannah Moushabeck.

Lastly, thank you, John, for making this book, and our rich life, possible. Jack and Sylvie, though it will be a long time before you can read this and much longer before I let you, thank you for arriving in the middle of it all and making me a mother. I love you more than all the words could ever say.